I0658559

MORVEN WATT

CURSES COME HOME

SHORT STORIES FROM THE DARK SIDE OF 21ST CENTURY EXISTENCE

MORVEN WATT

CURSES COME HOME

SHORT STORIES FROM THE DARK SIDE OF 21ST CENTURY EXISTENCE

MEREO

Cirencester

Mereo Books

1A The Wool Market Dyer Street Cirencester Gloucestershire GL7 2PR
An imprint of Memoirs Publishing www.mereobooks.com

Curses Come Home: 978-1-86151-879-8

First published in Great Britain in 2017
by Mereo Books, an imprint of Memoirs Publishing

Copyright ©2018

Morven Watt has asserted her right under the Copyright Designs and Patents Act 1988 to be identified as the author of this work.

This book is a work of fiction and except in the case of historical fact any resemblance to actual persons living or dead is purely coincidental.

A CIP catalogue record for this book is available from the British Library.

This book is sold subject to the condition that it shall not by way of trade or otherwise be lent, resold, hired out or otherwise circulated without the publisher's prior consent in any form of binding or cover, other than that in which it is published and without a similar condition, including this condition being imposed on the subsequent purchaser.

The address for Memoirs Publishing Group Limited can be found at www.memoirspublishing.com

The Memoirs Publishing Group Ltd Reg. No. 7834348

The Memoirs Publishing Group supports both The Forest Stewardship Council® (FSC®) and the PEFC® leading international forest-certification organisations. Our books carrying both the FSC label and the PEFC® and are printed on FSC®-certified paper. FSC® is the only forest-certification scheme supported by the leading environmental organisations including Greenpeace. Our paper procurement policy can be found at www.memoirspublishing.com/environment

Typeset in 12/18pt Century Schoolbook
by Wiltshire Associates Publisher Services Ltd. Printed and bound in Great Britain by Printondemand-Worldwide, Peterborough PE2 6XD

Dedication

For Mum, Dad, Iain and Forbes
I love you. You gave me all the world and all the words.

The Heated Minutes

The heated minutes climb
The anxious hill,
The tills fill up with cash,
The tiny hammers chime
The bells of good and ill,
And the world piles with ash
From fingers killing time.

If only you were here
Among these rocks,
I should not feel the dull
The taut and ticking fear
That hides in all the clocks
And creeps inside the skull –
If you were here, my dear.

Louis MacNeice

Contents

Acknowledgements

Fairytales are my lifeblood. Stories of the magical, the unexplained and the macabre spark something in my brain. I have to thank my Mum for providing me with the most outstanding collection of fairy tale anthologies that started before I could read and are still being gifted to me to this day. I also have to thank her for doing all the initial editing and listening to me untangle the stories in my brain. No thanks for starting the book addiction that keeps Barnes and Noble in business though.

Thank you to my Dad, who never stops arguing with me, never stops pushing me to be better and always has my back. Thank you also for taking me around the world and back, which influences just about everything that I write.

Thank you Iain and Forbes for your brutal/brotherly feedback on the stories, your vital input on the details and the inspiration you have given for my stories.

A huge thanks to Chris Newton and the team at Mereo. Your feedback, editing and everything else you did behind the scenes means so much to me.

Special thanks to Chad, who has to listen to me ranting about hypothetical ideas constantly – I do know I sound like I'm high on a mix of ayahuasca and speed. Thank you for being there when I freak out, panic, and don't know what to do. Thanks for letting me be me unconditionally. I love you.

About the author

Morven Watt lives in Flagstaff, Arizona with her five giant dogs and spends any time she isn't writing doing yoga, running marathons, swimming in wild bodies of water and climbing trees.

She is a native Scot and has a degree in English from Newcastle University. She loves travel, adventure, words and animals. One of her life goals is to open a canine rescue.

This is her first book and is the first in a series of short story collections

VIRTUAL

MONDAY

Kelly blinked at the screen. Eighty thousand bitcoins for a safari? That had to be some kind of joke. You could take a trip to the Moon for eighty thousand, maybe even less nowadays.

"Ugh... come on," she muttered as she clicked the link.

Experience luxuries like you've never known before. This isn't your regular safari... this is a global safari, taking you to the wonders of Botswana, where you run alongside lions and elephants, across to India, where you stalk the grass with tigers, and to the distant shores of Thailand, Japan, Borneo, New Zealand, and so many more places, to experience wonders you never thought possible. The reality of our safari will dazzle even the most experienced VR'ists, with enhanced smells, sounds and even a *touch option.

There was a small asterisk by the word touch, and Kelly moved the cursor over it.

[For an additional Twenty Thousand bitcoins. Must have VR Touch Hardware & Software.]

"Typical." Kelly shook her head as she scanned the pictures. Stock photos of dazzling blue beaches, fiery orange tiger eyes peeping out of pale grass, and thick dense jungles. She didn't bother clicking the video links. She had done a few similar trips before. The Kenyan safari had been the most disappointing. The entire VR had been spent in a nasty old Jeep, rattling around like a loose penny. The animals hadn't been programmed well either; no smells, glitching sounds, and poor movement quality. When she and Dad reviewed it afterwards she had been quite brutal.

"Kelly?" Her Dad called from the lower floor.

Their home spanned three floors in the chic Excalibur high rise. The uppermost floor, where Kelly had sequestered herself, was home to a large gym, a pool, and the Virtual Reality Room. The room itself was small, but it was attached to a larger viewing room, where you could scan the VR trips available or watch playbacks of your past VRs. Kelly was stretched out in a lounger, still in the sweatpants she had thrown on this morning.

"Coming." She called back, sliding the control over to the small star and clicking it. A small message popped up. *VR SAVED TO WISHLIST.*

The wish list had a stack of others on it already; *The Scottish Isles, Jupiter to Pluto, Beyond the Galaxies, Ancient Egypt & The Forbidden Tombs, The Lost City of Atlantis , Pompeii.*

"What are you doing up there?" Her father asked with a frown.

He was older, with tufted silver hair, and was dressed in the same threadbare V-neck and corduroy pants he had been wearing yesterday. His office was located on the central floor, with its own VR room solely for business.

"I'm bored," Kelly grumbled as she slid onto a stool at the island. She ran her fingers over the touch screen and selected a drink. It slid out from the chilled compartment nearest to her.

"Where is your mother?" Her father looked around with befuddlement. "Is there food in? Do we have to order in?"

"We could order pizza," Kelly said hopefully. "And Mom left for the VR convention this morning, remember? Ironically, it isn't held in VR." Kelly let out a dry laugh.

Her father nodded and tried to give off the air that he had known this all along. "Weren't you supposed to be at school today?" he asked after a moment.

Kelly chewed the inside of her cheek. Her mother mustn't have told him about her suspension. Knowing her mother, she would be completely swept up in the convention and would forget to call them all week. Kelly debated her options. She didn't want her father to know that she had attacked a girl and enjoyed every second of it. She sighed heavily.

"I have VR projects all week this week. I thought Mom told you." Kelly made an annoyed face.

"Oh, right... of course." He placed a small coffee cup in the dishwasher and paced around the other side of the island. Kelly changed the subject. "How's the VR coming on - Greece, isn't it?

"Oh fine. We're having some difficulty deciding what to keep in and what to keep out, the historical stuff that people will actually be interested in in their VRs, that sort of thing."

"Can't you just have different 'levels'?" Kelly perked up a little when her father furrowed his brow curiously at her. "Like, a level for tourists, a level for historians, for school kids? Like... erm... how do I put this... like have slightly different formats depending on the consumer?"

Both Kelly's parents worked in the VR industry. Her father, a technical genius, worked on the actual coding and design. Her mother, chatty, outgoing and stylish, worked in sales. Kelly couldn't understand for the life of her how they had ended up together. Her father was shy, soft-spoken and on the verge of being a recluse. Her mother was loud, bright and invited to every social event. That was why her mother had swanned off to Las Vegas for the largest VR convention in the world only twelve hours after finding out that Kelly had been suspended from school.

Maybe that was a good thing though, Kelly thought to herself.

"That isn't a bad idea, Kel," her father mused as he got out a fresh cup and put it into the coffee machine. "Would you... would you like to see what I am working on?"

Kelly looked up at her father. He gave her a small, hopeful smile.

"Sure." She hopped off the stool and followed her father into his office. Long transcripts of code filled one of the plasma screen walls. Pictures of ancient Greece, Greek gods and goddesses and archeological research papers flicked up in a rotation on the other two walls. The screen wall in front of her father's computer was blank.

Her father's fingers tapped softly on the opaque glass desk and a bunch of code scurried across the blank screen. A moment later a sunburst of small images came up, much like the ones on the other walls. It took a second before Kelly realized that they were actually videos.

"Wow! This is incredible." She looked at one video that played at the left side of the screen. "Can I?" Her father nodded. She pointed at it, and then swept her hand across the screen. In an instant the video filled the whole screen. "It's the Oracle at Delphi," she said. She always preferred the time travel VRs to the regular travel ones. Though, she thought, they are pretty much all time travel nowadays.

The video showed staggering cliffs and a deep cavern nestled just out of reach of the crashing waves. Tall pillars and a table, carved into the stone itself, ensconced an ethereally beautiful woman crouched at the center. She was dressed in diaphanous white clothes, and vapor streamed from a giant crevice in the cave.

"It's amazing... but I read that the Oracle was actually an old lady, Dad." She nudged him softly.

"No one knows for sure," he huffed.

"Those temples... they're gone now aren't they? The remains even?" Kelly bit her lower lip. She always did this to herself. She had done it with the tigers, and the elephants and the leopards. She had done it with the Amazon rainforest and the beautiful Scottish ruins that had been her favorite VR of all time.

"I'm afraid so, petal," her Dad said softly. "Do you want to see more?"

"Maybe later," Kelly said, swallowing down the lump in her throat. "I'm super hungry. Can we order some food?"

They ate in silence. The sound of two different news channels on different screens, and a fake fire crackling, gave the room a warm fuzziness. The pizzas were thin crust, Kelly's favorite.

Protestors are here outside Havelworth Prison to demonstrate against the newest wave of VR technology that will allow offenders to be held in varying levels of punishment. The offenders will be graded, depending on their crime, and they will be given a drip to ensure there are no VR-related starvation deaths such as those that occurred in 2304 at Markham Prison.

Kelly's ears pricked as she listened to the newscaster. "Does that happen?"

Her Dad nodded as he chewed. "Horrible technology, keeping people on a perpetual cycle of torture or fear." He shook his head and swallowed. "It's psychological torture."

Kelly nodded. "Yeah... but also the VR starvation deaths?"

Her Dad put down the rest of his slice of pizza. "Rarely nowadays. It used to, in the early days. Before we had set locks and alarms and whatnot. People would go into VRs on a loop, or even memory based VRs. Sometimes it was intentional, but mostly it was just terribly, terribly sad."

"Intentional?" Kelly's pizza dripped hot red grease onto her plate. Her father was always much more open with her than her mother was.

"You know... people who had lost loved ones, or were depressed, wanted to be someone different... somewhere different." He looked up at Kelly's shocked face. "Like I said, there are a lot more controls now."

"Mmm hmm." Kelly set her pizza crust down on her plate and thought about starving to death, trapped in a VR.

"Let's change the channel, shall we?" her father said. He pointed at the bottom of the TV screen.

LokTek is the innovative technology you've been waiting for. When you connect your VR chip to your VR Dreamer, you want to experience every second of it. You don't want to be jolted out by your own fear.

A young guy walked on to the screen. He had long, surfer hair, tattoos and a cap on. He smiled a pearly white, too-big smile at the viewers. He motioned behind him, where a man was preparing to jump out of an airplane. A parachute pack was nestled like a hump around his boiler suit. The man looked terrified. He jumped. A moment later, the same man, sweating and bashful was back to sitting in his VR room lounger.

I mean, isn't that the worst? You paid for your VR... and then you don't even get to experience it. Not anymore. With LokTek, you're VRs can be set to a certain ending time, or just till the end of the VR, so you'll never miss a moment again!

He looked behind him, where the same man was free falling, a cheesy grin on his face as he pulled out his chute and floated safely to land. A bunch of other people rushed up to him, smiling and high-fiving.

"Ugh, cheesy." Kelly wrinkled her nose. "These ads are awful."

Her Dad laughed. "Fair enough. That isn't even what LokTek is used for."

"What?" Kelly frowned. They had LokTek, she and her Dad had used it when they did the 'Swimming with Sharks' VR.

Her father coughed and blushed slightly. "It... it's used more for prisoners in VR nowadays... or people who love scary VRs."

"Like horror genre?" Kelly asked flatly.

"I suppose so, yes. Or people who love doing combat VRs." Her father tried to look for other reasons people might use it, but Kelly knew it was because there had been a huge rise in the horror genre. She had done a report about it for school.

Username: FAB_ABBY You there?

The message pinged on Kelly's screen in the upstairs VR room. The VR dreamer was fitted snugly to her head and her hands were covered with the paper-thin VR gloves. She hadn't connected her VR chip at the base of her skull yet, she was simply hanging out in the chat room.

Username: KELLY23 Yeah, just had dinner
Username: FAB_ABBY Are your parents still mad?
Username: KELLY23 Mom didn't tell Dad and she left for that VR Conv
Username: FAB_ABBY So lucky... when she back?
Username: KELLY23 End of the week
Username: KELLY23 And she is gonna kill me
Username: FAB_ABBY Not if you explain. Let's VR.
Username: KELLY23K. Where? Your pick.
Username: FAB_ABBY Beach party?
Username: KELLY23Sure. You pick and invite me. Keep messaging open!

A moment later a message popped up, *FAB-ABBY has invited you to 'Baja Beach Party'. Would you like to ACCEPT or DECLINE?*

Kelly hit 'accept' and a swirling spiral filled her screen for a moment. A message popped up on the side of the screen. *FAB_ABBY: I left the invite open... in case...*

Kelly chewed the inside of her cheek. She still hadn't connected the VR chip located behind her skull to the dreamer headset yet. She didn't want to tell Abby she hated leaving the VR invites open. Weirdos would sometimes try and hop in and talk to them. Her father's words bounced around the back of her skull: 'never leave a VR open, that's how predators and hackers can get in.'

FAB_ABBY: I'm hoping Brandon will join... I told him I might be doing this later.

Kelly's cursor blinked in her message box expectantly.

KELLY23: Sounds good. She typed, and then she clicked the *Link VR chip to Dreamer* button.

The VR panned over a busy beach. The sand was pristine and the water was clear turquoise. The waves were neat and free from debris. The sky overhead was azure, and a few choice clouds broke the expanse of blue.

Kelly could feel the warm air on her fingers and smell salt, sickly sweet mixers and coconut sunblock. The sound of dance music was loud, and happy shouting reverberated around Kelly's skull.

She slid her cursor down to the bottom of her screen. The VR set up at her home was state of the art and the bottom of the screen had a plethora of options.

VOLUME
INTERACTIVE-TOUCH-RECEPTORS
BRIGHTNESS
MESSAGES
AVATAR
DEPTH
INVITE
IMAGING
PANORAMA
LOKTEK
REPORT
EXIT VR

Kelly clicked on 'volume' and lowered it. She could see Abby's avatar already bouncing in time to the music a few feet in front of her. Her avatar was blonde, brighter than Abby's normal shade, and it was taller too. She wore a neon bikini with overlapping straps. Her boobs spilled out over the top of the cups. Some of the other Avatars would be real people, in their own private VRs, and Abby and Kelly could message with them if they requested to. Because they had left their VR party open, anyone could join in their chat regardless of whether Kelly and Abby wanted them to or not.

Kelly quickly selected the *AVATAR* option. She wanted the Avatar to look as close to real as possible. She had already been through the process of imaging, so it did look fairly accurate. She lengthened and layered the auburn hair, adding in some color to the pale skin and a smattering of freckles. The avatar had the same childishly chubby cheeks that Kelly had, and button nose, giving her a chipmunk quality. Kelly made a rodent face and the Avatar mimicked her. She smiled. Straight, white teeth with rosebud lips smiled back. She scrolled through the clothing options and decided on a demure green halter neck bikini with a pair of soft fleece shorts.

"All done," she murmured to herself.

Now she was inside the chat, she could use ALY, the voice-to-message software, to communicate with Abby.

"Hey, Abby!"

There was a pause.

"Hey!" Abby, or her Avatar, came jogging over. "Isn't this one awesome?"

"These VRs have so much money, it's crazy."

"No! No VR techie talk!" Abby chastised. "You're turning into your Dad." She grinned.

"Sorry." Kelly held up her hands and took a deep breath. She scanned the crowds over Abby's head. Several male avatars were checking her out. "You're getting some... er... attention," Kelly giggled.

Abby spun round eagerly. "Brandon?" she whispered.

"I don't see him, just... the others." Kelly waved a hand in real time and made a face when her Avatar did it. Luckily, the guys weren't looking at her and didn't notice her waving an arm at them.

"I hope he comes," Abby said wistfully.

"I'm sure he will Ab."

Abby kept scanning the crowds and Kelly looked off into the distance. She could make out a resort of some kind a little way down the coast, the white buildings gleaming in the bright sun. The beach was a half-moon shape, and the cliffs that rose up behind them were dotted with plants of some kind. Kelly was too absorbed in the scenery, and how incredibly real it was, to notice a guy come up behind her.

"Hey."

Kelly spun around. A male Avatar was standing close to her. He had messy, shoulder length blonde hair, deeply tanned skin and wore only a pair of navy board shorts. She quickly looked down at the bottom of her screen.

Username JACKW414

She tried to remember if she knew anyone with that tag. Did she even know a Jack? She tried to think of all the kids in her class, but her mind drew a blank.

"You go to Fairfield high right?"

Kelly didn't speak. She just nodded.

"I go to Palisades... it's the school just down the street. I've seen you around."

Kelly breathed a sigh of relief. He didn't go to Fairfield.

"Hey," she said.

A pale blue dialogue box popped up on the left of her screen.

"I'm Jack." He grinned and ran a hand through his hair.

"Kelly." She smiled back. "So... what's Palisades like?" She looked around for Abby, who appeared to be talking to another boy, though Kelly couldn't tell if it was Brandon or not.

"Oh... not like the palace that Fairfield is." He laughed.

Kelly laughed too. Fairfield was famous for being elitist. "Yeah... it's... well, it's got good tech and teachers." Kelly wanted to revisit the comment he had made about seeing her around. "So... Palisades, huh?"

"Yeah, my parents both work in the education sector.

They don't believe in private schools…" He paused awkwardly, "but I actually live in the Excalibur apartments."

"Really? Me too!" Kelly grinned and shifted in her seat. Her avatar wriggled on the sandy beach. She was about to continue when a message popped up on the bottom of her screen.

VR ROOM DOOR OPEN. PLEASE CLOSE FOR A BETTER VR EXPERIENCE. EXTERNAL SENSES MAY AFFECT YOUR VR EXPERIENCE.

A moment later, she heard her Dad's voice, "Kelly? Kel?"

"Shit!" Kelly cursed. She had told her Dad she was doing school projects, and now she was mucking about on a beach VR with Abby and someone she hardly knew. "Shit!" Kelly cursed again, remembering the open chat.

She exited the VR to the mainframe, not bothering to shut anything down. She quickly touched her ongoing Astral project, a detailed piece about planets in other galaxies.

"In here, Dad," she said. She prayed the others wouldn't try to pm her for a moment. Abby knew better, but Jack might wonder why her Avatar had suddenly vanished. She lifted her dreamer from her face.

"Hey." He poked his head in the door and glanced at the screen. "Sorry to interrupt… can I have a word?"

"Sure," Kelly replied quickly, pulling off the rest of her gear and hurrying out to the main VR room.

"I've had a call from your mother."

Abby's steps slowed and her stomach dropped.

"She wants me to join her in Vegas… says there is something I need to see… an opportunity," he mumbled. His face was flushed.

Abby's mouth fell open in an 'O' of surprise. Her mother might be bright and loud, but she never tried to push her father into doing things he didn't like. Whatever it was she wanted him to see, it must be a big deal.

"I... I should go, but I don't want to just leave you here all alone."

"I'm sixteen Dad, I'll be fine. I won't even leave the house," she said with a sigh of relief. "I'll be doing schoolwork the entire time," she added, thinking of the list her headmistress had given her after their meeting.

"Are... are you sure?"

Kelly wondered if her dad was trying to use her as an excuse not to have to go. "I mean... Mom must really want you to go."

"I know." Her father shifted from foot to foot. Almost, it seemed to Kelly, excitedly.

"And I bet there is a ton of awesome stuff to see at the VR convention. I've heard it's really hard to get tickets."

"Yes, yes," her father said quickly, "but your mother has got me a pass ready... if you don't mind me going."

"No Dad... that is cool... I bet you'll have an amazing time... I'm fine here by myself." She smiled at her Dad's worried face, "I promise."

TUESDAY

Kelly ambled through the empty kitchen. She opened the fridge door and stared inside. Her Dad had gotten her groceries and the fridge was stuffed full with things he knew she would like. She felt a little guilty. He had left for Las Vegas feeling terrible about leaving her home alone for a week. She still hadn't confessed about her suspension.

She felt especially guilty about the fact that her father had left her with 20,000 bitcoins to spend on any VRs she wanted to make sure she wasn't bored.

Her phone buzzed on the counter and she flipped over to see the display. It was her younger cousin, Paulette. Her halo of frizzy hair and cheery smile filled the screen.

"Hey Pauls, how's it going?"

"Good. How are you? Your Dad told my Mom to call and check in on you, but I wanted to talk to you first." Paulette spoke quickly, with an undercurrent of pre-teen excitement. "I can turn on Hologram?"

"Oh no... I'm in my PJs. I'm good. Just eating Chinese food and studying."

"Sounds *amazing,* I'm so jel." Paulette sighed heavily. "We're having some weird salad for dinner... and I'm banned from VR for a week," she flounced.

"Oh no!" Kelly scanned the muted TV. There was a film on that she wanted to watch. "That sucks. How come?"

"Well..." Paulette took a deep inhale. Kelly scrunched her eyes shut. Her cousin could talk endlessly.

"A kid at my school had some mega freak out. It was nuts... I mean... like, really nuts. He had been doing horror VRs." She paused, then her voice dropped to a whisper. "So, yeah, he had been doing a ton of VRs like, those, like, gross scary ones. Torture and stuff... I don't know, I hate that kind of stuff. Anyway, he had been doing them all with LokTek, like hyper real ones."

"Jesus!" Kelly murmured.

"I know, right? Isn't that insane? So, anyway, this kid got all weird and messed up and ended up attacking a bunch of kids at school."

"That's awful, Pauls. Are you OK?"

"Oh, yeah... he like, isn't in my grade or anything," Paulette said quickly. Kelly heard the clip of shoes and then muffled voices. "Kelly?" Her Aunt Mary's gentle voice came down the line.

"Hey Auntie. How are you?"

"Has Paulette been telling you about this awful business at her school?"

"Erm... yeah she did." Kelly smiled. Her aunt didn't sound angry.

"Silly parents, letting their kids lock their VRs and do them all unattended. I mean, do your parents let you do that?" Aunt Mary shook her head and Kelly heard her hair rustle down the phone. "I mean... I guess you're a little different, just like Bernie," Her aunt added fondly.

Kelly smiled, always thinking it was weird when she heard Aunt Mary talk about her baby brother, who Kelly only knew as Dad. "Yeah... I mean, they're pretty relaxed, but I don't really do much on the VR except school stuff, or stuff with Dad."

"You're a good girl, Kel. Well look, I'd better get dinner on the table. Call us if you need anything. Love you darling!"

Aunt Mary hung up after Kelly said goodbye. Kelly thought about the Baja beach party with Abby the other day and felt a twinge of guilt. She hardly ever abused her VR privileges. She knew her parents hated her using the party VRs.

Another wave of guilt washed over her; her mother's disappointed face when the Headmistress called about her punching a girl, her subsequent suspension, lying to Dad. It all added up and Kelly felt tears welling up in her eyes. She snuffled and went upstairs. She would only use the VR for schoolwork from now on.

WEDNESDAY

"Are you there?" Abby's voice carried through Kelly's bedroom. The room was tastefully decorated in pale grays and blues, with minimalist furniture and some vibrant shots from Kelly's favorite VR trips.

Abby's hologram rose up from the phone and she swiveled on the base, looking for Kelly.

"I'm just changing, hold on!" Kelly called as she stepped out of the closet. "Sorry."

"Oh my god, did you hear about that kid at Parkdale? Who freaked out?"

"Yeah, my cousin goes there. She told me last night. It's horrible."

"Everyone at school has been freaking out about it."

Kelly bit her lower lip. That probably meant everyone had forgotten about her attacking another girl. "It's crazy, for sure."

"So, I VR'd with Brandon the other night!" Kelly twirled excitedly.

"Were you talking to him in the VR the other night?"

"Yeah, where'd you go by the way? Did your Dad come in?"

"Yeah."

"S'what I figured." Abby sat down and crossed her legs on the floor. "So, Brandon and I got chatting and then last night he wanted me to VR on our own. He is so amazing." Abby sighed heavily.

"That's awesome, Abs." Kelly smiled.

"Who was the cute guy you were talking to?"

"Huh?" Kelly frowned, and then remembered Jack. "Oh... yeah, some guy Jack, he goes to Palisades."

"He was seriously hot."

Kelly giggled. "Yeah he was pretty cute," she conceded.

"We should VR now and see if he's on!" Abby chirped.

"I can't, I'm not supposed to use the VR machine for anything but school work or proper trips."

"Come on Kel, he was so hot! There are no guys even close to that hot at Fairfields."

"Except Brandon."

"Well, obviously." Abby beamed. "Please... come on."

"I really can't, Abby. My parents will kill me and I'm in enough trouble already."

Abby was quiet for a moment. She pulled her knees into her chest. "I'm sure your Mom will understand Kel... about the suspension."

Kelly smiled. This was why Abby was her best friend. Because she understood, and she always said the right thing.

"We can VR for a little bit I guess." Kelly smiled at her friend. "But this is for you and Brandon, I doubt Jack will even be there."

Kelly and Abby decided to check out the beach party at Baja once again, just in case Jack had logged into it again. Kelly's screen panned over the same generic beach as before. Looking at it impartially, she found it bland and a little basic. All the money for the VR had obviously been funneled into making sure that people could feel the warm air, smell the salt, sunblock and sugary drinks, and taste them too.

Kelly and Abby had their avatars in an open chat. Kelly waited whilst her VR chip synched fully with the dreamer. It was lagging.

"Sorry, chip was lagging," she said once she entered the VR.

"No sign of either of them." Abby replied promptly. Her avatar made a pouty face.

"I'm sure Brandon will be here Abs, he's probably just doing homework and stuff."

"Yeah," Abby replied glumly. Before Kelly could speak, a huge grin spread across Abby's face. "Ohmigod, they're both here!" She yelped. Her avatar shook out her glossy blonde curls and waved.

"What?" Kelly spun round to see Brandon and Jack walking over. Brandon was frowning slightly, but Jack appeared to be talking animatedly to him. Their conversation stopped when they reached the girls.

"Hey Abby!" Brandon smiled at her. "Hey Kelly!" He gave her a strange half smile.

"Hi!" Abby was cheery and her voice sounded bright and static-y in Kelly's ears. Kelly felt her stomach lurch as she wondered for the hundredth time what kind of things were being said about her at school.

"Hey Brandon. Hey Jack." She kept her voice neutral.

"Are you OK, Kelly?" Jack's Avatar leant in close to her. "You look kinda dazed."

"I… I'm OK," she replied slowly.

"You wanna go hang out away from all this noise?" Jack leant in towards her conspiratorially as Abby shifted towards Brandon.

"We can all go hang by that chill out pool," Brandon said quickly. Abby looked affronted, and then quickly rearranged her face into a smile.

"It's OK, you guys go, I have schoolwork to do," Kelly replied quickly. Her stomach felt queasy.

"I was hoping to see you again," Jack said softly.

"I mean... we could go hang in a more chilled VR," Brandon said once again.

"Let's leave these two." Abby nudged Brandon. "We can go hang by the chill out pool."

"I'd really like to spend some time with you, Kelly." Jack gave her a winning smile and Kelly pushed the strange fluttering in her chest aside. Abby tugged Brandon away, towards the chill pool.

"Do you wanna go hang in a different VR? There is this Scottish Isle one that looks amazing?"

Kelly perked up. She knew the VR, she had had it at the top of her own wish list for months. "Oh my god, yeah, I... I have wanted to do that one for ages."

Brandon squinted at Kelly's Avatar from the chill pool.

"Hey... hi... Hello in there?" Abby waved a hand in front of his face.

"Sorry, it's just..." Brandon's voice trailed off. His avatar shifted uncomfortably.

Abby had a lurching feeling in her stomach. Kelly was beautiful. She was tall and willowy, and her thick auburn hair cascaded down her back and framed her pale freckled skin. Her glasses made her look demure and pretty in a bookish sort of way, and her rosebud lips had a faint smile, making her look friendly. Abby suddenly felt a waspish jealousy creeping up her neck.

"What? What is it?" Abby's voice was pinched.

"I dunno." Brandon draped an arm across her shoulders. "Something about that guy Jack seemed off... like... I... like he didn't seem... real? I dunno..."

Abby looked up at him sharply. She suddenly felt awash with guilt about her jealous notions. "What do you mean?"

"I just asked him some stuff about Palisades and he didn't know anything... and he kept asking weird stuff about Kelly."

Abby felt a prickle on her neck and she swallowed. "I should go tell Kelly," she said quickly.

Brandon nodded, but when they turned to where Jack and Kelly had been standing, both avatars were gone.

Kelly didn't think too much about it as she paid the 5000 bitcoins for the Scottish Isles VR. It was very cheap, but her father said that there wasn't that much demand for remote VRs like that, even though most of them were labors of love and so they were actually very good. She knew her parents wouldn't have a problem with her taking a VR like that. She wasn't sure how they would feel about her going with a boy, but then again, they were only friends. She hadn't ever had a boyfriend before, not that she would call Jack her boyfriend or anything.

She took a deep breath out in the VR control room as she selected *The Scottish Isles* from her wish list. She fiddled around with the mainframe settings, making sure her dreamer was working properly and her touch gloves. She double-checked volume, brightness, depth perception and her avatar. Everything looked good. The door to the VR room was closed. There was no chance of her mom or dad walking in mid-VR. She had turned off her phone and set the room to 'Do Not Disturb', so none of the house electronics would interrupt her. She glanced around the room one last time.

"OK… just friends hanging out. No big deal. I've wanted to do this trip for ages. Dad gave me money for stuff like this. It's super cheap, and it's a pretty educational trip," Kelly said out loud. "Oh my god, get a grip," she muttered a moment later.

She walked into the tiny VR cube and firmly shut the door.

Slipping on the Dreamer and touch gloves she settled into the large recliner chair and got comfortable. She had told Jack she would only be five minutes. She clicked the *Link VR chip to Dreamer* button. She felt the strange tingling as the chip in her brain synched with the dreamer, and then everything went blank.

It took a moment as the VR loaded. When the screen appeared she was standing in a small, picturesque village. A white sign with black lettering said 'PORTREE.' She stood in front of a small port where a ferry was docking. The air was crisp, salty and faintly fishy. The houses stood in a row on the curved cobble street, in hues of pink, blue and yellow. Nearby, looming above them, a large church nestled among thick trees. The sea behind Kelly was choppy and dark, but the sky was a bright, cloudless blue.

She could feel the air on her fingertips, a little chilly, and excitement welled in her chest. For a moment, she forgot all about Jack. She turned and looked out. The scalloped, curved edges of the island weaved back and forth and she could see inlets and coves dotted with quaint white homes. She looked down and gently tapped the 'arrow' feature that nestled in the corner of the screen. Immediately arrows fell from above, each one neatly labeled with a local landmark; Portree, Fairy Pools, Talisker Distillery, Armadale Castle, Dunvegan Castle, Old Man of Storr, Neist Point Lighthouse, Boreraig, The Quiraing, Cuillin Moutains, Uig, Red Deer, Whale Watching, Caisteal Maol, Dunscaith, and Duntulm. On and on the arrows went, all over the island. Kelly jumped with excitement.

A stereotypical fisherman popped up in front of her in a thick Fair Isle sweater, wellies, and a knitted hat. He had a thick white beard and rosy cheeks. "Hullo Miss, ye're a bonnie wee thing, y'here for a tour?"

Kelly smiled. This trip must have an optional VR guide. She was about to say yes when Jack appeared at the small port.

"We don't need a guide, right?" Jack smiled at her. His avatar shifted uncomfortably.

"Oh um... are you OK?" Kelly looked him up and down. His smile had quickly faded and he shifted from one foot to another.

"Just Mom and Dad getting at me." He sighed. "Your parents must be chill."

"They're out of town." Kelly bit her lower lip. "We don't have to do this right now. We can come another time if you need to study."

"Nah, it's fine." Jack spoke loudly. "Come on. We don't

need a guide." He clicked the guide away and the computerized avatar wandered off down the street. "I really want to check out the Caisteal Maol ruins." Jack was back to bouncing from foot to foot.

"Oh... sure." Kelly chewed her lips. She wanted to wander around and relax in the VR and take her time to explore from arrow to arrow, not hop around and miss things. She did want to see Caisteal Maol ruins, but she could always revisit the VR later if she wanted to check things out at her own pace.

"Come on," Jack urged, hurrying her towards the small booth.

Most VRs like this had booths, cleverly disguised as phone boxes, market stalls or whatever was appropriate, but all with the blue arrow emblem, where you could 'jump' your Avatars from arrow to arrow, allowing you to see a range of things within a VR quickly.

They quickly 'jumped' to Caisteal Maol. Kelly stared at the ruins in awe. Two towers of rough-hewn stone rose out of an isolated mound, surrounded by brackish plants and icy seawater. The stone was moss covered and lumpy, and the bracken and heather nearby gave the area a colorful marbling.

"It's amazing," Kelly breathed.

"It's smaller than I thought," Jack said with a frown.

"It's said to predate the 15th century," Kelly said informatively. "They hadn't planned on doing excavations back in the twenty-first century. I believe the ruins were excavated sometime in the twenty-second century, they had better technology then and so they were able to keep the existing ruins safe." Kelly grinned cheesily. "Sorry... I'm just really into this stuff."

"Huh, it's cool." Jack stood away from her looking at the stones.

"So yeah... they excavated the ruins and found a bunch of cellars. I don't know, maybe with this VR we can go inside them, all depends on how much time and effort the VR designers put in." Kelly began walking around one side of the ruins as Jack skulked behind her.

The cavernous cellars were dark and dank. Kelly could taste the wet air and feel the chill on her fingers. Moss and ferns wormed their way through cracks in the stone and the ground underfoot was loosely-packed dirt. Kelly inhaled. The rich smell of loamy soil and vegetation filled the cellar.

"Oh my god!" Kelly turned to smile at Jack, but he wasn't behind her. "Jack?" She called out. Her voice carried around the cellar.

Kelly felt a strange clicking at the back of her skull. "What the...?" She looked around. The light in the basement seemed to be fading. "Jack?" She called out again, trying to fight the rising panic in her throat.

She looked to the base of the screen, but her control icons had disappeared.

Kelly started to walk towards the entrance to the cellar, but in the gloom, she had become disoriented and she walked towards a second room instead. When she walked inside she heard a strange keening, like that of a cat or injured animal.

"Jack? Is... is that you?" Kelly tried to keep her voice relaxed, but in the shadows she could see the figure of a hulking man, blood dripping from spade-like hands, a cruel sneer across his lips and a large knife held out towards Kelly.

"Oh my god!" Kelly stumbled backwards and tripped. Her hands hit something soft as she fell and she turned to see half-decomposed bodies and maggots writhing out of gaping wounds. She gagged and felt hot wet tears on her face. She looked up as the terrifying man began to walk towards her, a maniacal grin on his face.

"No! No!" Kelly held her hands out in front of her. "The Dreamer!" She mumbled tearfully, reaching for her avatar's face, for her face in real time. But her hands and the Dreamer felt locked. As the man got closer, she scrabbled to her feet and ran towards a small square of light across the cellar. "What's going on?" she sobbed. "Jack?" She called out again as she desperately tried to claw at her own face, but Jack had vanished.

Her Dreamer should be coming off, taking her out of the VR immediately. She looked at the bottom of the screen again, but her icons were still absent. "Come on!" she cried, gulping down panicked sobs. From within the bowels of the cellar she could hear slow, heavy footsteps, crying, and pained moaning. Were some of those bodies real people? Other people in VR? Kelly wondered with horror. Why didn't they just leave? She shook her head, and then she remembered the strange clicking at the base of her skull. LokTek. Someone had locked her VR, trapping her inside.

"No... no!" Kelly shook her head. She never used LokTek. She didn't even like using VRs that were thrill or horror genre. Something wasn't right. She thought about what her dad had told her about leaving VRs open, but before she could finish her train of thought, the man appeared again. He pointed a knife at her and began to lurch over. Surely he couldn't hurt her in VR, right? But as she saw his blood-drenched clothing she panicked and ran from him, going deeper into the warren of cellars. More rotting corpses littered the floors. Kelly tried to dodge them, but she felt her feet slipping on half-congealed blood. Her stomach churned.

"Help... help me!" A girl cried out. Kelly paused and looked down. The girl lay across the tunnel. Her blonde hair was tangled and matted with blood. Her clothes were dirty and torn. Kelly glanced down and quickly away from the girl's stomach. She had been eviscerated. She looked vaguely like Abby. "Help, please?" she said weakly.

"Got you!" Kelly heard the voice right on the back of her neck and she bolted, leaving as the girl began to scream. The noise carried down the tunnel and followed Kelly.

Kelly reached another quieter room, and took a moment to breathe. The cellars couldn't, shouldn't be this big. She shook her head. Someone had tampered with the VR. This wasn't supposed to be one of those horrible horror VRs. She scrunched her eyes and wracked her brains. Someone must have hacked her VR Dreamer, and when she had put it on, they had accessed her chip. Someone... Jack! Her stomach dropped as she realized. Her dad had been right. You never leave a VR chat open.

She felt her face crumple as she began to cry. Who was doing this? And why?

She gulped down air, trying to get a grip of herself.

"Tsk tsk... you mustn't run," a gravelly voice said from

the opening of the cellar. Kelly looked up, bracing herself to run, but her body went limp when she saw that the man was holding her mother by her hair, blood dripping from one temple and a knife pressed tightly to her throat.

"She's probably just chatting with him," Brandon assured Abby.

"I dunno... I mean, she usually answers my calls. And, like, all her responses are really short... it's not like her, it doesn't sound like her." Abby was trying to explain, but it wasn't coming out properly. Kelly was messaging her back, but it sounded snippy and strange, not at all the way Kelly messaged.

"Maybe she is just caught up talking to Jack?"

"I... I guess..." Abby frowned. Her hologram frowned, and Brandon frowned.

"Give it till tonight. I wouldn't worry," Brandon said, but his stomach was churning too. He hadn't told Abby about what he had overheard at school. He didn't want her to panic.

"No. Please. Mom." Kelly reached out. Her mother's Avatar whimpered and the man shook her roughly by her hair. More blood streamed out of her temple and dripped over her eyes. Mascara and blood coursed down her pale cheeks.

"Kelly," Her mother said softly.

"Mom," Kelly whispered again.

The man smiled, then let go of Kelly's Mom's hair and she crumpled to the floor. Before either of them could move, the man swiped his dirty hand and smacked her mom against the side of her face. Her lip exploded and she fell sideways.

"How…?" Kelly shook her head, and tears began coursing down her cheeks. Her mom was supposed to be in Vegas. If they had her mom, did they have her dad too? Kelly felt sick.

The man let out a scratchy laugh and kicked her Mom in the stomach. She let out a groaning scream of pain. Kelly ran forwards towards her mother, but the man lashed out with his knife. Then in one brutal movement he stomped a foot down on Kelly's Mom's face.

The screams kept carrying down the corridor from the other bodies. Kelly felt the breath leave her body. "This isn't real… this isn't real," she sobbed to herself.

"Oh Kelly!" The man laughed again.

"Kelly!" Another man's voice, safe and familiar. Dad. Kelly spun round hopefully. Her face fell when she saw her father. Another man was holding him, if you could even call him a man. He was tall, with a shaved head, pocked skin and a mean smile. He held a rusty saw in one hand and Kelly saw in an instant that her father was missing an arm. He groaned as the man threw him down. Blood dripped out from the stump, and the torn sleeve of his sweater revealed straggled muscle, sinew and bone.

Kelly felt acidic bile rise up in her throat. She uselessly clawed the back of her head one more time in the vain hope that her Dreamer had been unlocked, but to no avail. She felt her head swimming, and swallowed. The VR chip wouldn't let her faint, but her body desperately tried. She looked over to her father. His avatar lay semi-conscious on the filthy floor.

The two men looked over to Kelly, murderous looks in their eyes. "We've saved the best for you," the first man leered. The other man looked on lasciviously. Kelly looked back to her parents. In the half gloom – she almost missed it - her mother's face glitched, becoming blank and resetting. It wasn't her, not really, just a copy of her avatar.

Kelly sniffed and struggled to her feet. "No," she said, as firmly as she could manage.

"No?" The second man sneered.

"This is fake," Kelly said, louder now. "This isn't real. They're just copies of my parents' avatars. This..." She waved a hand at the cellar as her voice grew stronger. She was remembering everything her father had told her about VR, "all of this, it's fake, and you can't really hurt me." She stood up straighter.

"Kelly... Kelly... Kelly..." The voice was nasal and mocking.

Kelly recognized it instantly: JJ Barnes. The girl who had tormented Kelly for the past five years of her life. The girl who had pushed Kelly so far that Kelly had snapped and punched her in the face.

"You're just so fucking clever, aren't you? I can't believe you actually thought a guy was into *you*." JJ sneered. "I mean... Jack? Come on!" JJ laughed cruelly. Her disembodied voice taunted. "You're right, they can't hurt you, but my guess is that what we have in store for *your* Avatar next... that might push you over the edge." Her laugh tinkled over the VR and there was a moment of fuzziness.

Kelly looked around the cellar desperately. She had been duped. Jack was JJ in disguise. Before she could speak, a copy of her own avatar, virtually indistinguishable from her real self, walked in, completely naked. The two hideous men, real or fake avatars, Kelly had no idea, stared greedily at her body.

"By the way, this is all being recorded and live streamed," said JJ.

SATURDAY

"Hey, Mrs Simmons..." Abby gulped. She felt awash with nerves and guilt. It had been four days and she still couldn't get hold of Kelly on the phone. She had messaged her on the open chat room, but slowly Kelly had become shorter and meaner, and Abby had started panicking.

Last night Brandon had finally confessed to her that he had heard some rumors going around at school about a live stream link of Kelly, of something JJ had planned, and of people now watching this live link. Abby couldn't bring herself to click it, she was so consumed with panic.

"Hello? Kelly?" The voice was high pitched and panicked.

Abby felt nerves jump simultaneously in her jaw and stomach. Kelly's Mom sounded agitated.

"Er... no, it's Abby. Abby Hardwell." She felt strange saying her last name.

"Yes, of course, Abby. Is Kelly with you?"

There was a twang of desperation to her voice. "Oh... no... actually that's why I'm calling."

Abby heard Kelly's dad in the background, "Is that Kelly?"

"No, it's her friend Abby. Sorry, carry on Abby." Kelly's Mom sounded strained.

"I haven't been able to get in touch with Kelly apart from VR messages for like... four days now... I tried calling and I... I don't mean to sound crazy..." Abby babbled, "but... but I don't think it's Kelly."

"What? You haven't spoken to her on the phone either?"

Abby heard both Kelly's parents now, and she realized she must be on loudspeaker. Her stomach churned and she began to cry. This was all her fault. "There was this boy, Jack... she went to talk to him... that was on Tuesday... I, I..."

"Oh my god! Bernie, we need to get on a plane."

Abby was about to speak when the line went dead.

ONE MONTH LATER

Kelly was wrapped in a blanket on the sofa in the living room. It was an L-shaped sofa, with plush gray cushions and thick cashmere blankets draped over the back and arms. Her skinny body was sunken into the cushions and her eyes stared out blankly. Her e-reader sat ignored in her hand. The TV screen was black on the wall in front of her. She stared up at it.

Both her parents were in the Excalibur building. Her father was tucked in his office, unsure of what to say to her. Her mother had gone to the gym. She talked at, not to, Kelly now, efficient and cheery. Touching her hair, her shoulder, checking she was there, she was solid.

Kelly nodded and smiled when they spoke to her. There was a rictus grin on her face when she had to hear about the incident. About her mother saying it wouldn't last forever. About her mother saying it would pass. About the newscasters talking in clipped voices, their eyebrows knitted together in a frown as they discussed and dissected it. About the clips on social media that just wouldn't go away.

She stared at the TV. She knew that she would turn it on and there would be a daytime show talking about her or a news special about it. But she just couldn't not turn it on. She just had to see, to know, what the world was saying about Kelly Simmons, the girl who got trapped in a VR and preyed upon, mentally and sexually, by cruel school bullies.

"I mean... that poor girl... how do you deal with something like that at sixteen? With the internet nowadays... it's everywhere," a black woman in a soft cowl neck sweater said sympathetically.

"This is where the bullies really need prosecuted harshly," said a man sitting across from her on the sofa. He wore a slim-cut gray suit and he was overly tanned.

"The two older men who... participated" a third, smartly dressed older woman said delicately, "were prosecuted. Engaging in a sexual act of any kind with an underage avatar is a criminal offense. Especially since they knew she was being held against her will."

"I mean people have really focused on that aspect of this heinous crime, but these bullies actually forced the young girl to watch her parents' avatars being tortured and killed," the kindly black woman said.

"Yes, exactly," the man cut in. "And she was locked in for five days, with their bodies, even if they weren't real, the VRs nowadays... I mean they're so realistic..."

"Well, she could have died from dehydration," the older woman said severely. "That is why the bullies are being

charged with attempted manslaughter. They locked her VR and left her. Aside from the horrible psychological torture of having to witness what she did, and having them abuse her own avatar like that and live stream it for the world to see, these kids did actually commit a serious crime."

"Of course," the man agreed hurriedly.

Kelly switched channels. She had seen all this before. The world is on your side, Kelly. That was what her mother said. Her mother didn't know what the kids at her school were saying, what online forums and strangers said about her.

That she was a whore.

That it was her own fault.

That they were watching her on repeat.

That the video had been picked up by porn sites and pedophiles.

That she got what she deserved.

Kelly had overheard her parents the night before. She had not been able to sleep, in spite of the pills the psychiatrist had given her, and she had heard their hushed whispers through the crack in her door.

"How? How did this happen Bernie? I mean, she is our child. How did we... how did we not hear from her for four days? This is all my fault. If I had asked her about what happened at school, or called her more... I should have been more worried."

"Angela, we did, remember?" her father said soothingly. "We spoke to her online, we thought it was her."

"She is MY child Bernie, I should have known it wasn't her!"

"Angela, darling, that girl, that awful girl, she… she knew what she was doing. She messaged like Kelly."

Her mother sniffled. "But Mary said she spoke to her!" She had changed tack, a note of anger creeping into her voice.

"No, she said Paulette spoke to her. And when we pushed her about it, Paulette said she never said that. Mary said she did. Paulette admitted she probably wasn't listening to her Mom and just babbled," her father replied softly.

"Stupid, stupid girl!" Angela cried out, her voice rising to a hysterical sob.

"I know," her Dad replied sadly.

Kelly was about to head out of her room and let them know that it wasn't Paulette's fault, that she had let Jack into her messaging, that she had been duped, when her mother continued.

"I want that JJ girl prosecuted to the fullest extent of the law. I want that nasty little bitch not to see the light of day until she is eighty fucking five!"

Her dad said nothing. Kelly wondered if he was nodding along.

"We need to take care of Kelly right now. The lawyer will take care of the… others."

"They're not others, Bernie," her mother said coldly, "they are the fuckers who abused our daughter, and I will make them pay."

Kelly wrapped the blanket tighter around her shoulders. Her parents had found her, soiled and half-comatose, in the VR room, and manually pulled her out of the VR. She couldn't talk or explain what had happened, but it didn't matter, because it was all over the Internet. Police were called. Then doctors, lawyers and psychiatrists. Journalists were turned away.

A VR advertising channel was on. They were pushing a tropical relaxation getaway VR, complete with swimming with dolphins, kayaking on crystal-clear water, and long secluded beaches. The advert drew to a close, with one last panorama of a sunset.

A man walked on the screen, older and kindly looking. Safe looking.

"In this day and age, you just can't predict what might happen in a VR. That's why, here at LokTek, we have created the newest wave of kid-safe technology."

Behind the man, the image of a mild horror VR with a young teenage boy in it appeared.

"We know that no matter how good a parent you are, you can't always control what your kids are getting up to. With KnightSafe, you can rest assured that your VR can never be hacked, abused or locked. KnightSafe has three separate parts; firstly, you can set a series of controls as to which VRs can be accessed, fairly standard right?"

The man smiled as the kid in the background wandered further into a zombie-strewn wasteland.

"But that on its own is never bulletproof." The man smiled. *"That is where KnightSafe stands out. We have two further safety nets. The second is a patented anti-hacking software that keeps your VRs safe, and the third is a manual emergency release button."* The man beamed at the audience.

At the bottom of the screen a small asterisk appeared: **Manual Release Button KnightSafe TouchGloves must be purchased for this feature.*

On the screen behind him, a zombie stumbled towards the boy. The young boy panicked, screamed, and then touched a red button on his gloves, taking him back to the safety of his cushy VR room. Mom and Dad looked on from the doorway with smug, satisfied grins.

Kelly swallowed. How much money would they make from KnightSafe and KnightSafe TouchGloves?

She quickly switched channels.

"Good evening, I am Azumi Hawkins, and this is CNN News, where we have a special report on the recent VR hacking case that has taken over America." A beautiful, stern Asian woman in a tailored white suit looked out at the screen with a deadpan face.

"We are here tonight with a top VR tech, a lawyer, and a psychologist to take a look at this awful case that has shocked the nation to its core." She took a slow breath. *"The VR tech sector has taken America by storm, and whilst there have been reports of it being abused, this is a case that has truly shed a light on some of the very real and serious dangers of VR technology."*

The camera swiveled to two men and one woman sitting at a frosted glass table. *"Here with us tonight, we have people at the top of their profession to discuss the impact this case could have on VR, and on the public."*

The Asian woman joined the others and motioned to each of them in turn. *"This is Robert Clarendon, a troubleshooting VR engineer who has worked with all the top firms, Abigail Prince, a lawyer whose firm specializes in VR related cases, and José Maillol, one of the world's leading psychologists. Welcome."* She gave them a tight, formal smile. They nodded back somberly.

This wasn't like the daytime TV and sensationalist news reports, but Kelly felt the same shame and melancholy. The world was still gossiping and judging her. She had heard of Robert Clarendon. He was a British engineer who her Dad talked about with reverence.

"Well, from our side of things, the ruling on this case will set a precedent for anything that comes after," Abigail Prince began. Her words were decisive and rehearsed. She was a large woman, tall and broad shouldered, with a strong jaw and heavy framed glasses.

"The hearing for the two men who participated was yesterday," Azumi Hawkins added informatively. *"And the young woman who masterminded this, JJ Barnes, is to be tried next week."*

"Now, as a lawyer, let's play Devil's advocate here Abigail." Azumi narrowed her eyes. *"Could it be said, as some have, that this was all a horrible prank gone wrong?"*

"If I was her lawyer, that is what I would be arguing," Abigail said slowly. *"Or retaliation. The victim had been suspended a few days prior to the VR attack for assaulting JJ Barnes."*

"Come on!" José Maillol cut in harshly, *"it was clearly premeditated. The girls' lawyers are trying to argue that it was a prank to get back at the victim, but time stamps show that she was planning this for a while. She had contacted the two men involved, created a fake Avatar, and purchased hacking software. Maybe the assault was what set her off... but it is clear that this JJ Barnes had bullied the victim for years."*

Abigail looked at him coldly, annoyed at his

interruption. *"Yes, as I was saying, if I was JJ Barnes'*
lawyer, I would be arguing it was a prank. However," she
said emphatically, *"at sixteen you could well be tried as an*
adult. As she should be, since this was clearly a thought out,
abusive plan."

Azumi turned to Clarendon. *"Mr Clarendon, what are*
your thoughts on the new wave of LokTek and KnightSafe
technology?"

Mr Clarendon pursed his lips together and took a
moment to think about the question. *"It's all a front. Waste*
of money," He said in a clipped English accent. *The others*
looked at him sharply. *"We can't stop hacking. It's simply not*
possible."

Kelly's stomach dropped and blood rushed into her ears.
She felt sick and ashamed and her cheeks burned furiously.

"Hackers will always be around, but more importantly,
evil people who want to use technology in evil ways will
always exist," Robert Clarendon continued. *"They'll always*
be targeting people."

"Mmm hmm," José Malliol agreed. *"The key thing will*
be educating people on how to recognize signs of VR bullying,
how to cope with the aftermath."

Kelly cocked her head at the TV. She suddenly knew
how to cope with the aftermath. She knew exactly how. She
stood up from the sofa, her legs wobbly, and let the blanket
slide off her shoulders. She turned her head to look around
the house. It was quiet. The door to the bathroom was ajar.
Her sleeping pills, prescribed for her night terrors, nestled
in the mirrored cabinet above the sink.

"It's just so hard for kids nowadays, to really know… to
understand what to do in these situations. They seem, and

they are, at the time, enormous... and eternal." José Malliol continued. His voice was slightly accented and soft.

Kelly heard the words in pieces. Enormous. Eternal. Bullying. She sloped silently towards the bathroom. She closed the door silently, letting the catch click into place and then turning the lock slowly so it was soundless. She opened the cabinet. Her pill bottle, white and with the dense text of her prescription running around it, sat at the front. Yes, Kelly thought to herself, this was exactly how to cope in the aftermath.

Forgotten

Derek Mulberry raced through Terminal 5, past the hip sushi bar and the WH Smiths, towards the quieter end of the airport. Little Susannah Mulberry, sticky-fingered and close to tears, tried to nestle her chubby cheeks into her father's neck. He kept bouncing around and his collarbone struck her chin. She bit her thumb, which was tucked inside her mouth. She wanted to cry and scream, but even Susannah's infant brain could sense that something was deeply, horribly wrong.

"It's OK, OK." Derek murmured. He was tall, with salt and pepper hair cropped close to his head. He wore a tailored suit in navy pinstripe, but the trousers were rumpled and the jacket dotted with stains.

"Mm Ma-ma," Susannah whimpered.

"I know sweetie. I know." Derek felt heat radiating from his cheeks. Were people looking at him? He glanced around the airport. Some people were giving him sideways glances, but mostly people assumed that he and his little girl were rushing for their flight, and simply moved out of their way to let Derek pass.

'All passengers on Flight BA 179 to Stockholm, flight boarding is now closed at Gate B 11. Flight BA 179 to Stockholm is now closed. Flight AA624 to Montreal is now boarding at Gate C 52.'

Derek gulped. He stopped his jog and looked behind him. A cluster of people waiting in line at Pret à Manger had clogged up the main artery of the airport. He looked around. A parents' changing cubicle branched off to his right. He quickly dove inside and locked the door, jangling the handle to make sure.

"OK baby girl. OK darling." Derek lowered the changing table and carefully placed Susannah on it.

"I potty." Susannah pointed at the child-sized toilet.

"Okie doke." Derek tried to smile at his daughter as he lifted her down and helped with her panda print leggings and pull-ups. Susannah peed with a look of serious concentration, then pointed at the washbasin. "Hands."

Derek nodded, turning the tap on.

Susannah sniffed. "Mm hungry," she whined. Her stomach growled and she made a face.

"I know, darling." Derek was pacing around the small room. He patted his trouser pockets. He had a money clip with a few bills in it. He had thrown his mobile phone into a bin back on New Kings Road. Hopefully that would buy them some time.

"I know," Derek repeated, wondering if he should buy her some sweeties. He knew Angela hated it when their daughter had too much sugar. It got her all wound up. "We can get you a nice... a nice..." He mumbled, trying to think what it was Susannah liked apart from sweeties.

"Dadda." She reached up to him, her red cheeks inflamed and her eyes drooping.

"Come on then." He scooped her up and carefully unlocked the door. He poked his head out.

A woman was standing with a pram. She gave Derek a waspish look as he slowly exited the bathroom. Susannah fussed in his arms and Derek heard the woman making a 'tsk' sound as she shut the door.

Derek hurried to Huxley's, a dark and bustling bar. There were booths along the back wall and Derek hurried to sit in a small one. Dirty plates were still scattered across the mahogany wood.

"Sir, I have to clean this... and I'm going to need you to wait to be seated," a young waiter said. His cheeks were rosy and smooth, his skinny neck protruding from a too-big shirt.

Susannah chose that moment to pipe up. Her angel face crinkled and tears sprang from her green eyes. "I hungy," she sobbed, "home." She hiccupped, and the sobs came louder and faster.

"I'm so sorry," Derek smiled. His teeth were straight and white. "We've been travelling all night... I didn't realize." People were starting to look their way and Derek stood up quickly, not wanting to attract attention.

"Suse, we'll find somewhere else."

The young waiter looked back to the front of the restaurant. The young woman who had been waiting smiled at him. 'It's fine,' she mouthed, looking at the sobbing child. The floor manager nodded at him.

"Sir, have a seat, it's not a problem. Another table opened up, so you can stay right here."

Derek sighed. "Thank you, so much, are you sure?" He looked around, but the other diners had gone back to their phones or their food. The young woman he had cut in front of gave him a sympathetic smile as she was led to a nearby table.

"And how about we get you some apple juice and something to eat, huh?" The waiter said, smiling at Susannah. She grinned back, her face still snot and tear stained. She nodded. "Please." She said the word slowly and carefully, pulling apart the 'P' and the 'L' sounds.

The waiter smiled back. "I have a wee sister your age. Let me guess… two and a half?"

"I'm two," Susannah said proudly.

"Well aren't you a chatty wee thing!" The waiter exclaimed.

"Chicken fingys," Susannah said decisively.

Derek smiled. "Hold on sweetie."

"That's OK. My sister's the same, chicken nuggets and chips for every meal. I can get that for her if you like?" Derek nodded. "And anything for you sir?"

"Oh erm… just a coffee. Cappuccino." Derek smiled gratefully again at the young man as he left the table.

Susannah leant back against the booth and snuggled up to her father. Derek wrapped one arm around her and covered his face with his free hand. He was running out of time. Surely they would have tracked him to the airport by now. There were cameras everywhere. Derek was trained to look for the cameras.

He flicked his eyes up around the restaurant. One by the door. One pointed at the bar. He looked towards the gates outside the mouth of Huxley's. Three large gates sat in a U formation. Gates 12, 13 and 14.

Derek looked up towards the ceiling and the corners. The cameras were pointed down the U, but not towards the sides, which meant that someone looking at the footage wouldn't necessarily be able to see if someone was tucked into gates 12 or 14.

He pursed his lips together.

"Dadda. Juice." Susannah pointed. The waiter was back with a carton of apple juice and a cup of coffee.

"Oh yes, great, thanks." Derek gave the waiter a feeble smile. His body ached from fatigue, and he felt as if his eyeballs were about to fall out of his skull.

"I'll be right back with your nuggets little miss," said the waiter.

Susannah grinned a gap-toothed smile back at him. She sipped her juice happily as Derek returned to his musings.

There could be cameras further along that he couldn't see, nestled into the wall. There would invariably be cameras on the route to the airplane, but if it had already left, they would have a much harder job tracking Susannah and him.

Derek shook his head. They weren't tracking Sus, they were tracking him. He gulped as another thought arose. He sipped his coffee, the bitter liquid hitting his empty stomach and churning there angrily.

He looked up at the flight info displayed on a screen in front of him.

Gate 12 : HONG KONG : BA1729 : 15:15 [ON TIME]
Gate 13 : LOS ANGELES : AA62459 : 17:05 [DELAYED]
Gate 14 : NAIROBI : BA672 : 15:35 [ON TIME]

He looked at his watch. It was 2:55pm. The flights to Hong Kong and Nairobi were leaving soon. If he could slip Susannah on to one of them, then maybe he could get her away. Then he could give himself up. Once they had him, they wouldn't care about anything else, certainly not an infant. And he would never tell them which flight he had put her on. He wouldn't even think it. They would never find her. She would be safe.

Derek reached for his coffee. His fingers trembled as he tried to grasp the tiny handle.

"Here we go!" The waiter said, beaming cheerfully.

Derek jolted and knocked his coffee cup.

"Oh goodness, I'm so sorry," the waiter cried, yanking a towel from his apron and hurriedly mopping it up.

Susannah was engrossed in her chicken fingers and fries.

"It's fine… fine," Derek said, dabbing a napkin uselessly.

"Let me grab you another," The waiter said once the spill was cleared. Before Derek could stop him, he had dashed off.

He looked back towards the two flights. Most people had already boarded. Nairobi or Hong Kong? Derek had been to both places. Both were popular with expats, and lots of Brits were boarding. Derek focused in on them. He stretched his neck out as far as he could. He couldn't quite make out the group of remaining passengers waiting to board to Nairobi. Hong Kong it was.

Twenty more minutes until boarding closed. Derek had twenty minutes to decide to whom he would give his child.

Marguerite Allen

The woman looked tired, but motherly. She was half-slumped in her seat, a small bag clutched in her lap and a scarf looped around her neck and draped down in front of her chest, poorly covering several stomach rolls. She hefted herself in her seat and glanced at the other passengers left in the waiting area, but her eyes never met Derek's. She pursed her lips together and ran her fingers through her hair, trying to give some life to the curls she had styled. Her face was long, and there was a puffiness around her eyes and jaw. She reached into her bag for the chocolate buttons she had bought and popped one in her mouth. A moment later, with a sigh, she scooped a handful into her mouth.

Marguerite wrinkled her nose. She hated airports. She wondered why the others were still loitering in the waiting area. Were they hoping to get upgraded too? She exhaled sharply. She deserved a first class seat, or at least a business class one. The flight was nearly twelve hours, for God's sake. She shook her head, frowning at the others disapprovingly. She had been told there was a chance she might get an upgrade. Had the others been told that? She walked up to the woman at the check-in desk.

"I was told there was a good chance I might be upgraded."

"Yes ma'am. I understand. This is quite a busy flight, are you with our frequent flyer program?"

"No!" Marguerite snapped. "I was told by the check-in girl."

"Right. Well let me get the rest of the passengers boarded, then I'll see what I can do."

"I checked in very early." Marguerite cast a venomous glance over her shoulder at the other eight passengers still sitting down. "I was told first that there would likely be an upgrade."

"Of course, ma'am." The woman gave her a bland, placating smile.

Marguerite sighed angrily as she walked back to her seat. Her ankles and knees were sore. She had taken a cab and a train to get to the airport, to sit and wait for four hours. She didn't really want to visit her younger sister in Hong Kong. She didn't like Chinese food. She didn't really like Chinese people, either. Marguerite frowned; was Hong Kong China? She would figure it out on the flight, she thought.

She knew the only reason her sister had invited her was to gloat over her engagement. The man was some British hedge fund guy she had met a year ago at a bar in Sloane Square. It baffled Marguerite how her sister had managed to talk to a man, as she was usually such a mouse. And, in Marguerite's opinion, a bit of a bore, always yakking on about the hospital where she worked.

A slow smile spread across Marguerite's face. She was the prettier one of the two. She had been in TV commercials, and worked in theater. Let's see what the new man thought about his bride when he saw her sister.

"Ma'am?" The woman from the front desk motioned to Marguerite.

Marguerite hurried over. "I'm being upgraded?"

"I'm afraid all the first and business seats are full, and unfortunately all the exit row seats for this flight were booked."

"Well…" Marguerite spluttered, "can't you move them?"

"No ma'am," the woman said firmly, "they paid extra for those seats."

"I have bad knees," Marguerite hissed. "I can't be cramped."

"Do you have a doctor's note?" the woman asked sweetly.

Marguerite glared at her. "I was told there would be an upgrade."

"A *likely* upgrade. Unfortunately, everything is booked up," the woman said with finality.

Derek watched the woman walk back to her seat. The airline agent had been smiling the entire time, though Derek could tell it was a strained smile. He looked at the chubby, middle-aged woman again. She had returned to her seat and opened a fresh packet of chocolate buttons. Susannah did like treats, Derek mused to himself.

Nathan Illingworth

The elderly man three seats down from Marguerite Allen looked decidedly grumpy. His lined, weathered face was rumpled. His mouth was turned down and his gray eyebrows were knitted together. He wore a thick V-neck sweater, well made, with a small emblem on the left breast. A well-thumbed copy of a non-fiction World War II book lay on the seat beside him. He glanced around at the others still seated in the waiting area. His eyes flickered over Huxley's, but Derek didn't know if the man had seen Susannah, still engrossed in her chips, or himself.

Nathan wasn't so much angry as frustrated. He willed the feeling to dissipate. It was always followed by the same tugging depression over the feeling that he wouldn't be feeling this way if Betsy were still there. She was so good at the airport stuff. Not the ticketing and what not, but the calm, breezy attitude to crowds or delays. Nathan missed that more than anything in the world. She was always so happy, warm and smiley, even when everything else was falling apart around them. For sixty-one years she had been there, and now... now she wasn't.

Nathan peered at his phone. Their daughter, Cecelia, had sent him a text. She would be there when he landed. Nathan smiled. Cecelia had given birth to his third grandchild a week before. They had named her Norah Betsy. Nathan scrunched up his face as a photo of the baby popped up on the message thread. How Betsy would have loved to see this little girl. A lump worked its way down Nathan's throat. He scowled again.

Using the aluminum cane the airline had given him at check in, he walked slowly to the help desk. He glanced up at the board behind the woman. N. Illingworth was first on the wait list.

"Can I help you, sir?" The woman smiled.

"Oh... er..." Nathan grumbled, "I was wondering if I'll get on." He nodded his head at the screen. He placed his phone on the counter.

The woman took a glance down. "Oh my goodness, look at that little gem!"

Nathan looked up at the woman. She smiled at him, a trace sheepishly, but he suddenly beamed back at her.

"That's my granddaughter, Norah Betsy, named after my late wife." His loose skin moved slightly as he spoke. "My daughter Cecelia, it's her third. First two are boys." He smiled again. "Big family. Those boys are terrors, but maybe now they have a sister they'll calm down."

"That's wonderful, congratulations!" The airline agent was smiling more genuinely now. "Are you off to see them?"

Nathan nodded and sighed. "They, my daughter and her husband, moved out to Hong Kong for work two years ago. Just before... well, it'll be nice to see them."

The woman nodded. "Hold on a moment sir. You're Mr Illingworth?"

Nathan went to get his passport but she waved it away. Her fingers began moving quickly over the keys, tap-tap-tapping.

"You know sir, it looks like we have one seat left in business class I can put you in. Will that be all right?"

Nathan looked worried. "Oh - I just bought a standard ticket." He frowned.

"Oh no, Mr Illingworth. This is an upgrade, I believe you missed your connection down from Edinburgh this morning on the 9am flight?"

He nodded glumly.

"Well hopefully this makes up for the wait." She smiled and clicked some more buttons. "Give that baby a big smooch, and enjoy your flight sir."

Nathan's eyes began to mist and he tried to hide behind a cough. "Thank you. Thank you so much."

Nathan returned to his seat and slowly began to gather

his things. Norah Betsy. His granddaughter. He smiled. He had a Jellycat bear in his bag for her. He knew she would love it, because it was just the kind of thing Betsy would've picked out.

Derek tilted his head and examined Nathan. The airline agent was smiling, a real smile now, and also watching him. He had taken a seat to gather up his things. Nathan man was smiling too. Derek watched. Nathan man moved slowly, his knobbled hands tracing over his lower back from time to time. Derek shook his head. He was too old to care for Susannah.

Jacob Heatherton

Derek quickly noticed that he wasn't the only one watching the elderly man. A portly, suited businessman was smiling benignly at him. The suited man was wearing a Savile Row number, with a pink shirt and a wide cherry tie. A gold tiepin caught the artificial light and glinted. A slim briefcase was leaning close to his feet and a new iPhone was nestled in one thick-fingered paw. He glanced away from the old man, at Derek. He caught sight of Susannah and her ketchup-stained face. He smiled at them both in a relaxed, fatherly way. Derek gave him a tight smile in return.

Jacob liked airports. He liked people-watching. It was an unusual thing to find himself the focus of such attention. He was a realist. He knew he wasn't handsome or particularly striking in anyway, and yet this man had been staring at him in Huxley's with quite some intensity. The daughter had grinned too, gregariously. She had been waving a chip, though Jacob suspected that this signified a personal triumph rather than a greeting.

He looked down at his boarding pass; he was in business class. He had heard the airline agent during both her conversations. He had felt a small victory on her behalf when she had refused that abhorrent woman and gifted the elderly man with the business seat instead.

Jacob worked at a corporate real estate firm. He was Senior Executive, in charge of all the employees scattered from Hong Kong to Malaysia and as far as Australia. He had been back in London for two weeks to see his ailing mother. He was glad to be leaving her. Mean as it was to admit it, she had spent the entire two weeks haranguing him about the fact that he was unmarried, childless, and obsessed with his job.

"You have Pikachu socks," a voice said. A little boy, being tugged along by his listless mother, was pointing.

"I do indeed," Jacob replied.

"I like Pikachu," the boy said proudly.

"Me too."

"Really?" The little boy frowned.

"But not as much as I like Hitmonchan."

The little boy's eyes went wide. Only people who knew Pokémon knew Hitmonchan. "Me too!" he cried.

"Come on, Brendan," the mother snapped nasally.

"Sorry," Jacob said. His eyes narrowed at the woman. She was yanking on the boy's thin arm.

"Oh... s'fine," she replied, suddenly realizing he was there. "I don't want him to bother you."

"He isn't, at all." Jacob smiled.

The mother nodded and walked off, and little Brendan

gave him a forlorn wave. Jacob waved back. He relaxed back into his seat. He didn't like to be on the plane any earlier than necessary. He didn't want to admit it, but the seat arms had been digging into his stomach more and more with each flight. He smiled at the retreating back of the little boy. Yes, he would be quite happy to get back to Hong Kong. He was particularly fond of children, though more the motherless ones that could be bought on seedy backstreets, which was exactly why he had taken the position in Hong Kong in the first place.

Derek felt a bubble of hope. The little boy had left the businessman grinning and waving. The man had seemed genuinely happy to talk to the little boy. Maybe he had kids of his own? Perhaps a friendly wife who would be happy to take on Susannah? She was a particularly sweet and outgoing child, most of the time. Derek looked down at her. Her head was lolling. Ketchup rimmed the edge of her mouth, making her look somewhat vampiric. He looked back up towards the businessman, whose hands were folded in his lap. He looked up when Derek looked to him and gave him a warm smile. Derek smiled back.

Amelia Woo and Carrie Vaughn

Derek let his eyes rove over the two women who were bickering a few rows behind the businessman. He couldn't tell what they were arguing about, but both women looked strained, tired and exasperated with the other. One of the women was part Asian, and her long black hair was so shiny Derek was momentarily bewitched by it. She pressed her hands together as if praying for a moment, closing her eyes, and then reached out a hand and gently tucked a lock of hair behind her partner's ear. Her partner shook her head softly, then reached out and embraced the Asian woman, tears rolling down her blush pink cheeks.

Carrie didn't mean to start crying - she knew Amelia wasn't a fan of public displays of emotion - but this time Amelia just rubbed her back and let Carrie snot on to her shoulder.

"I'm sorry." Amelia's breath caught in a ragged gasp.

"It's not your fault, Carrie." Amelia took hold of Carrie's shoulders and leant back from her. "It is not anyone's fault."

Carrie looked at her wife. Amelia had a kind of beauty that intimidated people. She was petite and always wore personally-tailored suits. She had long hair that swished at her mid-back, but her most striking feature was her bright green eyes. She had got those from her Irish mother.

"I know, I just… I thought this time, I thought… it was *the* time."

Amelia bit her lip. "I thought so too." She inhaled and sat Carrie back down on the hard plastic chairs. "We'll figure this out, Carrie."

Carrie looked up at her. Her blue eyes were red and watery, and her normally cheerful face looked gaunt and gray. In fact, in the past year she had gotten painfully thin. Her normally strong, athletic body looked bony. Her flowery dresses hung off her shoulders and billowed around her like blankets.

"How, Lia? We don't have any money left for more IVF. We've been turned down by so many adoption agencies. I quit my job to make sure one of us could be a full-time carer, and we still can't seem to find somewhere that thinks we're fit to be parents."

Amelia's mouth pinched. She lowered her voice to just above a whisper. She was about to argue, then thought better of it. "I know, it sucks. Maybe we wait..."

"Wait and get older, and less likely to be deemed good parent material?"

"We're mid-thirties Carrie, not mid-sixties, we just need to find the right agency."

Carrie shook her head but said nothing. Amelia sat down on the seat beside her and placed one hand on Carrie's thigh. Carrie remained rigid, stiffening into her anger.

"We can't borrow any more money from our families!" Carrie burst out. "I... I could go back to work, but then, if we were applying for the adoption agencies they might..."

Amelia shook her head and pursed her lips. There was no arguing with Carrie about this. "I don't know what to say, Carrie. I..." She shook her head. A tiny spark of anger came into her voice. She wanted a child as badly as Carrie did.

"Nothing. There's nothing to say," Carrie snapped, and they fell into a sullen silence.

Derek frowned. The women had finally stopped bickering, but now they glared out into space in angry silence. They were obviously a couple, but Derek couldn't read them. The Asian woman was dressed in a smart tailored suit, and she seemed reserved, whilst the blonde woman was rail thin and on the verge of hysterics. As Derek watched, the blonde woman reached out an arm and wrapped it around the Asian woman's shoulders. She leant in and planted a loud kiss on her ear. The Asian woman yanked herself away, grinning, and shoved the other woman away. Derek saw the blonde woman say, 'I'm sorry.' The Asian woman smiled and they hugged. Derek chewed the inside of his cheek.

David Waters

"Flight BA1729 to Hong Kong, this gate will be closing in ten minutes. All passengers make their way to Gate 12."

Derek watched the straggle of passengers thinning as the airline agent checked everyone in. "Come on," he mumbled to himself. Susannah had curled into a ball on the booth seat with her head in his lap and was blissfully sleeping.

Derek's eyes flicked quickly over the remaining passengers in the area. A handsome black man jogged over. He threw his bag into a seat and began rummaging through it. A mobile phone was lodged between a shoulder and an ear, and he was talking enthusiastically to someone. His smile was wide and happy.

"Come on Benji, come on. You've got to be good for Mum," said the man, laughing. Derek leant his head forward hopefully. He seemed awfully young to have a child of his own, but Derek had to choose someone.

David tried to reason with his baby brother. He looked around at the other passengers who were still in the seating area. He was kind of surprised that the hippie chick hadn't noticed him - usually girls noticed him – but this one seemed engrossed in her iPad. David knew he was good looking; he had known that long before the modeling agency had offered him this job in Hong Kong.

David flopped into a seat beside his bag. He still had ten minutes.

"Benji, come on man, you gotta be good. You gotta do what Mum says." David was getting irritated, but he couldn't stop himself from smiling. He was going to Hong Kong, to model. He had an apartment that was paid for by the agency. They told him he had the right look; he was going to be a star.

"Benj, I get it. Look, is Jane there?"

Benji muttered angrily at his big brother, but went to get his big sister nonetheless.

"Hey Jane. What's going on?" David asked through gritted teeth. He couldn't wait till this wasn't his problem anymore. "Hold on, lemme switch to headphones."

A moment later he heard Jane's voice crackling through the new Beats headphones.

"Jane, what's going on?" David chided. His sister was sixteen; she should be able to take care of this.

Jane sighed and static carried through the earpiece, "Mum's had another one of her episodes." Jane's voice wobbled. "I don't know that I can do this without you, Dave."

David bit his lower lip, "Janey, look hun, we don't have hardly any money so I had to take this job," he reasoned. That was what he had been telling himself for the past six months.

"I know, it's just… she had a bad anxiety attack last night, went off on Benji and the little ones." Jane replied softly. The little ones, Gayle and Gavin, were only three years old. They had been the final straw for David. They were only his half siblings, and David had already spent the past five years raising Jane and Benji.

"Is she out of her meds?" David tried to say it lightly, like it was normal and OK that his mother had been taking Oxycontin for the past five years, since the car crash.

"No, she bought some the other week. I think... I think she upped her dose, David." Jane lowered her voice. David heard his mother yelling from the living room. The younger children were shrieking happily. Obviously she was medicated at the moment then, David thought.

"Jane look, I'll be back at Christmas, and I'll send money. I told Ange to check in on you guys. You know you can call her if you need help." David tried to sound encouraging, but he knew Ange didn't really want to involved with his family. Since the car accident five years ago, no one did. David's dad had died. His mother had broken her back and developed a serious addiction to Oxycontin. Which meant that David, at fourteen years old, has left to raise his two younger siblings. Then, three years ago, she had given birth to twins. David still didn't know who the father was.

"Look Jane, I've got to board. It'll be fine, all right? It'll be fine." David hurriedly got off the phone to his sister. He hadn't booked a flight back for Christmas. He said that was because he didn't have the money yet, but David knew, deep down, that it was because he had finally managed to escape his family, and nothing was going to drag him back.

Derek saw the black guy smiling as he put both his earphones in. His head began bobbing around to the music. He could have a child, Derek reasoned. Susannah was barely two, and it was more than likely that if he did have a kid, he or she would be close in age to Susannah. That could work, Derek thought, feeling a growing excitement. The guy was obviously young and energetic. He was well dressed too, not in a suit, but expensive trainers and a luxury designer backpack.

Derek shifted in the booth, careful not to wake Susannah.

Flick and Jason Getz

There were only two others left in the waiting area. Derek paid his bill absently as he looked at them. The girl was, in Derek's mind, unusual looking and attractive. He couldn't place where she was from. She had dark, almost caramel-colored skin, full lips and thick chocolate hair that was dreadlocked and streaked honey blonde. Jewelry adorned her ears and arms, and tattoos were visible across her back, shoulders, arms and even creeping up her neck. The man she was with was engrossed in a book, though Derek couldn't make out the cover. He too was dappled with tattoos, and yet strangely his hair was cropped neatly and he wore a smart polo and slacks.

"I'm nervous." Jason said, without looking up from his book.

Flick smiled. "You're nervous?"

"Well, yeah... I mean... your mum and dad love me." Jason grinned.

His wife raised her brows at him. "You know they do, but I mean - these are your birth parents."

"Birth mother," Flick clarified. Butterflies fluttered in

her stomach. She was nervous too, though she hadn't told Jason why. She wasn't worried about whether or not her birth mother would like her – frankly, she didn't care. It was more that she knew nothing about the Aboriginal Australian woman who had given her up thirty-three years ago. Flick hadn't learned anything about Aboriginal culture. She simply hadn't known that element about herself until a few years before, when she had sought out more information surrounding her adoption.

"It'll be cool though, to see Australia." Jason smiled again.

Flick smiled back. "I'm surprised you didn't go over there on your travels." She leant back in her seat.

Jason wrapped an arm around her. "You know, I always felt it was kinda... too similar to the UK. Which is weird, because they have all this awesome stuff that we definitely don't." He waved his notebook at her.

Flick smiled. One of the reasons she loved Jason was his nose for amazing locations and adventures. "We aren't there for long. We'll be heading back over to Cambodia pretty quickly."

"I know, I know. But still, we should squeeze in what we can." Jason flicked through a few pages. "Have you heard from the rescue?"

"Yeah, it's all fine. We've got some new kid coming out, eighteen, gap year, wants to be a vet," Flick surmised.

"Nice."

"Yeah he seems lovely. Did a big fundraiser for us back in... I want to say Devon, but he raised about four thousand pounds, so I sent him a detailed explanation of what it would all be used for - medical supplies, neuters and spays, food, and rebuilding some of the kennels."

"Sweet." Jason had taken out his phone. "You should send him some pictures of the dogs."

Flick nodded. She had started the Buddha's Best Friend Rescue eleven years ago, when she was twenty-two. She had been in the middle of her veterinarian degree when she went out to Cambodia one summer. Eleven years later, she and Jason were living in Cambodia and spent most of their days rushing around in a beat-up van rescuing strays. Dogs mostly, some cats, and more recently two horses and a donkey.

Jason looked over at Flick. She was staring into space. "Flick?"

"Yeah?"

"What do your mum and dad think about all this?"

Flick tilted her head to one side. "I mean... they didn't know when they adopted me. They said the orphanage in Sydney had a record of a white male dropping me off. He said he was my birth father and that my birth mother was dead. I don't know... my parents want me to do what I need to do."

Jason nodded. "Oh, here you go." He handed her a bag of sour Haribo.

"Yep." Flick looked at him out of the corner of her eye. He was smiling amiably. She smiled to herself and took her favorite sweets.

"I couldn't do that to a kid," said Jason.

Flick's smile deepened. She wondered when she should break the news to him that she was pregnant.

The couple looked happy, Derek reasoned. Something

niggled in the back of his mind. He didn't like tattoos and dreadlocks. Not that he would ever say that, he just felt something nagging him. They were lounging as well, almost lazily. Derek frowned. They were probably off on a lengthy travel stint. They did look kind, but they wouldn't be able to provide a stable home for Susannah. Derek reached down and fondly stroked her blonde curls.

'Last boarding call for Flight BA1729. Could all passengers remaining please board at Gate 12.'

Derek rushed out of his seat, carefully cradling Susannah's sleeping form in his arms, making sure not to wake her. He hurried over to the gate. He had made his decision.

48 Hours Later

Angela found her husband at the Natural History Museum. He was loitering in one of the upstairs displays, in a dark, cloistered corner.

"Oh my god, Derek!" She breathed a sigh of relief. She grabbed her mobile and called her sister, "Harriet, I've found him. Oh thank God. Yes. Level 2 – " she looked around - "in the geology display."

A moment later Harriet and two police officers appeared around the corner. Derek stared at them all wide eyed. His hair and clothing were disheveled and his face gaunt.

"Stay away from me, Angela!" he warned.

"Where is Susannah, Derek?" Angela spun around the room. It wormed its way in a long circular tunnel. From around the corner, she heard a child's shriek. "Mummy's here, Susy!" she called out. A small child appeared at a run, but she continued on past them all, towards a woman with outstretched arms. The woman looked at Angela with curiosity. Her eyes took in the policemen and the agitated-looking man.

"Why don't we go somewhere more private?" Harriet suggested.

"Derek, where is Susannah?" Angela snapped. She took a deep breath. "Darling, where is our daughter?"

"She wasn't safe." Derek looked around the area as if he were plotting an escape.

One of the policemen stepped closer. "Sir, what do you mean she wasn't safe?"

Harriet leant in and whispered, "Derek is a paranoid schizophrenic. He gets worried he is being followed, or going to be attacked. He's done this before. He hides Susy. She'll be tucked in the earthquake display eating Gummi Bears." Harriet smiled tightly.

The officer nodded. Derek was nodding maniacally. "She's much safer where she is." He glared at Angela. "You're safer away from me too, Ange... they're after me."

"They're not darling, it's OK, you just forgot your medicine. Now, where is Susy?"

Derek looked around, confused. He looked at his wife. The flight had left long ago. The passengers would have cleared customs. Susannah was safe now... but *they* had got to Angela.

"Derek, please, where is she?"

Derek was sweating. "Heathrow."

Angela clenched her fists. "No Derek, you *were* at Heathrow. We've been there already. I'm asking where

Susannah is *now*?" She turned to Harriet. "Call Heathrow."

"Already on it," one of the policemen said.

"I'll go talk to the front desk." The other one hurried off.

"OK, right... yes, we'll need to talk to that young man." The policeman nodded into his mobile. He turned to Angela.

"What is it?"

"A young waiter remembers seeing Susannah. Two days ago. He said your husband seemed agitated. He saw Derek a while later, but he didn't have Susannah."

"So she's at the airport?"

"No Ma'am, they checked that first day we were there. They haven't found any sign of Susannah."

"I gave her to someone who could take care of her," David murmured, his eyes now glassy and unfocused.

Angela felt something in her stomach drop sickeningly, but when she turned back to her husband, his head had lolled into his chest in a stupor.

72 Hours Later

Jacob Heatherton felt giddy at his luck. He walked back to the Mandarin Oriental with a spring in his step. The small wreath of jasmine he had been given as he had walked back in was hung around his neck. The girl would like that.

He had worked diligently, eager to return to the delights the hotel offered; luxury spa, excellent room service and aquamarine swimming pools. He had made the child stay in the room, and had informed the front desk, repeatedly, that no one was to go into his room.

A twinge of nervousness struck his belly. What if they had ignored him? Or misunderstood? They were fastidious about cleaning after all. His pace quickened as he turned off the busy road into the expansive sweeping driveway of the hotel.

In his room, the little Thai girl sobbed small hiccupping gulps of fear and loneliness. She had tucked herself inside the wardrobe, hoping that this would serve the way it did in hide and seek. She was invisible until she decided to come out. She heard the beeping of the door lock and tucked herself into a smaller ball.

Then, a soft, crooning voice. The sound of rustling sheets and opening closets. The tiny crack of light of the closet widened and the sweaty face of the man appeared.

"Shh, it's OK," Jacob said, smiling, padding the sweat on his forehead with a handkerchief. He looked at the girl's tearstained cheeks and cocked his head. "Come on now," he said. He gripped her arm and dragged her from the closet.

In the Natural History Museum, only the display lights were still on. A loudspeaker was announcing that the museum was now closing, and any remaining visitors should make their way to the exit.

Brandon, schlepping around the geology display, shone his flashlight over the displays, under benches, into rubbish bins, all to make sure no one was hiding away in the museum. The walkie-talkie on his belt crackled periodically as areas were fully swept and shut down.

Brandon heard the nasal voice of his supervisor and groaned. He was desperate to head out and get to the pub. "Brandon? Do you copy? Over."

"Yeah. I'm here. Over."

He continued strolling down the corridor, out of the

geology museum, towards the dinosaur exhibit. It was his favorite part, especially when there wasn't the swarm of visitors.

"I need you to check the proboscidea display. Over."

Brandon's mind drew a blank for a second. "Like, the elephants?"

There was a sigh of impatience, and Brandon knew his supervisor had deliberately held the walkie talkie to his mouth so he would hear it. Brandon put his middle finger up at the device.

"Yes, elephants, mammoths, mastodons. You are familiar with these beasts? Over."

Brandon mouthed a string of curses. "Yes, I am. I think Dave already swept it. Over."

There was a long crackle of static. "No, he hasn't yet. Apparently some kid came running out from there a second ago and said he heard a child crying. We need to check it out. Over."

Brandon, thinking of a tall glass of cider and a chicken potpie, tried to dig his heels in. "Has a parent been separated? Over."

"No. Just go do it, Brandon. Over."

Brandon skulked around the rest of the dinosaur exhibit. Some dumb kid had probably walked past one of the interactive figures, probably one of the baby mammoths, which did make a strange keening sound. It could be mistaken for a child crying.

He reached the end of the suspended 'skywalk' above the dinosaur skeletons. Left took him to the proboscidea displays, right took him back to the front desk, where he could check out and head home. He chewed his lower lip.

His mobile phone beeped in his pocket and he checked the screen. Jenny, the girl he liked, had sent him a text asking if he was coming to the pub.

"Brandon, you check that display yet? Over."

Brandon heaved an enormous sigh, then reluctantly turned left down the dark hallway.

SKELETONS

"Danny, right?" A small mousy woman holding a Styrofoam coffee cup in one hand and a cookie in another smiled at him.

"Uh huh." Danny barely managed to muster the grunted response.

Melanie smiled gently. The guy had glazed eyes, stained clothes and three days of stubble on his gaunt face. "I'm Melanie, I'm the group leader tonight."

Danny's eyes roved over her briefly. "You, huh?" He raised an eyebrow. The woman was dressed in loose jeans, a thick sweater and heavy-duty snow boots.

"Oxycontin." Melanie said it with a smile and a shrug.

Danny nodded knowingly. "I'm on day three," he said. "Heroin."

Melanie placed a hand on his bone-thin arm. "Come sit over here. Do you want a coffee? Something to eat?" Melanie led him to two free chairs. The chairs had been arranged in a ring. They were slowly filling up for the 5pm meeting.

Danny shook his head. "Will I have to speak?"

"You can introduce yourself, say something, or just listen. It's totally up to you."

Danny nodded and scratched at his hands. He swallowed the nausea that welled in his throat and sat down beside Melanie. She smelt of fabric softener and coffee.

He wanted to touch her, just to feel her soft sweater and remember for a brief moment what it was like before, when his house had smelt of clean laundry, coffee, Violet's perfume and sweet cinnamon milk from Annette's cereal. Melanie didn't look like Violet. Violet was dark, skinny and brooding, with a loud laugh and a wicked sense of humor. She would be able to make him laugh even when he was at his most vulnerable.

"Right, shall we get started?" Melanie rose from her chair.

Danny folded his head into his hands.

"My name is Melanie, and I was, still am I suppose, addicted to oxycontin. I've been clean for six years now, seven this coming April." There was some scattered applause.

Danny felt his head swimming as Melanie told her story. He tried to listen, he really did, but his brain just wouldn't work.

"Let's take a break, shall we?" Melanie said. "Danny?" She rubbed his shoulder.

"Huh?" He looked around. People were dispersing, flocking back to the watery coffee and stale baked goods. Driving rain lashed at the windows. It was a wild and wet Seattle evening.

"Danny, do you have somewhere... anyone?" Melissa

pursed her lips as she thought for the right words.

"I've got a place," Danny said, thinking about the cockroach-infested room he couldn't afford the rent for.

Melanie raised her eyebrows. "Because I know somewhere clean, safe, for people... like us."

"It's fine... fine." Danny looked away nervously.

Melanie could almost feel his discomfort. She looked around the room, "Tsk, I hate those things." She wrinkled her little nose.

Danny had been watching her, thinking that she looked like a timid fox, but he glanced over to where she was gazing. A guy in skinny black jeans, a carefully-curated 'threadbare' T-shirt and a chunky cardigan was chatting to two women. Danny frowned.

"Those video-information glasses by SpecTech."

"Oh... er, I think they're called the Iris-Plus."

Melanie snorted. "Is that what they're calling them now?" Melanie opened her mouth to say more, but the guy wearing the glasses walked over.

"Don't worry, they're not live." Melanie raised her eyebrows. "I'm Michael." He smiled sheepishly at Melanie. Danny realized that the guy had a crush on her.

"Live?" Melanie's voice dripped with skepticism.

"Recording. I can take them off if you'd prefer."

"Does it make a difference either way?" Danny laughed. "I mean... recording or not, it's not like there is anything we could do about it."

Michael looked down at his feet. "I know they're not popular at NA meetings. I wear them for work, I travel a lot. They're very helpful with translation, history, meeting reviews."

"Mmm hmm" Melanie sighed. "We should get back to the meeting."

Michael took the glasses off. "And I know, nowadays... recording is... OK. Well... legal... but I don't want to upset anyone, or make them not want to be here."

Melanie softened. "Michael," she put a hand on his arm, "look, everyone here, they're just trying to be a better person. The idea that someone is watching, videoing, gathering information, or looking it up, looking up their records..."

"But, I'm not I swear," Michael said earnestly.

"They don't know that though." Danny nodded towards the NA participants, who were heading back to their seats.

Michael took the glasses off and folded them into a case. "You're right."

Melanie gave him a warm smile. "Thank you Michael," she said with sincerity.

Danny looked at her closely. He wondered if he could ask her to be his sponsor.

****

"That is enough TV, Mabel!" Corinne leant around the doorframe.

"Mom, mom... just... it's a Skeleton's marathon!" Mabel waved her hands to try and express the gravitas of the situation to her mother.

"Just record it." Corinne stuck her tongue out. Mabel ignored her, so Corinne walked out and stood behind the couch.

On the TV screen, a woman was crouched in the fetal position, sobbing uncontrollably in a seedy bathroom. More like a girl, Corinne thought. She was young, maybe fifteen, with chalky skin, ratty hair and poorly-done makeup. She wore a tight, glittery Spandex dress. A wad of money was clutched in one hand.

"What is this, Mabel?"

"It's this show. So like, people nominate someone they know and they video them so you see all the stuff happening with them."

"Does the person - this girl - does she know?"

"No, but like, they get her help, or whoever, or they try to, at least at the end of the show."

"What kind of 'stuff'?"

"Oh y'know... drug addicts, prostitutes... runaways, rape victims... like... anything like that," Mabel said nonchalantly.

Corinne felt sick. "That's horrible. How is this even legal?"

"Well, they changed all those laws." Mabel rolled her eyes at her mother.

Corinne thought back and nodded. She remembered it being in the papers about a year and a half ago. Since Spec Tech and other video information glasses had become so popular, they had changed the laws about being filmed without your consent. There had been too many frivolous lawsuits against people wearing the glasses. "But, surely this... I don't understand."

"I dunno Mom, ask one of your lawyer friends about it." That dig was aimed at Corinne's ex. He had been the stereotypical slimy lawyer type, but she had only dated him for a month.

Corinne snorted, "Never mind. Dinner is ready. This show is vile. You shouldn't be watching it."

"Uh huh." Mabel ignored her.

"Aunt Jackie and Uncle Troy are coming over for dinner tomorrow. So you need to be back from school sharp to help with dinner."

"Fine!" Mabel snapped. Her voice was brittle.

"Mabel! I know your Aunt can be..."

"A bitch," Mabel muttered.

"Difficult. But she's family."

Mabel pursed her lips until they disappeared into her face.

"Up next week, we meet Andrea, a young girl with severe anorexia and bulimia. Nominated for the show by her mother, we'll get a glimpse of how these addictions have torn apart a family - and what secrets lie beneath."

There was a tense silence in the room, as if mention of the word 'anorexia' was an exploding bomb. Mabel remained rigid on the couch, swathed in baggy clothing and layers.

"Honey, come on," Corinne said gently.

Mabel swallowed. The red light for 'record the next episode' blinked on the screen. Mabel clicked slowly over and unchecked it. She stood up on wobbly, stick-thin legs.

"I'm not hungry," she said, storming out of the living room.

Corinne nodded, and tears rolled down her cheeks. "You never are," Corinne whispered to herself as her daughter stomped up the stairs.

****

"Guys, come on, we can do better than this." Ariadne jabbed a finger at the sheaf of papers in front of her.

"We're getting swamped with submissions," One guy in a charcoal suit said.

"We need a timeline - make sure we're not pushing out similar episodes week after week," another chimed in.

"That's good." Ariadne nodded. "But we've got to be more flexible - go with topics that get great ratings, what's hot… " She frowned as she looked at the screen that displayed their ratings. It was set at one end of the conference room. "What was this?" She pointed at a spike.

"Kid, runaway… sort of… anorexia, prostitution, drug abuse," said a young intern in a too-short skirt between chewing her thumbnail.

Ariadne frowned at her. She hated people who didn't dress professionally. The girl looked away awkwardly.

"Let's focus on more of those for now. That spike is where we want the ratings to stay. Let's get people watching addictively, then we can throw in the bunk episodes every once in a while." Ariadne was still frowning.

"We need better people," an older man said. He was dressed in smart jeans, a suit jacket and a V-neck tee. Tattoos crept up his chest and neck.

Ariadne looked at him inquisitively. She knew he was a producer - Tyler something?

"People liked that episode because the girl came from a decent family. They don't want to see run of the mill crack whores, druggies and gangbangers. They want to see people like them… sort of."

Ariadne nodded. "Yes. This is good." She pursed her lips and rubbed her chin.

Jesse, the intern, thought she looked positively Machiavellian. She knew she shouldn't have worn this stupid skirt; she could see Ariadne giving her a once over and deeming her unprofessional. It wasn't her fault the washer-dryer in the apartment wasn't fucking working.

"We could offer more money - to the nominators," Jesse blurted out. Everyone turned to her. "We'd get better people... not better, but..."

"She's right." Tyler gave her a roguish smile. "We get junkies and that lot because the cash payout is average. 'A Closer Look' is nearly double what we pay out."

Ariadne nodded and sucked in her cheeks. Her broad jaw and wide-set eyes would have been attractive and peaceful, but a sharp bob and perma-scowl made her look like an angry alien. "We'll up the ante then, double the money, pull in the middle-class crowd, so the other middle classes can watch and see them suffering with glee." She smiled.

"It's called Schadenfreude," an intern standing beside Jesse whispered to her. He had acne and was wearing a cheap, too-big suit. "It's when you get pleasure from seeing someone's misfortune."

"I know what it is!" Jesse snapped. She tugged the hem of her skirt down. "I know what it fucking is!"

****

Danny leant against the doorway of his room, "look, I'm in NA, I've been clean for five days. I've got an unemployment check coming, I can pay the rent man. Please Carl, please. I swear Carl, please!"

Carl's phone buzzed in his pocket. He looked lazily away from Danny. Danny felt a hot rage bubble in his chest momentarily. He used to be better than this – begging and wheedling to stay in a shitty bedroom with a moldy shared bathroom. He used to have a condo with his wife and kid, breakfast in bed on Sundays and movie night on Fridays. They had bills to pay, but they were happy. Tears pricked at his eyeballs.

"Fuck man, you don't need to cry. Get the money to me by tomorrow." Carl turned on his heel and stomped away muttering, "fuckin' druggies."

Danny sank down onto the floor, tears spilling over his lower lids. Violet made spaghetti. Annette would giggle and pretend to be the dog from *Lady and the Tramp*. Danny would always play along. They would put Annette to bed after apple pie and cartoons and then cuddle on the sofa watching dark thrillers.

His phone buzzed again. A text, from Melanie. *We have NA tonight at the Presbyterian on 5th and Pine. Are you coming?*

He hadn't found the nerve to ask her to be his sponsor, but maybe she sensed how much he needed someone, anyone, to anchor him.

His fingers were shaky as he tapped out the response. *Yes*

Moments later: *Great, we start at 6pm, if you could be there 15 mins early I'd love to talk to you about some stuff.*

Danny felt a prickle of sweat in his armpits. He hadn't used to be a nervous person. With Vi, everything felt safe.

His job as a production manager at an up-and-coming 3D design firm was stable. He liked his coworkers. He loved his family. Then the accident happened and the aftermath, and then, Violet was gone. After that, everything was a blur. Except Annette. Annette was still here, and that was why he needed to get better.

His phone said 5:23pm. The Presbyterian Church was just down the road, but Danny gathered his wallet and keys and headed out into the bitingly cold evening.

On the walk over, he thought about Annette. He hadn't seen her in months. A wave of paranoia flushed his system; what if she had forgotten him? No, she was nine, it wasn't as if she was a baby. He exhaled. Maybe that was worse... she had had to watch as her beloved Daddy moved from oxycontin and then to heroin. Maybe it was better that she was with Vi's parents. Even though they hated him. Even though they wouldn't let Annette near him. Even though they blamed him for Violet's death.

"Danny?" Melanie was in a thick sweater, with a battered anorak over the top and a fuzzy hat.

Danny looked up startled. "I... um... it didn't take long..."

Melanie smiled warmly. "It's good you're here. I wanted to talk to you about a sponsor for you. I remember being where you are, it's really important you have a sponsor at this stage."

"You?" Danny smiled hopefully.

"No, actually, this is Tyler. He volunteered - said he thought he would be a good sponsor for you."

Danny frowned. An older guy in hipster clothes with neck tattoos gave him a half smile. "I don't know you," said Danny.

"I... uh... I read about you. I had to..." Tyler shrugged. "My brother."

Danny felt himself deflate. "I do need a sponsor."

Melanie grinned. "This is good. Really good, Danny." She squeezed his arm. "Come on, let's get inside."

"Wouldn't want the other druggies to snaffle the cookies, would we?" Tyler joked, and Danny let out an unexpected chuckle.

Danny followed Melanie in. Tyler turned back to the shadowy figure of Carl, standing in the doorway of a greasy falafel joint, and gave him a curt nod.

****

Mabel arranged the mini PriceCo entrees on the platter with the utmost precision. Shrimp toasts, doll-sized quiches, teeny eggrolls. They were so small, Mabel wondered if they would count. She reached for one and then drew back when she heard Aunt Jackie's shrill voice in the living room. Uncle Troy boomed and chortled and Mabel shuddered. God, she hated them so much.

"One second, another beer Troy?" Her mom called. "Lordy lord!" she said as she leant back against the kitchen counter. "Are the snacks ready?"

"I don't know why you bother. Aunt Jackie will just bitch about them being ready made before stuffing them all in her fat face," Mabel snapped.

"Mabel!" Corinne chided. She looked at Mabel and softened. She wore skinny jeans tucked into thick winter socks and an oversized fisherman's sweater pulled down over her thumbs and held in place by two strategically-cut holes. Her neck and wrists stuck out like a child playing dress-up. "Come on." She pointed to the platter and Mabel picked it up carefully.

Corinne grabbed a few beers and followed her daughter back into the den.

Aunt Jackie was splayed out beside Uncle Troy on the couch. She wore cheap clothes from Target, designed for teenagers, with tacky, shiny words splashed across them. Troy grinned and stood up to hug Mabel.

Mabel nodded and thrust the platter out in front of her. Corinne put down the beers and sat on the love seat. To her surprise, Mabel quickly curled up beside her.

"So, Miss Mabel, how's school?" Troy said, grinning.

"Yes, tell us about high school," Jackie added. Her eyes were glistening eagerly. Rimmed with electric blue eyeliner and topped with purple eye shadow, she looked possessed.

"S'fine. Good."

"She's being modest. She has a 4.0 GPA and she won the Mathematician of the Year award."

"Oh that's great... good news for scholarships?" Troy smiled amiably.

"Yes, really good." Corinne smiled.

Jackie looked sour. "Don't you want a bite, Mabel? You look like you could use a burger, honey - although, I get why you might not want to. All this PriceCo stuff is so greasy." She smiled. Her teeth were streaked with candy-pink lip gloss.

Her phone chimed out with a pop song. "Gotta get this." She heaved herself to her feet and rushed out of the den.

Jackie walked out the front, onto the freezing porch, before she answered. "Yes, this is Jackie."

"Hi Jackie, this is Jesse from Skeletons?"

"Yes, yes I'm using the mini-cams on my person, like you said."

"Great, we are getting that feed. I just wanted to call and let you know we need to install the house cams tomorrow, so we'll need you to get Corinne and Mabel out of the house."

"Right - OK, I can do that."

"Great, I'll call and let you know when they are there."

Jackie signed off and rushed back inside.

"Who was that?" Troy asked when she came back inside.

"Are you free tomorrow, Cor?"

"Uh... it's a Saturday. So, yeah."

"I have to go to a memorial for a work friend. Can you come help me pick out something at the mall?"

"Oh sure, sure..." Corinne looked baffled. "You want to come, Mabel?"

"No."

"You could come help me finish setting up the new TV and gaming set - brain like yours would be a lot of help." Troy sipped his beer.

"I have to study."

"I thought you finished studying?" Corinne frowned.

"It's settled then," Jackie squawked happily. "We'll go to the mall and Mabel can help Troy with the TV."

Mabel looked beseechingly at her Corinne, who looked back oblivious. "I have to study... I..."

"Don't be silly. It's good for you to get out the house." Jackie narrowed her eyes.

"Mom?" Mabel nudged her mother.

"It's fine honey, it's only for a couple of hours."

Mabel stood and rushed out of the room, stamping her

foot on each step of the stairs before slamming her bedroom door.

"Teenagers, right?" Corinne said as the house trembled.

"Right." Jackie smiled back slowly.

****

Ariadne pinched the bridge of her nose in her sleek glass office, which took up an entire corner of the 19th floor.

"What is the problem here exactly, Tyler?" She exhaled loudly.

"There's just a lot of distractions at the NA meetings with this guy... Danny. Like, he doesn't speak."

"But we know his story, right?"

"Yeah... Carl, the landlord-slash-mate, told me the story, plus some of it was in the papers. This Danny guy was in an accident, car accident. Wife was driving. He broke his back, which is how he got addicted to painkillers."

"And the wife?"

"In a coma, brain dead. He had power of attorney and turned off life support."

"And they had a kid, right?"

"Yeah, the in-laws were furious he turned off life support, so when his drug problem got worse they jumped at the chance to take the kid."

"Do we have access to them and the kid?"

"So, the kid..." Tyler glanced down at his phone, "Annette. She was taken into foster care. Turned out the grandfather was pretty rough with her, school stepped in."

"Does this Danny guy know?"

"Nope, he was on the streets for a bit, now he is in this

shitty room and in NA getting clean."

"Hmm… could relapse if he finds out his kid is in the system." Ariadne furrowed her brow. "But the issue is the material we are getting is dull?"

"Right. NA meetings are just a bunch of other druggies telling their stories. Danny sits there like a mute. Doesn't do shit in the apartment that Carl gave us access too, and we don't have video at the in-laws, or know where his daughter is."

"I like this story though. Hold on a second." Ariadne adjusted the sleek Iris-Plus glasses on her nose. Streams of data scrolled up in front of her eyes. "So the daughter, I've found her."

Tyler raised his brows and didn't ask. He didn't want to know where his boss was getting that kind of information.

"Her case worker is a woman named Corinne. Placed her with a family she trusts whilst they try to work through the situation with the grandparents. She has been digging for info on Danny, it looks like, trying to see whether he should be involved. Looks like before the accident they were a pretty normal happy family."

"Sounds like the in-laws don't like Danny then."

"Indeed." Ariadne smiled. "This is good. This is really good. What are the odds we have any footage from when Danny was on drugs? Heroin, right?"

Tyler grinned. "Well. you are in luck. Our seedy little fucker Carl videoed him multiple times when he was high, used them as part of the reel when he nominated Danny for Skeletons."

Ariadne made a small fist and a little twitching motion. "Excellent. Let's get all that footage, plus what you have, to editing and start getting the back story mapped out."

"Any word on who else is going to be part of the hundredth episode special?" Tyler looked up from his phone.

"Well, as fate would have it, Jesse the intern, who I must admit I wasn't a fan of, has found a real gem." Ariadne smiled secretively. "But you'll have to wait and see at the team meeting." She tapped her nose.

"I can't wait." Tyler smiled roguishly back. He wondered if he had a shot with Ariadne. "Back to work, later, boss." He smiled again and ducked out of the glass office.

****

Melanie fiddled with the Thermos flasks and the baked goods. They were picked over, and the glazed sheen was turning dull. She suspected that Danny was a step away from homelessness. She also suspected he was a step away from suicide or a relapse. He was so much like her brother. She knew she was projecting her guilt onto Danny, but every time she saw him she had to resist the urge to mollycoddle him.

"Mel, right?" Tyler said, smiling.

Melanie blushed. She flicked her eyes up to his face and her smile faded. "Are those Iris-Plus? Like the SpecTech ones?" They didn't look like them, not exactly.

"No, cheap knock off regular specs, made to look like the real thing." Tyler looked down bashfully.

"Of course, right, nowadays it's all keeping up with the Joneses!" Melanie bit her cheek and felt like an idiot. "My parents both have them, so I get why people like them. Info at your fingertips... or eyeballs!" She heard her voice, nervous and higher pitched than normal.

"Must be nice. But maybe not for people like us... too much y'know."

"Yes, exactly." Melanie nodded.

"I hope I wasn't too forward with Danny. He hasn't been exactly forthcoming since I became his sponsor."

Melanie nodded again. "I know... he... well... I know a little about his past. I think he's happy to have you as his sponsor, more than you know. He told me after last week he wants to share his story - get it off his chest in his terms - so maybe that'll help him open up to you."

Tyler smiled and placed a warm tattooed hand on Melanie's arm. She felt her stomach somersault. "That's so great, just what he needs."

Melanie nodded and tried to get her tongue to work. "He'll be here any minute, I'll have a chat with him."

As if on cue, Danny appeared, skulking at the doorway of the NA meeting room. Melanie hurried over and Tyler watched as they chatted – well, mostly Melanie - and Danny reluctantly nodded. Tyler breathed a sigh of relief, and then turned his back to them to subtly turn on his Iris-Plus glasses. They were specially made for the Skeletons team to look like cheap knock-offs.

"Right, most of you guys will have seen Danny around. He wants to share a little bit of his story with you tonight." Melanie smiled at Danny as she sat back in her seat.

To Tyler's surprise, Danny looked at him with startling vulnerability. Tyler managed an encouraging smile back.

"Right." Danny stood up and shifted back and forth. He was rail thin, and his clothes were old, but looked clean. He wore old Levis, a check shirt and a thick V-neck sweater. His scarf and coat were draped on the back of his chair. "So, um... my name is Danny, and I'm addicted to heroin... been clean... um... ten days now."

There was more clapping than Tyler had expected. He'd have to do some more research on heroin addiction when he was back at the office.

"I uh... I... was addicted for about two years. I lost my wife, not from the heroin... from before, and then I lost my daughter - because of the drugs." Danny added nervously. The room was filled with sympathetic smiles and nods. Tyler kept his head still and his eyes focused in on Danny's face.

"My in-laws... they uh, they took my daughter, Annette... I was really angry, but now I know she's better off with them... I mean, I want her with me, but not like this."

Tyler subtly rubbed his temple and zoomed in on Danny.

"They're angry with me still, after Violet and I were in the accident... see..." Danny's eyes misted, "I had to turn off the life support. It was what she wanted... they didn't see the letter, but I knew what she wanted."

Tyler adjusted his glasses, making sure to increase the volume. This was interesting; a letter the in-laws hadn't seen. It could provide them with some great leverage, Tyler mused.

"After that, they just couldn't forgive me. I get it... she was their baby girl. Then I was in so much pain, so much... which was no excuse, I had... have a kid..." Tears were flowing freely from Danny's eyes now.

As Tyler looked around he noticed some of the others crying, some nodding along sadly.

"So now, I've made a promise to myself, to Annette. Get sober. Get a job. Get my life back so I can get my baby girl back." Danny sat down in his seat with a thud, emotionally and mentally spent.

Melanie rubbed his arm and gave him a sympathetic smile. Tyler frowned. This was too nice. Too safe. Danny was in recovery. Skeletons needed drama, tears, danger... Ariadne wanted something that horrified viewers, but it had to be something they couldn't look away from.

Tyler leant back in his chair. What he had to find out was exactly what would push Danny back over the edge.

****

"That bitch doesn't know what's coming to her. I'm fuckin' Jaylee y'know, who the fuck is she?" The girl on the TV drawled, pulling each word out as she smacked her gum between her teeth.

The shot panned to a small suburban house nestling in a cul-de-sac. The homes were small but well kept, with neat lawns and cutesy mailboxes.

Diane – Jaylee's Mom.

"I don't know... maybe when she was around eleven, she started rebelling, her and some of her friends from school. They started hanging out with older boys down by the 7/11 on 17th street. Jayne – sorry, Jaylee - she was so sweet when she was a little girl. Her father and I, we don't know what happened." The woman looked bewildered. "Her father died about two years back. Jayne had been bad before that, but after, she just... that was when she left the house and started..." Diane's chin wobbled.

The screen cut back to Jayne, or Jaylee as she preferred to be called, standing on a street corner. Her hair was in a high ponytail and she was in another cheap-looking bodycon dress. Dark red lipstick and heavily-lined eyes finished the ensemble. She was smoking a cigarette and looking boldly into the camera. A magazine was clutched in her other hand. It was a tabloid rag. Her picture was emblazoned on the front with the headline '*WILD CHILD SET TO DO LIVE PORN*'.

"Have you seen this?" She grinned. "I'm gonna be fuckin' famous. My mom didn't know shit. She said I'd be dead, that I was makin' my father ashamed." Jaylee smirked and shook her head. "I'll show that bitch Kiki too. Tryin' to get on my fuckin' turf."

The cameraman watched as a car, license blurred out, pulled up and Jaylee was beckoned over. She got in the car. The camera filmed the area, prostitutes catcalling the crew and the cars as they drove by.

"Our team waited while Jaylee was with the 'John'. She was gone for about 15 minutes."

Jaylee was back. Lipstick smudged. A few bills poked out the top of her dress. "Got enough for a hit." She grinned fervently. "Gotta go find my dealer."

The cameraman filmed her as she sauntered off down a seedy back alley. A moment later, the screen transitioned to a suave-looking man and woman in a clean, well-lit studio.

"You know here on Skeletons we don't normally film people once the reveal is over, but Jaylee... well we just had to follow up." The man smiled. His voice was rich and smooth.

"Right, and I have a feeling we haven't seen the last of her!" The woman chipped in perkily.

****

"Disgusting." Uncle Troy switched the TV off and hoisted himself out of his chair. "Little fifteen-year-old slut doing porn and drugs - what the hell next."

Mabel stood frozen in the doorway. She had been at Uncle Troy and Aunt Jackie's for thirty minutes and all she had done was watch Skeletons and listen to Troy comment on Jaylee and her Mom.

"Well, best be getting this TV sorted, otherwise Jackie'll be on my case." Troy grinned, revealing yellowing tombstone teeth. Mabel remained rooted in the doorway.

"Head on down to the basement," Troy said as he walked into the kitchen to grab the toolbox that was sitting on the dining table.

"The basement?" Mabel felt her stomach cinch.

"Yes, we put the TV down there till I could install it. I'll need help bringing it up. Think your scarecrow arms can manage?" Troy chuckled at his attempted joke.

"I don't think..."

"Hurry up and get down there, Mabel," Troy snapped. The laughter was gone from his voice.

Mabel backed out of the doorway. What would happen if she just fled right now? She pulled the sleeves of her holey sweater down over her thumbs. What would happen if she refused to help? Thoughts darted across her head as her leaden legs carried her, as if of their own volition, down the rickety wooden steps, into the dank, dark basement.

Neither Mabel, nor Troy when he followed a few minutes later, noticed the tiny glow from a single red LED in the corner of the basement.

****

Vianne and Charles Foxton looked at the social worker with undisguised dismay.

"And why exactly can't we see Annette?" Vianne's voice was crisp.

"We have to assess the environment, home life, personal life and so on before we can return Annette to you," Corinne replied calmly. "And she deeply wants to see her father."

Vianne snorted. Charles remained stony faced, as he had been since Corinne arrived.

Corinne had read the file. She suspected that Charles wasn't a bad person, but favored old-fashioned punishment methods. She pitied the father, Daniel or 'Danny', but they were adamant that he should not be allowed near the child.

"A child of Annette's age can be quite determined. She lost her mother. Losing her father too…"

"He let her go when he chose to turn off life support, and when he started shooting up with a needle." Flecks of spittle frayed from Vianne's lips, and her cheeks flushed.

Corinne took a deep breath and refrained from shaking her head. "Danny is now in NA. He's got a long way to go, but it could help both Danny and Annette to heal if they can see one another. He is her biological father."

Charles' frown deepened further. "Can he make a claim

for her, now that she isn't with us... now she is in the... system?" He waved his hand at nothing in particular.

Corinne knew what he meant. Since Annette had been taken from the Foxtons, Danny did have a right to request full custody again. "Yes," she replied simply. "But, it's more complicated than that - I actually received word from a lawyer." Corinne frowned. She could've sworn she saved the email, but it had vanished from her inbox that morning. Thankfully, she remembered it. "Danny would love to meet with you to discuss some things now that he is sober."

Both the Foxtons stiffened. Charles' florid cheeks turned deep claret. "Fine," he snapped, "but if that filthy murdering druggie thinks he's going to try and take our granddaughter, he's got another think coming."

Corinne bit her lip. Violence and rage emanated from Charles. She'd note that on their file when she got back to the house.

****

Danny whistled at his workstation. He was packing boxes at a firm that did custom apparel and stickers. He hadn't felt a craving all day. He'd got a letter from a lawyer saying that Charles and Vianne wanted to talk to him about Annette.

"How's it going, Danny?" Jeremy, his boss, perched on a stool.

"Really good, man. I can't tell you... thanks for this."

"I know you can do more, I get that, you know. I just want you to learn the ropes, build trust, you know?"

Jeremy talked a lot about building trust, building one

another up and so on. He had been a drug addict and had built his company by hiring other NA and AA members who were struggling to find work. They had team NA meetings. They did team events. The healthcare was great. The entire corporate culture was built around support. Danny actually preferred it to his old job. The pay wasn't great, but there was a team therapist, and everyone who worked there had been in NA or AA, so Danny didn't have to make anything up or pretend to be someone he wasn't.

"I totally understand. I... I've only been clean a month. I really appreciate this, more than you know." Danny grinned. He thought about the night before. He had gone for dinner with Tyler. The guy had seemed strangely stand-offish at first, unusual for a sponsor, but then they had started talking. Turned out they had more in common than they realized. They were both into the same films, same books, and had the same upbringings. Hours had flown by and Danny realized how much he missed having a friend. Someone he could just chat to about normal stuff.

"I do know Danny, I really do. My history is more checkered than most." He looked down, his smile fading for a moment. "You'll be at the team barbecue on Friday right?" He grinned.

"Yeah man, looking forward to it." Danny smiled back. To his surprise, his smile didn't feel fake or stiff.

"You talking to the staff therapist today?" Jeremy asked lightly.

"Yeah." Danny bit his lip. "I'm meeting my in-laws... who have custody of my daughter. First time in a while, since I... well... it's a big deal," he blurted out.

"That's great man, really great." Jeremy nodded and

stood up. "It's great to have you on the team, OK, and my door is always open."

Danny nodded and smiled before returning to packing. He had texted Tyler that he was going to be meeting Charles and Vianne.

Want me to come along? Tyler had texted. Another text followed quickly. *I have a decent amount of legal knowledge.*

Danny frowned. He thought Tyler did something for TV... he had been vague about it. Cameraman maybe, or editing? Danny couldn't remember.

My parents were both lawyers! Sucked when I got into trouble as a kid ;)

Danny exhaled. *Yeah man, that would be great, if you have time.*

****

Annette lay down on the faded bedspread and looked at the ceiling. Her foster parents were in the kitchen cooking, and a sour smell permeated the house. Her favorite teddy, Puffball, had been left at Granny and Grandpa's, along with most of her clothes and belongings.

"Ann?" her foster mother, a shrill, rat-faced woman, screamed from downstairs.

"Annette," she whispered under her breath.

"They're not that bad... not like some of the others." An angelic-looking black boy leant in the doorway. "I'm Michael. Or, Mike now."

"Was Michael too long?" Annette smiled as she pushed herself up from the bed.

"I guess so. I'm eleven."

"I'm ten today."

Annette held up a hand before the boy could say anything. "Don't tell anyone, I just wanted someone to know. I haven't... my family... it's like they've forgotten about me."

Michael nodded. "I know. We should get downstairs, you don't want to piss her off. And call her Mommy - she gets really mad."

Annette swallowed and bit her tongue. She was a good girl. She was going to do whatever she had to so that she could go back to Daddy.

"So, why're you here?" Michael whispered as they descended the stairs. Other foster kids were emerging from cramped bedrooms.

Annette wrinkled her nose. "My Dad was ill, so I had to go live with my grandparents. They - well my Grandpa, he isn't a very nice person."

Michael again gave a sage nod. "Is your Mom dead? Both my parents died in an accident. No one else in the family wanted to take me in."

Annette nodded. Michael was the first foster child who had been nice to her so far. He was also honest. Annette had realized quickly that a lot of the other kids lied, stole things, or were just plain mean. "Yes. She died before though - before my Dad got sick." She frowned. That wasn't really true. Dad getting sick was because Mom died.

Michael nodded and fell silent as they entered the kitchen.

"What are you two staring at?" their foster mother screeched. "You need to help lay the table for dinner. And you?" She jabbed a dirty spoon at Annette. "Ann, you have a meeting with your social worker at 9am tomorrow."

"Yes."

"Yes MOMMY!" their foster mother snapped, rapping the spoon on one of Annette's knuckles.

Annette winced but stayed silent. "Yes Mommy."

****

Ariadne paced in front of her desk. The 100th episode special was her chance to really make an impression at Sintertainment Inc. She could move up the chain, or use her status as the lead on Skeletons to get a better gig over at another company.

She had been skimming the footage from the six different people they had been filming to try and discern which two would make the best options. They would run all six eventually, but the 100th episode needed to be special. She wanted that shock factor that would leave the viewers unable to tear their eyes from the screen.

"What about a happy ending?" Tyler said, leaning around the doorframe.

Ariadne looked at him. "What?"

"Most of our episodes don't exactly have a sunny outlook, right?" Tyler grinned. "What if we could sort out a happier ending?"

Ariadne frowned. "I don't know... I mean... the story would have to be pretty cutting. I'm not talking cheesy lifetime movie heartbreak."

Tyler thought about some of the footage he had seen of Violet in her comatose state and the horrendous videos Carl had shared from when Danny was in the depths of his addiction. "It's... cutting."

"I... I don't know."

Tyler sat down in one of the sleek gray chairs which were artfully placed in the luxurious office. His knee jiggled. He had to meet Danny at his apartment by 5pm, since the entire meeting with the in-laws had been orchestrated to happen there, where Tyler already had hidden cameras rigged to catch every angle.

"Look, I know we don't go for the cheesy happy ending, but I think this could be a hit for the 100th episode, and draw in viewers who say we exploit the disadvantaged."

Ariadne drew in a sharp breath. "I don't want to cater to those looking for some manufactured happy ending," she snapped.

"I get that, but what if this wasn't manufactured? And it worked? And it involved a little kid and a struggling dad? Skeletons' whole premise is that we fill the gap between celebrity drama and the dark underbelly of everyday people; we raise people up to quasi-celebrity and then we can show the seedy or sad backstory. But, every once in a while, people want something good..." Tyler paused, trying to think of another way to pitch it to her. "C'mon Ariadne, you gotta admit it's pretty perfect."

Ariadne's face remained pinched. "Maybe if the other story was particularly dark as well? Could be a good contrast."

Tyler nodded and looked at his watch. It was already 5pm. He was going to have to speed to get to Danny's. He could feel his phone buzzing in his pocket, no doubt Danny asking why he hadn't showed. "Look, just think about it..." But then the door flew open, cutting him off. It was Jesse, panting and breathless. Ariadne looked nonplussed, but Jesse was too flustered to notice, or to care.

"Oh my god, Ariadne... I... the footage..." Her eyes were round. She was wearing a fashionable suit, but her cheap highlights and scruffy makeup made her look out of place.

"I have to go." Tyler began to stand.

"The footage," Jesse gasped, "from the mother and daughter, nominated by the aunt... um... the anorexia?"

Ariadne nodded quickly, urging Jesse to spit it out. Even Tyler remained momentarily rooted to the spot.

"There's child abuse... I didn't know... pedophilia."

"Show me the footage. Now!" Ariadne snapped.

"I better get going."

"No, Tyler, come with us to the viewing room. I need your take on this."

Tyler resisted the urge to frown and kept his face placid. "My take?"

"Yes, whether or not we can show it. Come on."

Tyler remained rooted to the floor, "I have to go meet...

"All the cameras are set up for this Danny guy, now come on." Ariadne's voice turned hard. "It's not like he needs you there." She beckoned Jesse and Tyler out of her office and marched off down the corridor towards the darkened viewing room.

Tyler's phone buzzed in his pocket again. "Shit," he muttered. He had been out for dinner a few times with Danny now. He hadn't thought he'd like the guy, but Danny was nice. Genuine. In fact, he was the first person Tyler had hung out with in years who wasn't full of himself, or full of shit.

Jesse looked at him and blushed guiltily. "Sorry, I didn't mean..."

"It's OK, not your fault," Tyler said. His stomach churned as he walked out of the office and turned his phone on to airplane mode.

****

Mabel lay on her bed, rigid, eyes glued to the ceiling. When she'd been a little girl, her Mom had put glow-in-the-dark stars on the ceiling. About three years before, Mabel had insisted on redecorating her room and she had picked them all off. Now she stared at the pale pastel blue ceiling and wished they were still there. She contemplated crying, forcing tears to leak from her eyes, but she knew it wouldn't make her feel better. She had learnt that long ago.

She heard the front door open and tensed as she waited. The sound of her mothers' chunky, 'practical' heeled shoes clunked on the hardwood hallway. Mabel relaxed.

"Mabel? Honey?" Corinne yelled. She plonked her briefcase down and quickly dug her laptop out. The Foxtons had lied to her about the time and location of the meeting, and she suspected that they had gone to meet with Danny on their own. She had never even met the guy, but she had read all the reports and notes on him.

"Mabel?" She called again. "Are you home?" She leant around the bottom banister. She felt damp underneath her thick sweater. Irritation rose. "MABEL!" She shouted.

"Jesus Mom, I'm right here!" Mabel hissed back, opening her door a crack.

"Well you could tell me when I called your name the first time!" Corinne snapped back. Immediately, she softened. Her daughter's face looked particularly drawn, and her nails were bitten to the quick.

"Come on downstairs and tell me about your day, or at least let me tell you about mine, I've had a crap one." Corinne bit her lip. She wasn't really supposed to disclose cases, but she had told Mabel the odd tidbit in the past, and today she really needed to vent, even if it was only to her teenage daughter.

Mabel nodded and came downstairs; her footfalls were so light they didn't make a sound. Corinne clattered around the kitchen, unloading about the Foxtons as she made chamomile tea. Mabel sat in the breakfast nook with her feet underneath her.

"So, how was your day?" Corinne asked as she sidled into the seating bank.

"Weird." Mabel blew on her tea. It smelt of oats and chamomile, and she inhaled deeply.

"Weird? School?"

"No, school was fine. I got an A in my biology test." Mabel paused and sipped. "No, weird 'cause Aunt Jackie came round and was being... super..." Mabel pulled her mouth to one side.

"Super what?" Corinne frowned. She didn't like the idea of Jackie being around Mabel when she was alone. She knew her sister could be cutting at the best of times, and she seemed to particularly enjoy picking at Mabel.

"Just... kinda nasty." Mabel looked down. She didn't want to tell her mom the truth. Jackie had come around and tried to force her to eat something, then yanked up her sleeves to question her about the deep scars that ran from elbow to wrist. She had been fervently insistent that Mabel 'talk about things'. Mabel had locked herself in the bathroom and refused to come out until she heard Jackie's car drive away.

"Oh well, you know Jackie. She's had that tongue on her since we were little." Corinne waved a hand.

Mabel felt a little hot wave of anger. "No, it wasn't like how she normally is. She was really mean."

"About what?"

Mabel looked at the floor. "She was saying nasty stuff about you, about me... about how I am..." she shrugged. Her eating disorder and self-harm weren't topics she wanted to talk about. She had already been through the same verbal dance with her mom so many times there wasn't really any point.

"Y'know, your Aunt Jackie had it tough when we were kids. Our dad, your grandfather who you never met, was really hard on her, and our mom, well... she always wanted her to be thinner, smarter, prettier. She... well, when I came along, she thought we would be best friends, but my parents... they were so different with me. I think it hurt her even more - alienated her."

"Ok-ay... so I get it. But that doesn't make it fair that she is horrible to me." Mabel felt her body getting stiff.

"I wasn't saying it was fair, honey, I just think sometimes you don't get why..."

"Forget it." Mabel edged out of the banked seating.

"Come on Mabel, don't be like that."

"Be like what? Not wanting my aunt to verbally attack me? Oh, why silly me, I didn't realize that was so horrible of me." Mabel's face was twisted and her voice dripped with sarcasm.

Corinne opened her mouth, shocked by the rage on her daughter's face, but before she could speak, Mabel had stormed upstairs to her room.

Ensconced in her pastel blue room, Mabel felt a torrent of hot, angry tears spill down her cheeks. She clenched and unclenched her fists, wanting to shriek, scream, smash everything in her room, but instead she reached under her desk lamp. Taped to the base of the lamp were two new razor blades. Carefully, she peeled back the tape and examined the one of the blades under the light. Then she reached under her bed and pulled out the old burgundy towel and a stash of gauze that she kept hidden. She laid it flat, in front of the full-length mirror, and placed the blade ceremonially where the base of the mirror met the towel.

She stepped back and began peeling the layers of her clothes off. The thick sweater, the fleecy socks, the multiple layers of long sleeve tops, her jeans, and finally the matching cream thermals, dotted with little posies.

When she was in her underwear, she looked up at the reflection in the mirror. She turned left and then right. She wore an elasticated training bra and a pair of boy shorts in matching pastel blue. Her ribs, collar bones and hips jutted out like the bars of a cage. Her skin was a strange shade of gray. Mabel's fingertips traced along the scars on her arms. She moved down to the scars on her thighs, upper and inner, and finally her fingers grazed over the deep scars on her stomach, up and down her ribs, like the notches on the cell wall of a prison.

Mabel stepped forward delicately and folded herself down into a cross-legged position. She picked up the blade and examined it once more. It glinted in the soft light of her bedroom.

Mabel heard voices and she paused with the blade held between her finger and thumb. She heard the voices change, then change again. The TV was on. Mabel let out a long, defeated breath and brought the blade to her abdomen. There was a gap of untouched skin on her right side, from her rib to her hip.

With a practiced, decisive motion, she pushed the blade in and down, watching the small pearls of blood turn into streams. She picked up some gauze before they could stain her underwear.

She waited a moment, and then drew the blade again, vertically alongside the last line. She was so good now the lines were artistically straight. She bit her lower lip and wondered when it would be enough. When the thinness would be enough. When the scarring would be enough. When she would no longer be pretty little Mabel.

****

Danny was curled into the fetal position when Melanie found him. Out cold. She went round the room methodically, cleaning, tidying, and destroying the paraphernalia. The room was disgusting. Mold crept up from the rank carpet. The air was stale and the window jammed shut. The sink, bathroom and hotplate were all crusted with decade-old dirt. Melanie shook her head. How much was Danny paying for this place? The landlord had even heckled her for rent when she went into the room.

"Danny?" A muffled voice came through the door.

Melanie tensed and wrapped her coat tighter. The room was freezing and frost gathered at the corners of the windowpanes. Danny had no heat. No kitchen. A bathroom in which the shower didn't work. His bed, presumably once a futon, was now a fetid lumpy thing that emanated a sour smell.

"Danny, it's me, Tyler." Tyler rubbed his face with his hands. The 100th episode showing was tonight. Tyler didn't have much time. He'd already called in all his favors with the crew at Skeletons. He'd probably be out on his ass tomorrow.

Melanie flung the door open. "What the fuck are you doing here?" she snarled.

Tyler stepped back. Melanie was usually so... bland. She wore cream sweaters, jeans and boots like a uniform. Her undyed hair was always in a ponytail and her face was always devoid of makeup. Now, fury lit her up.

"You weren't here when he called you!" She took a step forward, forcing Tyler further back into the hallway. "You weren't here when he texted you, begging, pleading for help." She shook her head with vehemence. "Did you even listen to his messages?"

Tyler nodded. Danny's messages, his voice cracking, slowly becoming more panicked, more stressed, then as he passed in and out of consciousness, pushing Tyler's conscience over the brink. "I... I did."

"So you know about the letter? About the Foxtons? About Annette?"

Tyler thought he nodded, but he felt sick and numb.

"Well I'll tell you. He showed them the letter, thinking

it would help them understand why he turned off life support. The mother-in-law, Vianne, broke down. Confessed about little Annette being taken, but Charles went off on Danny. Attacked him. Badly. You should see his face. He looks like he went ten rounds in the bloody ring. And his daughter? They don't know where the hell she is, except in some random foster family. Danny went online and tried to find out some information. Found out about a little girl who was in the news recently for being abused and murdered by her foster family. Danny had a panic attack... well, you can guess what happened."

"Tyler?" Carl's head poked out from a doorway. "Are you here?"

"We have to go and help Danny now!" Tyler stepped up to Melanie.

"Tyler?" Carl rubbed sleep from his eyes.

Melanie looked at Carl, confused. "What's..."

"We have to go inside and I can explain." Tyler, as gently as he could manage, pushed Melanie back into the room and slammed the door.

"What the hell is going on?" Melanie snapped, flinging Tyler's hand off her shoulder and turning to Danny, who was groaning. "Shhhhit, he's in bad shape."

Tyler knew he wasn't a particularly nice person. Nor was he a person who delved much into his conscience or his personal failings as a man. He still couldn't fathom why Danny and his story had got to him so much.

As if Melanie could read his mind, she sighed and turned to him. "It's hard seeing a life with a hand that has been so unfairly dealt. Lose your wife to a car accident, but not really, you have to make the decision to end her life. In agony from a broken back and given painkillers up the wazoo until you can't live without them. Lose your kid to your in-laws, who are supposed to be on your side, and then get assaulted and find out your kid is in the system, sending you into a relapse from your first serious recovery." She was laying it all out succinctly.

Tyler nodded. "I... my life has been easy. Danny grew up like me. In the suburbs. Nice family. His parents died, y'know. That's how he met Violet. She was a nurse."

Melanie frowned. "I thought... didn't you have a brother?" She tried to remember what Tyler had told her.

"Danny is so like me... our lives... it makes me wonder. I... I have to tell you something Mel, and I'm going to need your help." Tyler looked up to one corner of the room, then to Mel, then to the bloodied, bruised heap that was Danny. "You're going to hate me, but we don't have much time."

****

Jesse nervously moved from foot to foot. Tonight was the big night. They were showing her pick, the girl Mabel, and Donovan's pick, a father who was a closeted gay man having an affair with his wife's brother. Ariadne was equal parts foul and excited. She had wanted to use Tyler's pick, the drug addict, but a bunch of the files had been corrupted. No one was sure how, and now there wasn't enough footage. She had been on the warpath for a few hours until she had seen Donovan's cut. It was pretty incredible. The wife was going to lose her shit when she saw the footage.

Jesse felt bad for Tyler - kind of, but not really, since her pick had been chosen for the special and that was all that really mattered. Now Ariadne was taking her seriously.

"Ok, live shows aren't our norm." Marianne, the production director, stood beside Ariadne. Her cheeks were flushed. "There are going to be anomalies that we can't edit, cut or control. We all have to stay on our toes. Everyone knows what they are doing?"

Everyone in the room nodded. A ripple of tension and excitement flowed through the group.

Ariadne turned to Jesse. "Do you have everything you need?" Jesse nodded. Ariadne gave her a tight nod in return. "Both of these could go south quickly, and we could end up with some explosive reactions" Ariadne paused, savoring the thought, "so be ready to manipulate the situations to how we want them to go."

Jesse swallowed. She had four people at her disposal, along with the filming crew. She turned to the intern with the acne, Tom, and gave him a small smile. "The film crew has their van ready, and we have a car right?"

Tom nodded and scratched an angry outbreak on his chin. "We do. I think the others are just getting their stuff." He looked down at the faded Jansport backpack on the floor.

Jesse picked up her faux leather handbag, sack shaped and filled with crap. She didn't know what to bring. She didn't know what she was doing.

"It's gonna be a real mess," Tom said cheerfully.

Jesse gulped. "I know," she snapped. "I can handle it."

****

Jackie sipped coffee at her kitchen counter and watched the TV with her mouth hanging open and a faint smile playing on her lips. A plate of cookies was sitting, half eaten, beside a pile of tabloid magazines that were now dusted with crumbs.

A Closer Look was on TV, but Jackie preferred Skeletons. A Closer Look was a bit more like watching a therapy session play out on TV, whereas Skeletons was like watching a daytime drama.

Jackie hefted herself on the stool and moved out to stop the counter digging into her belly. She grabbed the pile of magazines and drew them towards her. The headlines were all in thick black lettering; ASHLEY A GAINS 20LBS AFTER SHOCK SPLIT!; 'SEX, DRUGS & LIES... Inside the BELLADONAS' marriage'; FROM CHUBBY CHICK TO PORN QUEEN – MEET ROSIE DOUBLE-D!; 'SICK SCANDALS ON THIS WEEKS' SKELETONS – Looking back at some of their most insane episodes before the 100th episode bombshell hits!'

Jackie grabbed the last magazine and flicked to the pages dedicated to Skeletons. The girl from last week, Jaylee, was posing in a ludicrous caricature next to the headline. A flurry of doubt passed through Jackie's skull. What if Skeletons made Corinne and Mabel famous? It was more like infamy, but knowing her sneaky sister, Corinne would turn it around.

Jackie shook her head and stuffed a cookie in her mouth. Mabel wasn't anything like this Jaylee girl. She was mousy and shy, and Jackie doubted any men would be interested in such a scabbed-up bag of bones. As for Corinne, she was still pretty, but she always looked plain. Jackie smoothed her glittery T-shirt and ran her fingers through her hair. Unlike her sister, she made an effort, and now she was the pretty one of the two. Maybe she would get famous from it.

Slurping her coffee, she scanned the article. It detailed the dark family secrets that had been spilled on national television: Jaylee, the drug-addicted teen prostitute, Brian, a violently abusive father of two, Caterina, the mother with Munchausen's syndrome, and Bethanny, the woman who was systematically sleeping her way through her husbands' friends, her friends' husbands and as it turned out, shagging her brother. Jackie let out a cackle as she read about each person and the fallout from them in the press and on TV.

"Unbelievable," she muttered as she read about Caterina. She let out a huff of air. "I wonder how they'll show Corinne - terrible mother, distracted." She chewed her lip fervently. She smoothed her shirt again and stuffed another cookie in her mouth. Her phone buzzed on the counter.

"This is Jackie," she said.

"Hi Jackie, it's Jesse."

Jackie didn't hear the flutter of nerves in Jesse's voice. "Yes, hi!" she trilled. "Is it the big day?" She fanned a hand and stood up off the stool, and her earrings and bracelets jangled.

"Mmm hmmm." On the other end of the line, Jesse looked at her watch. It was 2pm. She had been up, at the studio, since 2am. The entire week had been a blur of editing, cutting, adding, re-editing and then 'glossing', which was the term the team used for adding in all the final touches. All that footage would make up the first forty-five minute segment of Skeletons, the 'backstory'. Then the bombshell would drop, and the second forty-five minutes was dedicated to the fallout. Normally it would all happen several weeks prior to airing, so the team would cut, edit and do their thing. But today they would drop the bombshell around 5pm, ready for the airing time of 6pm.

"The show is airing at 6pm," Jesse said. "If there is anything else you want to make the cut before then, now is the time to make sure it gets in."

Jackie nodded. She had been round at her sister's house, fully made up, of course, to try and ruffle feathers and prod Mabel.

"Well Mabel has Mathletes club tonight till 6pm."

Jesse closed her eyes. The girl wouldn't know anything until it was live on TV. Because she was over sixteen, they didn't need to blur her face, but Jesse still felt queasiness in her belly.

"Right, Friday night… well, we just need to clear some logistical things up with you prior."

"Of course," Jackie crowed. She had already received ten grand, and another ten would fill her bank account when the show aired. $20,000 for shoving Corinne's faults in her snooty, stuck-up face. Jackie grinned.

Jesse tapped her iPad screen and pulled up the list of 'guide-probes' Ariadne and Marianne had gone over with her. Jesse's pick had turned out to be the trickiest one to date, but the one with the biggest shocker. The guide-probes were all designed to set up the situation the way Skeletons wanted it. Normally the 'nominators' knew about the guide-probes, and they helped the crew set up the situation and the reveal. This time, Jackie had to be kept in the dark as much as Corinne and Mabel did. After all, she was as much a part of this as they were.

"Do you and Troy want to be at the house when we do the reveal?" Jesse forced her mouth into a smile and tried to sound cheery.

"Well... it'll just be Corinne if you do it at five."

"We can do it at 6pm," Jesse blurted out. She scrunched her face. That would give them no wiggle room. The footage would be going directly live.

"Great!" Jackie practically screeched. "I'll organize a dinner."

"Great." Jesse felt her phone buzz with another call. "OK Jackie, you get that set up and call me back when it's all sorted. You're doing a fab job!"

"Will do!" Jackie hung up quickly.

Jesse could practically hear her acrylic nails clicking Corinne's number. Jesse shook her head. That woman was in for one hell of a shock.

****

Melanie seethed as she drove through the darkened streets. Danny, passing in and out of consciousness, was in her back seat. Tyler sat rigidly in her front seat.

"What was that about?" Melanie managed to force the words out quietly, but her tone was still sharp.

Tyler held his phone in his lap. "They recovered some of the footage, the beating... I think was all... I'm not sure, but..."

"So they might have seen the relapse? Fuck Tyler!" Melanie smacked her hands on the steering wheel. "Sorry," she muttered bashfully.

"No, you're right to be angry." Tyler looked down at his phone. He wasn't sure what they had recovered, and did this mean that Ariadne wanted to show Danny's story? No. Then she would have called him. He frowned. "I don't think they have the relapse. The tech guy just kept talking about the beating, about the fight... then something about new material from the foster home." He furrowed his brow.

"Annette..." Melanie went pale.

"Shit." Tyler rubbed his face. "I didn't think Ariadne followed through on that. Fuck... fuck."

Melanie shook her head and her face turned sour. "Let's just get Danny to a hospital. My Dad's a lawyer, I can ask him to help with the legal side of things. We need to get a hold of the social worker too." Melanie started making a mental list of things that needed to happen.

"If they see... the relapse... the assault..."

"Then Annette will stay in the foster system... and likely won't be able to return to her father *or* the Foxtons."

"Shit, Jesus! What've I done?"

"Something horrible that a bad person would do." Melanie's face was set in a grimace. "Y'know, I'm sure you and your co-workers like to sit back and watch people like us, druggies, fuck-ups and the like, but my god, you think you're better?"

Tyler was silent.

"B... elanie..." Danny mumbled through thick lips. "I fink... um... I'm sorry."

"It's OK Danny, you didn't do anything wrong," Melanie cooed.

Danny sobbed. "No, I used..." He mumbled something else that sounded like 'Annette' and then passed out.

"What do we do?" Tyler gulped.

Melanie glanced up at her rear-view mirror and snuck a peek at Tyler. He seemed genuinely remorseful. She had made her fair share of awful mistakes.

"We need to get Danny a place to live, that's nice. Get him to the hospital, make sure they don't get any footage or results of the blood tests. I don't know... we need to get hold of the social worker, if there is..." she lowered her voice to a whisper, "abuse in the foster home, god forbid, it might mean Danny can get Annette back - I don't know."

"I have a place he can live," Tyler volunteered.

"No!" Melanie snapped. "I have a mother-in-law suite above my garage. It's been sitting empty, but I can let Danny move in for a low rent. He has a decent job, but if they find out about the relapse... it might jeopardize that."

"What can I do?" Tyler looked ashen.

"We need to find out what happened in the care home, find out about the social worker. Find out what footage they do have." Melanie paused. "Will they do a story regardless?"

Tyler wanted to shake his head, but he knew Ariadne would want to make use of every piece that had had money sunk into it. "Probably," he admitted.

"Spin it - in his favour. You already said you pitched it as a happy ending. Go do that. Maybe - maybe it will help get Annette back. I don't know." Melanie glanced in her rearview mirror again. Danny was so very much like her brother. She was terrified of what her parents would say when they saw him. Would it bring back all the memories of the fire? She shook her head.

Tyler had dropped his head into his hands. "If this doesn't work, I'll fuck up his whole life. He might never see his kid again."

Melanie opened her mouth for a retort, then closed it. "When I was on drugs, my brother and me - he was a few years younger than me - we were living in a shitty house on the outskirts of Seattle. We got high one night, there was a fire... I woke up to smoke and crawled outside. Passed out. The firefighters found me, on the grass, shivering and semi-conscious."

"Your brother?"

"Never woke up. Burned to death. My parents didn't blame me, but they should have. I could have woken him up, got him out, I don't know... done something."

Tyler exhaled as though he had been punched in the gut.

"We all fuck up, Tyler. But you can fix what you did." Melanie turned to him as they pulled into the ER parking lot. "Get an Uber to the studio and fix this."

****

Mabel kept her head down in the classroom. There were eight of them in there for Mathletes club. She did the equations methodically, her pencil making a soft, soothing sound as she completed each one. When she was done, she placed her pencil down but didn't hit the buzzer in front of her.

Adam looked at her and grinned. He rolled his eyes and hit his buzzer. As soon as he did, Mabel tapped hers.

"All done Adam?" Leah, the captain of the Mathletes smiled at him.

"Yeah." He pulled the word out.

"Great job, you were first!" she gushed.

"Uh huh." Adam glanced at Mabel and raised an eyebrow.

"Good job for you too, Mabel. Of course," Leah added quickly. A few more buzzers sounded as people finished.

Leah looked at the times. "We need to be faster if we're going to beat Evergreen High." She frowned, her crush on Adam forgotten.

"I have to go. Family dinner," Mabel said quietly.

"Ok – well, I might need you or Adam to coach the others, bring up times," Leah said with a smile. She liked Mabel, even if the poor kid looked like she had one foot in the grave, and rarely spoke.

"We can do that." Adam smiled.

Mabel gave a noncommittal move with her head and gathered her things. "OK, bye." Mabel hurried out the room without waiting for a reply.

"Hey honey! Figured I'd pick you up."

"And take me to the depths of the underworld," Mabel muttered.

"It's dinner with your aunt and uncle," Corinne sighed, "so I suppose that is a fair comparison."

Mabel looked up at her mom and smiled. "Good day?"

"Well, I had a fun conversation with your aunt," Corinne said. Looking at her pinched face, Mabel could tell it had been about as much fun as her conversation had been a few days ago. "And I keep getting called from a number I don't recognize, Seattle number. I'm worried it's a parent of one of the kids under my supervision." Corinne chewed her cheek. "How was school?"

Mabel gave a non-committal answer as they navigated out of the school parking lot. Corinne chatted as they drove home; Mabel looked out the window and gave the odd grunt of agreement.

"Ready?" Corinne asked.

"They're here already?" Mabel's face fell.

"Your aunt cooked."

"Oh Jesus," Mabel grumbled as she yanked her backpack out of the footwell. "Let me guess, Mac'n'cheese and hamburger helper?"

"Lasagne, I think." Corinne bit her lip. "Honey, are you OK? You... the past few days..."

Mabel tried to force the frown off her face. The cuts on her tummy had split and she could feel blood starting to trickle. "Yes Mom, just busy and school and stuff." She wriggled out of the car and away from her Mom.

Corinne sighed and eased herself up out the car. Her phone began buzzing again. "Hello?" she said with exasperation. Mabel was loitering by the front door. "Yes, this is Corinne Beaumont... uh huh... I see... and you are?... This is very unorthodox, you're not supposed to contact me directly... wait, how did you find out about that? And you're sure?"

Mabel sidled closer to eavesdrop.

"A report needs to be filed formally... no... look, I understand... and he's at the hospital? OK, right... well I can't make it down tonight, we'll have to talk tomorrow... No, I really can't. Uh huh... I understand... I'll do what I can."

Corinne hung up the phone. Her skin had turned gray.

"You OK Mom?"

"A... one of my charges... I don't know how they got my information." Corinne walked towards the front door in a daze. Neither of them noticed the long Mercedes van parked in the neighbors' driveway, or the two cameramen camped out around the edge of the house, just waiting to burst inside.

****

"Welcome to the 100th Episode of Skeletons! It's been one hell of a rollercoaster, and this ride isn't slowing down tonight."

The montage of past episodes scrolled across the giant flat screens in the sleek brick and wood studio. The presenters, Abbie-Rae and Jono, were seated on a curved gray sofa. She was in slim fit pants and a T-shirt, her hair in effortless waves, and he was in close-cut jeans and a distressed Henley. They looked like those thirty-year-olds that get cast as popular eighteen-year-old high school students.

"So, it seems like our stories are getting ever crazier, but we can promise you, we don't make this stuff up or ever intervene. As you can see from tonight's LIVE show, this stuff is as raw as it gets." Abbie-Rae revealed a wolfish, gleaming white smile.

"And man, are you guys in for a helluva shock tonight," said Jono. "Both nominees are going to find out tonight that they were nominated for Skeletons, but before we do that, let's take a look at their backstories."

Both the presenters smiled at the camera and then shifted their bodies ever so slightly so they were angled in towards the main flat screen.

"OK, backstory is rolling. Where are you guys at?" The static crackled in Jesse's earpiece.

"We're lined up outside the house. Ready when you are."

"We'll give you the go ahead in about twenty minutes. We're getting the live feed of the dinner and editing it as it comes in for the first part of the live reveal." Marianne's voice was calm and collected, and Jesse took a deep breath. From outside, she could make out Mabel's face. It was a mask of misery.

Jesse looked down at her iPad. Maybe she was doing the poor kid a favor. "OK, perfect. We'll wait for your instructions," Jesse said, looking back up to study the family.

In the glossy studio, Mabel's sad life story was playing out, carefully curated and edited to leave out the most shocking detail. Right now the audience, and likely the millions of viewers at home, were letting out sad sighs and pained sounds. The girl was deathly thin and scarred beyond belief. The footage of her eating, or not eating, was agonizing. The cutting was so stark and visceral that the audience couldn't look away, as if they were sadists or dacryphiliacs. They watched the blood tear out, over and over again, and watched Mabel suppress winces as she cleaned it all up.

By the time they went to a commercial break, the audience had been well and truly gripped by the sad cycle.

"It's hard to watch, but hopefully after this, Mabel can get the help she needs." Abbie-Rae did her best attempt at a sympathetic smile.

"There is a lot more to come though, so stay tuned for the bombshell reveal... that'll bring more than one thing to light in Mabel's story." Jono gleamed at the cameras as they panned back and cut to a commercial for depression medication.

"How's the incoming edit?" Marianne peered over the editors' shoulders. A team of three were quickly sifting, cutting and glossing everything.

"Aunt's a fuckin' bitch," one of them mumbled.

Marianne let out a sharp bark of laughter. "Yes, I think the audience hasn't quite realized that yet... that's the first part of the second half, right?"

"Uh huh," another guy mumbled. "We've cut together a bunch of scenes of her goin' after the kid. Girl, Mabel. An' her sister... the mom. Right up to the start of dinner." He continued clicking his keyboard.

"We'll come in to do the reveal, and that is when we'll show the footage from the basement cam." Marianne was nodding to herself.

"S'gonna be a fuckin' train wreck." One of the tech girls, dressed in a punky outfit, was transfixed on the screens.

"We can only hope," Marianne said ominously, before turning back to Ariadne and saying something inaudible.

****

Danny awoke to faint beeping. The lights were low and someone was curled in a chair across the room. He had a vague memory of when his mother was sick, and he was the one curled in the chair. Pain ricocheted inside his skull. It felt like there was a bowling alley between his ears.

He groaned and tried to roll over. Tubes lassoed him to the bed. That was when he felt the tube in his throat, and the panic set in.

"Unghh." He scrambled with his hands, coughs

spluttering and smothering his breath. A volley of beeps sounded and a nurse came in. Her shoes squeaked.

"Shhh... it's OK, Danny." Her voice was soft.

Danny felt sick. He didn't deserve niceties. He had relapsed, and god knows what else he had done whilst he'd been high. Tears rolled down his cheeks.

"It's all right. You had a collapsed lung, so you've got to leave this tube here for now."

Drowsiness tugged at his eyelids. He nodded.

"Is he awake?" Melanie stood from the chair and tried to work a knot out of her low back.

"In and out. Poor guy's in a state."

Danny saw her put a hand on the nurses' arm and give it a squeeze. "Thanks for this, Cath."

Melanie picked up her phone and sent six texts one after the other. Responses started pinging in almost immediately. Danny felt a vague inkling that something was going on when she picked up her phone and began talking in hushed tones about blood tests, cameras and footage, but he pretended to be asleep and kept his eyes half-closed.

"Tyler?" Melanie picked up her phone. "Uh huh... OK, that's great news... any word on Annette yet? Uh huh... . OK, keep me updated... oh, I suppose you should..." She bit her lip. "OK, see you soon."

Danny knew he had heard Annette's name before. Something tugged inside his head, a string yanking on a lobe... Annette... something had happened and it was about Annette. He tried to grasp at it, but he felt himself slipping off to sleep instead.

****

"OK, ready?" Jesse turned to Devon, the 'on-site' presenter. Devon wasn't like Abbie-Rae or Jono. She was curvy, with honey skin and soft wavy hair that was flecked with gray. Dressed in slim fit pants and a sweater, she exuded warmth. Her smile crinkled the corners of her hazel eyes and lit up her chipmunk face.

Devon exhaled sadly. "This is going to be awful Jesse, are *you* ready?"

Jesse gulped. She wanted this. She wanted to be in this industry. She had picked the best nominee. "Yes," she replied firmly, ignoring the churning in her gut.

"OK then." Devon made sure her earpiece was snug. "Marianne, Ariadne, team, do you have me?" Jesse heard the voices from the earpiece confirming. "I'm good to go." Devon walked up the pathway to the house.

Jesse stayed behind, in the van, with the rest of the on-site film crew.

Devon, along with two of the Skeletons 'specialists', waited at the front door for the signal before knocking.

"Well, isn't Aunt Jackie a real piece of work." Jono looked at the cameras dramatically as caws of cruel laughter erupted in the audience.

"As you can see, Mabel has had to deal with a lot from her aunt, without much help from her Mom along the way, but things are about to get real in the Beaumont household. Let's step in and get those skeletons out of the closet with Devon!" Abbie-Rae chirped out the tagline.

The audience hushed as the screens panned to Devon, waiting patiently on the doorstep.

"Welcome to the hundredth episode of Skeletons. I'm here at the Beaumont house where Mabel and her mom Corinne live. They're inside having dinner with Aunt Jackie and Uncle Troy right now."

An older, fatherly-looking gentleman smiled genially as the camera roved to him. The caption on the bottom of the screen read 'Dr Greer/Child Psychologist'. The camera shifted again to a homely woman in a pantsuit. 'Dr Johnston/Family Therapist.'

Devon knocked on the door. A moment later a flushed and excited-looking Aunt Jackie yanked it open. A manic grin was spread across her face, emphasized by the strange orange lipstick she had chosen. She was in a tight dress with sequins running in zigzags from neck to hem. Something was spelled out in black sequins, but it was lost in the folds of her stomach.

"Hi, I'm Devon."

"From Skeletons, I know." She ushered them inside. "Oh good, you're the kiddie therapist - that's what Mabel needs." Jackie tried to reform her features to make herself appear concerned, but it failed to hide her glee. "Come on. We're all in the dining room."

Off camera, Troy and Corinne could be heard asking who was at the door.

Devon, the doctors, and the film crew crept along the hallway behind Jackie, who turned and theatrically mimed to indicate that the arched gap in the wall was the entrance to the dining room. Devon nodded and smiled. She took a deep breath, but before she could enter and break the news to them, Jackie had leapt around the corner and announced them, leaving Devon and the crew to rush in after her.

"Skeletons are here!"

The camera panned slowly across their faces. Corinne and Troy looked utterly baffled. The camera moved to Mabel. Her eyes went wide and she began to tremble. Her head shook slightly from side to side and she mouthed something. The sound guy edged closer to try and catch what it was.

"No... no... no..." Mabel whispered, over and over.

Back in the main studio the audience gasped, then held their collective breath.

"Skeletons? Like that awf... ahem, that show Mabel watches?" Corinne stood up from the table. "I don't understand."

"What's going on Jackie?" Troy had a deep crease in his brow.

"I'm Devon, a presenter of the show Skeletons, and this is Doctor Greer and Doctor Johnston. Corinne, you and your daughter were nominated for our show."

Corinne paled and turned her blue eyes to Jackie, "What did you do?" Corinne spoke slowly, turning her gaze from Jackie to Devon. Devon heard faint static in her earpiece, then the instruction "show the reel".

"We actually have something you need to see." Devon stood up straighter and her tone bordered on stern. "If you could all take a seat." She gestured to the table.

Dr Greer moved to stand closer to Mabel. A TV was rolled in by one of the crew.

"What's going on?" Jackie frowned. Then, remembering the cameras were there, she smiled and tried to pout seductively.

"OK, this might be hard to watch, but Mabel, the whole team at Skeletons and everyone watching at home really wants you to get better."

Mabel, still stunned from the ambush, barely registered Devon's words. She stared vacantly at the TV screen that had been rolled in, her head still shaking and her hands trembling.

"I really don't think..." Corinne started, but she was cut off as the TV sprang to life. There was a moment of silence. An empty, dark room was on the screen. After a few moments you could make out a bench and some tools hanging to the left. A rack of camping gear, unused, alongside old sleds, spare crockery and tubs of hoarded belongings filled the back of the room.

"That looks like..." Troy squinted at the screen.

A beam of light illuminated the room. The sound of gentle footfalls; Mabel appeared. Mabel had stopped shaking. She stared at the screen, completely inert.

"What is this?" Jackie looked utterly bewildered; the first genuine expression on her face since the cameras had appeared.

Troy appeared on the TV screen. He walked down the stairs and each footfall was amplified. Mabel was leaning against the table, her thin arms wrapped around her body, her head bowed to her chest.

"Get undressed." Troy's voice was menacing.

The camera panned to him, sitting at the dining table. His face was turning beetroot. "Turn this off!" He snarled.

"Please... please don't." It was the first time Mabel had spoken. Her eyes were glazed and fixed on the TV. She looked up at Devon hopefully and the presenter looked away from her.

"What is this?" Corinne's head was snapping from Jackie, to Mabel to Troy. The TV kept rolling and the camera crew was filming the reactions of the four of them seated around the dining table.

In the studio, and in homes across the US, the TV screen was divided, one half showing the basement cam footage, the other showing live feed. People were transfixed in horror. The Mabel on the screen began forlornly peeling off her clothes, and the on-screen Troy began to unbuckle his belt. "

No, stop this!" Jackie screeched. Mabel's face crumpled and for a moment it looked as if she would faint. Then, remarkably, she stood. "Excuse me," she said softly, pushing past Dr Greer and the film crew.

Corinne's face had flushed. "What the fuck is this?" she snarled, but no one answered her. "Mabel?" Corinne turned to her daughter as she calmly walked out. "Mabel!" Then she turned to Jackie, who was quivering and pale as she watched the TV screen. "You fucking bitch! It was you - you nominated us. Mabel - your niece!"

"They weren't s'posed to put cameras in my house." Jackie whined.

Troy, panicked, tried to flee, but the camera crew were blocking him in. "This isn't... you don't understand." Flecks of spittle flew from his mouth. "She... she wanted it."

Corinne saw Mabel come back into the living room. She saw the glint of the large carving knife, freshly sharpened in her hand, but she said nothing. The camera crew was too focused on Jackie and Troy to notice her daughter's silent footsteps. Jackie, seated beside Troy, opened and closed her mouth like a fish. "Turn that off!" she screeched, jabbing a thick finger at the TV. "TURN IT OFF!"

"Be ready, crew," everyone heard in their earpieces. "This is about to erupt."

"TURN IT OFF!" Troy thundered.

Mabel thought about Flopsy Ferret, her favorite childhood toy. She had been seven when she threw it away after realizing it offered her no comfort to the horrors in her life. She still missed Flopsy Ferret. She held the kitchen knife in her palm, blade tucked upwards into her wrist. She could feel the cold steel grazing against her skin tenderly. She could end it in one quick flash. Neck. Thigh. She knew it would be almost painless.

"You don't understand," Troy was saying, as Devon and the doctors looked away from the TV screen in disgust. "Mabel and I... we... she..."

Corinne's eyes were hard chips of ice. "I'm going to kill you." She looked from Jackie to Troy and back.

"This isn't my fault!" Jackie spat back, and her chin wobbled.

Mabel was standing close to Troy and Jackie now. Her blood would spray them both if she slashed her carotid, she mused.

With one swift motion, the knife glinted in the camera's lens, and then blood rained down in the dining room.

****

Tyler sat in the waiting room with Melanie and waited till the doctor had left before he even glanced at her.

"Look, I know you hate me…"

"I don't hate you. I think you did something bad, but you're trying to fix it and that is all any of us can do in this life when we mess up," Melanie said. "My parents have got hold of the social worker. They're going to try and get a temporary custody of Annette on Danny's behalf whilst we sort this out."

"That's amazing!" Tyler beamed.

"They see my brother in him, so that is the good news. You said they recovered some footage, did you find out what?"

"The beating… it's hard to watch, but not even close to what else is going on tonight. I don't know if Ariadne will still be interested, unless she wants to spin it as a happy ending - father gets his daughter back."

"That's hardly Skeletons' *thing*." Melanie said scathingly.

"I know, but it's how I pitched it to her before - to try and ease my guilt, I guess."

"And?"

Tyler shrugged, "I don't know… I don't know what's going to happen. The studio is totally focused on the 100th episode special, so at least Danny's out of that. Corrupting the main bulk of footage bought us some time."

"Will they try and get hold of his medical records?" Melanie looked panicked.

Tyler nodded. "Yeah, they already dug into the social worker records to find Annette. Did the nurse…?" Tyler went silent when he heard voices outside the door.

"She altered them. But if they dig…"

"I'll try and make sure that doesn't happen." Tyler gave Melanie a reassuring smile.

"We'd best get back in there. I don't want him to wake up to no one." Melanie patted Tyler on the arm. "It'll be OK. I contacted his work, told them he was attacked. The boss was very understanding."

Tyler looked down at his $600 sneakers. "I hope my boss feels like being understanding too."

Melanie nodded. "All we can do now is pray."

Three Months Later

Corinne was led along the hallway in a daze. Everything was white, sterile and barren. She pursed her lips and fought back tears. The nurse who was beside her snuck a peek. "It's OK Ms. Beaumont, this outer bit looks worse than it is."

Corinne nodded and tried to unclench her jaw. They arrived at a small window in the corridor.

"You'll need to sign in." The nurse smiled at Corinne encouragingly.

'PSYCHIATRIC SIGN IN' was printed at the top of the sheet. There were only four other names on the paper. Corinne felt sick as she signed her name.

"This way," the nurse said, leading Corinne away down a different corridor, to a door marked 'Dr Abone'. "You can take a seat, the doctor will be with you any second."

"Oh." Corinne sat on one of the pale gray chairs. "I... is... " She turned away from the nurse and slumped. The nurse thought about saying something, but thought better of it, and went to get Dr Abone from the common area where she was talking to other patients.

"Ms. Beaumont?" The doctor, an elderly African-American woman with long twists neatly coiffed, smiled as she came into her office.

"Corinne, please."

"I'm so glad you could make it."

"Of course, anything…" Corinne felt herself stammering and flushing, but she no longer cared. "Is she here? Can I see her?"

Dr Abone took a seat and relaxed back into it. "Yes, she very much wants to see you. But first, I'd like to talk with you."

"I didn't know… I didn't…"

"I know that. No, I want to talk about how you are doing."

"I'm a bad mom." The words sounded small and childish as they fled from Corinne's lips and she felt awful for saying them. Especially after what Mabel had gone through.

"You're not a bad mother, Corinne. Or a bad person. That is clear to me."

Corinne looked up and sighed dejectedly.

Dr Abone frowned. "I'm sorry you had to go through what you did."

Corinne began to weep. "I really didn't know… I really didn't," she hiccupped.

Dr Abone nodded kindly. "Look, before she comes in, there are some things that I need to make clear to you."

Corinne looked up and managed to get a hold of herself. "Yes, yes. Please, tell me."

****

Danny, dressed in slim dark gray jeans and a button down, leant back on the sofa and tried to radiate a calm he didn't feel.

"Everything is going to be fine," he heard Tyler say in his earpiece.

On the couch beside him were Melanie and her parents, Don and Teeny. Abbie-Rae and Jono entered from the left as the opening montage of Skeletons rolled across the screens.

"Welcome to Skeletons. And after the shock that was the 100th episode, we know that Danny's story has really been a ray of sunshine." Abbie-Rae smiled at Danny. He was thin, but undeniably handsome.

"It's been tough for you man, we all saw that, but you've been so strong, you've come out the other side. Truly inspirational." Jono gave Danny a typical 'bro' backslap.

Danny gave a humble smile and looked at Melanie and her parents, "it's all these guys... I mean, without them..." As if on cue, a single tear appeared in the corner of his eye. Behind the scenes, Tyler could almost hear a million women swooning across America.

"Good job on this, Tyler," Ariadne whispered, appearing behind him. "Just what we needed after the 100th episode."

"Highest ratings ever, wasn't it?"

"Messy but successful," Ariadne said with a smirk. It had bought her a fat pay rise, along with a slew of offers from other networks.

"Uh huh." Tyler kept his eyes on Danny.

"Right, Melanie, you were Danny's NA liaison?" Jono gave her a charming smile.

"That's right," Melanie said sweetly. She chose to ignore the odd wording. Her and Tyler were friends now; she wasn't going to drag him on live TV.

"And you were there after the attack?" Abbie-Rae's eyes widened. They had all seen the footage – or at least, the first part of the footage.

"I was…" She paused, "it was hard to see, but Danny… he's a friend."

"He's like family now," Teeny said, squeezing Danny's arm. The camera zoomed in on the sweet old lady, who was giving Danny a motherly look.

Danny smiled back. "The Beaumonts… they're wonderful people."

"And, weren't you tempted to use again, after finding out your daughter was in an abusive care home and after being assaulted by your former father-in-law?" There was an edge of gleeful menace to Jono's tone, but the camera zoomed in on Danny.

"Just breathe man, tell the truth," Tyler said softly through the earpiece.

"I was… that's what being a drug addict is… wanting to use… being tempted."

"But he didn't – that's what matters," Melanie said, staring Jono down.

"And that is why we are here today!" Abbie-Rae chirped, her eyes twinkling. "We have a pretty wonderful surprise for you, Danny!" The audience started clapping and cheering. Danny looked around, perplexed. The presenters stood, and Melanie and her parents followed suit. Bewildered, Danny got to his feet.

Don leant in so that he could whisper something to Danny, who smiled and let out a silent huff of laughter.

Annette, in a pale pink dress, her long dark hair flowing behind her, came running high speed out of the wings. Danny bent, arms outstretched, and swooped her up in one fluid motion and held her to his chest. The audience erupted with cheers and awws. People wiped away tears and parents hugged their kids.

"Annette, how excited are you to see your dad?" Annie-Rae asked when Danny put Annette down.

"Super excited," she said gravely. "It's the best day," she added, with a wide smile.

"Wrap it up, guys" came through the earpieces.

Annie-Rae and Jono blathered on some more, as a montage reel of Danny and Annette scrolled on the screen behind them. Annette leant in to her Daddy. "Why did we have to pretend we hadn't seen each other for ages? I've seen you bunches since I've been with Granny Teeny and Grampy Don."

Danny smiled. It was nice she had taken to Melanie's parents to quickly. He was so grateful they had taken to him.

"Just for TV honey. It's all just for TV."

"But why do people want to see it if it isn't real?" she whispered as the credits began to scroll.

"I don't know." Danny said, kissing the top of her head. "I really don't get it either."

****

Corinne waited nervously. She had waited three months. Three agonizing months seeing the vitriol being spewed out all over the papers and TV stations about 'that' Skeletons episode. She had been asked to take 'leave' from work, paid, so she accepted. She was suing Skeletons. Her lawyer said they had a good chance of getting a solid payout. Dr Abone had gone, and she waited nervously. What if she broke down? What if she wasn't strong enough yet?

"Come on Jackie," Dr Abone said gently, as Jackie allowed herself to be led into the room. She stopped when she saw Corinne. Her hair was frizzy, and the roots showed. She had lost some weight, and loose gray skin hung from her jowls.

"Why don't we all sit?"

"Doctor!" There was a commotion from outside the room and a loud, blaring siren carried along the hallway. A nurse, out of breath, came running in.

"Emergency!"

"I'm afraid..."

"Ward Four, doctor," the nurse added gravely.

"Come sit down, Jacks," Corinne said gently, guiding her sister into the deep couch. She smiled tenderly at her. Dr Abone looked at the sisters, seated side by side on the couch. "Excuse me one moment, I won't be long," she said. She hurried off with the nurse as the siren continued to blare.

"Corrie," Jackie said, in an affected child-like voice. "You came." She looked up at Corinne. Corinne smiled, but her eyes were hard as flint and Jackie shied back. "Of course I came, Jackie. I came to give you something." She reached into her handbag and pulled out a fat wad of tabloid and mainstream newspapers. "These."

She fanned them out on the coffee table. Each one was covered with pictures of Jackie and Troy, mostly from the month following the Skeletons 100th episode. "Just a small selection," she said.

Jackie tried to look away, but Corinne grabbed her wrist in a vice. "Look at them, Jackie."

The headlines mocked everything about Jackie and Troy, flayed every aspect of their lives, all whilst an angelic photo of Mabel looked on. Pictures of them trying to clean their house, egged, trashed, and smeared with shit. Pictures of Jackie taken with a telephoto lens as she undressed, every bit of cellulite revealed. Their personal information splashed all over the web and the torrents of abuse transcribed.

"Why... why..." Jackie whined and sobbed.

Corinne grabbed her other wrist and wrenched Jackie round, forcing her sister to look at her.

"You killed my daughter. You and your sick fucking husband killed my baby."

"I didn't... didn't know..."

"Didn't know about Mabel, or didn't know about the girls at all? He might not have been convicted, because she was seventeen and wasn't there to testify, but some friends online uncovered some other information about darling Troy - and it looks like you did fucking know, Jackie!" Corinne hissed.

"Corinne, I didn't..." Jackie trailed off as a glob of snot dripped from her nose. "It... it was Troy."

Corinne let out a bark of laughter. "Oh, don't worry, I have much, much worse planned for your darling husband. But don't worry, I'll make sure you hear about that too." She stood up from the sofa. "Oh, I thought you should know... I told them you're here."

"No... no..." Jackie moaned. "I came here to escape - why?"

"You didn't afford us the luxury of anonymity, and I'm certainly not going to give it to you," Corinne said as she walked towards the door. "Goodbye, Jackie." Corinne turned and gave her sister a twisted smile before walking off down the deserted corridor.

DEMONS

DECEMBER 2018

Anthony hunched down over his steering wheel on the 101 eastbound freeway and glared through the windows of the other cars. So far, he hadn't seen one Demon this morning, which was surprising. There had been an increase in Demon activity in the past few weeks. He had seen some loitering near his house and at Tom's Thumb trailhead. He was certain that his neighbor had been turned into a Demon, but her aura kept changing and it was hard to be sure.

Anthony felt on edge. Any one of them could lead him to Jessica and Ollie. As soon as the lane in front of him cleared, he jammed his foot down on the accelerator and wove between the near-gridlocked cars. Jessica and Ollie had been taken nearly a year ago now. Their home still smelt of her. Her sweater was still slung over the back of her favorite armchair.

When Anthony had discovered she had been taken by a Demon, his only option had been to rescue her. The only problem was that he still didn't know which Demon had taken her; the Archangel was refusing to tell him. Apparently, he needed to discover it on his own.

"Fucking hell!" Anthony yelled as a driver cut in front of him. He slammed on his brakes and glared out through his windshield. A strange aura emanated from the car, reddish brown. The hairs on the back of his neck prickled. A Demon.

Anthony edged his car closer to their back bumper and turned on his indicator. He wanted to pull up alongside the car and catch a look at the Demon inside. He drummed his fingers on the steering wheel.

"Come on... come on," he urged, but the traffic had slowed to a crawl and no one was letting the dinged-up Subaru in.

His phone began to buzz in the passenger seat. He had been ignoring it for two days. Brian had left six voicemails already.

"Go away." Anthony didn't turn his head. The phone continued insistently.

"Hello?" Anthony snapped.

"Anthony? It's Marcus... where are you?" Marcus was his boss at the Newhaven Literary Agency in downtown Phoenix.

"I'm on my way... traffic is bad."

"But you're two hours late."

"I know, Marcus." Anthony's heart rate quickened and he could feel his breath coming heavier. "I have to... there were some things I had to do." His mouth pinched as he tried to control his anger. Marcus had been telling him to give up on his Quest to save Jessica and Ollie for a while now.

"Is this... is this about..." Marcus's voice sounded tense and clipped.

"No no... I just had to finish reading that new manuscript we got the other night." Anthony racked his brains for the name of it. It had been good. He had fallen asleep at 3am with it in his lap. Why couldn't he remember the name?

Marcus sighed with relief on the other end of the line. "Pangea?" He smiled as he spoke, his voice lighter. "That's great. Did you like it? Donna said it was amazing."

"Yeah, great," Anthony said through gritted teeth. The traffic had begun to move. The Demon was going slow; slow enough for Anthony to pull up beside him.

"Fantastic. I'll have Donna get in touch with the author."

Marcus sounded jovial now and Anthony seized the opportunity. "Sorry about the tardiness." He pursed his lips and pushed his glasses back up his nose. A film of sweat had broken across his face. "But traffic is awful, I'll be there ASAP."

"Great... great, Anthony." Marcus' voice was loud, authoritative. "See you shortly."

Anthony hung up quickly and flung the phone back into the passenger seat. It bounced off the fabric and disappeared down the crevice between the seat and the door. Anthony didn't care. He was about to see the Demon.

Anthony stood in the leafy park, close to where Jessica and

Ollie had been taken. He had failed, once again, to get a Demon. The Archangel had told him that the Demon who had taken Jessica and Ollie had taken them to another realm. He had even gifted Anthony with powers to help him get them back.

He slowly walked the loop around the park. It was the end of summer, but the air was still hot. The waterway running through looked meager and dirty. The ornamentally placed saguaro cacti were mangy.

The Archangel hadn't visited him for over a month, and Anthony wondered how long his 'gifts' would last; he could see Demons all the time, not only after dark, he could manipulate time, and he could communicate telepathically with Jessica. The last gift was what kept him going. Hearing her asking, begging, him to help.

Jessica had been telling him that she and Ollie were safe. She said she was more worried about him; the Demons knew he was hunting them and now they were hunting him back. That was why he was carrying a Colt Python revolver, tucked safely into a holster on his hip.

"No chance." He shook his head. He couldn't let the Demons get to him first. What would happen then? The Archangel wouldn't tell him. He would only say that he didn't have forever, that his Quest to rescue his beloved wife and child would end in despair if he didn't hurry. "None at all."

He looked around. There were Demons in the park. Plenty of them. He could see their vile stale-blood auras skulking around the edges, waiting for a chance to swoop in and take an innocent, just as they had done to Jessica and Ollie. Jessica should have known better. That was the only thing that still rankled with Anthony. Jessica knew how to defeat Demons better than anyone. She wouldn't have been taken down easily.

He stood at the gate to the park, watching the cars pull in and out of the lot. Jess and Ollie had been taken right here, right from this spot. Anthony was surprised to see a Monk standing in the small asphalt entrance to the park. He carried a book with the St. Jude Insignia. It was harder and harder to find Monks in this day and age. Most of them had vanished as Demons had increased. People were scared, too scared to fight for what was right. Maybe if there were more Monks, Jessica and Ollie wouldn't have been taken, Anthony thought bitterly.

"Nice day," the Monk said casually.

Anthony grunted. There were no nice days anymore. The last nice day he could remember was coming home from the literary agency, a fresh manuscript in his bag, to Jessica sitting on the living room floor. She worked as a stationery designer. Paper covered with her incredible calligraphy and careful detailed filigree was strewn about her. As soon as Anthony walked through the door she smiled and held a finger to her lips. She scrunched her eyes up in concentration for a second. Anthony smiled back and leant down to kiss her.

Pay attention to the Monk Ant, he can help you find me.
Anthony was jolted from his reverie. Jessica.

"You know she isn't gone forever." The Monk smiled knowingly at him.

"I know." Anthony replied calmly, though most days it didn't feel that way.

"There are just so many... so many of them around

nowadays. Demons," the Monk replied, waving his hand at the parking lot.

Anthony's head snapped up and his ears pricked. He turned his head towards the parking lot. The car from this morning had just pulled in and whipped into a space.

The Monk frowned. "Awful." He shook his head.

"I know… it has to stop."

"It has to stop now." The Monk looked pointedly at Anthony.

The gun. Anthony felt the metal digging in to his side. He looked back over to the parking lot. More Demons had come in. A group of them stood around looking over the park eagerly. Looking for more victims. Anthony felt bile rise in his throat. Had they done this? Looked at Jessica and Ollie and decided upon them? Had it been a group like this? Is that why the Archangel wouldn't tell him who the Demon was?

"That's it." Anthony spun away from the monk.

"Be careful," the Monk warned, but Anthony wasn't listening. He unholstered his gun and strode over to them. It held eight bullets, pure silver, nestling in their dark little chambers, waiting to pierce the heart of a demon. Anthony raised the gun. The Demons turned to him, their eyes glowing red through the nasty haze of their auras. No one else could see it, but the park goers knew what was happening and they froze.

Anthony smiled at the Demons. Their lips pulled back, revealing jagged rows of teeth, bloodstained and sharp. Their faces stretched unnaturally, the skin gaping in places and showing bone and muscle, half-rotten, beneath.

Do it.

Jessica urged him forward. Anthony released the safety and began to fire the bullets at the Demons. Each one hit its target with a satisfying thud. Some went clean through, to the Demon standing behind. The echo from the gun carried across the park, but Anthony kept striding towards the Demons, closer and closer, until he could smell their fetid blood. Seven of them lay in a tangled heap at his feet. One, half curled and snarling, leant back against the car.

"Where is she? Where is Jessica? Where is my son, Ollie? Tell me!" Anthony demanded. He only had one bullet left.

"No!" The Demon rasped, a faint sneer on his lips.

Anthony pulled the trigger. Blood splattered over his face as the Demon's skull exploded into a million pieces.

OCTOBER 2018

The Demon watched Anthony carefully from her manicured garden. He was being shifty, a common thing lately, and peering out between his curtains at the street. She didn't like it one bit. She had been trying to get close to Anthony ever since Jessica and Ollie had been taken, but he was sharp, too sharp, on edge.

She pretended to water her flowerbeds. Pansies. She didn't like pansies, but the last owner had planted them. They bloomed well, and she couldn't really be bothered to change them. She was too busy scouting for souls. Searching out the most damaged and vulnerable ones.

She kept her eyes down. Recently Anthony had been particularly suspicious of her. She had told him to give up on his Quest to rescue Jessica and Ollie one too many times. Now he avoided her like the plague. Perhaps he knew. She chewed the inside of her cheek and worked to avoid looking over to his twitching curtains. Soon, soon enough, his soul would become weak, and he would come to her on his own.

Anthony cursed under his breath. His neighbor was loitering outside. He strongly suspected she was a Demon, but he hadn't been able to read her aura properly. If she was one, she hid it well.

He was late for work again. He had been up all night trying to connect the dots. Trying to figure out where Jessica and Ollie could be, trying to work out how to get there. The Archangel had visited him in the small hours with depressing news: Anthony must find Jessica and Ollie soon, they were growing weak. He told Anthony to kill more Demons. He told him how to use the gifts. He just didn't tell him the one thing Anthony wanted to know: where Jessica and Ollie were.

His basement looked like a police investigation room. Pictures of Jessica, pictures of Demons, surreptitious videos Anthony had taken of suspicious people, barely-eaten power bars and empty soda cans; it was all strewn in a chaos only Anthony could understand.

"Anthony?" There was a banging on his front door. Anthony jumped out of his skin. He licked the inside of his mouth. It was thick with fuzz and his breath was stale. He quickly glanced to his neighbor's yard. She was still there, fussing, so it wasn't her at least.

"Who is it?" he snapped.

"Are you kidding? It's me. Tabitha, Tabby." A woman's voice. Soft. Sad. Anthony felt his head swim.

Anthony's head slumped to his chest. "Hey Tabby," he said stiffly, opening up the door. He glanced behind him at the living room. The shafts of sunlight caught the dust that had settled on everything.

"Hey." Tabby looked around. She hadn't been over in weeks, but the living room looked unchanged, save for the layer of dust. Pictures of Jessica still covered every surface.

"How are you?" Anthony tried to smile, but it was more of a grimace. He had work to do.

"I'm good," she said slowly, taking in a picture of Jessica on the mantle.

Anthony wondered if the Archangel had visited her, told her something, or if the Demon had. Maybe Jessica had been able to communicate with her. They were best friends after all.

"Do you want a drink?" Anthony knew that there was nothing in the fridge and the best he could offer was lukewarm tap water or stale herbal tea.

"No, I'm fine." Tabby swallowed. "I spoke to Brian."

Anthony squinted. Brian? "Like... my friend Brian?"

"Mmm hmm. I'm dating his sister."

"Oh, I didn't know that."

"It started a few months ago." Tabby pursed her lips together. "He told me that you're on a Quest to find Jessica. To save her from a Demon."

Anthony stayed silent. He knew that not everyone could understand. Most people just gave up when a loved one was taken by the Demons.

"I... I don't think it's a good idea," she went on.

Anthony's face hardened. He ushered her to the door, pushing his hands between her shoulder blades to hurry her along. "I have to, Tabby. I have to save her, to save my son, even if you don't care anymore."

Tabby turned, her mouth agape, to try and argue, but Anthony slammed the door in her face.

He had his new gun. It felt heavy, but then, Anthony wasn't used to guns and he supposed that they all felt quite weighty. The weight of the steel, the weight of the lead, the bullets, and the weight of the crime all added up. He had ordered special bullets off a dark site, made from silver, the only ones that would properly kill the Demons.

The gun was tucked into the side of his jeans in a black holster. Another special order. Anthony had left the house soon after he had forced Tabitha out. Every time he thought about her, nasty bile came into his mouth and it twisted his lips strangely. He saw people looking at him and crossing to the other side of the street. He didn't care. He wandered towards the city canal and walked down the bleached steps to the walkway. Several underpasses were spaced along the canal, and Anthony had found that the homeless often hid Demons, or knew where to find them. He had taken to lurking in the hope of hearing something helpful.

His phone buzzed in his back pocket, the ringer off, but the vibrations still unsettled Anthony.

He reluctantly picked up, turning his back on the oncoming underpass and looking out at the shimmering canal. "Yep?" he said tersely.

"You coming in to work today Dude?" It was Walter.

"I…" Anthony looked down at his watch, confused. He had thought it was Saturday. "Shit, it's Friday." He reached for his wedding ring with his thumb. A bud of thought bloomed in his mind, why was he still wearing this? Before he could dwell on the thought, Walter's voice cut in.

"Um, yeah." Walter sounded annoyed.

"Sorry, I just got caught up in some stuff…"

"Demons?"

"Yeah."

"Nice." Walter gave a tired laugh, "but you still have to come into work. Marcus might shit a fucking watermelon if you miss another day."

"Shit." Anthony rubbed his eyes. "I'll be right in."

Anthony turned and began heading back to the Trader Joe's parking lot.

He sensed the Demons before he saw them. He was still on the canal sidewalk. Several trees with wide branches lined one edge of the walkway, and half obscured the steps back up to the main pavement.

"Nice glasses," a Demon called out. The edge to his voice was razor sharp, and he let out a cackle. Two female Demons stood behind him, their eyes flicking over Anthony in a serpentine manner.

Anthony kept his head down but slowed. He had the gun. He felt it, a rich warmth that spread through his body and made him feel powerful and strong.

"He's like a sadder Harry Potter," one Demon snickered. Her voice was nasal and Anthony looked up through lower lids. Her aura was particularly noxious in color.

"Uh huh," Anthony grunted quietly to himself.

"You say something?" the Demon said with a sneer.

Anthony looked up. He had a choice. "Do you know where Jessica is? Do you know where Ollie is?" He was already snarling.

"I don't know no fucking Jessica," the first Demon hissed back.

Anthony looked at the two female Demons. They looked shifty, uncomfortable. They exchanged a surreptitious glance.

"They know!" Anthony jabbed a finger at them. "They know something." He took a step forward and the male Demon lunged towards Anthony.

"Mother..."

"Stop right there!" Anthony screamed. He yanked the gun from his holster and waved it at them.

"Jesus fuck!" The Demon held up his hands, but he was shaking his head and sneering.

"Tell me what you know about Jessica." Anthony turned to the two female Demons. "Please!" The word slipped out without him meaning too, and Anthony felt hot tears on his cheeks. "Tell me where my son is. Please." He couldn't stop himself.

The male Demon was sneering, but the two others were shaking their heads and backing off.

"We can't... we can't... sorry." One Demon said. She tugged on the others and they hurried away, leaving Anthony holding the gun limply and staring at their quickly vanishing backs.

SEPTEMBER 2018

The stranger had approached Anthony in the bar. He had been nursing a whiskey, which he didn't much enjoy, in a darkened booth. Walter had said this particular bar was a hive of information and would help him with the answers he needed for his Quest.

"Heard you were after a Demon." The man had his hood up and his face was barely visible in the low light.

"Yup." Anthony shivered. He felt exposed and awkward talking to a stranger about this.

"For your girl?"

"My wife, and my son... were taken." Anthony said after a pause.

"Fuckin' Demons."

"She a fighter?"

"The best."

The man shook his head and tsk'd. "Damn shame. W said Archangel visited you."

Anthony stayed silent. The Archangel had said he couldn't tell anyone about his powers, and yet he felt he could trust this stranger.

"He visited me... a long time ago."

"For a Quest?"

"Yeah." The man's head bobbed inside the hood.

"Demon?"

"Demons." The man breathed in hard. "If you want my help – I need to know what is going on."

"A Demon took my wife and son. The Archangel gifted me with some... skills, to help see Demons, to help fight them so I can find my family."

"Good, good. That's good. So you need weapons?" He was blunt and gruff, but Anthony felt awash with relief.

"Yes, exactly."

"Not a problem. Colt Python. Silver bullets. We'll have

you good to go in no time." The man patted a scuffed black bag on the seat beside him.

"And the cost?"

The man lifted up his hood. His face was deeply scarred down one side. He waved to the waiter, mumbled for a drink, and then turned back to Anthony.

"I'll need something... gold. Valuable. Priceless."

Anthony's gut churned. "Gold?"

"Something that ties you to her... to them." The man's face was fixed on the gold band around Anthony's finger.

"I... oh..." Anthony searched blindly in his shoulder bag for something, anything else, to give the man.

Anthony nodded. Sickness coursed through him in waves. Jessica had the matching ring. Gold, thin, engraved. She would understand though, when he got her back, she would get it.

"OK." Anthony slid the ring off his finger. The man took it in his open palm and folded it inside his thick fingers. Anthony's head swam. He felt faint and leant back on the plasticky booth. A moment later he slid into darkness.

He didn't remember getting home, but he awoke in his bed, the covers wrapped snake-like and cloying around his legs. He had stopped calling out for Jess and Ollie in the mornings. Finally. He walked through to the kitchen to make coffee. Outside, the sky was a bruised purple, and warmth was already creeping through the dawn.

Anthony made coffee and stared at the fridge while the hot liquid dripped at a snail's pace. It was a mess of ticket stubs, stained recipes, tiny cards with snippets of calligraphy, and pictures. Mostly pictures. Jessica had them printed on to paper and then drew designs around them; words or sayings mostly, but sometimes she would draw small animals or flowers.

Anthony sighed and poured himself a cup. He and Jessica had known one another since they were twelve. They had both attended Desert Canyon Middle School. They were nerds, not outcasts, just more into books and Pokémon than house parties and football. They had their own social circle, and everyone was interested in Demon hunting. Back then it had seemed more like a game.

He had been in love with her from day one. It had taken her a year to really notice him back. They had been on an enforced school trip to Sedona. They had hiked together, uncomfortably, and from then on they were a couple. Through high school, university, moving out, travelling and first jobs, they had been so happy with one another, it never crossed either of their minds that there wouldn't be a wedding and a happily ever after.

Anthony slid out the picture of them from their Senior Prom. Jessica had written 'I would walk into Mordor for you.' The script was written in a wide-nibbed fountain pen, deliberately cracked and exactly the same as the LOTR title on the films.

Anthony swallowed and slid the picture behind a recipe for chocolate chip cookies. He had to find her.

JUNE 2018

Anthony was slumped on the couch, wrapped in a filthy blanket. He felt stale; eyes crusted with sleep, and unbrushed teeth. He had hunted Demons all night, returning home at 4am, eaten some ancient ramen that was loitering at the back of the cupboard, and then passed out on the couch. He wasn't even sure what time it was. It was light outside but both the blinds and the curtains were closed. The room was dull and it smelt of old coffee and that sour, sleep smell.

He grabbed his laptop. Several emails pinged into his inbox, which he ignored, and a message from Marcus popped up, *Are you coming in to work today?*

So it was a weekday. Anthony's fingers hovered over the keyboard. Marcus knew about the Demons, and the Quest. He was the one who encouraged him to do it, along with Walter and Brian.

You need to stop this Quest stuff.

Three dots bounced up and down as Marcus continued typing.

You've already missed nearly a week of work. I'm your boss Anthony… I can't keep ignoring this stuff.

Anthony seethed. Marcus was his boss, technically, though it was more of a title than an actual hierarchical structure.

Brian and I both think you need to give up this whole Quest. It isn't good for you. You have to let her go.

Anthony was about to reply, the scathing words already flowing into his fingertips, when an eerie howling echo filled his house.

"What the…"

Anthony turned. An elderly gentleman in a pale gray-white suit stood by the sofa. The insignia of the Archangels, St. Jude, was stitched onto the lapel. It was this insignia that adorned Monks who were sympathetic to the cause. He looked around the room and cleared his throat. He had a white cloud of hair and a weathered, kindly face.

"I..." Anthony's eyes went wide. "Um..."

"Um," he said back to Anthony. "Yes, indeed." He chuckled softly.

"Hello?" Anthony lifted his hands helplessly.

"I am the Archangel. You are on a noble Quest."

Anthony gulped. He nodded vigorously. "I am. For Jessica. And Ollie."

"Yes. Quite." The figure moved closer to Anthony. "I am here to help you."

"Help?"

"You have not found the Demon who took her?"

Anthony shook his head.

"Nor have you been able to find out much," the Archangel said with assurance. Anthony didn't bother to confirm. It obviously knew.

"I am here to give you a gift. A few gifts actually."

"W... why me?"

"Your Quest is noble. All Questors need help from time to time," the Archangel said gently.

Anthony nodded. He would take any help he could get.

"This'll show Marcus." He mumbled.

"You must not tell friends about these gifts. They will make you a target..."

Anthony nodded quickly.

"I will give you three gifts." The Archangel held up what Anthony assumed was a hand. "First, you shall see Demons all the time, not just at night. Second, you shall be able to manipulate time."

Anthony was now enraptured. "Thirdly... you shall be able to communicate with Jessica."

Anthony flinched as though he had been struck.

"What? H... how?"

"You shall hear her. She is not gone from this realm, only being held in limbo. I shall open up the channels."

"When?" Anthony demanded. He didn't care about the other gifts, but he longed to hear Jessica's voice.

"Anthony, you must save her soon," the Archangel said severely. He vanished, the same keening echo carrying through the house, leaving Anthony with the foreboding sense that he was running out of time.

Anthony practically skipped to work. He could talk to Jessica again. Not all the time, but he would hear her, like she was talking through the phone and Anthony had an earpiece in. She would pop up. Sometimes she cried, and begged him to help, and Anthony would spend the entire night hunting Demons. Other times she would tell him that she and Ollie were OK. Anthony spent every moment waiting to hear from her. Now, nothing else mattered.

MARCH 2018

Anthony sat at his work desk and looked at Walter. Walter was engrossed in a manuscript, his red pen poised over the fresh white pages. He scribbled, shaking his head, then laughed and a big red tick appeared on the page.

"This is so good, so good." Walter didn't look up as he spoke. He was the editor in charge of comedy literature, fiction and non-fiction, and he continually struggled to find great books. Whereas the rest of them found good manuscripts fairly regularly, good comic writers were few and far between.

Anthony felt he should ask Walter what was so funny. He knew that he should, but he didn't. Since Jessica had been stolen from him, he simply couldn't care about anything else.

Walter kept mumbling to himself and scribbling. Anthony breathed a sigh of relief, then looked back down to the manuscript in front of him. It was a poorly-written, overly long fantasy about werewolves and demigods. He rubbed his eyes, confused.

"You OK, Anthony?" Marcus had stepped out from his corner cubicle.

"Yep." Anthony didn't look up.

"Right." Marcus shifted uncomfortably. Walter had stopped reading and Brian stood and stretched his legs, subtly eavesdropping. "Well... we still on for takeaway at yours? Hobbit marathon." Marcus smiled.

"Oh, I..."

"Yes, you said Anthony, you said. Come on dude!" Walter grinned. "But no takeaway, I'll bring some of my Mom's lasagne." He nodded at Anthony. "Come on, Ant." His tone was more serious, and he looked at Anthony expectantly.

"Yeah... yeah, fine." Anthony tried to smile, but found there was a lump in his throat, so instead he looked back down at the manuscript and pretended to be engrossed in demi-gods and werewolves duking it out.

A fine patina of dust dulled the gaming console. Three smallish screens, an Xbox One and a PlayStation, as well as a plethora of mics, controllers and an unopened VR headset, sat on top of the beech Ikea stand.

"When did you get this?" Brian picked up the VR headset and looked at the box.

Anthony didn't answer, he just turned away from the gaming set up, studiously ignoring Jessica's black and green controller. It had small biohazard signs on the side. It was one of her custom ones.

"So, Hobbit?" Marcus came into the living room with a fake, jovial smile. Walter had portioned out the steaming lasagne onto plates. The TV was on; spewing out adverts about Viagra medicine, lunchmeats and awful reality shows.

Anthony sighed. "Sure." He picked up the remote. At least he wouldn't have to talk to everyone once the movie was on.

They watched the final Hobbit movie in a stifling silence. Walter and Marcus tried to banter, but Anthony glumly stared at the TV screen, unresponsive. Brian was glued to the TV too, but in a much more enraptured state.

When it finally drew to a close, Walter stood and began busying himself with the dishes scattered on the coffee tables.

"So... um... you guys got any weekend plans?" Brian said through a yawn.

"No, just chilling at home with Brenda." Marcus rolled his eyes. "Probably get roped into doing chores or DIY."

Brian and Walter gave halfhearted laughs.

"There's the product launch for the new Lost Tombs." Walter came back out of the kitchen. "The game designers are local guys, so they're having a thing down at the Hyatt conference center."

"That's cool," Marcus chipped in enthusiastically. "You should go Anthony. You're into Lost Tombs right?"

"Oh uh... yeah." Anthony shrugged. "I guess."

"When's the last time you gamed?" Brian had stood and walked over to the gaming set up. He ran a finger on top of the black Xbox console. A clear line was left behind. Anthony looked down at the floor and gritted his teeth. Why were they all still here? He had stuff to do. He didn't want to be discussing his hobbies right now.

"You haven't been on in weeks," Walter said, earning a black look from Anthony.

"Come on Ant, we all knew," Marcus chimed in.

"I just... I haven't felt like it, OK?" Anthony heard the whine at the tail end of his voice. "I... I..." He stopped, the lump in his throat threatening to spill into choking sobs.

"I know." Walter walked over to Anthony. "I mean... I don't... but I get why." He held up a hand as if to pat Anthony on the back, but then pulled him into a hug instead.

Anthony stood stiffly. He hadn't touched another human in weeks. He couldn't even remember the last time. He ducked his head, not wanting to see pity on the other guys' faces.

"I actually have something for you," Walter said.

From the corner of his eye, Anthony saw Marcus subtly shaking his head. Brian pursed his lips together thoughtfully.

"What?"

The three guys were standing around Anthony in a

semi-circle and he felt claustrophobic and irritated. "What is it?" he snapped.

Walter went to his bag, leaning against the siding by the front door, and pulled out a slim DVD case. He handed it silently to Anthony.

"It's the expansion pack. I got it before... for, well..." Walter trailed off.

Anthony nodded and put the DVD case by the Xbox. "I'm really tired..."

"We should head home," Marcus said quickly, nodding.

Anthony watched them leave eagerly, feigning yawns. As soon as the last set of headlights disappeared down the road, he hurried to the console and powered it on for the first time in three months.

Welcome Anthony.

Do you want to FastTravel to Jessica?

YesNo

Anthony's hand shook as he selected *Yes.*

Jessica is Online at the Park.

Anthony gulped. He felt sweat beading on his forehead. The park was always her favorite place, in every world.

Anthony's fingers worked without thinking, casting the spell needed to enter the park. A portal opened. Anthony stepped inside. He looked around. Jessica was there, her long hair in a thick braid over one shoulder. A knife on her hip. A tiny gamer tag for her baby hovered above her stomach: 'Ollie'. Anthony shook his head. It was bright and summery. A thick band of sapphire water ran through the leafy area.

Anthony just stood there, watching, smiling for the first

time in months. He was about to walk over to her when a thick fog of muddy brown, streaked with red and black, filled the park. Anthony spun around, trying to fight his way to Jessica through the miasma.

Demons.

Anthony stumbled, blind, but when the fog finally cleared Jessica was gone.

He rushed to the town, his fingers pushed down on right toggle, a fast sprint. He went to the bar, just like the one off Market Street, and ducked inside. He spun, searching for the barkeep.

A man in a deep, hooded jacket stood next to the bar.

'You look troubled, friend.'

The barkeep still hadn't appeared, so Anthony turned to the hooded stranger. 'Demons, they took my wife... have any of them been in here?'

'Demons have been taking many innocents these days.' The man said gruffly.

'How do I find her? How?'

The man turned to Anthony, the dim lighting catching his face. Anthony stifled a gasp. A thick ridge of scar ran along one cheek, but what caught his eye was the small St. Jude Insignia on his jacket. A Monk. 'I know where you can find the one you seek,' he said.

'What?' Anthony leant in closer to the Monk.

'I know the Demon who took her. You can still save her.' The stranger finally looked up from his glass of amber liquid. 'You must embark on a Quest.'

Anthony nodded dumbly.

He selected Quest menu to the left of his screen and selected 'Begin Quest.'

JANUARY 2018

Anthony sat in the small, warm room beside the crematorium. Hydrangeas, blue and white, nestled in small alcoves around the wall. His face felt stretched and it stung where fresh tears kept running over dry skin. People milled around the room in a state of muffled melancholy. David was around somewhere, and Tabitha kept coming to check on him, handing him glasses of water or small nibbles that he didn't eat.

"Hey you." Anthony's mom sat down beside him. She reached out a hand. It was warm, and her gold wedding band was worn and scratched. Anthony studied her hand. It was lined, with nails painted a pale gray, and it was wrapped tightly around his shaking knuckles.

"I can't," Anthony started before dissolving into a fresh bout of tears. "I can't do this without her mom." He pushed away from his mother, away from the people who stood in small groups and watched him over the rims of their glasses. He pushed through a door marked 'Staff Only.' The room was painted an ugly rust color. Anthony felt his head swimming, the sludge color of the walls closing in on him.

"Sir, you can't be in here," an elderly gentleman in a light gray suit said. His voice was firm but kind. "Come on now."

The man led Anthony out of another door, not back into the function room. They were in a small kitchen. A Formica counter held a toaster, coffee maker and kettle. A white fridge was tucked beside a table and two chairs.

"Have a seat," the man said. His voice was deep and comforting. He had white hair, longer than usual, down to his shoulders. He was big, but he moved around the small staff kitchen gracefully. "Coffee? Tea?"

Anthony nodded. "OK," he said obediently.

"Things will get better."

"Uh huh," Anthony said with a rueful shake of his head. "No," he added, letting his chin slump to his chest.

"Listen son. I've been where you are. One day, you won't see the bad all around you, you won't feel like time has stopped... you'll be able to live again."

Anthony kept shaking his head as he began to weep.

The man leant forward and placed a comforting hand on Anthony's shoulder. A small St. Jude medallion dangled from his neck. "She isn't gone forever son, she just isn't with us on earth anymore. She's dead, but not forgotten."

JANUARY 2019
Phoenix New Times
Thursday 17th

MAN ARRESTED FOR MASS SHOOTING IN DOWNTOWN PHOENIX

by Brianna McCain

Phoenix Police arrested Anthony Mifford yesterday for a mass shooting that saw six people killed in Cielito Park in Phoenix. The victims were six high school students. Five were pronounced dead on the scene. One student, Martin Lewis, was taken to hospital with traumatic head injuries and died shortly after midnight. Two others were taken to hospital with minor injuries and are expected to recover.

Police spokesman Sgt. Abigail Alves said the Phoenix Police Department were called after the suspect drew a Colt Python on the students in the Cielto Park parking lot and began shooting. Bystanders saw the suspect draw the gun on the students, but were unable to stop him.

An elderly man, Bob Reynolds, spoke to the suspect moments before the shooting began. 'He just came right up to me, made a kind of, beeline. I had just left the service, at the St. Jude Episcopal, and he kept on staring at my hymn pamphlet. I thought he was odd, you know? But I had no idea he was dangerous,' Mr Reynolds told reporters on the scene. 'He was talking to me like he was having some whole second part to the conversation. He was real agitated by those poor kids in the parking lot about them smoking and larking about'

Mr Reynolds watched the suspect walk over, thinking he was going to talk to them, when the suspect suddenly pulled out a gun and began firing.

One of Mifford's neighbors, local psychiatrist Vivica Shields, spoke to us about the suspect. 'He is, or was, a nice man, but he's been having problems since his wife passed. I suspected he was struggling. I tried to talk to him. I spoke to his friends and family. We all knew he was losing his grip on things. We tried to help. After Jessica died, he seemed depressed, and then things changed. He started acting erratically, mumbling to himself, suspicious of everyone. It's terribly sad. To lose so much.'

Police say Mifford is facing multiple first-degree murder charges.

A teen driver killed Jessica Mifford and their unborn son in a tragic, unrelated accident. The case shook Phoenix and prompted harsher crackdowns on texting and driving fines.

LEARNING MURDER

LESSON ONE – Know Thyself

Bea was small. Smaller than anyone else at the facility at least, she knew that. In fact, there were no other children there at all. In fact, if she really boiled it down in her six-year-old brain, she would have guessed that not only was she the only child there, she was the first child to ever be there, judging by the awkward looks the doctors and staff gave her. The other patients (not that she was supposed to know there were other patients there, but of course she did, because she was crazy, not stupid) had told her the kind of things that went on at the facility. She nodded along sagely, because, as she had told her parents, she thought the facility was her only chance of being a 'normal' person.

Her mother, being wonderful, told her that there was no

point in being normal. Her father, who agreed with this sentiment, said that they would pay for it if she truly wanted to go. Bea, who had already thought about it extensively, told them that yes, it was what she wanted to do. Bea told them that she had been considering killing the neighbor's dog for quite some time, and that she was aware that this wasn't normal. Admittedly, she was only aware that this wasn't normal because she had sneaked downstairs and caught half of a *Criminal Minds* episode that her older brothers were watching. Nevertheless, since she wanted to like the dog and not end up some kind of deranged killer who ate her own family, she had decided upon this facility. She did not divulge that she had already tested out her ability to take a life on three rabbits, two mice and an unfortunate robin.

"Bea?" The psychiatrist knocked on her door.

Bea stood up solemnly from the edge of her bed.

"Are you all ready?" The woman smiled condescendingly and Bea gave her a stony look.

"Obviously," she replied witheringly.

The woman swallowed and her cheery smile faded. Bea's black eyes bored into her face and the scruffy bob that frizzed away from her pale cheeks. The psychiatrist motioned for Bea to head out of her room. She did something strange with her hand and Bea wondered if the woman actually thought Bea would need or want to hold her hand. To be on the safe side, Bea folded her hands in front of her tummy, away from the stranger's clammy paws.

Present

"Oh my god, Bea, come *onnnnn!*" Atlas, her brother, stood

in the doorway with his arms folded. He kept glancing over his shoulder distractedly.

"Stop looking over your shoulder. You won't find any pretty girls down here, in fact, you won't find any other humans down here. No one else has offices in my little basement."

Atlas mimicked his sister silently, but then turned back to face her. She was probably right.

"Mom is going to be pissed if we are late for her birthday lunch."

"I don't know what to tell you Atlas, I have to finish this."

Atlas pursed his lips and exhaled slowly. "Bea, remember when we were kids and me and Artemis took away all your pencils and books and stationery and we wouldn't tell you where it was?"

"Yes." Bea didn't look up from her notes. She wasn't kidding, she did have to finish the applied mathematics work, but there was no real urgency to it, other than her own desire to complete it.

"Remember how first you got angry, but you couldn't really do anything to us, and then you tried to figure out where we had hidden it?"

"Uh huh."

"And then we realized that we had put it in the trash and Marta had taken the trash out, and it was books you had collected from all over the world, that Dad had bought you and that you had made notes in?"

"Yeeees." Bea looked up and dragged the word out.

"And?"

"I was upset?" Bea queried. She could vaguely remember

her brothers tormenting her, but after the facility, nothing seemed quite as clear as it had before.

"Very upset."

"Oh... kay..."

"That's how Mom will feel if we are late to her sixtieth birthday lunch."

Bea stood up. She quickly shuffled the papers into order and carefully put her pens and pencils away. She powered down the Mac and looked around. "I get it."

Atlas smiled and tried to usher his sister out of her office. She got all squirrely by the door.

"I have to go out last."

"Whaaa..." Atlas stopped and smiled. "Sure." He stepped into the corridor and sighed. It was going to be a long drive from Berkeley to Santa Cruz. Thank God they were picking Artemis up along the way.

LESSON TWO – Control

Bea quite enjoyed the doctor. He was a self-professed psychopath and sociopath, just 'well medicated and even better educated' than the rest, as he put it. He did not talk down to Bea, although now that she had been at the facility for three years, no one did, apart from new staff.

"And how are you feeling after yesterday's treatment?"

"Fine. Good. I mean... no different."

"Mmm hmm... and how are your studies going?"

"Fine." Bea sighed.

The doctor turned and looked at Bea and leant against the metal counters that hemmed the treatment room.

"Bea, you can't stay with us forever. This isn't a school,

and we're never going to truly know if the treatment is working if you are ensconced here."

"Yes but…" Bea clenched her little fists. She was only nine, but her eyes felt gritty from lack of sleep. The newest therapy was giving her dreams. Strange, frightening dreams. Bea had realized that she had never felt frightened before these dreams.

"What if…"

"If 'ifs' and 'buts' were candy and nuts then we'd all have a Merry Christmas."

Bea looked up at the doctor, about to give him a filthy glare, but he was staring darkly at her.

"Bea Medusa Braithwaite, no one knows your struggle better than I do, but I swear to you, you will not know if our treatments work unless you give them a chance in real life. I can personally attest to the fact that self-control, self-discipline, these things must be practiced to be fully mastered."

Present

"Artie darling, pass your mother the champagne." Lillemor Braithwaite smiled at her eldest son. "Artemis!" She snapped, when he appeared to be checking out the waiter rather than listening to her.

"What?" Artemis turned back to his parents and siblings. "What, Mom?" He smiled winningly, revealing a row of straight white teeth.

"Champagne. Mother wants champagne." Rodrigo Braithwaite widened his eyes and looked fearful. "Quickly! You know how she gets."

"Oh fuck off!" She said witheringly to them as she yanked the bottle away from Artemis.

Bea watched each of her family members in turn and swallowed a glug of her coke. She was trying to block out their voices so that she could concentrate on the math problem she had left behind in the basement office at Berkeley. Her brothers' loud voices and her mother's chatter made it hard to properly concentrate.

Her father nudged her gently, trying to rouse her from her daydream, "where are you BB?"

"Berkeley." Bea smiled.

Her mothers' voice cut in. "So where are all my pressies?"

Artemis and Atlas grinned and began digging through their bags with a boisterous energy. They added small parcels onto the table, all poorly wrapped in brightly-colored paper.

Rodrigo reached down and grabbed three parcels from beside his chair. Bea reached for her phone and fired off a few text messages, but otherwise remained still. The phone continued to vibrate on the table as everyone began to watch Lillemor unwrap her goodies. She squealed with childlike glee at each gift. Bea looked at the trinkets piling up. Crazy jewelry, some books, an antique spoon, and all the things their eclectic mother loved. Lastly, Rodrigo handed her an envelope. Inside was a picture of an enormous fiberglass figurine. Made by Colin Christian, it was an exaggerated model of their mother in the eighties, in a glitter bodice, with punk hair, enormous shiny black lips, and sparkling sapphire eyes the size of dinner plates. Lillemor let out a scream of delight and leant over to give Rodrigo a kiss. Atlas and Artemis made faces.

No one looked at Bea expectantly. She knew no one expected her to get gifts. She had tried, in the past. But no one seemed to like her gifts. She was smart enough to see through their protestations.

"Excuse me." Bea stood up suddenly, her chair scraping on the patio. She hurried off down the street and disappeared around the corner. The rest of the family watched her, bemused. She reappeared a moment later with a white cardboard box in her arms.

"Ohhh Mom, you get a Bea gift." Atlas whispered under his breath and Artemis snickered.

"Boys," Lillemor chided, but her face was a frozen smiling mask.

"Here." Bea thrust the box at her mother.

Lillemor smiled. "Oh darling, you..."

Rodrigo gave his wife a warning glance.

"You sweet girl, thank you." Lillemor smiled and took the box. It was heavier than she thought, and unbalanced. She placed it on the table.

Gingerly, she lifted the lid and let out a little gasp.

Atlas, Artemis and even Rodrigo leant in to look.

"Oh my god! Bea, is that...?"

"It's a puppy." Lillemor lifted the sleeping nugget up out of the box with a grin.

"I know, we couldn't... when I was little." Bea's words were stilted. She wrinkled her nose, changing tack. "It's a French bulldog. Blue is what they call that color. Eight weeks old. He's a boy. He doesn't have a name. It's good, right? It's cute." Bea looked around at her family. A shadow of concern fell over her gift choice. No one had said anything yet.

"Bea..." Artemis slung an arm around his sister, "it's amazing." He reached out for the puppy, but Lillemor had it cradled like a baby.

"Do... do you think it's cute?" Rodrigo smiled gently at his daughter.

Bea looked up. They were all looking at her. "Um... yeah, I mean... I looked at a bunch of different breeds. I figured this would be the best one for Mom... for you guys." She motioned at her parents. "Plus, this one seemed real cute. It's..." Bea looked for the word. She reached over the table and rubbed the puppy's little face, "it's smooshed."

"Oh my fucking God!" Atlas exclaimed. "She is a fucking human!" He grinned and reached out to grab his sister into a hug. Artemis laughed and kept an arm around his sister who was, at this point, trying to wriggle out.

"Group hug, group hug!" Artemis exclaimed as Bea futilely tried to escape her brother's arms. "Bring it in Mom, bring the smooshy puppy, Bea can be at the center!"

Raucous laughter erupted with the scraping of chairs and the yipping of a tiny puppy as other diners craned their heads to look at the commotion.

LESSON THREE – Love

"Do you love anything, Bea?" The therapist, Anita, was leaning back in her chair. Bea had wanted to not like Anita, but the treatment facility, and the doctor, had recommended her. She looked, Bea's thirteen-year-old brain searched for the right word; she looked too relaxed. Yoga pants, a draped sweater, a brunette ponytail. Slightly overweight. Bea still went back to the treatment facility every six weeks, but she saw Anita twice every week, Tuesdays and Thursdays, 5pm sharp.

"I love mathematics."

"You're good at mathematics."

"I am."

"I meant, do you love anything, like say... a sweater, or a place, or a person?"

"A sweater?"

Anita laughed, "OK, more generally, any specific objects or possessions?"

Bea shrugged. "No."

"Places? People?"

"I..." Bea raised her brows quizzically for a moment and then fell into silence. Anita said nothing.

"I do know what love is." Bea said eventually.

Anita smiled warmly but stayed silent.

"I love my family," Bea said eventually, although she frowned as she spoke.

Anita nodded. "And friends?"

"I don't have any friends," Bea said simply.

Anita raised one brow and leant forward slightly.

"I'm a thirteen-year-old surrounded by people in their early twenties. I'm a freak, firstly because I'm a genius, but secondly because... well y'know." She shrugged. Her young face was smooth and untroubled by her pronouncement.

Anita nodded. Before they started the sessions, she had been given a detailed explanation by Bea's parents and the doctor regarding Bea's situation, treatment and capabilities.

"Are you lonely?"

Bea chewed her cheek as she thought. Lonely. The word didn't mean much but she knew she had to talk to Anita. The doctor had been very explicit about not 'bottling things up.'

"You know we have new neighbors? They have a dog. It... it's a husky mix. They call him Palmyra. He's named after a mountain."

Anita nodded and waited for Bea to continue. She did this sometimes. Changed tack. Anita had first thought she was trying to avoid certain questions, but she had come to realize that her prompts would trigger other thoughts in Bea's complex brain.

"They... they let me play with him last week. They saw me staring. They thought... they thought I would want to play with a dog. Which I suppose is a normal thing for them to assume. Mom and Dad were inside, I was on the patio working." Bea paused with her head cocked. A shimmer of her long caramel ponytail rippled back and forth. Her green eyes narrowed.

Anita braced herself. Bea had told her a few things that had shocked her, deeply, even after the doctor's warning. But the things Bea had told her had only been thoughts before; ideas, never actions.

"I played with it for an hour." Bea nodded grimly. "It was fine. I mean... I liked the dog."

"You liked the dog?"

Bea nodded. "Mom came out and nearly had a heart attack and the wife just laughed, she didn't get it... obviously. She said I can play with him whenever I want."

"When you were playing with the dog... did you have

any urge to hurt the animal?" Anita waited, breath caught in her throat.

Bea looked up at her, an anguished look on her face, "No." She swallowed.

Anita scooted to the edge of her seat, "Bea?"

"Not the dog..."

Anita waited and tried to unclench her jaw.

"The... the owners, the guy. When Palmyra wouldn't listen to him, to go back inside, he grabbed him by the neck and the dog was crying and yelping." Bea had gone pale and she looked up at Anita. She inhaled and her nostrils flared. "It wasn't the dog I wanted to hurt, Anita, not at all."

PRESENT

Bea sat in the car whilst her brothers argued over who got to choose the music. She never got a say, which was fair, since she didn't care about music. They were heading back to their parents' palatial home in Santa Cruz.

"Hey, earth to Bea?" Atlas turned around in the passenger seat. "Bea?"

"Huh?" She looked at her brother.

"Are you still doing kick boxing?"

"Oh... no, I... I mean I still practice but now I'm doing capoeira and krav maga." The redwoods blurred as their car sped along the Cabrillo highway towards the house. Everything was wet and vibrant green.

Artemis rolled his eyes and the twins went back to their bickering.

"Can you drop me off in Gordola?" Bea said, cutting in to their sniping.

"Gordola?"

"I want to go to the beach."

Atlas and Artemis exchanged a glance. "OK, but don't you want to wait, till like, tomorrow?" Artemis ventured.

"No."

Atlas shrugged but Artemis frowned. The facility that Bea had spent many years at was located near Gordola, or used to be, before the Government stepped in and contracted them out to Quantico.

"Do you... were you wanting to... um..."

"No. The facility has closed, Artemis." Bea's voice carried an edge.

"Right." Artemis swallowed.

"Just let her go," Atlas mumbled quietly to his brother.

LESSON FOUR – Pain

Bea's screams carried out from the small treatment room, down the long, echoey corridor, all the way into the deserted front hallway where no receptionist stood and the heavy steel doors remained locked.

The doctor didn't ask if she wanted to stop. He knew the answer. The thick cabling from the equipment jumped and dragged on the floor as Bea writhed in the plush leather seat. Half reclined, it almost looked like she was in the middle of a video game. The display monitors were angled towards the doctor, Anita and Rajul, a leading psychologist. They all watched, transfixed by the barrage of images.

Anita held her breath. The doctor watched dispassionately. Rajul pursed his lips. Anita and the doctor had forewarned him, obviously, but he was still feeling shell-shocked.

"Will this really help?" Rajul leant in towards the doctor.

"It has in the past."

"But with her…"

"Bea!" Anita cut in firmly.

"But will it help Bea?" Rajul pressed on.

"It has in the past."

"Like this?"

"Just like this." The doctor exhaled as a new realm of images sprung to life.

"That's new." Anita nodded her head towards the screen.

"What?" Rajul normally would have hated being the person who knew the least, but frankly he was so awed to have been invited to the facility to work on a case like this that he didn't much care.

"Historically, Bea's psychosis and sociopathic tendencies were… unbiased. Animal or human," Anita said slowly.

"When she started here, we noticed a definite interest in becoming less… ahem… she had a desire to become less violent towards animals. She had already killed some small rodents… she was aware of what she was." The doctor's face softened as Bea suppressed another scream in the chair.

"She was only six," said Anita.

"Yes, so we capitalized on that and channeled her behavior towards helping animals, from those who wanted to harm them… that's how the neurological reprogramming works, in stages. It was a good first stage since she already showed the inclination."

"So you're reprogramming her." Rajul sniffed and looked back at the computers. "With this?"

"No, this is a way to channel some of her desires - get them out, help them find a more… productive home. And help her understand the dynamics of physical pain, emotional pain."

"Is that... is it legal?"

"She consented to it," the doctor said stiffly. "And essentially 'this' is what has helped Bea return to the world as a functioning human being who isn't afraid of herself."

"Until the other day," Anita said wryly wrinkling her brow. Working with Bea had been an incredible opportunity, but Bea had, for the first time in their sessions, frightened her. She had seen Bea's face when she made her confession. She had been ashen and shaky, but the emotion in her eyes was unmistakable; eager, excited, and filled with longing.

Rajul nodded along and turned away from the screens, sickness creeping from his belly, up his esophagus and into his throat. "Ahem... yes... and I am here because?"

"You are here because we are both, Anita and myself, concerned that Bea has reached, perhaps, a point where we can no longer..." The doctor cleared his throat. The words stuck, unwilling to venture out into reality.

"Where you can no longer reprogram her?" Rajul finished. He was getting into the swing of things now. This was a once in a lifetime chance.

"Exactly." Anita looked at the monitors. Two of them had gone dark. Bea was winding down. "She's nearly done. Time for you to meet her, Dr Rajul."

PRESENT

Gordola was quiet. There was one man walking his dog along the beach; both man and dog were ancient. He wore a blue rain jacket and the dog hobbled along with a stick in its mouth. Bea smiled at them both as they shuffled past her. The salty wind swept in off the ocean and flicked the ends of Bea's ponytail round into her face. Bea watched as the elderly duo climbed the narrow stone steps up out of the half moon bay back towards the small main street that made up the entirety of Gordola.

Bea looked along the length of the coastline and sniffed. The salty air took her back to long, dark nights in the facility; to meals alone and studying in the tiny back office that had been reassigned for her, to watching the doctor as he set up equipment or explained another new treatment option to her. She missed the facility deeply and the safety that it's walls held for her. Perhaps, Bea wondered as she strolled along the dark sand, it made her feel safe because she knew the world was safer without her in it.

Clouds rolled in overhead and Bea walked towards the narrow steps. She climbed slowly, making each step decisive, and didn't stop till she neared the top. Her legs burned slightly, heavy with fatigue. She kept her eyes down on the mossy, slippery steps, worn smooth with age.

There was a scuffle, something grated, metal on metal. Bea snapped her head up, a moment too late. White male, stubble, scruffy hair, a baton; black and scarred.

Bea's eyes fluttered, roving around for some last-ditch attempt... at what? She didn't know. Then hands, rough, and darkness.

LESSON FIVE – TAKE HEED

"Bea, I'm Rajul," he said in a measured voice, careful not to reveal the frisson of excitement he felt.

Bea nodded and exhaled slowly. She looked exhausted. Her pale skin was gray and her green eyes were ringed with dark purple circles. She slumped in the chair, comfortable in the facility, but exhausted by the most recent treatment.

"I know the doctor already explained why I am here." Rajul shifted in his seat. Bea's eyes looked past him, glazed and unseeing, and she didn't even acknowledge that he had spoken. "But, I wanted to know if there was anything you wanted to share with me before we got started."

Rajul waited hopefully. It all felt very basic. He hadn't done this type of one-on-one since he was fresh off his PhD.

Bea exhaled forcefully. She had wanted not to like Anita, but she found the woman tolerable, even likeable. Rajul, however, watched her like a dog eager to gobble down raw meat. She was a commodity to him, even if he was the 'best in his field'.

Rajul put down the silk handkerchief he had in his hands. "I must confess, I am very interested in working with you Bea, but I understand if you... I understand that you've spent your whole life doing..." Rajul waved a hand around the office, "this. You might not be inclined to share with me." He bowed his head gracefully.

"Huh." Bea nodded.

Rajul's stomach fluttered hopefully. The doctor had told him that honesty was his best chance at getting Bea to communicate with him. Authenticity was something she valued highly.

"And I do know that I am probably coming across as over eager, like a teenage schoolboy no doubt." Rajul chuckled, but inside, he cursed his choice of analogy. "I just... I just find your particular brain incredibly interesting."

Bea let out a dry scraping noise that could have been a laugh or a scoff. There was a heavy silence in the room.

"So what do you know about my brain, Rajul?"

Bea's question was guarded, but there was a thin veil of anger and menace in her voice. Rajul cocked his head; there was something else there too, perhaps curiosity.

Rajul breathed in deeply. He chuckled, "I'm nervous."

A faint glimmer of a smile played across Bea's lips. "Don't be. I've heard it all," she said, as the smile faded.

"You're fundamentally different from most, if not almost all, psychopaths and sociopaths, in that your intelligence is incredibly high, and yet you are also very self-aware," Rajul began.

Bea nodded. This was nothing new to her.

"Your problem comes in that whilst you are aware of your diagnosis, you are not able to relate to any emotions, so there is a gap there that is very tricky to bridge. I know that is what the doctor and Anita have been working on with you." Rajul steepled his fingers. Bea had shifted a little straighter in her chair. "I know you have also been trying to figure out this conundrum by yourself," he went on. "The doctor told me of your desire to work in applied mathematics, but also to work on the statistical analysis of serial killers in an attempt to map or predict their behavior."

Bea nodded slightly and raised an eyebrow.

"Not the best idea. Obsessing on a focal point in an attempt to understand the whole picture is rarely conducive to understanding." Rajul took a steady breath. He felt calmer now. "You are unique in that you realized your desires were…"

"Murderous?"

"Wrong." Rajul held up a finger. "At least by our modern society's standards." He gave Bea a wry smile. "And you took steps to correct that. You recognized that you were…" Rajul searched for the word.

"That I was struggling." Bea leant forward in her chair. "Anita and I have spoken about it."

Rajul frowned slightly but nodded. "OK, we'll use struggling. So you realized that, and at such a young age, and you came here. Now, you have a new challenge facing you, and that is when those same desires manifest in more adult realms of understanding. As a child your desires were uncommon, but still basic in terms of psychotic and sociopathic. Now, your general world view is much more informed, thus your desires are more logically informed."

"You're making it sound like it's normal, like it's OK." Bea shook her head and arched one dark eyebrow.

"Bea, normal is a relative term. We have to work with what works for you, not try and make you like every other 'normal' human being out there." Rajul said bluntly.

"So tell me. What am I supposed to do?"

PRESENT

The darkness was patchy, a strange crosshatch across Bea's eyes. A bag or some kind of fabric sash was over her eyes. Loose, so a bag, sacking probably, Bea surmised. There was talking, so more than one of them. Both male – accents - local, Northern California… one of the voices sounded thick, like a speech impediment or perhaps a fat lip. Bea tried to roll over slightly. She knew she must be facing the back of the van, because the voices were behind her and a low rumble emanated from in front. She didn't want them to think she was awake.

"Yeah... I know... well tell him then..."

"Can't seem to get... cell service... shitty."

"He'll be down... anyway..."

Bea frowned. There was a third man it seemed, or at least, that was highly likely. That wasn't good for her. Her hands were bound, in front rather than behind her, which was good. Rope, smooth and tight, circled her wrists. Well wrapped and tied. She would struggle to get out without something sharp. Or help.

She tried wiggling her fingers. They were achey and swollen with blood. Blood filled her mouth as she bit down hard on her lip. Someone, one of them, had prodded her in the back to see if she was awake. The shock and determination she had exerted to stop herself from crying out now filled her mouth, hot and metallic.

"'Still out... you must've got her pretty good."

"She'll be fine."

"Sure is a pretty one... John will be happy."

The other man grunted.

"Looks like that one... what was her name... Annie? Ally? Remember?"

Bea could smell the man's breath as he leant close. Light filtered in as he lifted the sacking hood slightly. Bea kept her eyes almost completely closed.

"Yeah... Ava."

"It wasn't Ava."

The light went away, and the men continued to argue, presumably over another woman they had abducted. What concerned Bea was that their conversation about 'Ava', or whatever her name was, had been in the past tense.

LESSON SIX – BEATRIX MEDUSA BRAITHWAITE

"Well, you're the one who wanted my help," Rajul hissed at the doctor. They were standing, he, the doctor and Anita, in a semi-circle. The Mac injected a blueish tinge into the otherwise white and green office. The enormous window looked out over lush woodland.

"I just… Bea…" The doctor frowned. Rajul could be pompous, condescending, and a prat, but he wasn't a liar.

Anita splayed her hands and let out a long, steady breath as she sat down in the gray armchair. "A vigilante complex?" She looked up at Rajul.

Rajul sat down across from her on the sofa and the doctor leant against the edge of the white desk. Anita suppressed a smile. She was good at defusing situations.

"I don't think it was deliberate, obviously." He looked at the doctor with a nod. "I think it was the only way Bea could rationalize her desires."

"But… all the pain understanding treatments?" The doctor waved a hand at the door, imagining the long hours spent in small rooms hearing Bea screaming.

"Yes." Rajul nodded in agreement. "She understands pain very well, which I think is why this complex presented itself. She wouldn't hurt a random person. She understands pain and suffering too well, but someone who she thought 'deserved' it, well…"

"Have you told her this?" Anita leant forward in the chair.

"No. We discussed it a lot, but making her understand the logistics behind what is and isn't fair versus what should happen and what shouldn't, what can happen and what can't - they aren't things that can be taught. We can explain a fair trial and Bea's knowledge and understanding would surpass ours almost immediately, but..." Rajul pursed his lips.

"You can't explain ethics to her." Anita leant back and folded her hands in her lap.

"Exactly." Rajul leant back too.

"Bea... Bea knows ethics. She understood that as a child. She knew that wanting to hurt animals was wrong." There was a whining edge to the doctor's voice. Rajul was already shaking his head, but Anita spoke before he could.

"No, she didn't know that was wrong. She only inferred it from catching thirty minutes of a TV show. She was able to make the logistical bridges between herself and a fictional serial killer. She told me she snuck onto the family computer and researched serial killers, which took her to 'sociopath' and 'psychosis' and a number of other things she hadn't heard of. She realized her thought patterns were considered 'wrong' and in her six-year-old mind she thought it was a foregone conclusion that she would end up killing her family or go to prison." Anita smiled.

"I just don't think you're giving her enough credit." The doctor managed to keep the snarl out of his voice.

"I disagree," Rajul replied in a clipped voice. "I have no doubt she has a brilliant mind, but a beautiful one? Alas my friend, she does not. Even she knows that. Her desires... they are darker than any of us could possibly imagine." Rajul's voice lost its pomposity as he finished his sentence.

"So what do we do?" Anita looked at the men. "What are the next steps for us now that we have inadvertently created a sociopathic, psychotic serial killer, with genius-level intelligence and a propensity to kill those who have done wrong?"

Anita and Rajul turned to the doctor, but he had turned away to look out of the bay windows. He watched a rabbit nibbling nervously on verdant grass and tried to stop his hands from trembling.

PRESENT

Bea found herself being thrust out of the van, arms still bound tightly behind her back, a blindfold around her eyes. The step out of the van fell away to rough ground and she stumbled, nearly tripping. One of the men grabbed her upper arm to stop her falling face first. He smelt of deodorant, Old Spice Sport, and mints, Mentos, sickly sweet.

Bea let her breath steady, taking small steps. The ground was rough, and lumpy like mud. They had only travelled a few hours. Bea could vaguely smell mud and salt. It was chilly. Southern Oregon or Northern California. So they hadn't gone that far. A farm? A ranch? Bea let her mind process each smell and sound. Birds. Sea birds. She wasn't that far from home. Being close to the sea was a risk though. It was one great big untraceable grave.

Bea let the man guide her over the ground. He wasn't the one who had prodded her in the back. His grip was tight, but not deliberately painful. The one who had prodded her had smelt sour. He was still standing by the van. She could hear the sound of him pulling things out of the back. Metal things.

A door. Old. Wooden. A screen. Creaky. Linoleum underfoot. Potatoes boiling. Another door. Bolted, heavy. Bea fought the urge to struggle as she heard the bolts being slid across. A woman, nasal and sharp. Then a hollow echo, and the slow descent of a staircase. Bea stepped carefully. Basement stairs, narrow and unfinished. Cold and damp permeated the air. Earthiness.

Then the sound of metal on metal. Rattling. Chains? Bea grimaced. There was a squeaking as something swung open, then a whimpering. Bea's ears pricked. The hand on her arm released. The snap of a knife blade. Bea stiffened, but then her wrists were freed. Before she could think anymore she was shoved, a big hand in the middle of her back, forward and down. She stumbled through a small opening. Thin metal scratched her arms and face.

Metal clanged quickly as she fumbled with her blindfold. The click of a padlock.

Bea's fingers worked the knot quickly.

She unwrapped the blindfold and pulled it away from her eyes.

Shit.

LESSON SEVEN – BLOOD

"I mean, come on, she can't possibly think that's uh... I mean... normal." The sounds of clinking champagne glasses and mild-mannered chatter floated in through the open bay windows.

A lone waiter stood at the far end of the kitchen plating

up hors d'oeuvres on a silver platter. The two women leant their heads close together and sipped sauvignon blanc.

"Well, I suppose... what else are they supposed to do?" The second woman said, in a snide tone that suggested she had a myriad better ideas.

"Not go around publicly hashing out your divorce with the entire social circle. Christ! And look at her, she'll be after the husbands next, let me tell you." The first woman, blond and coiffed, watched the garden party over the rim of her glass.

"I know, I'm surprised Lillemor lets her come around here all the time."

The other woman, shrewish and dark, let out a little huff of laughter. "Oh, I doubt anyone could steal Rodrigo away from Lil."

"Don't say I didn't predict it."

"Come on, Lillemor looks like a thirty-five-year-old, and she's got the body of a twenty-five-year-old." The darker woman scanned the crowd with her tiny eyes for the lithe form of Lillemor.

"Yes, but Lillemor also comes with baggage, that wretchedly creepy child of theirs, Bea. Beatrix Medusa, what a name! I mean what man wouldn't want to get away from that?" The blonde woman suppressed a cackle and her friend gasped and giggled.

Beatrix watched their neighbor, Anne, frozen in the doorway of the kitchen. She looked mortified. Tears brimmed on her lower eyelids. She still lived next door. Bea played with Palmyra a lot. Anne was not trying to steal her father. Anne was, in fact, relieved to be free from her abusive husband. Anne was also a lesbian, and far more likely to make a pass at Lillemor. Anne hadn't told Bea this, but Bea was more astute than most thirteen-year-olds.

Bea was stuck on the back staircase. She had been trying to find a copy of an astrophysics textbook that she suspected Artemis had taken.

Instead of walking into the kitchen, Bea silently turned left, one ear cocked to the two witches cackling in hushed tones in the kitchen. She walked into the pantry, rummaging around on the lower shelves where spare kitchen supplies lived.

Bea smiled, finding what she wanted, then turned to the fridge and carefully pulled out the raspberry meringue that was the grand finale. She tinkered with the back of the fridge for a moment. She looked at the meringue and sighed. Her mother would forgive her.

"Hello girls, what are we whispering about?" Lillemor's accented voice, bright and happy, filled the kitchen. The two women began fawning over the garden party, the food, and the flowers. Bea listened to their nauseating voices for a moment and then carefully sliced her palm with the carving knife.

"I think Rodrigo wants to make a little speech," Lillemor said, and Bea heard the sound of the big doors being thrust open wider. The sound of the guests grew quieter. Bea picked up the meringue, sliding a small metal skewer just beyond the front rim of the plate. She gripped the plate, the pain in her hand bringing shocked tears to her eyes. Good, she thought, with a smile.

She hurried out of the pantry.

Lillemor was facing the guests.

The blonde, coiffed witch was half facing Bea.

The guests were turned to Lillemor.

Anne remained frozen in the bathroom door, too embarrassed to come out.

Bea began to run, "Mama, the fridge..."

She tried to slide to a halt, as if seeing the blonde woman for the first time. Her bare feet were gliding over the wooden floor. The meringue plate was becoming lighter in her hands.

Bea subtly pitched herself forward. The thin metal skewer, invisible to the guests, slid forward so that it caught the blonde woman in the ribs, sharp and painful. She lashed out, screaming, sending the meringue up into the air. Her clawed hands struck towards Bea angrily.

All the guests' eyes were on the blonde lady, and then the glass platter, as it turned mid-air. Bea had been knocked backwards, but she kept her cut hand carefully balled into a fist.

Lillemor let out a gasp. The platter came crashing down on Bea. Glass exploded as Bea tried to cover herself. Bea unclenched her fist and blood spurted out, a split second after the glass shattered.

"What did you do that for?" Lillemor snapped. "Pauline?" Her eyes blazed. The blonde woman looked stunned as Bea's blood splattered over the white cabinets.

Guests rushed forward, toward Bea.

"Something caught... I..." Pauline's face was growing ashen.

Bea let out a pitiful whimper.

"Oh my Bea!" Lillemor leant down and reached for Bea's gushing hand. Bea looked over, pointedly, at Anne. Anne looked gobsmacked. Bea gave her another pointed look with narrowed green eyes.

Anne stepped out. "Oh my god Pauline, why would you push her? She's just a kid."

Anne rushed to Bea, who reached for her in pathetically sickly way. Lillemor shuffled to let Anne take a look at the wound.

The dark woman sidled away from Pauline nervously. "I didn't…

"Yes you did!" Bea snapped, and then remembered to let out another sad snuffle.

"For goodness sake Pauline, she's a child. What, you didn't want get meringue on that nasty Prada outfit?" Lillemor's trademark tongue lashed out as Bea's hand continued to bleed.

"I didn't…"

"Get out of my house!" Lillemor snarled, rising to her feet. Her loose waves and crisp white sundress were splattered with meringue, raspberry jam and blood.

Pauline, now ghostly pale, swallowed a few times. She backed out of the kitchen. Rodrigo, jovial as ever, clapped his hands and diverted attention outside as he shut the patio doors.

Lillemor, Bea and Anne stood in the kitchen. The waiter proffered the first-aid kit he had retrieved, then quickly hurried off.

Bea turned to Anne. "Can you bandage this?" Anne nodded and grabbed the kit.

"I was just going to slap her," Lillemor said, carefully picking a piece of meringue from her hair.

"What?" Anne looked up from wrapping Bea's hand.

"Nasty Pauline, I heard her," Lillemor said. Anne looked mortified. "I take it you did too." Lillemor nudged Anne. "I know you aren't a husband stealer."

"I just... I should've stepped out, said something," Anne sighed. "All done, Bea." She had finished bandaging the hand.

"Well, instead she got a dose of Bea justice. Very messy. Fucked up my meringue. So much drama."

"You did... you did that on purpose?" Anne looked shocked.

"I don't like Pauline." Bea cocked her head. "And I really like Palmyra - and you, I guess." She strolled back out of the kitchen.

"I know she's..." Lillemor held up one hand and tilted it side to side. "But that was pretty spectacular."

Anne swallowed as Lillemor embraced her in a hug. "I think I'm just glad she's on my side," she mumbled, her wide eyes looking at the dark doorway Bea had just vanished into.

PRESENT

"Shh... shh..." The girl in the cage beside Bea rocked back and forth on her heels, her arms wrapped around her knees, her lank brown hair falling in front of her gaunt face.

Bea rolled her eyes. She had always thought that in this type of Criminal Minds-style scenario she would be on the other side of the cage . She resisted the urge to mutter and instead slunk to the back of her cage and slowly looked around.

She let her palms rest on her knees and thought about

the facility at Gordola, then about Anita's pale green office with its abundance of plants and cream seats. She took a breath and looked calmly around the room. There were at least six other cages. By the snuffling sounds Bea assumed that there were, therefore, six other women. The smell was bad, but not hideous, so they were at least slightly bothering to clean the basement. The women she could see, two others, were close in age to her, but not similar in looks.

So young women was their thing.

They were thin but not starved, so they were being fed. Bea frowned. If they were being fed, it meant they were being held for some time. That was good and bad.

The room was a basement, bare, with one ominous-looking workbench at the center. Bea couldn't see any blood on it though. There were some splatters she had noticed on the floor, but nothing that would exceed a bad cut or bloody nose.

"Wh… what day is it?" A voice came, tired and groggy, from the darkest corner. Bea looked at the corner. She felt numerous sets of glistening eyes turn to her in the gloom.

"Tuesday June 5th. It is a little after 4pm."

"June." The voice echoed.

There was a sniffling from one of the women beside Bea and someone else let out a stream of incoherent mumbling. Bea felt her throat grow tight. She didn't really want to talk to anyone, but she had to get more information.

"How long have you… been here?" She asked slowly. She was trying to remember what Anita had told her about communication. She hadn't been listening back then, but bits of it still floated inside her skull.

There was a long silence. Then the voice from the corner, "four months."

Bea nodded. That was good. They weren't just going to make it quick and painless. She had a shot.

"Three." Another voice said. Bea could make out a dark-skinned African American woman in a cage across from her. More mumbled voices came from each cage. One month. Two. Three. A few weeks. The voices were unsure.

The lock on the door at the top of the basement stairs rattled and silence quickly fell.

Bea watched a pair of Converse trainers, dirty and threadbare, descend the staircase. Heavy duty work pants, also filthy, and a T-shirt with a long faded logo. A man, straggly beard, but young, with straw colored hair and hazel eyes, looked into her cage.

"Nice," he leered. His fingers slid through the cage and gripped around it. Bea saw dirty fingernails. She looked up at him carefully.

"I'm Bea," she said.

The man smiled. His teeth were a little crooked, but not dirty.

"Yeah." He leant in and studied her. His nose was a little crooked and his eyes sloped down on the outside edges.

"What is your name?" she asked evenly.

"Nice try," the man said, with one last look at her. He walked to a cage in the far corner. Not the darkest cage, but one that Bea couldn't quite make out. He unlocked it and dragged a red-haired girl out. She was beyond pale, with frizzy red hair and still a soft layer of puppy fat on her. She whimpered but didn't struggle much.

"Come on." He yanked her arm, hurrying her up the

stairs and out of sight. The sound of the lock clicking carried down the stairs and silence fell again.

"That's Jacob. He's the worst," came the voice from the dark corner.

Bea nodded and smiled to herself. She was willing to bet that of all the sick fucks upstairs, none of them had anything on her.

LESSON EIGHT – PHYSICAL THERAPY

Bea's small fists pummeled the bag.

"That's good, but try to hold your fist like this." The small Japanese-American instructor took Bea's hand gingerly. Bea looked down at her hand as if an alien had taken it.

"See?" The woman quickly let go, apparently as uncomfortable as Bea was with the physical contact. Bea looked at her from under her eyelashes. She was petite but well-muscled, with solid shoulders and visible muscle along her arms and back.

Bea nodded. She was fourteen, by far the youngest person in the class. Her mother had come to the first one and bounced around in one corner with her blonde ponytail swishing. Then the first sweat bead had appeared on Lillemor's brow and she had decided she wouldn't accompany Bea any further than the front door from then on.

Bea had been studying karate, but she found the classes childish and boring. Instead she had settled upon jiu-jitsu and kickboxing. She also wanted to learn knife fighting, but whilst Anita and the doctor agreed that the physical exercise would help her, the knife skills were 'taking it too far'.

"Ok, we're going to work in partners and practice that last sequence," said the instructor. Everyone paired off, but Bea remained focused on her bag. "You can work with me," she heard the instructor say to her. Bea sighed. She hated other people.

"Excellent, Bea." TJ, the instructor, nodded as she walked past. There were only four of them in the class: Bea, one other lady in her thirties, and two heavyset mid-twenties guys.

Bea smiled. TJ, as it turned out, had quite bad Asperger's which she managed successfully with her therapist, Anita, and physical exercise. When Bea had run into her at Anita's office she hadn't been sure which of them had been more uncomfortable. TJ's brother had started the Warrior Academy and she had become fixated on jiu-jitsu at fifteen. Now, she was their best instructor.

"Excellent," TJ remarked again.

Bea had been practicing for two months. Every day, for hours, she would practice Jiu-jitsu or kickboxing. She would back both her parents' cars out of the garage and lock herself in. She wasn't allowed to partner with anyone other than TJ, or TJ's older brother Shaun. There had been an unfortunate incident with a young man who had tried to be a tad heavy handed with Bea. No one was precisely sure what had happened, because the young man was too ashamed to admit he had done something that would provoke a fourteen-year-old, and that he had then been badly injured by an adolescent girl. Bea wasn't very helpful either, but given that she was a psychopath, no one had really expected her to divulge much beyond "he deserved it".

PRESENT

Bea lay back down on the floor of her crate. It was the middle of the night. The girl who had been taken still wasn't back. She was tired, her body clock not yet warped by the lack of contact with daylight, and she let her eyelids close in a half-sleep.

She didn't believe in fate, but Bea wondered at this moment, if she was somehow, 'supposed' to be there. She heard one of the girls whimper in her sleep and Bea knew that they were terrified. Bea wasn't terrified. Bea didn't really feel anything. Well, that wasn't true. She felt some vague black humor settle over her at the irony of it. Gordola. Fucking Gordola.

"Mrs... Braithewaite?" The young police officer was ludicrously handsome. Dark stubble, chiseled jaw and cheekbones, honeyed skin, all well put together on a tall, lean frame. Lillemor smiled luxuriously.

"Oh for God's sake." Rodrigo elbowed Lillemor to one side. "Come on in officer, what can we do for you?"

Lillemor followed the officer and let her eyes trail to his buttocks. She smiled and looked up to see Rodrigo making a face at her. "What? What can we do?" She corrected quickly, looking at the police officer's face.

Rodrigo wondered where Atlas and Artemis were. The noise blared from the cinema room. What had they done this time?

"Um... well, this is a little unusual, but we had a call from someone..." The police officer shifted from foot to foot. His radio crackled. There was another knock on the door and the police officer turned to it with relief. "That'll be my partner."

Rodrigo hurried to the door. "Come in." He waved an Indian woman inside. She was tall, almost six feet, with dark, smooth skin, a hooked nose and jet-black hair and eyes. Lillemor had found a new wondrous subject, and she stared at the woman with delight. "I'm Lillemor," she said, smiling.

The woman nodded. "Officer Karina Laghari." She looked around the palatial home with a dispassionate eye. "Is there somewhere we can sit and talk?"

"What is this about?" Rodrigo was looking between the two officers.

"This way." Lillemor motioned towards the kitchen. They tromped there in a tense silence.

"So, what is this about?" Rodrigo pressed as Lillemor went to the enormous stainless fridge and grabbed a jug of lemonade.

"Well... we had an unusual call," the handsome officer began.

"What is your name?" Lillemor cut in. Her voice was cold and brittle now.

"Officer Damian Athol. Sorry." He nodded at Rodrigo and Lillemor.

Officer Laghari cleared her throat and scanned a small black moleskin notebook. "We had a call from a Mrs Pippins."

"At the Yeneral store in Hordola." Lillemor's breath was

short and her accent was thicker, warping her G's into Y's. Rodrigo placed a hand over hers. "Bea."

Officer Laghari remained calm. "She called us because she believed she had witnessed your daughter, Beatrix, being taken." Officer Laghari barely took a breath. "now, we don't know anything, so we came to check with you before we looked into this further." She held up a hand.

"We just need to ask a few questions." Officer Athol pursed his lips together in an attempt at a comforting smile. Officer Laghari watched the Braithewaites carefully. They were nervous and frightened, as she had expected, but they had exchanged a look that she couldn't quite place.

"We should get the boys in here, they were the ones who dropped her at Gordola earlier."

"ARTEMIS! ATLAS!" Lillemor screamed. Everyone jumped. The boys came skidding in. Officer Laghari was surprised to see two young men, twins. She had expected teenagers.

"Jeez, Mom, what?"

"Your sister has been taken," Lillemor snapped.

Officer Laghari caught it again, that look, quickly exchanged.

"We just need to ask a few questions. I'm Officer Athol, and this is Officer Laghari," said Athol, smiling again.

"Let's sit." Laghari motioned to the smooth, bleached dining table, free from clutter.

Bea heard the door go. She shifted herself to the very back of her crate. She wasn't afraid, but she wasn't a moron. A deathly silence fell over the room. Bea peered through the dim light. Were they going to bring the redheaded girl back?

Clunk. Scrape. Metal on metal. A padlock, Bea guessed, heavy duty, likely around some kind of catch.

The door was heavy, but wooden, not metal. The basement was cold and had a faint earthy odor. They were on an old farmstead, Bea guessed. None of the newer homes had basements like this. She hadn't heard or smelt any animals when she arrived, but they could just be somewhere else. So far there had been three men and one woman upstairs. There were at least six women down here. Weak, frightened women.

The house was big, but dilapidated. The people were dirty and unkempt. Not a lot of money; probably not selling the women, then. So not smart either, Bea wagered. That was a blessing and a curse.

Bea exhaled slowly, flexing each finger and toe, then both wrists and ankles.

'Jason' was back, the redheaded woman in tow. She was semi-conscious. Blood was trickling from cuts on her belly and arms. Her already dirty, ragged clothes were even more torn and skewed. Her face was puffy. Beaten, raped and tortured, Bea wagered. Bea was the 'new' toy, so whatever had happened to the girl, she was likely to face next.

Jason flung the woman back in her crate and stomped over to Bea. He licked his lips. Bea looked at him calmly.

"We're saving you," he chuckled.

Bea smiled. "Lucky you," she said coolly.

Jason was momentarily silent. He stared at her. "You'll see," he snapped menacingly before heading back upstairs.

Bea let out a dry laugh that followed him up the stairs and carried around the basement.

A faint smell of fatty bacon wafted down for a moment

and the sound of a screeching woman carried out of the kitchen. Bea looked around the room. Some of the women were staring at her.

Bea bit her lower lip. "I need you to do something for me," she began. Her voice was stilted. She didn't like speaking to big groups of people. "I... um... I need details."

There was silence. A cough. Then the ebony-skinned woman nodded. "There are six of them, that we know of," She began.

"Kidnapped?" Rodrigo's skin paled and his eyes widened.

"No... no, you don't understand," Lillemor began, but Rodrigo squeezed her hand.

"We understand that Beatrix has mental disabilities." Athol pursed his lips.

Atlas shook his head. "it's Bea."

"What?" Athol frowned.

"Her name, it's Bea, she doesn't like being called Beatrix," Atlas muttered.

"She does have some... mental peculiarities, not disabilities," Rodrigo said after a pause.

"The woman, Mrs Pippins, said Bea was very particular," Officer Laghari said delicately, "and she wouldn't have gotten in a car with anyone."

All the Braithewaites shook their heads and agreed. "No one," Lillemor repeated twice under her breath.

"A van..."

"Oh my god - a van!" Rodrigo half stood, his chair scraping on the floor. "There was a van?"

The officers looked at one another. "The van in question was a black Mercedes, fake plates," said Laghari. "Does Bea know..."

"No. She doesn't know anyone." Atlas looked pale and Artemis was swallowing the lump in his throat.

"We know sometimes... we have an idea of a family member," Officer Athol began.

"No, you don't understand." Rodrigo waved a hand at the officers. "What my son is trying to say is that Bea doesn't know more than a handful of people outside her family and medical staff because she has severe psychopathic and sociopathic tendencies."

"She... what?" Laghari stiffened in her seat.

Lillemor stood up and walked away from the table, "I need to call Anita and the doctor."

Laghari looked alarmed. "Ma'am, Mrs Braithewaite, we need you to keep..."

"No, you need to talk to them," Lillemor insisted.

LESSON NINE – SILENCE & NOISE

Bea walked slowly down the corridors of the facility in Gordola. The doctor had told her yesterday that he had been offered, and had taken, a position in a new facility in Virginia. He made it seem far more like he wasn't really being offered, but commanded. Bea didn't question him. She only had a few more months of treatment with him. Beyond that, she could travel to Virginia. The doctor had expressed his wishes for her to do so, and she would continue her weekly therapy with Anita.

A scream rang out and disappeared down one of the smaller arteries of the hospital.

Bea kept placing one foot in front of the other. She was heading to 'her' room. She was fairly certain no one else had treatments in her room. It felt like her hospital. The doctor was her doctor. How was she supposed to be any kind of normal without the regular treatments? How was she supposed to not kill someone?

Bea leant back in the chair. The treatment was new, experimental. That is why the doctor had been called to Virginia. More security. More funding. More lab rats to use.

"Are you ready?" The doctor and Anita were looking at her.

Bea nodded.

"Anything we need to know?" Anita smiled gently at Bea.

Bea gave a close-lipped smile back. Long ago, when she first started this, she found Anita's question and her smile each week incredibly annoying. Now it felt familiar, safe and overwhelmingly reassuring.

Bea nodded. "More thoughts. They're getting worse."

Anita nodded. She already knew.

Bea began strapping herself into the chair. Anita and the doctor leant their heads together and whispered. The doctor looked up at Bea, not quite alarmed, and then nodded at Anita.

"Okay. Let's begin," he said. His voice was a delicate tenor that carried across the room like a songbird.

Bea was 'in' a small room. Smaller than the pool shed at home. It was narrow, with tiny windows that were blacked with grease and covered with chicken wire. She looked around. They had used this one before. She sighed and wondered if she should stop the treatment.

She sniffed and walked forward, towards the back of the room where it was dark. There were panels that were loose and she could push them to get outside, into a derelict cityscape where murderers roamed the streets. Bea pushed on the broken wooden panels. They jiggled, but didn't move. Well, she thought, this was new.

She smiled. The doctor had some more tricks up his sleeve. Bea was turning when she felt a searing pain across her back. She heard shouting, indiscriminate and deafening, and she instinctively dropped low to the floor. It was stained with blood. That was still the same then.

Someone was moving around her, still yelling, but they had backed up a few feet and she heard clanking as they rifled through tools or weapons. Bea knew she had to act quickly, otherwise there would be more pain. She wasn't used to this. Usually it was 'suffer' or 'cause suffering'. A clear separation, but now the lines were blurred.

Bea felt a prickle. Excitement. Fear. Nerves. Desire. Her eyes narrowed as she skulked to the back of the room. She couldn't get out, so she needed a weapon. Her synapses bounced around from one thing to another, quickly making calculations. An image popped into her head, unbidden: Anita and the doctor, their heads bent together, moments before she entered the experimental 'murder' VR, whispering. Was this what they had been whispering about? Was this something new altogether?

PRESENT

Lillemor paced back and forth in the police station. The doctor had been notified and would be heading to Santa

Cruz as soon as he could get away from work. Anita was already on her way. The new puppy was asleep in a Louis Vuitton handbag that Lillemor had purchased, his snuffles dampened in the buttery leather.

The officers had gotten them all down there and locked them in some cramped 'family room', where they were being held. A small Keurig was tucked into one corner and a rotating stand held different K-Cups. A bowl of creamers sat beside that. The walls were a soft yellow and pale blinds, half closed, covered the outside windows. Pictures of nature and animals were dotted on the walls. There was a sofa, with one cushion and a freshly washed, though old, blanket draped over the back.

Lillemor flung the door open and the cheap plastic blind rattled. "Anita's parking," she announced.

Anita walked in a moment later. Her black yoga pants were dotted with dog hairs and her sweater sleeves were pushed up. Her hair was in a topknot and her usually calm face was scrunched with worry.

She embraced Lillemor and Rodrigo in turn. "What do we know?" she said, smiling at the twins.

"Nothing." Artemis shook his head.

"There was a van," Rodrigo said hollowly.

"Bea is a smart girl, we have to stay positive," Anita said firmly.

"The police aren't telling us something." Atlas stood up from the sofa. "I can tell that woman cop, Laghari - she knows more."

Both his parents stared at him. "Do you really think so?" Rodrigo asked.

Before Atlas could answer, Officers Laghari and Athol knocked on the door and immediately entered.

Officer Laghari looked at Anita. "Ah, you must be Dr Anita."

Anita smiled at the woman kindly. Officer Laghari's face remained stern as she surveyed Anita.

"We'd like to talk to the Braithewaites," Officer Athol began.

"You can talk to all of us," Rodrigo said angrily.

"She probably knows more about Bea anyway," Lillemor said with a mirthless laugh. "Poor Anita." Her breath caught and she turned to Anita and fell into her arms.

Anita made soothing sounds as the officers looked back and forth. "OK then," said Officer Laghari, "let's all remain in here."

"Tell us what's going on. You wouldn't bring us in here if this was just some random kidnapping," Atlas demanded.

Officer Athol cleared his throat as if to argue, but Officer Laghari held up a hand.

"You're right." She nodded, her face softening ever so slightly. "We came as soon as we received the call from Mrs Pippins, for two reasons. Firstly, your family is very well known." She paused for a long moment. "But we also believe Bea may have been abducted by a group who have also abducted at least twelve other women and girls."

"Twelve!" Lillemor looked horrified.

Anita narrowed her eyes. "Have any of these girls been found? Alive?"

"What?" Rodrigo turned to Anita.

"Do they still have all twelve of them, or have some been rescued, or... found?"

The officers looked at one another. "Some have been found," Officer Athol said quietly. "None alive."

"And the layout goes bedroom, bedroom, bathroom, unidentified room on the left, yes?" Bea was grilling one of the girls whose face she couldn't see.

"Yes... yes I think so." The girl swallowed nervously.

"This doesn't even matter." The redhead who had just returned had been silent during the hours while Bea had been absorbing information on who their captors were, on what they did to them, where they were, what was going on, and on and on Bea went with the questions. "They'll take you - and you'll see."

Bea turned in the direction of the cage where the redhead was held and stared at her blankly. "No, I won't," she snapped.

The redhead glared at her. "You don't even know!" she hissed. Gulping sobs leapt out of her throat.

Bea shook her head and snorted. "But I am about to, right? I mean, I'm not an idiot." She gave the redhead a black stare. The girl began to whimper and cry, but Bea turned away from her indifferently.

The door bolt scraped. Boots clunked.

The girls fell silent.

Bea stood up as best she could and shuffled to the front of her cage. She arched a brow at the redhead. The black girl gave her a nod, but her face was pained.

'Jason' and another man came downstairs. Judging from what the girls had told her, he was 'AK'.

"Mmm, all ready for us?" AK leered at Bea.

"You bet," Bea smiled. "Are you ready for me?" She tilted her head to one side.

Jason's face was red with anger. "Come on, bitch!" he snarled, unlocking her cage and grabbing her by the hair.

Bea relaxed and let herself be dragged from the basement. The only person who could see her face was the redhead. Through tear-filled eyes she could have sworn she saw Bea smiling.

LESSON TEN – TYGER, TYGER

Bea slumped back down in her seat. She had been forced to take core classes throughout university even though she felt them utterly useless, and had said so. Another hour wasted, Bea mused, as she watched the hands of the clock move at a glacial pace. English literature had to be her least favorite subject in the world. She didn't like English, or literature; in fact, if she was honest, she didn't like words at all.

The professor was handing out a little stack of papers, neatly stapled. He was a new professor. He was old, with wiry, unkempt salt and pepper hair. He was dressed in a way that was now stylish, albeit unintentionally: skinny pants, sharp-toed shoes, and a patched sweater that wasn't bought from an expensive store.

"You have a collection of great works in front of you." The professor smiled. "Some of them are excerpts, some poems, some non-fiction, just... greatness."

Bea's fourteen-year-old self resisted the urge to snort.

The other students looked rapt. Bea studied their faces.

"We will be reading them today and comparing them.

They all have something in common. I'll give you twenty minutes to read through them and make notes."

There was rustling, brief words, pencils and pens were exchanged. Bea quickly read the pieces but made no notes. She didn't know the answer; she wasn't going to waste brain cells coming up with incorrect theories.

"OK then," the Professor said after the excruciating twenty minutes was up. "Let's see what you've got."

An aggressively hipster girl with dreadlocks and a lip ring held up her hand frantically. "They're all about resilience," she said smugly as soon as the Professor nodded at her.

He pursed his lips. "Hmmm... well some of them are, but not all."

She opened her mouth to argue, but the Professor had turned away from her.

"They are all about God, or a higher power, in some way," a bespectacled boy said. He must have been twenty, but he looked fifteen.

"Very good, and?" the Professor pushed.

"Oh... um..." the boy blushed.

A preppy guy piped up. "They are about us - about humans and our... our, like... how we act."

A second later everyone was adding things into the conversation. Everyone except Bea, who had begun doodling a math formula at the bottom of her paper. Her idea that one could mathematically calculate serial killers' next moves had been getting a lot of attention recently. Schoolwork had taken a back seat.

She looked up to find the Professor staring at her. He raised his hands to shush the chaos. Students were bickering or waving their hands as they tried to make a point.

"OK, OK - settle down," he said.

"So what's the thing?" The preppy boy asked. "They're all about God, or Gods... or whatever, but what else?"

The Professor smiled. "Well, do you have any thoughts... Miss Braithwaite?"

Bea cringed. She felt eyes turning to her. She imagined the sound of eyeballs moving to be like nails on a blackboard.

"Nope." She shook her head.

"None?"

Bea looked at the poem that was first in the pamphlet: "The Tyger" by William Blake.

"It's about evil." She pointed to the paper.

"Good. Yes, all the pieces are in some way about evil, and also good." The Professor looked around the classroom.

A quiet girl raised her hand. She had black eyes and a blunt fringe. "Are they all about how good and evil can exist in the world at the same time... like... God creates both and we can choose..." She frowned as she searched for the word.

"Something to add, Miss Braithwaite?" The Professor was looking at her, and so was everyone else.

Bea looked up. "Huh?"

"You were shaking your head."

"Oh..." Bea tried to think of something to say other than what she had been thinking. "I was just going to say that they all seem to have an element of doubt."

"Doubt?" The hipster girl looked positively affronted.

"Yes, doubt." Bea replied crisply. "As in, how can you possibly believe in a God, if believing in him means you must also believe that everything dark and horrific and evil is done by design?"

There was a silence.

"Challenging the church?" The bespectacled boy had shifted straighter in his seat.

"More like challenging their own beliefs," the Professor said. "Very good." He began striding back and forth across the front of the room. "The cadence to all of them, you will also notice, is one of patience. All the authors of these pieces are questioning, but understand that they cannot come to conclusions without deep thought and time."

The preppy boy laughed, "So what? Like in the face of evil you've just got to be patient?"

The Professor fixed him with a serious stare. "Yes. Exactly."

PRESENT

Lillemor glared at Officer Laghari. They were back at their house, and a veritable command center had been set up in the Braithwaite's formal dining room. Laghari studiously ignored Lillemor.

Rodrigo had insisted they bring the investigation surrounding Bea back to the house, and that meant bringing a huge quantity of the investigation that revolved around the other girls back too. Laghari wasn't happy about it, but there wasn't much she could do against the Chief of Police's wishes: "Give Rodrigo Braithewaite whatever the fuck he wants for God's sake. Do you know how much he's donated and how much of the media he can get on his side?" Those had been the Chief's exact words. Apparently Lillemor wasn't happy about it either.

Artemis and Atlas were hovering, their faces pale, as the officers tacked up pictures to pinboards and splayed maps across the dining table.

"This is all my fault," Artemis murmured. "I shouldn't... I knew Gordola was a bad idea."

Officer Athol, not much older than the twins, had overheard and he beckoned the boys over to him. "This has nothing to do with you. I promise, you didn't cause this."

"But... but what if they were following us to get Bea?" Atlas was wide eyed.

"All evidence indicates these guys are picking girls at random, not ransom based. They didn't stake out and wait for Bea."

Lillemor cocked her head to one side. She was, or at least, she had been, the foremost astrophysicist back in Sweden, before she had had the kids. Her brain ticked so loudly Laghari could almost hear it. She looked questioningly at Lillemor.

"Why don't we offer a reward?" The word came out thick and heavy with Lillemor's accent.

"They aren't..."

"I know they aren't looking for a ransom." She cut Athol off. "But they might be inclined to think about it if it's big enough."

There was a silence in the room. Then a clean, clear voice carried across it. "She was abducted 24 hours ago. I'd wager her captors don't have much more than that left." The doctor had arrived.

When Bea was finally brought back downstairs even the black girl, who had been there the longest, was shocked. Her hair was red with blood, both eyes blackened and her lower lip swollen and split. Her arms, legs and torso were riddled with cuts, one of which, on her thigh, bulged strangely. She shuffled slowly, from pain, the girls knew, right down in her pelvis and abdomen.

Jason threw her in her cage. "Thought that might shut you up," he leered.

There was silence and Jason began ascending the stairs. He reached the door.

"Just promise me you'll come back and do that again tomorrow," Bea said, voice husky.

The door was flung open to a brief snapshot of sound from upstairs, then it slammed and scraped as it was locked.

"Oh, are you..." One of the girls began.

Bea let out a low frightening laugh that sent the hairs on the other girls' necks upright. They couldn't see through the gloom into her crate. She took off her bloodstained shirt and carefully spit on her hand, then wiped her face so that it looked better. She needed them to pick her again tomorrow. She needed it more than she had realized. "Oh, I'm better than ever," she said, repeating her manic laugh. In the darkness, she squeezed the bulging cut in her leg until the small buck knife emerged, folded, out of it. She placed it carefully to one side, and then continued to groom herself back to presentable.

LESSON ELEVEN – THE DOCTOR

"What was the goal then?" Bea asked calmly. She had wanted this visit to be more than it had been. Virginia had been a disappointment. It was too hot and the new facility was full of unrecognizable faces and rooms. "What was the goal with me?"

"There was no goal, Bea," the doctor replied.

"Really?"

"I wanted to help. I want to help."

"But you can't, can you?" Bea shrugged. "I mean... I'm not getting any better. I wouldn't say that I'm worse, but I am certainly not better."

"You can't say that," the doctor insisted, rising from his chair.

"Oh really, can't I?" Bea said, back to her usual cool indifference. "Do I still want to hurt other people? Yes. Do I still want to kill people? Why yes, I do. Do I understand any human emotions yet? No, I do not," she finished witheringly.

"But you haven't, Bea. That is why we know the treatments are working. Because you haven't hurt or killed anyone." The doctor waved his hands vigorously at Bea's file that lay, papers scattered, on his desk.

"Yet," Bea said darkly.

"Yet?"

"I haven't killed anyone... yet."

PRESENT

"What are they doing to her?" The red-haired girl whimpered.

"Why did they even take her again? They never normally go back to back." The black girl shook her head.

"She kept antagonizing them." Another girl shook up from the cage beside Bea's. "Like she wanted them to take her."

"We're never going to get out of here," the red haired girl sobbed. "Never. Never!"

"That's enough," the black girl chided. "Listen.." she began. Another horrific scream came from upstairs.

The girls collectively shuddered. They never normally heard one another during the 'sessions', but now, screams and thuds carried into the chilly basement every five minutes. Guttural and pained, each scream sounded like it would be the last, but on and on they went for hours.

Rodrigo leant close to the doctor. "Do you think... she has... a chance?" He knew about what had happened in each of the sessions with the doctor, but he didn't know how relevant it would be in helping Bea.

"I do." The doctor spoke slowly and carefully.

Anita came over and leant her head in close. Lillemor and the boys had finally passed out in the den.

"If she gets a chance, there's no telling what she'll do," Anita said softly.

"She might not even be able to separate reality from her VRs, depending..."

"Depending on what they've done to her? My god, I never thought I'd say this, but why shouldn't she?" Rodrigo fumed. "Why shouldn't she fuck up those sick bastards?"

Anita placed a hand on his arm. "Shhh, Rodrigo." She glanced at Laghari and Athol, who were looking curiously at the three of them.

"It would still be murder," Anita said after a pause.

"What?" Rodrigo looked furious.

"If she does something to them, whoever they are, it would still be murder."

The doctor lowered his voice even further. "It would be self-defense."

"If she killed them, yes," the doctor said. "But I don't think…" He sucked in his cheeks. "Once she gets going, I don't think she would be able to just kill them."

"But…" Rodrigo looked panicked.

"This is all hypothetical," Anita reminded them. "The police are working hard to find her."

"Oh my god, she wouldn't even know… she just… this is on you," Rodrigo said with a low growl. He glared at the doctor for a moment, and then marched off to the kitchen.

"Is it?" Anita looked up at the doctor.

"Maybe." He nodded to himself.

"We couldn't have known something like this, I mean…" Anita widened her eyes and motioned to the police and the evidence boards.

"No. We could not have." The doctor licked his lips. "I read about the bodies. The other ones they found that they think are connected to Bea's disappearance."

Anita didn't ask how he had got hold of that information. "And?"

"And if she does do something, she will be one hundred percent justified."

Anita swallowed. Tears slipped from her lower eyelids and streamed down her cheeks.

72 HOURS LATER
Interview One – Abigail Monroe

Officer Laghari pointed to the recording device. "It's OK if I record this?" She gave the girl a half-smile. The girl in front of her was brunette, too thin, and had been held for four months, the longest of all the girls. She was exceptionally attractive, with large doe eyes, Cupid's bow lips and a smattering of freckles on her cheeks and nose. Laghari resisted the urge to wrinkle her nose. The abductors had liked the pretty ones. Pretty, and just legal.

Abigail nodded and pursed her lips. The room was bare, with two chairs and a wooden table. She was holding a large hot chocolate. Not from the station either. Someone had gone and gotten them coffees and whatever else they wanted from Starbucks.

"No one can be in here with me, can they?" she said.

"Like your Mom and Dad?" Officer Laghari frowned. Abigail nodded. "No. But you aren't in any trouble, we are just trying to figure out what happened."

Abigail nodded wearily and sipped her drink.

"Let's get started."

Officer Laghari: So, you were held for four months? I'm afraid you will have to answer rather than nod or shake your head.

Abigail: Yes.

Officer Laghari: And you didn't know any of the other girls?

Abigail: No.

OL: Did you ever try to escape?

A: No.

OL: Why not?

A: When I arrived... there were two other girls. They both disappeared. They told me there were six people, or maybe five holding us. I was too scared."

OL: I understand. You are incredibly strong and brave to have survived for so long. Can you tell me about the other night?

A: When we were rescued?

OL: Before that, before anyone came to help you.

A: How much before? It's hard... I lost track of time.

OL: I understand. I just meant, earlier, like 24 hours before.

A: They took the new girl... it was bad. She was in bad shape. I thought they might have killed her by accident.

OL: By accident?

A: They usually like to keep us... keep the girls for a while.

OL: I see. So they took her and brought her back?

A: Mmm hmm. Yes. And later, I don't know how long, we heard screaming and banging... we didn't know what was happening. It was all a blur. I was trying to stay conscious.

OL: And then you were let out of the cages you were being held in?

A: I think so.

OL: When you went upstairs, do you remember that? Do you remember seeing anything?

A: Mmm... there was a lot of blood.

OL: From your abductors?

A: I think so.

OL: Someone had mutilated them, killed them (paper rustles as Laghari moved her notes). Someone ripped out fingernails... drove nails into them, gouged out eyeballs... They were tortured for a long time.

A: No... not long enough. I think I'm done... I don't know anything.

OL: You don't know who did this?

A: No. I just want to go home.

Officer Laghari switched off the recorder. "Thanks for talking to us, Abigail."

Abigail nodded wearily as Laghari indicated the ceiling cam. The family liaison officer came in with Abigail's parents. They rushed to hug her, again, and she stiffened.

"Can we take Abby home?" Mr Monroe asked. He was chubby and balding with a helpful face.

"Yes. If we have any more questions, we can give you a call."

"Of course." Mrs Monroe said, as they ushered Abigail from the room.

"If you think of anything else..." Laghari didn't know why she bothered to continue, the girl's face had shut down completely, "just let us know."

Interview Two – Felicity Fernville

Felicity looked at the young police officer. He swallowed a few times and offered her another drink. She lifted her Starbucks cup at him in reply.

"Of course." He nodded quickly and sat down across from her.

Felicity was the most groomed of all the girls. Her

mother, a single parent and a beautician, had taken the time to cut, color and wash her hair, do her nails, fix her eyebrows and put her in a new set of clothes. She had peroxide blonde hair, wide set brown eyes and a now skinny frame. There was something alien about her, Officer Athol thought.

"It's OK to record this," she said quickly. Felicity had already spotted the recorder when she was escorted into the room, now she just wanted to get this over with.

Officer Athol: OK... OK then, let's get started.

Felicity: OK.

Officer Athol: Can you tell me how long you were held?

Felicity: I think a month or so... maybe.

OA: And how... do you remember being abducted?

Felicity: I was coming home from work. I work at a vet practice on weekends. I cut through a side alley. They grabbed me.

OA: They?

F: Mmm hmm... more than one. I don't know. There were a lot of them at the house.

OA: OK, can you tell me a little bit about the last week at the house?

F: Do... do you know what they did to us?

OA: (coughing) Yes, the doctors told us.

F: But... do you get it? Do you get what it does?

OA: No.

F: I can't remember much. Just pain. Fear. Trying to block it out. Switching between wanting to live and wanting to die.

OA: Anything you can tell us…

F: They're all dead, right? What difference does it make? (Felicity sighs heavily.)

OA: The people who abducted and tortured you, they had been tortured.

F: I know. I saw it.

OA: You saw?

F: As I was leaving. One of them, Jason, he was the worst one… he had his dick cut off; there was blood all down his thighs. It had been shoved down his throat. Something was wrong with his face… like it had no skin.

OA: (rustles his papers) Did you see anything else?

F: The woman… she used to laugh at us when she would see us being raped. Her tongue was nailed to the dining table. All her fingernails were ripped out… chunks of her scalp gone. I didn't see the others.

OA: And the person who let you out?

F: I didn't see them. We were all panicking… running around. We couldn't think straight. Last thing I remember was Stacy pulling me out and up the stairs.

OA: And the torture? You remember seeing that?

F: Yes… yes I do.

Felicity had glowed when she mentioned the torture in a way that alarmed Officer Athol. She didn't seem horrified by it, or even remotely shaken.

"We're all done," he said.

"OK." Felicity stood up from the table. "I can go?" But she left before he could reply.

Interview Three – Diana Hamlin

"Diana Hamlin?"

"You can call me Deedee," the girl said. She was petite, Eurasian, with a sharp bob and a nasty laceration under one eye. Her voice was soft and melodious, when she spoke, which was rare.

"I'm Officer Laghari, and I just need to ask you a few questions."

OL: OK, you were taken just outside the Santa Cruz campus?

Diana: Yes.

OL: And held for three weeks?

Diana: Yes.

OL: Can you tell me a little bit about the past 72 hours, Deedee?

D: I... um... I don't know much. Stacy knows more, she was there for a really long time. They took her the most. She took care of us.

OL: Anything you can tell me can help.

D: Help with what?

OL: Help catch the person or persons who killed-

D: (whispering) the abductors.

OL: What?

D: You want to catch whoever killed the abductors... I just don't know why.

OL: We're just trying to figure out what happened.
        And the person who killed the abductors... well,
        they did some bad things.
D: They can't be that bad.
OL: (Sighing angrily) One of the men had had all his
        teeth ripped out, and his hands, feet and genitals
        burned with a blowtorch. He was finished off by
        someone cutting out his tongue with a pair of
        secateurs.
D: I don't... I don't think I can... I want to leave
        now.
OL: Can you tell me anything else about what
        happened two nights ago, Deedee?
D: (muffled crying) No. I can't

Officer Laghari met up with Officer Athol outside the
interview rooms. "None of them are talking," she fumed.

"None of them know anything."

"So they say."

"Why are we interrogating them like this, Karina?"

"You know perfectly well why, Damian. You've got
LouAnne Och next, the redhead. She's scared. She might be
the one who breaks."

Interview Four – LouAnne Och

Officer Athol frowned. LouAnne Och had been escorted into
the station by her father and three older brothers, all of
whom were extremely rankled that she had to be dragged
through this process. All of whom seemed more than happy
about the deaths of the abductors, or as one of them put it,

"I only hope you find him so I can thank the guy".

LouAnne was eighteen, with milk white skin and frizzy red hair. She was slightly soft around the edges, and her round face was angelic.

OA: I just need you to tell me what happened, LouAnne.

LouAnne: (sniffling) I don't know much... what they did to us...

OA: I know... I know (rustling)

LouAnne: (Blowing her nose) I was there for a week... not like some of the others. I heard that some of the girls had been there for months... I can't... I...

OA: I just need you to tell me about the past few days.

LA: When Bea arrived?

OA: Sure, let's start there.

LA: She wasn't afraid.

OA: Of your abductors?

LA: Of anything. Of them, of the torture... I thought she was fakin' it, but even after they got her the first time she didn't care.

OA: The first time? I thought she was only taken once?

LA: She was - I meant, usually we all got taken a few times. Her first time she got taken she wasn't scared.

OA: So she wasn't taken upstairs by your abductors again.

LA says nothing.

OA: You have to verbally respond, LouAnne.

LA: No, she wasn't.

OA: OK, so then you were all downstairs for the night and then you started hearing screams and banging?

LA: Uh huh.

OA: And how long did that last?

LA: I dunno... like twelve hours, maybe more. It was hard to tell times.

OA: What did you think was happening?

LA: That they were... that they had another girl. Got another girl or something.

OA: OK. So then, the person, whoever it was, came downstairs. Were you scared?

LA: No.

OA: You weren't scared of a new person coming downstairs?

LA: No. I want to leave.

OA: Oh, OK. I just have a few more questions.

LA: No. I wasn't scared. What else were they gonna do? Stacy had been looking after me, after all of us. She said, what else are they gonna do, kill us? (long silence) I wanna leave. NOW!

Officer Athol stepped back from the table and LouAnne screamed. "OK, OK!" He raised his hands in surrender. Shouting carried in from outside. Someone yelling LouAnne's name.

"Daddy!" she yelled, rushing the door. She yanked it open and fell into his arms.

"Haven't you done enough?" shouted LouAnne's father. "You fuckers didn't even find our girls, and now you're after the goddamned hero who did?"

The family liaison stepped in and ushered the Och family to the door, murmuring words of comfort that seemed to soothe them. Officer Laghari looked at LouAnne, and then at Stacy. An infinitesimal nod passed between the girls. Then, LouAnne was gone.

"Fuck." Laghari rubbed her eyes.

"I know, she definitely said 'first time'. I questioned her about it, but that's when she shut down."

"Fuck and double fuck," Laghari muttered. "Chief's here."

"Oh fuck." Damian snapped his head around.

"Athol. Laghari." Chief Whipplewhitt stepped into the task room and looked at them both witheringly. "Still questioning the victims, I see."

"Sorry to interrupt, mind if I come in?" Andi, the family liaison officer stepped into the room.

"It's fine." Whipplewhitt smiled at the petite woman. Her smooth skin glowed and her cornrows were pulled back to reveal sharp cheekbones, pearly teeth and enchanting yellow-brown eyes.

"Look Chief, something happened in that house..." Laghari ignored the Chief's raised eyebrows, "other than what happened to those girls. I mean... someone used a power sander to sand off one of their faces. Jesus, the vice, the scalping. Without any hesitation? I mean, who was this person? Some vigilante who we're just going to let go?"

"Well that isn't your theory, is it now Laghari?" The Chief cut right through her bluster.

"I just think, with all things considered..."

"If we could see her medical records..." Officer Athol began.

"Well you can't. The girl was raped, beaten and tortured, and, I feel like I shouldn't need to mention this again, her father is Rodrigo Braithewaite. I do not want you to push this. You have no evidence, no proof, nothing. Do you hear me Laghari? Jesus! I mean, Beatrix is 120lbs soaking wet, how exactly did she get control over five people, four of whom were adult men?"

"Sir, we have to finish questioning them," she replied stiffly.

The Chief muttered something under his breath that sounded like "I'll fucking scalp you", but Karina Laghari ignored it. "Fine. Fine," he went on. "But so help me God, if this goes fucking sideways, it's your ass on the line."

Interview Five – Stacy Baker

Officer Laghari smiled at the gorgeous, albeit emaciated, black girl sitting out front of the interview room. Her parents were sitting with her, quiet and calm. She herself seemed calm, although Laghari had noticed a faint tremble when she sipped her coffee. "Ready?" he asked.

Stacy nodded and stood, and that was when Laghari noticed the unmistakable bump of pregnancy under her T-shirt.

OL: I'll try to make this as fast as possible.

Stacy: That's OK. I've not got anywhere to be.

OL: If you need anything, or need a break... just let me know.

Stacy: (laughs softly) Cause I'm pregnant? Don't worry about it too much, Officer. I'm getting an abortion.

OL: Just... let me know. You were held for three months? That must've been hard.

S: It wasn't easy.

OL: Can you tell me about the past three, four days?

S: (sighs and lets out a laugh) You mean since Bea arrived?

OL: You know her name?

S: Yeah. Our cages faced one another. The way they were set up, it was easiest for us to talk.

OL: And did you?

S: Yeah. I told her what they were gonna do to her.

OL: Really? Why?

S: She wanted to know.

OL: Did you think that was strange?

S: Not really, I mean... fear of the unknown is the worst kind, right? Can't prepare for it.

OL: So you told her what would happen to her for when she was taken?

S: Yes.

OL: And the second time she was taken, was she 'prepared' by then?

S: She was only taken once.

OL: You know Stacy, one of the men was found in a bedroom. Someone had slit his abdomen and pulled his organs out slowly. Whoever it was had gone to the trouble of shooting nails into all his finger nails and toe nails.

S: Sounds like someone really didn't like him. Can't say I blame them.

OL: Doesn't that scare you? That someone could do that?

S: No. What humans can do no longer scares me at all, Officer. Doesn't that scare you?

OL: So Bea was taken, and then returned to the basement.

S: Yup.

OL: You all heard screaming, banging, anything else?

S: Shouting. Pleading. We all thought they had another girl.

OL: More than one girl upstairs?

S: (chuckle) No, another poor soul like the rest of us, to be slung in the basement like an animal.

OL: And then this mystery person let you out?

S: Yup.

OL: Any idea who it was?

S: Nope... fuzzy pregnancy brain I guess.

OL: Did you know one of the men, the one... AK? His legs were crushed in a vice. An eye was gouged out. He was whipped with electrical cables. Doused in brake fluid.

S: uh huh.

OL: Was he the worst one?

S: What?

OL: Did he treat you the worst?

S: I guess. None of them were exactly Prince Charming.

OL: Hmm. It seems like someone, whoever it was, really had it in for him.

S: You think Jason got off easy? Half his face was sanded off and he had been choked to death with his own dick. Hah. (sharp laughter)

OL: You saw that?

S: We all did.

OL: And you don't think the person who did that should be caught? You don't think it's scary that someone like that is free in the world?

S: Officer, I am pregnant by some hillbilly cunt, which one? I don't fucking know. I have spent the last three months in a cage. I have a law degree, I know how it works, but believe me, there is no one who deserved that kind of death and torture more.

OL: The person, whoever, killed the woman too.

S: (a chair scrapes as Stacy stands) Good. I told them I was a virgin. I wasn't lying. You want to know what she said? She told them to make sure that the word 'virgin' was no longer in my vocabulary, ever again.

Interview Six – Beatrix Braithewaite

"Beatrix?" Officer Athol smiled warmly at her.

"This way." Officer Laghari motioned to the interview room.

"Ah, I get the double. Special me," Bea murmured.

"Can I come with her?" Lillemor reached out for her child but didn't make contact. Consciously, carefully didn't make contact, Laghari noticed.

"I'm afraid not."

"It's fine. I'll be right back." Bea smiled wolfishly and turned back to the officers. Officer Athol smiled dumbly back at her and Laghari wanted to hit him. There was no denying how attractive the girl was. Long caramel hair, smooth skin, a delicate nose and emerald eyes sat in a Slavic face. Her body was powerful and muscular. Her hair was pulled back into a ponytail, nothing hiding the black eyes or her bruised face and neck. She moved gracefully, oblivious to her injuries. The others had winced a little, looked away, embarrassed to be victims, to know that others knew what had happened to them.

Officer Laghari clicked the recorder on, although she had a feeling this was a conversation she would never forget.

OL: Ok Bea, can I call you Bea or Beatrix?

Bea: Bea is fine.

OL: I'm Karina, and this is Damian. We just want to ask you a few questions.

Bea: OK.

OL: You were held for five days.

Bea: One hundred and three hours.

OA: You counted?

B: I like math.

OA: You work at UC Berkeley in applied mathematics?

B: Yes.

OL: You also work on a private project where you work out the statistical likelihood of serial killer attacks, and how and when active serial killers will strike again, don't you?

B: It sounds like you already know the answer, but yes. It's a hobby.

OL: Pretty strange hobby for a twenty-year-old?

B: I know that you know that I have sociopathic and psychopathic tendencies. Anita and the doctor are here.

OL: Hmm... it's almost like, of all the people in the world who could be called a serial killer tactician, it would be you.

B: Almost. (Laughing) I'll have to tell Anita and Rajul that when they tell me to stop with the serial killer math. Tactician sounds much more normal. Almost like a job a qualified professional would have?

OL: Almost.

OA: Bea, can you tell us about what happened for the 103 hours you were held?

B: Well, I take it you know what they did to us, so can I safely assume you want to know if I have any insights into what happened to them?

OL: You seem very calm for someone who has gone through so many traumas.

B: Not as much as Stacy, or... the others.

OL: Nevertheless, still a lot.

B: Do you know the traits of people with sociopathic and psychopathic tendencies, Karina? I'm going to make another assumption and say you do. In which case, my calmness should be par for the course.

OL: Did the contact bother you?

B: The what?

OL: The physical contact with your abductors.

OA: We can take a break if you need it, Bea.

B: It was necessary.

OA: What?

B: They had deemed contact necessary to their endeavors. And I wouldn't go too far down this route, since you're asking me to say whether or not I was OK being raped and tortured. I can't think of a good outcome for you on that line of questioning. (Shuffling papers. Athol coughs and sips his coffee)

OL: Do you know what happened to them? Did you see?

B: Some of it. Not all.

OL: Which?

B: Jason. The woman. They were the only ones in the kitchen.

OL: How do you know that?

B: Because we left through the kitchen when our mystery savior let us out.

OA: And you didn't see who it was?

B: Oh no, no I didn't see a thing. (Laghari snorts)

OL: So no one saw anything? Do you know what happened to those people? Half of them were partially scalped, burned, sodomized with farm equipment, lacerated, eyes gouged out...

B: I'd shed a tear for them, but I think I'm all out. If you don't have any more questions, officers, I really don't have anything else to tell you.

"Fuck." Laghari fumed. "She's going to get away with it." They were watching the Braithwaites leave the station.

"It might not have been her, Karina," Damian said, "I mean, how did a girl her size subdue five people?"

"She has advanced martial arts training, intelligence and tactics on her side. I mean, yes, it's crazy, but not impossible. What if she had a weapon? She could have gotten her hands on one, then taken them out one by one?" Karina slapped a hand on the desk. "I don't know!"

"We can keep looking, but the crime scene is a mess. There is enough DNA to populate a small country and no way we can pinpoint hers. All the girls' DNA was on all the dead bodies."

Karina shook her head and pushed away the mug of cold, stale coffee. "Y'know the worst part? At the end of the interview when I listed the torture, she looked fucking happy. Gleeful... no, she looked like she was reveling in it."

48 HOURS EARLIER

"Hmm, only peanut butter. I shall have to add that to your

list of transgressions. I'm not a big fan of the stuff," Bea said as she carefully smoothed the peanut butter she had found across a slice of bread. She took a bite and felt her stomach cinch hungrily. "Although, I must say, right now, it tastes pretty good."

"Please... please..."

"You know what always bothers me about all those crime shows?"

"I don't... I'll do... whatever... just..." Jason lisped. One of his lips was hanging off.

"It always bothers me that every single time they find out who the killer is there is always some hideous backstory that 'made' the person into a monster. Was that how it was with you?"

"Ungh... please..."

"Come on now, this is your chance. Tell me. Was there something that sparked it in you? Or, were you just 'like' this?"

"I don't know," Jason whimpered. Blood dribbled out from the raw wounds on his face. The long nail that was driven through his penis into the chair wasn't moving, not that he could anyway; his hands were lashed to the kitchen chair.

"You don't know?"

"I think I was just... I'm just like this."

"Mmm, me too. I was just like this." Bea strolled around the back of his chair and fluttered a hand through his dirty, straw colored hair. She felt him stiffen even though he attempted to remain still.

"I wonder if she was just like this." Bea indicated the woman, whose name she still didn't know. Her face was mottled with blood and saliva. Her scalp hung off the back of her head. "I forgot to ask her."

"Please…"

"Stop whining!" Bea chided Jason. She looked around the kitchen. She was down two, and once she was done with Jason, she only had AK and the old man left. She was saving AK till last. They had gone down like flies. She had just ticked them off, one, two, three, subduing them, tying them up, and then going back and taking her time to savor the fun. "I shouldn't tell you this, Jason, but I have a feeling you won't tell." Bea leant in close with the knife; a big Bowie she had found in one of the rooms.

"Please," Jason whimpered as Bea knelt down by his crotch.

"I consider you abducting me a golden opportunity. It's almost like… it's almost like fate, which I don't believe in, set this up for me." Bea giggled. "Now," she looked down, "I don't think you'll be needing this anymore."

Jason began to scream. AK writhed in the vice, desperately moving his body to try and loosen the ties around his wrists.

"Fucking bitch," he muttered.

"That's not very nice," Bea said from the doorway.

"How the fuck you get out, anyway?" AK was playing for time. The vice around his left shin was tight, but not doing any damage. His eyes flicked down to it.

"Oh, yes, I'd forgotten about that," Bea said, as she carefully slid the knife down the plastic cover of the electrical cable. She peeled off the outer layer and then placed the long, whip like material on the workbench. AK eyed it suspiciously.

"I thought you were into kink, AK?" Bea taunted him. She was bone tired, and she knew she would have to let the girls out soon. She and Stacy already had a plan. Stacy should be doing her part right now. Bea already knew she would. She would have done it for free, but Bea had figured she'd sweeten the deal.

"Time for a little security. Can't have you hopping out of my clutches." Bea smiled as she tightened the vice. AK did try not to scream, but once his shin and ankle started to splinter he let out an ear-splitting howl.

"Fuck!" He spat at her when she finally paused.

"To answer your earlier question, I got out because my IQ is higher than those of your entire inbred family added together." Bea looked at him sweetly.

"Ahhh!" AK had tried to wrench himself out of the vice.

"I saved you for last, AK. Doesn't that make you feel special?"

"The police are gonna get you for this, bitch."

"No they're not. The crime scene was already destroyed... thanks for that by the way. Too much DNA. No witnesses."

"The girls."

"Ah yes, the girls you abducted, raped and tortured definitely don't want to see you punished." Bea's voice dripped with sarcasm.

AK fell silent.

"See, that's the other problem will all these TV shows, Jason and I were talking about this earlier, the end of the story is always the police saving the day... like that makes everyone sleep better at night. The cops getting the bad guys."

"Fuck you, bitch!" AK screamed.

Bea tightened the vice incrementally. "Or the victim kills them in some feeble last fight scene - a gunshot in a moment of panic."

"I'm gonna fucking kill you!" AK grunted. Sweat poured from his face and he gritted his teeth together.

Bea leant close, so close they were nose to nose, and she brought one hand to his throat. "No AK, you're not. See, that is why this is so satisfying, because no one is coming to save you and I won't be punished for this, and you, and all your family, are getting exactly what they deserve."

She let his neck go and his head snapped back.

"Now, enough chit chat. I'm not usually a talker." Bea turned away and picked up the electrical cables. She unscrewed the cap on some brake fluid and left it ready on the workbench. "I just figured I probably wouldn't meet many others like me again," she mused quietly.

"Look... just... just let me go." In desperation, AK had turned to wheedling.

Bea turned to him, her face serene. "No." She swished the electrical cables in the dirt. "I've always wanted to try this."

THEORY 2.0

Hope rolled over and swiped her phone. She fumbled and the phone dropped on to the floor, still bleeping. She leant halfway out of bed and grabbed it. Rolling onto her back, she relaxed into her pillow. Yawning, she swiped right and blinked her eyes open properly. Her phone background was a foliage-carpeted archway that looked out towards a solitary white beach and tropical blue seas. She had taken the photo on a trip to Thailand four years ago.

"That's a whole lotta nope," she groaned. It was a fucking Saturday and she had forgotten to turn off her work alarm. "Nope." She rolled sideways, still clutching her phone, and nestled into a fetal position.

Hope opened her gmail first, like always, and deleted the junk. Sale emails, random notifications, some group threads that she didn't really need to be cc'd in on. Then she checked Instagram, Snapchat and Twitter. She scrolled slowly down, randomly hitting 'like' here and there. She went back out to her homescreen. She swiped across the two pages of apps, back and forth, wilfully ignoring the pink and blue globe emblazoned with the engraved style 'T'. She chewed her lower lip.

Hope shifted in her bed, pushing herself out of the swirl of blankets, and leant back against the pillow. She had arrived back home from a three-week trip to South Africa five days before. Since then, she had spent the entire week in the Edinburgh office, calling vendors and clients, sorting out her agenda, setting up meetings for next week. She deserved a lazy day. She deserved a day to just do whatever she wanted.

A minute later, she clicked on the colorful globe. Butterflies fluttered in her stomach.

"Hope?" came a voice from the other side of her bedroom door.

Hope bit her lips together and gripped her phone tightly.

"Hope darling?" The thick wooden door muffled her mum's voice.

Hope had moved back to Edinburgh from Australia six months before. She was trying to find a place to live, but she refused to buy somewhere that wasn't exactly what she wanted.

"Yeah Mum?" She was about to add that she was having a lie in.

"Did I wake you?"

"Nope. What's up?"

"Can I come in?"

Hope slammed her head silently back into the pillow. "What do you want, Mum?"

"Don't get your knickers in a twist. I just wanted to tell you that your father and I are going out for a wee walk with Greyfriar."

Her mum sounded miffed as she huffed and puffed her way out of the house. She heard her dad's thick Scottish accent as he wound up the dog, repeatedly saying 'walkies' to the poor terrier in a silly high-pitched voice.

Hope relaxed back into her bed. "Oh my god. Just take the damn dog out," she muttered. She needed to find her own place today. She was starting to think that perfect was anywhere but living at home with her parents at thirty-one.

She swiped right without thinking. She held her breath as the screen came alive.

THEORY 2.0 was emblazoned at the top of her iPhone. Below it a series of videos played on loops. She was on her daily feed. Hope exhaled. The videos were neat squares and ran from between 30 seconds to 10 minutes. Alice Beasley had posted one five minutes ago, of herself, leaving her house with a full face of make-up and bumping in to Jason Armor, the celebrity of the moment. He smiled dreamily at her and then asked her out. Hope watched it and scanned Alice's sarcastic comment "So glad I didn't wear make up to grab milk this morning… " Three blushing and three facepalm emojis were beside it. It had already been liked 47 times. Someone had commented "OMG I can't believe you saw JA tho! That's still awesome!"

Hope was about to keep scrolling when her phone buzzed. "What up?" she said, smiling.

"Nothing," Sarah replied. "Just saw your mum and dad out… surprised you weren't with them for a brisk walkie!"

"Fuck off." Hope smiled. Sarah knew how Hope was suffering being back at home. She hadn't lived at home since she was twenty-one.

"What you doing?"

"Scrolling Theory. Alice Beasley bumped into Jason Armor this morning."

"Yeah, I saw that." Sarah's voice was strangely tight.

"You OK?"

"I'm taking a social media break."

"Cool." Hope didn't use social media much, but she knew Sarah struggled with body image. "You OK?"

"Yeah, I mean IG and stuff, it's just... y'know? Well you don't know because you are always off someplace amazing and I just... Theory is the worst, I just need to delete it. I just like... I hate seeing all those choices I could've made played out. Or like... all the fake... 'Look how shitty my life could've been' ones that are obviously kinda staged, but... whatever." She laughed suddenly. It was a shrill, sharp laugh and Hope leant away from her phone.

"I get it."

"Hmmm." Sarah sighed. "Well anyway, I wondered if you wanted to have some lunch and... dun dun daaa... I think I have found your dream home."

"Don't tease me, temptress." Hope swung her legs out of bed and padded to her door. She poked her head out to make sure her parents were gone.

"I'm serious."

"Then obviously yes, where do I buy you champagne and when can I move in?"

Sarah laughed, a real, happy laugh. "Let's meet for lunch at Café Andaluz on George Street?"

"Perfect, one?"

Sarah agreed and hung up. Hope put on her running gear and looked at the chart on her wall. A twelve-mile run. She was competing in the Hawaii Ironman later in the year. "Not too bad," Hope assured herself as she dressed.

Her phone lay face up on the bed. The videos from Theory still scrolled down, each being bumped by the next post every few seconds. Celebrities posting their 'what if' moments, friends, family members, even her work colleagues.

Hope picked it up. She clicked a small pin icon in the top right that took her to her home screen. A glut of brightly-colored videos with a play arrow on them filled the screen like a jigsaw. Most of the play arrows were blue, indicating that they had been watched, but four bright pink ones lit up the top row.

Hope's finger danced over each one and a title came up.

What if you hadn't moved back from Australia?

What if you'd talked to that cute client from work the other day?

What if you got a cat?

What if you see Michael this weekend?

Hopes gut churned. Every day. Every damn day. She looked down at the videos that sat on a random, frozen still. Half of them, at least, were of Michael.

What if you talked to Michael?

What if you called Michael?

What if you and Michael hadn't broken up ten years ago?

What if you had got back together at the end of uni?

What if you had stayed?

Hope angrily clicked on the 30-second video *What if you*

got a cat? It played; her and a ridiculously cute fluffy kitten in a rustic, yet modern flat, padding around and getting breakfast. Hope in her pajamas eating toast and drinking coffee as the kitten wove between her ankles. A bright Scottish sun, just like the one this morning, beaming in through high windows. The kitten chasing a small toy across the wooden floorboards.

Hope looked at the other three videos. She closed the app, synched her headphones and raced out into the fresh chill of the Scottish summer morning.

Bryn Hartshaw looked out of the windows of the real estate agency and let his mind drift blissfully to a tropical beach somewhere. The boss was out of town for the week so he, Archie and Sarah were keeping the office nice and relaxed.

He turned to Sarah and Archie. "How was your weekend?"

Archie was leaning back in his chair sipping a Pret coffee and fiddling around with his phone.

"Good. Went out. Had a shit Tinder date, watched rugby." He grinned. Sarah raised her eyebrows at him. She wondered if every date was 'shit' for Archie because he was a posh twat with a big ego.

"Lovely." She flicked over the paperwork on her desk and continued scribbling. "Well, I closed on the Great King Street property."

"Really?" Archie looked up from his phone. "Who?"

"A good friend actually, from school." She replied loftily.

"From school?" Bryn leant forward with knitted eyebrows. "But that place is like 1.5 mil, isn't it?"

"Yep." Sarah carried on with her paperwork.

"Jesus... so, who's your friend?" Archie had a smug smile on his face.

"No one you know."

"Was it that girl, woman, I mean..." Bryn blushed. His sister hated it when he called grown women 'girls'. "That woman who you were having lunch with on Saturday?"

Sarah looked up. They had run into Bryn. She had already forgotten. "Oh yeah, yes. It was her."

"She hot?" Archie raised his eyebrows at Bryn, who ignored him. "Or she marry rich?"

Sarah looked at him, and an angry flush rose to her cheeks. "She started her own company actually," she snapped.

"Riiight." Archie enjoyed baiting Sarah. He found her highly strung and condescending.

"Yes. She founded Pulse Travel." Sarah smiled as she saw Archie's face lose its smugness.

"Like... *the* Pulse Travel?"

"Yeah. Her family owned a small travel agency that did boutique stuff growing up, and she was always super into fitness, like even back at school, so she started it as a side venture to her parents' business. After a year she set it up as an independent thing. A few years ago she bought out her parents' business."

Archie was scowling slightly. "So why does she still hang out with you?"

Sarah's nose flared. "Excuse me?"

Archie barked out a laugh. "Jesus, I'm fucking kidding."

Sarah swallowed and glared. She wondered that same thing from time to time. Hope had let her take several free trips with Pulse Travel. She had got Hope a great deal on the Great King Street Property.

"That's cool, Sarah." Bryn smiled and looked back to his computer. He wanted the conversation to end. He didn't want to hear about someone his own age who was a multi-millionaire, world traveller and business mogul. She was also pretty damn hot, not that he would tell Archie that.

"So, you wanna set me up on a date with this hot rich friend of yours?"

"I didn't say she was hot. What if she's a mutant?"

Archie smiled. "She isn't. I googled her." He turned his phone around and waggled it. Hope's vibrant red curls and emerald eyes filled the screen. A company promo shot.

"Ugh. You're vile." Sarah shook her head and bent back over her work.

Archie turned to Bryn. "Hot though."

Bryn ignored him and went back to his work. He was more depressed than he had been before he started daydreaming about tropical beaches.

His phone buzzed. His flat mate wanted him to grab milk. Bryn sent a thumbs up back and then flicked over to THEORY 2.O to see if there was anything new going on. A bunch of celebrity videos were trending. Some goofy 'what ifs' that mostly appealed to the public desire for 'down to earth celebrities'. Bryn tapped his home pin and looked at the videos that had appeared this morning.

What if I'd gone out on Friday night?
What if I'd gone for a run on Sunday?
What if I'd asked out Sarah's friend?

Bryn cringed. They were so dull, so mind-numbingly trivial. He knew a lot of people used the PVs, which were basically ideas that everyone had had at least once; *what if I was famous? What if I was a pro athlete? What if I visited Paris?* There were a bunch of them, but Bryn found it a struggle just to see every tiny option in his life splayed out in a sunburst. He sighed heavily. There were just too many options, he thought, as he clicked the first of his videos, and watched another version of himself dance in the dank underbelly of the Opal Lounge.

Archie yelled out a goodbye at five minutes to five. Friday meant pub, beers and clubbing. He was the only one who was pleased to have their boss back, because it meant Sarah would stop acting like some pseudo-manager.

His phone buzzed. Mum.

"Hey Mum, what's up?" He kept a brisk pace as he weaved through the madness that was Princes' Street at rush hour.

"Hi darling. How are you?"

"Good, Mum. What's going on?" He loosened his tie with his hand.

"Oh well, it's your father." His mum's voice was soft and wobbly.

Archie slowed fractionally. "How is he?"

"He won't stop working - he's getting sicker by the day," she whimpered. Archie wondered if his father was home in his study.

"Mum, I can't make him stop." Archie had said this to his mother a thousand times.

"Oh I know, it's just... he's killing himself!" She had turned shrill. "I can't just watch it."

"I know, Mum." Archie was trying to placate her. "I'll come home on Sunday, yeah?"

His mother sniffed and Archie heard teacups clinking. "Yes, yes. Your sisters will be home for the day too."

"Great," Archie said cheerily, desperate to get off the phone. He hung up and hopped on the bus, which had appeared right on time. It was going to be a great Friday night. His mother, in Berwick, slammed the phone into the cradle and cursed at her eldest child.

From the study, Allan coughed. "Was that Archie?"

"Yes. Coming home for Sunday lunch," she snarled. "Obviously," she muttered under her breath.

Allan didn't get up from his chair. He knew Polly didn't like the fact that he was still working, still in and out of the hospital every day. He had tried to explain to her that he didn't just stop being a pediatric neurologist because he got sick. There were still sick children, interns who needed mentored, and special cases that needed his expertise.

He put down the medical journal he had been reading as he heard Polly's shoes tapping on the stone floor. "Sunday lunch," she repeated. Her face, once chubby and cheery, was now lined and slightly paunchy.

"Darling, come here." Allan beckoned to his wife of thirty-six years and she stiffly walked and stood beside his armchair. "I'm not killing myself. Cancer is killing me. And I can't just give up on life."

"But all this stress and strain…"

"No darling, no." Allan took her hand. "The work makes me happy. You know that. I'm on the outbound train anyway. I may as well help as many children as I can before I have to depart."

Polly's face crumpled and her stout body shook. Tears rolled over her cheeks and dripped off her chin.

Allan stood up, "Oh my love." He wrapped Polly in his arms.

"I just... I don't want..."

"I know, Pol." He tightened the hug, pressing her close to his chest. He rested his chin on her shoulder. He wasn't afraid, not really, nor sad. He smiled at the family picture on the mantle across the room. It had been such a good life.

Hope directed the guys from the furniture store around her new flat with decisive jabs. She had left every single stick of furniture in Australia. The only few things she had kept were some pieces of art that she loved and her own personal belongings. A fresh start, she thought, watching as a cool gray new sofa was placed in front of the fireplace. The walls were already a nice shade of slate and the floors had recently been redone with a beautiful washed limestone. Everything about the flat was minimalistic and modern. Hope smiled. It was a good Monday.

She gave the main guy a few more instructions, then went into the kitchen. It was all white, and as yet unsullied by her attempts to cook. She slid onto one of the bar stools and flipped open her Mac. She dutifully responded to all the pertinent emails, and then lazily scrolled through Facebook whilst she waited on a call from an advertising and PR manager.

She held her phone in her left hand and pulled up Instagram. Curated pictures of food, cats, and travel filled her feed. Alice Beasley had posted a selfie, fully made up, with a sad-pouty face. Two other girls from her old school had posted gym selfies, the same one, it looked like, captioned 'twinning'. There was a bunch of ones from her Aussie friends, mostly of bright sunny days and brunch. Some of her colleagues had posted snaps from the exotic locales that they had been assigned, always captioned 'world's best job!!!'

Her phone buzzed. "Hello, this is Hope."

"Hello Hope, this is Meredith from Global Strike Advertising."

"Hi Meredith, how's it going?"

"Good, good."

Meredith sounded young, not much different from Hope herself, she guessed. She clicked open her notes app and closed the door to the kitchen.

"So I spoke to Henry, and he told me you were interested in a more global outreach for Pulse Travel."

"Yes. I mean, we do have a pretty good reach right now, though mostly with Australians and Brits. I would love to start weaseling into the US market." Hope smiled.

"Yes, yes, completely." Meredith was obviously doing something, note taking or filling out a form. "And do you have a timeline?"

"A year. Initially. If we start getting a lot of US clients then I would have to reorganize some things, adjust pricing and so on." Hope remained vague. She hadn't met Meredith.

"And budget?"

"That's more negotiable."

"Great."

Hope sensed Meredith smiling. "Look, I would love to meet so we can discuss this more thoroughly. I am actually moving in to my new place today, which I didn't know before

I scheduled this call."

"Oh my goodness, congrats! Yes, we can meet. When is good for you?" Meredith said eagerly.

Hope smiled. When she had started Pulse Travel, no one had wanted to work with a twenty-five-year-old with no budget. "Does tomorrow work, Tuesday?"

"Yes. We can either meet here at the office, or we can grab lunch?"

Hope had a few errands to run at Harvey Nichols. "How about the Forth Floor bar in Harvey Nicks?" she suggested cheekily.

"Yeah, that works great." Meredith replied. "12:30?"

"Perfect." Hope hung up and closed her Mac. The movers were still clunking around in the living room and bedrooms.

She slid off the barstool and leant against the counter. A moment later she opened the THEORY 2.0 app. She scrolled down the feed, clicking on random videos from athletes and celebrities, some models or IG famous people. They were all fairly dull. One of her friends from Australia had started doing his own PVs, which were all just blindingly awful, stuff like *what if I could have babies? What if I had strangled my lying ex-girlfriend*?

Hope wasn't too sure how he'd done it, since Theory always did happy or lighthearted videos. It was rare to get a 'bad' alternative outcome from a choice. He was a tech guy though, Hope thought, so maybe he had tinkered with the algorithms. She sighed and went to her home pin.

What if Paul hadn't cheated on you?
What if you'd married Michael, not Paul?
What if you got a kitten?
What if you bump in to Michael?

Hope looked at the kitchen door. Still closed. "I guess I need to get a cat," she said quietly, before clicking on the second video.

She and Michael sitting on a small balcony overlooking the Edinburgh Old Town. Cups of tea in hand. A dog snoring by Michael's feet. A book sitting on a coffee table above a stack of Michael's legal paperwork.

Hope swallowed, sick to her stomach. Something niggled though, as she watched the alternative Hope sitting on the balcony, smiling at Michael. Her alter ego sipped her tea and watched as he began leafing through his work. She patted the dog on the head and relaxed back into her chair.

Hope closed the app. She pushed herself off the counter and grabbed her Mac. She had work to do.

Bryn scratched the point behind his ear where his AppChip was located. He needed a new one. Something was faulty with this one. It kept glitching. He waited in line at the AppChip store, inching closer towards the help desk. He had taken a long lunch so he could get it fixed, though he'd told the boss he had a doctors' appointment.

A young guy with gauged ears and a mustache beckoned Bryn over to his desk. "How's it going man? What can I do for you?"

"Hey... good... er... yeah, my AppChip's been glitching a lot lately."

"OK, OK cool man. We can get that fixed for you no probs."

Bryn smiled nervously. He adjusted his tie and looked around the shop as the guy tapped something into his touchscreen.

"Can I?" The young guy held up a scanner.

"Right, of course." Bryn leant forwards and the guy roved the scanner around his neck and behind his ear. It beeped.

"OK, cool. So you have the 2054 Everest model." The guy frowned.

"Can it be fixed?"

The guy shrugged, "I would just replace it. Cheaper and you'll get better interfaces on all your synched apps, plus better imaging quality and memory retrieval for stuff like Theory 2.0."

"Shit," Bryn cursed, then looked at the guy. "Sorry, I just have to be back at work soon."

The young guy smiled, showing crooked teeth. "No worries man, we can have you outta here with the 2057 Mariana chip in ten."

"Really?"

The guy grinned and his fingers tapped away furiously. "For sure man, it's gonna change your life."

Bryn settled back into his desk. His boss hadn't even noticed his absence, it seemed. He fiddled around on his computer for a second and then slid his phone on top of his keyboard. The guy at the store had updated and synched everything. Bryn felt a strange flutter of excitement, followed by a guilty shame. It was an app, social media and crap for Christ's sake, he chided himself.

Still, he opened Instagram, Twitter and Theory 2.0. Twitter's new feature was that you could hear the person saying their 140 characters. Great if you were trapped in an office or on a commute. Great for comedians too, since they could properly convey their jokes. Instagram was on a whole new level. The images could be used with Theory 2.0, so you could save someone's IG pic and use it for your own video. You could also do special IG videos which people could be part of remotely with their AppChip.

Bryn opened Theory 2.0 last. His feed sprang to life. The videos were vivid, smooth and hyper-real. They didn't look like hypothetical imagined scenarios that people had dreamed up, but real events.

"Jesus…" he muttered as he clicked on one. Some random blonde girl on the back of an elephant dressed in a sari.

He clicked on his own videos. The usual boring detritus of choices that made up his life; meal choices, to go out or not to go out, what if he'd spoken to some random chick and on and on they went. He noticed a small star by his home pin. That was new.

He clicked on it and a new, fresh green page opened on the app.

Welcome to THEORY 2.0's newest feature. We are pairing with the hottest celebs, brands, locations and events to bring you the best Theories yet! The best thing about these PV's though, is that you can actually be a part of them in real life! THEORY 2.0 is offering great deals on these events. check them out here first, and then be part of them… FOR REAL!

Bryn scrolled further down, to where a beautifully-curated selection of videos appeared. These must be the new ones everyone was posting; vids of themselves on a beach dancing to some rapper, or riding an elephant in India.

Bryn looked around the office. Sarah was engrossed in

paperwork. Archie was frowning at his computer. His boss had spun his chair around and was sipping coffee and murmuring on the phone to someone. Bryn scrolled to an image of Machu Pichu. He hovered his finger above it and *'What if you took a trip with Give Back Co. to the incredible Macchu Pichu? Enjoy local foods, events and adventures, all whilst helping local children!'*

Bryn had always wanted to see Peru, he thought, as he leant back in his chair and clicked play on the 8-minute video.

Allan rubbed the tender spot behind his ear where the chip had been implanted. He hadn't really wanted one, but his daughters had been very persuasive. It meant that they could HoloChat. He did want to HoloChat with them of course, it was just that he would rather they came home and actually spoke to him face to face. They didn't like seeing him ill. Well, Genevieve, their youngest, didn't. He could see it in her face. She looked wide-eyed and frightened and tried to pretend she didn't see the pale, sagging skin, or the dark circles under his eyes. Allan tried to reassure her that death was nothing to be frightened of, but her eyes would well up and he would be forced to stop.

"Dad?" Archie hollered from the front hallway.

"In here, darling," he called as Archie came clomping in. Their ancient Labrador, Cadbury, thumped his tail on the rug in front of the fire.

"Hey!" Archie engulfed his dad in a bear hug. "You look fucking terrible."

"Bugger off." Allan smiled. "I swear to God if that bloody dog outlives me... I'm taking him with me when I go."

Archie laughed. "Hear that, Cad?" He shook his head and the dog's tail wagged harder.

"How are you?"

"Oh fine. Work is a bit dull, though we did get a whole load of new high-end properties this week, which are a bit more fun to sell than some of the dingy flats around Sighthill. I'm getting a promotion too - small one, but still." Archie flopped onto the sofa. Cadbury began the laborious process of clambering up beside him. "How are you?"

"Jolly good." Allan sat back down in his armchair. "Your mother might kill me if I don't die soon. She's quite furious that I'm still working."

Archie raised his eyebrows. "I know. She calls me. A lot."

"I got an App thing. Chip?"

"An AppChip? That's awesome. Did Gen convince you finally?"

Allan nodded.

Archie grinned wider. "Oh my god, there are so many apps you need to get. You need to get Theory 2.0 and oh, you'd love OnPoint, it's a new one. Give me your phone." Archie reached out and took it from his dad. "I'm gonna load Theory. Dad, seriously, you're gonna wake up tomorrow with all these videos. It'll be cool, I promise."

Hope and Sarah looked out at the dull sky from the coffee shop and the people huddling under umbrellas and bus shelters.

"Christ, I have to walk all the way around Old Town showing houses later," Sarah grumbled as she sipped her coffee.

"Yikes!" Hope smiled at her sympathetically.

Sarah looked up at her friend. Hope looked exhausted. Her normally china-white skin was dull, and her hair was frizzy.

"Are you OK?" she asked.

Hope looked up at her and smiled weakly. "I'm just on the verge of being quite overwhelmed," she said softly. "I've been training for the Ironman a lot. I have a trip to Vietnam to check out some junk boats for a new trip planned for next month, then the whole moving in thing. And yesterday I had to meet with this advertising and marketing strategist and ugh…" she made a face and stuck her tongue out.

"Awful?" Sarah smiled into her cup of coffee.

"Like…" Hope looked conspiratorially around. "OK, so the woman, Meredith, was just so intense and pushy. I felt like… you know when you're in a nightclub and some drunk dick won't leave you alone?"

"Yeah?" Sarah giggled.

"It was like that. Over lunch. With a business woman." Hope shook her head and sipped her coffee, "She was trying to sell this new thing that Theory 2.0 is doing for advertising." Hope shook her head. "It wigged me out."

Sarah raised her brows inquisitively.

"It's basically…" Hope sat up and put her coffee cup down so she could gesticulate. "So, they would take all of our trip info; hotels, daily activities, WOD plans, adventure trips, restaurants, basically, as much as we can give them, and they create PVs for people to watch. Then these PVs are embedded in some new part of the app, so people can check them out and then book a trip with us through Theory 2.0 with a 15% discount."

"I mean… it sounds like a good idea." Sarah frowned.

"Yeah, except, for one, they track people's mental data. Which is weird, right? I mean, they track if people want to get fit or travel or both, and then suggest Pulse Travel to them, which I mean... fine, but then I got thinking and I figured, people use Theory to imagine things a lot of the time that they have no intention of doing. The last thing I want is people imagining a trip with us in lieu of doing the real thing."

Sarah leant back in her chair, her cup still gripped in her hands. "You're right."

Hope shook her head. "Meredith didn't think so. She's calling me later to check back in and see if we can 'figure something out'."

"I got rid of it y'know. IG, Facebook, Theory 2.0. Twitter too." Sarah looked around the coffee shop.

"Yeah, you mentioned that."

"Do you ever..." Sarah looked at Hope and bit her lip, "I just kept imagining certain scenarios over and over, and seeing them played out - it was like... torture. I kept imagining what it would have been like if I'd moved to Paris after uni." She shook her head. "Did you ever get stuff like that, like, all the time?"

Hope swallowed. "Um... yeah, like, if Paul hadn't cheated." Sarah nodded sagely. "And whether or not I should get a cat," added Hope, to lighten the mood.

Sarah smiled, seemingly satisfied with the answer. "Well now I know what to get for your housewarming present."

Bryn lay in bed and grinned. It was a Saturday. He was going out tonight. Sarah's friend Hope had stopped by the office today and chatted with him for a bit. It was going to be a great weekend. He could hear his flatmate on the Xbox and smell bacon cooking. He scrolled down Instagram and Twitter, smiling to himself and hitting 'like' on almost every other picture.

He opened Theory 2.0. His feed had been markedly better in the past few days. He had a whole bunch of videos this morning, not just the usual four.

What if you worked in the pro athletics industry, and hanging out with celebrity athletes was just part of the daily job?

What if you were dating model and actress Hailey Demovich?

What if you took a year off to sail around the globe with Sail Sport Worldwide?

What if you could party in Ibiza with DJ Van?

What if you took an adventure trip to Patagonia, horse riding, climbing and hiking, with the GSA team?

Bryn shrugged himself deeper into his pillow and duvet and methodically clicked on each video.

Allan shuffled around the kitchen. Polly was already outside with Cadbury, feeding chickens, checking on her plants, and just generally being her busy self. He made a cup of tea and yawned. His phone buzzed a few times on the kitchen table. He ignored it in favor of sneaking a chocolate biscuit into his mouth before Polly could get back and tell him it wasn't a nutritious breakfast.

The phone buzzed a few more times and he wondered if maybe the hospital was trying to reach him. He had consulted recently on a small boy who had a large tumor located near his pituitary gland.

He got his glasses out of his dressing gown pocket and peered down at the screen. A bunch of white notification bars, each with a blue and pink globe on the left, filled his screen.

Welcome to THEORY 2.0. *You can check out tips, tricks and our T&C's from the app by clicking on the menu bar.*

Your first videos will be live at 7:00am GMT. Get excited!

Your first video is LIVE! Welcome to the THEORY 2.0 *family.*

Ohhh, looks like there's more, be sure to check out all your vids and our new features to get the most out of THEORY 2.0.

Allan raised his eyebrows and leant closer to the screen. It took him a solid minute to get into the phone, clear the notifications and actually locate the app that was bugging him. THEORY 2.0 swooshed to the top of his screen. Allan squinted. There was a whole page of small squares and a little white speech bubble that said "Why don't you check out these?" Another one pinged up near the bottom of the screen. "You can click this button on a feed you like, or a friend, so their posts will show up in your daily feed."

After a moment both speech bubbles disappeared. As Allan tried to navigate the screen, more appeared. "You can hit this button on videos you don't want to see." "Click this pin to go to your video and see what theories have been curated for you."

Allan clicked that pin and his screen swooshed again. The screen was mostly white, with four small, bright squares at the top. They were all emblazoned with a bright pink 'play' arrow. A small info bubble popped up: "hover your finger over the videos to see what each one is about".

Allan obediently obeyed the app.

What if you got another Labrador for Cadbury to play with?

What if you went on that trip to the Grand Canyon?

What if you had become a heart surgeon?

What if you had taken the CA84-BR1 drug five years ago?

Allan's gut swooped and his head swam. Archie had told him that Theory 2.0 worked by gathering all the data from your thoughts, memories and ideas, even subconscious ones, to create the videos.

Allan didn't think all that much about the experimental drug he had been offered five years ago, shortly after he had been diagnosed with cancer. At least, he thought he didn't think about it too much. He sat down heavily on a chair and leant his forearms on the kitchen table. He had only been offered the CA84-BR1 because of his senior position at the hospital. He knew someone who knew someone, that sort of thing. He had declined it at the time. Too many risks, too few trials. Now, his finger hovered over the video. The pink play button throbbed. Allan clicked it.

He saw himself sitting at his hospital office, a stack of papers rising up on one corner, his phone ringing in its cradle, the hubbub of the hospital just beyond the office door. He stood up from his desk. He looked lean, his face tanned and healthy.

Allan gulped as the video continued. It faded out to another scene.

The other 'Allan' and Polly at the beach, south of France,

eating a picnic. HoloChatting the kids. Eating baguettes slathered with brie and pâté. Polly smiling in a carefree way he hadn't seen in years.

The video faded to another scene again. 'Allan' on a treadmill in their garage. Jogging and laughing along to a rerun of *House*. Cadbury snoring beside him. 'Allan' looked healthy, vibrantly so. He got off the treadmill and walked to the kitchen. Archie sprung out. Gen and Sally were there grinning. Polly walked over to him holding a cake with candles. 'Allan' looked down. '5 Years in Remission!' was iced onto the top of the cake.

"Allan?" Polly hollered as she came in to the house.

Allan quickly exited the app.

"Oh my god, Al, are you all right?" Polly rushed over.

Allan couldn't speak. His eyes were glossy and his mouth hung open.

"Allan, are you OK? Do you feel OK?" Polly grasped his shoulders. Allan tried to nod, but instead a fat tear rolled out of his eye. "I... I should've taken... I..."

Polly shushed him. "Come on now Allan. You need to rest." She hurried him to the sitting room, forcing down the lump in her own throat. She nestled him on the sofa with a blanket and Cadbury and went to get him a cup of tea.

In the kitchen, she called Archie. Before he could even say hi she cut him off. "You need to get over here now. Something is wrong with your father."

There was a pause, and then she said, "No, not like that, it's like... it's like he realized today that he is dying. I don't know Archie, I haven't seen him like this... yes... yes OK... I'll see you in an hour."

Polly hung up and leant against the Aga. For the past

five years she had desperately wanted Allan to fully understand the implications of his impending death. He always seemed so happy and positive, and she had felt like she was alone on a sea of grief. Today she realized how deeply she had been mistaken.

Hope wasn't really watching the TV. She was staring, angrily, at her phone. It lay, face up, on the sofa beside her. A new kitten, tortoiseshell and unnamed, was peeking out at her from the top of its new cat tree.

"You don't have to deal with shit like this, little man," she said, looking from the kitten to her phone. The kitten meowed and poked his head out further.

Hope leant back against the sofa. It had been an awful Saturday night. She had gone out with Sarah and Alice Beasley. They had been to dinner, which was lovely, and then decided to dip into a club. Michael had been there, with his new girlfriend. Long-term girlfriend, Hope reminded herself. A Slavic beauty with willowy limbs and a striking, angular face. Nothing like Hope at all.

Hope scrunched up her eyes and rubbed her face. She had cried. She had actually cried. They were laughing and grinning. They seemed in sync. Alice offhandedly remarked that they were great together, really happy. That was when Hope burst into tears. To add insult to injury, Sarah's cute work friend, Bryn, had ignored her completely and just stared at his phone the entire time they were at the club. Then some drunk idiot had spilled his drink on her dress and she had lost one of her earrings.

Hope glared at her phone. Alice Beasley had posted a pic this morning on Instagram. The three of them at the club, a random shot where they were all grinning. Hope didn't remember it being taken. Alice had captioned it #bestnightever #girlsnightout #opallounge #clubbing #pulsetravel.

"Ugh!" Hope slammed her hand down on the sofa cushion and the phone bounced. The kitten leapt from the cat tree and stalked over.

Then, in one final knife twist, she had gone on Theory 2.0 and the woman with whom Paul had cheated on her with had posted a PV of them getting married. She had captioned it #hinthint and #putaringonit.

"FUCK YOU!" she snarled at the phone.

It rang. Hope glared at it. Tessa. She picked up. "Hey Tessa!" Tessa was one of her best friends back in Australia. She was coming to Edinburgh to visit in two months. Hope was already excited about it.

"DUDE!" Tessa exclaimed in her thick Aussie accent. "Dude... oh my god."

"What?" Hope sniffed miserably.

"Oh my god you don't even know... you don't even know."

"What is it?" Hope sniped.

"Stop being bitchy and mopey. Have you seen that post that she who must not be named posted?"

"Yes." Hope sighed.

"DUDE!"

"It's tacky." Hope knew she sounded more than a little bitchy.

"Well yeah, but he fucking cheated on her!"

"What?"

"Ummm yeah. So, you remember Jax? That super hot, super gay, guy I lived with?"

"Yeah."

"So Jax and I went to brunch and Jax was telling me how his sister hooked up with this twat who said he was single and then she found out he actually had a girlfriend."

"Oh, that sucks."

"Mmm hmm, and Jax was pissed on his sister's behalf and wanted to tell the girlfriend, but couldn't find her. So Jax messages his sister and puts her on loudspeaker and she is telling me about this guy. She said, he says his name is Adam, which is Paul's middle name, but I didn't think about that immediately, and then she is saying he is super tall, works in website design, and I'm like, huh this is weird. She then goes on and it's like he had this cheesy ass fucking tattoo of a phoenix on his left pec."

"Oh my fucking GOD!" Hope exclaimed. That was Paul all right.

"I KNOW!" Tessa yelled.

Hope launched into her own tale of how hideous last night was, and then they chatted for a bit before hanging up.

The kitten mewled and leapt up on to the sofa. Hope leant back and put her phone back down on the sofa beside her. "It's all so fake," she whispered. There was a lump in her throat. How many hours had she wasted on Instagram, Facebook, Twitter and Theory 2.0? And how much of it mattered? How much of it was real or lasting or even meant anything?

The kitten mewled and padded a little closer to Hope's soft voice. He stepped on her phone, his soft pads lingering until all the icons began to shake. Little 'x's appeared at the top corner of all of them.

"That is a good idea, lil' man," Hope said, seizing her phone. The kitten followed the phone as Hope drew it towards herself. It clambered into her lap. Its orange fur glowed against the black and white patches.

Hope systematically deleted all the social media apps, one by one, until that folder was empty. She smiled and looked down at the kitten. "Verum," she said.

The kitten mewled.

"It's a good name," she said. "It means truth."

Bryn walked into the office with a wide grin on his face. He had felt hideously hung over all day on Sunday. It was pouring with rain today, but Bryn didn't really care now that he was ensconced in the warm heat of the office. He nodded to Archie, who looked decidedly glum, and to Sarah, who barely flicked an eyebrow at him. He sat down, checked his emails, then surreptitiously brought his phone out and shifted his keyboard out of the way.

He placed his phone down carefully and clicked open Theory 2.0. He felt a frisson of excitement. A text pinged up from a group chat he was in.

"Bryn, you were so smashed on Saturday!"

"Can't believe you got kicked out the club!"

"Saw a hot redhead hitting on you tho."

"You guys up for a Thursday pub crawl?"

The messages continued. Bryn had already posted a bunch of blurry pics and videos from the night out, not that he could remember much, and he had already posted a few

PVs about what would have happened if he hadn't been kicked out of the club.

The door jangled for a second and Hope walked in. Bryn nodded hi, and was about to speak to her when Theory 2.0 pinged.

'Six new PVs... what are you waiting for? Get watching!'

He dropped his head and clicked on the first video eagerly as Hope walked past him and went to Sarah's desk. Sarah glanced back over her shoulder. Archie looked red-eyed and unusually glum. She leant to Hope and whispered something, and Hope nodded. "Hey Archie, you wanna come grab a coffee with us?" said Sarah.

Archie looked up and sighed. "Yeah, yeah for sure." At the door, he turned. "I've gotta grab my phone."

Sarah frowned. Archie was rummaging for his phone, and Bryn was so glued to his screen he didn't notice the three of them leave.

"You OK?" Hope asked when Archie returned, phone clutched in his hand.

"Oh, um... yeah..." He swallowed, and then lowered his voice. "My dad is really ill, I'm just... we're just... y'know."

Hope nodded and the three of them left to the sound of Bryn guffawing over a video of 'Bryn' doing something that the real Bryn would never do.

Allan hadn't gotten out of bed in five days. He refused all calls from everyone, including the hospital. A call had come in from a doctor in desperate need of Allan's expertise, and he had told Polly to tell the doctor that he was too sick. Polly had wanted to scream, to drag him out of bed and back to his old self, but she had nodded and made the call from the kitchen.

"Mum?" Archie called. He had gotten off work early and decided to pop home to check on his parents.

"How are you, darling?" His mother appeared from the kitchen and beckoned him inside.

"I'm OK. How's Dad?"

"Same as he was on the weekend, won't talk to me. Won't say why this sudden change hit." She shook her head and her cheeks wobbled. Archie nodded. "How's work? I'll get you some tea and then you can head on up and try to get through to him."

"Work's really good actually. This guy at the office has kinda dropped the ball recently and so I've picked up a bunch of new clients this past week. So that's good... and I got asked out."

His mum turned and smiled. "Really?" Archie had always been an outgoing boy, but he hadn't ever seemed to really click with girls.

"Yeah... yeah, this girl from work. I think I told you about her maybe, Sarah? We actually didn't get along, but we... It was kinda strange we got chatting about stuff and she erm... she yeah. We're going to go have a drink after work tomorrow."

"Lovely." His Mum smiled and handed him a cup of tea.

Archie took it and slurped. "I'll go up."

"Hey Dad?" He knocked and poked his head around the door. His Dad was half covered by the quilt. His phone was in his hands and tears poured down his lined cheeks. "Oh, Dad, are you OK?" Archie rushed to his side.

"Why did you show me this?" Allan thrust the phone to Archie. The Theory 2.0 logo shimmered out from the screen.

"Theory? What? I don't understand, Dad, is this why you've been sad?"

Allan gulped and roughly wiped away a tear.

"It's not real Dad, it's like… a daydream you can see, that's all."

Allan shook his head, "I know, it's just… you don't understand Archie." Allan handed his son the phone and clicked the video. It was the only video he had played. All the others were still pink and unwatched, but this one had been watched 112 times already. Archie watched it with growing horror.

"Oh Dad, I… I didn't know…"

"I know son, and neither did I. I didn't want… I never wanted to know." Allan said, as fresh tears flowed down his face.

"I was sorry to hear about your Dad," Hope said with sincerity as she handed Archie a glass of red wine.

"Thanks Hope." Archie took a sip. "We'd been expecting it for a while, but it's never what you want to happen."

Sarah rubbed his back gently. "How was Halong Bay?" She asked. "I haven't seen you in like… three weeks?"

"I know, I know." Hope held up her hands apologetically. "It was great. I started this thing with the guides, the ones who are actually out on location, that they cut down their social media usage, and actually write pieces about why our trips are so good; emotionally, for health, travel, mentally and all that kind of thing. It's been really good. Sales are up, since we push the stuff, ironically, on social media. But, once people read the article we offer discounts and stuff. I just want to encourage people to actually go out and DO stuff." She thrust her hands forward in a decisive gesture.

"That's awesome." Archie smiled. His phone was in the kitchen, on silent, behind the closed living room door.

"Are you two excited about your trip to Brazil? You guys will have a blast." Hope grinned. "It's such a great place. One of my favorites."

"Yes, thanks by the way, we can only go because of the deal you gave us." Sarah sipped her white wine, "although work is shitty right now and will be till we leave."

"Oh no! How come?"

"Bryn got fired," Archie said flatly.

"Oh shit, when?"

Sarah cocked her head and looked to Archie for a second. "Like, two weeks ago? He was always on his phone, not selling, not communicating with clients. He's obsessed with the new PVs from Theory 2.0. Like the ones you told me about, the sales pitch ones?"

Archie nodded, trying to ignore the choking guilt sensation that he got every time someone mentioned Theory 2.0.

"That's so sad," Hope said.

Sarah shrugged. "Yeah, I mean, he was being a total idiot."

Hope smiled ruefully. "I know. I mean, it's so sad that he takes Theory 2.0 so seriously when in the end it's all just a bit of fun. Well, it's not exactly life and death, is it?"

BRECADH

July 12TH 2084

The news reports were all the same, blaring out across every screen in the room. Aodh looked dismayed as he saw the swarms of journalists crowding around the site.

"For fuck's sake, they could be a wee bit more careful," he muttered as he watched over Tina's shoulder.

"Aye, it's sad. They're gonna wreck it all."

"Bet we won't even be allowed in, even though it's right on our bloody doorstep." Aodh shook his mop of brown hair. His Fair Isle sweater was stained with soup, and his grandpa's old pants, two sizes too big, gathered dust at the hems.

"You might," Tina consoled him.

It was a hollow statement. They both knew the World Government would swoop in and privatize it. It was the only way to actually protect anything nowadays.

"Mmm... well. What time is Hamish coming over?"

Tina's boyfriend worked down at the new marine institute by Lerwick, on the east coast of the Shetland Isles. They lived in Aith, on the west coast. It was a fun 30-minute drive on narrow roads between the two towns.

"Gosh, I dunno. He's supposed to be here soon, but I reckon he'll be held up by all this."

Aodh nodded. Tina ruffled his hair as she walked into the kitchen. "Tea?"

"Aye."

Tina watched him as he sank into the sofa, transfixed by the plasma screen. She and Hamish had known Aodh since they were kids. He had left for university young, a brilliant career ahead of him, so they all thought, until they discovered he was a target for bullies and there wasn't much work for cryptologists.

Aodh was agender and asexual. Tina thought he might well have been bullied on the Island, except for the fact that he had two older sisters and a pappy who would level anyone with a shovel if they blinked wrong at his son. He let everyone refer to him as a 'he' only because he got tired of explaining that he didn't feel like he had a gender at all. Plus, even he would admit that with his mop of hair, strong cheekbones, and geriatric man's style, he leant more towards a masculine ideology.

"It's just... y'know, this is what I should've been doing," Aodh muttered. He had never finished his degree at Glasgow.

"Here you go." Tina handed him a cup of tea and a plate with a few digestive biscuits on it. Tina sank down beside him, gingerly holding her cup out in front so she didn't spill.

"I cannae imagine... must be incredible."

"Well it fucking isn't!" Hamish boomed from the doorway. His crisp English accent was at odds with the red hair and tartan shirt he had on.

Aodh snapped his head round. "Oh my god, tell us everything."

"I need a bite first Aodh." Hamish slumped down at the kitchen table and Tina hugged him from behind.

Tina, upon hearing the words, reached for the oven door and opened it. The homely smell of shepherd's pie filled the room.

"Is that real lamb?" Hamish's eyes widened and he inhaled deeply.

"Mmm hmm, the McCullough's farm... killed a few. Rest's in the freezer."

Even Aodh had moseyed into the kitchen and sat down at the table. He eyeballed Hamish.

"I can't get you in there Aodh."

"I know! Just tell me about it." He hissed back.

"Come grab it." Tina said, as she ladled peas and spooned lamb, rich with gravy and mash, onto three plates.

"Well..." Hamish said, sitting back down. With food in front of him he seemed much more jovial and glad to be the focus of the attention, "we're going to have a devil of a time keeping it from the Norwegians. I can tell you that."

"But... what about the *actual* ruins Hamish?" Aodh rolled his eyes in exasperation.

"Oh right, yeah... didn't see much."

"I thought you guys would've been first on the scene, so to speak." Tina said between forkfuls.

"Well, Garrett wasn't too happy we weren't, what with

it being in our backyard an' all, but the coastguard got there as soon as the tide pulled out."

"S'already on the news." Tina nodded at the sitting room TV.

They all turned, forks paused. On the screen was a TV reporter, buffeted by wind till his cheeks were raw and dressed in an unflattering rain jacket.

"As you can see, the ruins were discovered in the early hours of the morning by local fishermen. The coastguard was called in, you can still see the choppers, drones and hoverboats over by the Lerwick coast." The newscaster pointed to a gray, drizzling area of fog. Spots of light pierced the gloom. "They're heading back in and out as new portions appear. It's become clear the ruins show no sign of returning beneath the waves either, and local tidal experts put this down to the damaging change in tidal flux known as the 'Helios Flux' that was discovered two years ago."

"Can you tell us anything about the ruins?" A woman in a snappy red suit, planted firmly in an anchor's chair, leant towards the camera.

"We haven't heard much, though initial speculation suggested that they are around 27,000 years old. How they have survived with so little damage underwater is the real conundrum here, Alice." The reporter tilted his head towards the screen. "Until we start getting archeologists down here, which won't be till later tomorrow, we just can't make any definite statements about the ruins."

"There has already been chatter about the ruins being tied to Stonehenge."

The reporter shrugged and pursed his lips, "You know, we really don't know much at this point. I can tell you that the military and the World Government have been called in so that the same thing that happened at Stonehenge doesn't happen here."

The TV zoomed back to the cushy news desk.

"Thanks, Marlon. We'll be updating this story live as more news breaks, but for now, let's take a look at the weather."

Aodh sat at the window seat and stared glumly out into the hills. It was surprisingly sunny after yesterday's stormy weather, but clouds were gathering on the horizon, just past the white-tipped waves. The TV was off. Tina was at work. Hamish had refused to let him come along to the marine center and poke around the ruins.

Bear, his service dog, a Labrador, was curled and inert on the sofa. The dog's foot twitched occasionally. When Aodh shifted, the dog's ears pricked and he watched as Aodh made his way into the kitchen.

"It's fine, I'm just getting some food," Aodh grumbled. He felt watched in the house. Watched by Tina and Hamish, watched by his mother and sisters, who came round every bloody day. Now apparently Bear was watching him too. Just 'popping in' they would say, but he knew they were all checking up on him.

Aodh made toast. He spread Marmite on one piece and peanut butter on the other. "I don't know why Hamish is being such a twat about it, Bear. You ken? I mean… it's not like I'm asking to be made lead cryptologist," he grumbled. The dog's ears twitched. "Not that I could be," Aodh murmured to himself.

"Aydeee? Ayyyydee?" His mother crooned from outside.

Bear let out a half-hearted bark and stretched luxuriously from the sofa.

"Come in Mum." Aodh sat down at the kitchen table with his toast. "Just having some lunch."

"Oh Aodh, that's nae lunch!" she chided as she planted a kiss on his head. "Here, I brought some lasagne, and a wee spot of chicken pot pie, not a proper one mind, just the leftovers." She plonked four silver foil trays down on the table.

"Just the leftovers, was it?" Aodh raised his eyebrows, but slid the trays closer. His mum was a fantastic cook.

"Mmm... have ye been watching the news?"

"Aye." Aodh bit into his toast until his mouth was stuffed with buttery toast and the sharp tang of Marmite and he couldn't talk.

"Oh Aodh, you have to stop skulking around here at Tina's!" His mother slapped her hand on the coffee table.

Aodh continued chewing. "I live here," he said eventually.

"You know what I mean." She jabbed a finger at him angrily.

Aodh gave his mother a black look and stood from the kitchen table. Bear snuffled under the chair for any toast crumbs.

"Mum, look, what d'ye want me tae do?" Aodh snapped. "Go over there and barge past all the security, the military police and just say 'Oh hello, I dinnae have a degree or anythin' but I'd sure like to take a wee look at the ruins? I cannae dae much and I'm no a cryptologist cause I failed uni, but NAE MIND!" He screamed the last words before slumping back into the seat. Bear nuzzled his ankles comfortingly.

His mother stared at him stony faced. "Don't you speak tae me like that laddie," she said quietly. "You need to get your act together."

Aodh was about to speak, but his mother knelt down, gave Bear a pat and then stalked out of the house. Aodh got up and paced around the kitchen.

"What the hell does she know eh, Bear?" He fumed. Bear's droopy eyes followed him back and forth. "She does nae know what it was like. She does nae know." Aodh felt a lump in his throat rising, so he quickly grabbed his Barbour jacket and thrust his feet into wellies.

"Enough. We're off for walkies." Aodh was looking out of the window towards the beach. At the last word, Bear sprung to life and scurried to the back door. "Aye, get away from that witch," he muttered, with another black look at the door. "I can tell ye want to as well."

JANUARY 2085

"Aodh, come on!" Tina shrieked from the living room of the Campbell household. She practically counted Aodh's family as her own anyway. His sisters jostled for places on the sofa; they were broad, sturdy girls and they elbowed one another for more space. Mrs Campbell was whipping up some sandwiches for them all and Mr Campbell was half asleep in his recliner.

"AODH!" his eldest sister, Bessie, screeched. "COME THE FUCK ON!"

Aodh whipped his head out from his old room.

"I'm nae deaf," he grumbled.

"Aye. Just fucking slow," his sister Bertha quipped back.

"Language!" Mr Campbell muttered from his chair without opening an eye.

"It's starting," Bessie announced as rolling credits began. "Shhh."

"Tonight on WorldWatch, for the first time, an in depth look at the recently discovered ruins, now known as 'Brecadh'."

The image opened to a selection of artistic shots of the site, juxtaposed with the headlines that had been taking up websites and media every single day since it was discovered. WorldWatch had cherry-picked the real attention-grabbing headlines: 'IS THIS THE DAWNING OF THE END OF DAYS?' 'Dig site swamped with bad luck... is it CURSED?' 'Proof that ALIEN LIFE once existed on earth!' Or the more political ones, "Is Norway after our heritage?' 'WORLD ORGANISATION SWOOPS IN ON SCOTLAND.'

"Dramatic much?" Aodh whispered theatrically.

"Shh Aodh!" Bessie hissed.

Aodh rolled his eyes but went quiet. He glanced at Hamish, who was still sitting at the kitchen table, away from Tina. He was eating his sandwich slowly and frowned every time he looked at the TV. Aodh pulled his mouth to one side and made a mental note to keep an eye on Hamish as well as watch the TV.

"I'm Daniel DeMarco, and this is WorldWatch. The lost city of Brecadh, subject of spiritual, political and historical debate, blew up on our screens six months ago and hasn't budged from the number one spot since then. Two political sex scandals and one celebrity feud couldn't push the ruins out of the headlines.

"We're here tonight with a panel of experts, with exclusive access to the site, and with never seen before footage from the initial discovery of the Lost City of Brecadh."

There was a pregnant pause in the room as they all stared expectantly at the TV. It cut to a commercial break.

"Milkin' it for all it's worth," Aodh's mum said, taking the words from his lips as a McDonald's jingle played on the screen. "Food's in the kitchen, an' crisps. Grab what ye want," she said, smoothing her apron across her ample stomach.

Bessie and Bertha leapt up but Aodh stayed, leaning in the doorframe. Hamish had migrated towards Tina, but he still sat stiffly away from her on the sofa. Aodh remained still and silent as he eavesdropped.

"Come on Hamey, just tell me. I cannae help you if you willnae say nuthin'."

"Tina, I already told you, it's a work matter that doesn't concern you."

"I'm your girlfriend Hamish, we practically live together, for God's sake."

"I don't want to talk about it."

"Is it about Brecadh?"

"Tina!" Hamish's voice was low and threatening and Tina huffed.

"You've been there 24 hours a day, you don't tell me anything, if you didn't want to come tonight you didn't have to but I want to know!" Tina's whisper became shrill and squeaky.

Hamish stood abruptly from the sofa, leaving Tina looking baffled and pouty. Bessie and Bertha had settled themselves back on the sofa as WorldWatch resumed, but Aodh followed Hamish into the kitchen.

"First up, we'll be talking to Professor Jameth Comey, the world's foremost archeologist in subaquatic ruins, to see how Brecadh survived so well underwater."

"What's she made this time?" Aodh grinned as he carefully lifted the top of the soft baps to check the sandwich innards.

"I had a roasted onion, peperoncini, salami and provolone, with some salt and vinegar crisps. I'd highly recommend it." Hamish smiled and relaxed. "I don't know how your Mum gets her hands on all these rare goodies."

"One woman Mafia." Aodh grinned, grabbed a packet of crisps and balanced them beside the sandwich.

Hamish gave a halfhearted snicker. "Uh huh."

Aodh sat down at the kitchen table beside Hamish. "I'm getting a wee bit sick of all this Brecadh talk." He bit into his sandwich and smiled. "Mmm, s'good. Y'know I read a good book recently about a Marine, he was out surfing off the north coast and he got swept out – stranded. Anyway, he survived for like, 16 hours in the sea before being rescued. You reckon it's true? Like, could someone do that?"

Hamish leant back in his chair, a look of relaxed relief crossing his face for the first time since he had arrived.

"Well it would depend on a lot of factors," Hamish began, rubbing his chin.

"Quiet you two, some of us are trying to listen, Tina snapped.

Hamish looked at her and pressed his lips to a hard line.

Aodh looked down at his food.

"Can I ask you something, Aodh?"

"Fire away."

"About uni."

Aodh swallowed and then gave a short nod.

"How far along were you, before… well… How close were you to graduating?"

"Very. Nearly done."

Hamish nodded. "Right."

Aodh tilted his head and mused. Perhaps this wasn't about him. "Why?"

"Oh, I just… well…" He glanced quickly at the sitting room, but everyone was immersed in WorldWatch. "There's some stuff at the ruins… they just… they're bugging me."

Aodh nodded and swallowed his excitement. "Did you talk to Garrett?"

Hamish nodded and sighed heavily, "it's just…" He looked both ways again, "it's just that something is off."

"And the cryptologists and researchers and archeologists?"

"None of them know a damn thing."

"Look Hamish, if there is something you need me to look at, I can take a wee glance."

Hamish nodded and chewed his lip. "Yeah… yeah that'd be great."

Aodh was practically hopping at the door waiting for Hamish to arrive. He had shuttled Tina out as quickly as he could, valiantly trying not to arouse her suspicions. As a result, Aodh was fairly certain she thought he had a date of some kind, so he just let her think that.

His heart hammered in his chest. Hamish had texted saying he was going to be bringing over some extremely sensitive documents about Brecadh, and it was imperative none of Aodh's family 'drop in'. Hamish didn't say it, but Aodh got the distinct impression that if anyone found out Hamish had taken copies of the documents, or Aodh had seen them, they would likely both end up in a World Government prison.

Aodh fluttered from the kitchen to the sofa and back. Bear snuffled at the doors and windows, as agitated as Aodh was.

There was a soft knock and Aodh did a strange hopping dance before smoothing his holey cashmere sweater and exhaling slowly through pursed lips. "OK Bear, I'm chill... no big deal, no biggie. I am not going to make a big deal outta this for Hamish. Right?" he whispered.

Bear gave him a lazy look of agreement, and stopped barking.

"Aye. Good lad."

"Aodh?" Hamish poked his head around the door gingerly, as if he hadn't barged in a million times before.

"Aye, aye, come on in. Kettle's on," Aodh said casually. He was about to turn away, as if he didn't really care about hearing the clandestine details of Brecadh, when he caught sight of the woman behind Hamish.

"Um, Hamish..." He pointed urgently at the woman, as if she might be some World Government employee Hamish had failed to notice hanging on his coattails.

"Yeah, this is Mercy." Hamish ushered her in and closed the door behind her, locking it and checking before he turned back to Aodh.

Mercy looked at Aodh. She was shuffling, nestled inside an old anorak, looking warily at Bear.

Aodh looked back at her, perturbed by her presence. "Tea?" He finally said in an acid tone.

"Oh Aodh, don't get a face on. She's the resident lead archeologist at Brecadh."

"What?" Aodh couldn't stop his jaw from dropping open.

Mercy looked bashful as she edged towards the table.

"Please sit," Aodh said quickly, yanking out a chair and waving at the table. He glared at Hamish with a 'why-the-fuck-didn't-you-tell-me?' look before smiling sweetly at Mercy.

"Milk, sugar? Well, not real stuff, but you know... "

"Black is fine," Mercy said softly. She unzipped her jacket a fraction and looked around the kitchen. It was all scrubbed wood and exposed brick. "It's a nice house."

"Better than where you're being put up, no doubt." Hamish said with a humorless chuckle.

"Mmm... well, yes."

Aodh flounced down into a chair, inserting himself into the conversation. "Mercy, I'm Aodh, Hamish's friend." He pushed her cup of tea towards her.

"I know. Hamish has told me a lot about you."

"Oh really? Has he?" Aodh glared at Hamish. "He hasn't told me anything about you. I didn't know you were coming over. I would have..."

"Made a cake?" Hamish arched his brow at Aodh, who gave him a withering look in return.

"I know this is a little... invasive, Aodh, but I asked him to bring me along. He tells me you are a brilliant cryptologist."

"I... um..." Aodh gave Hamish a brief, pained look. "I did nae even finish my degree."

Mercy let out a chuckle. "I know. I looked at your file."

"I have a file?"

"Everyone has a file," Mercy said with a close-lipped smile. "Regardless of your degree, you were quite the extraordinary student." Aodh's mouth had twisted strangely. "I was - I am - very close to Professor Mulhaven. He told me about you." Mercy continued, either oblivious or deliberately ignoring Aodh's grimace.

Hamish watched and fiddled with the handle of his teacup. Aodh had never told him what had happened in Glasgow. He knew vaguely, tidbits from Tina, about why he had quit his degree, but he had never asked him to share.

"He told me about what happened. I understand why you quit."

Aodh opened his mouth, ready to snarl, but Mercy held up a hand.

"Trust me Aodh. I understand." She gave him a pointed look, holding eye contact until the anger left Aodh's eyes. "What those boys did to you was unforgiveable, but not greater than what we need you to do."

"I..." Aodh looked around the room, avoiding Hamish's face. "I don't understand," he said finally, awash with confusion.

"The lead cryptologist was hired by the World Government. He is a friend of the Directors. We don't know exactly what he is doing, but it looks a lot like he's withholding information." Hamish looked grim.

"O... kay," Aodh sighed, glad to be on a new topic. "And you need me?"

"We have some images from Brecadh." Mercy reached into her coat and pulled out a thick manila file, held by a stringy red rubber band.

Aodh's eyes widened.

"And you need to help us figure them out."

MARCH 2085

"Aodh!" Tina scuttled away from the windows. "Aodh, your mam and dad are here!" she hissed.

Aodh swooped the papers that were sprawled across the coffee table into a pile and shoved them under the sofa.

"Oh my god, there's someone with them... he looks military. Oh fuck, fuck," Tina panted. She ran into the kitchen, leaving Aodh sitting on the sofa like a lemon, and began making tea.

"Ayyyooodahh?" His mother crooned.

"For god's sake Margie, ye can just knock," his father grumbled.

Presumably the knock got forgotten, as both his parents came striding into the house.

"Aye, good job on tha knock, Mum." Aodh raised an eyebrow at his mother.

She gave him a furious look and her cheeks turned a deep shade of Merlot, but she held her tongue.

"This is Commander Barick." Aodh's father indicated the tall, sturdy man who had followed him inside. He was in his early fifties, but still good looking, with a strong jaw and cheekbones, thick salt and pepper hair, a hooked nose and sharp blue eyes.

"Right-o." Aodh gave Tina a mildly alarmed glance as

the Brigadier nodded his hellos. "I'm Aodh." He turned to his parents, bewildered.

"Commander Barick is here with the World Government Military. He wanted to meet you," his father said in his Scottish lilt. Aodh could have sworn his father raised his eyebrows as he said this.

"Aye, did he? Um..."

"He's an old friend of your father," His mother supplied.

"Can I get everyone some tea?" Tina chirped. Aodh exhaled through his nose. He was the one who had suggested to Hamish that they should let her in on the secret. If she blew it, Hamish would never forgive him.

Aodh gave her a look, before smiling cheerily at his parents and the Brigadier. "Oh, I'm sure they're not staying Tina. Just popped in to say hello, eh?"

The Commander chewed his lower lip thoughtfully. "Actually, I wanted to have a little chat with you. If that's all right?"

Aodh knew he didn't have much of a choice. "Why don't we all have dinner?"

"We can let them have a chat. We'll be back in a bit, Wilson." Aodh's father nodded at Commander Barick and placed a large hand on his wife's back as he thrust her out into the bleak windy evening.

"We're actually expecting company." Aodh pursed his lips at the Commander.

"Hamish Waters," The Commander said softly.

Tina remained frozen by the kettle, like a rabbit in headlights. "I... tea... tea's ready."

"I know about your little... research project."

Aodh felt his stomach drop and a wave of acid rose in his throat.

"I'm actually very interested in Brecadh, for personal reasons." Barick paused.

"Look, Commander..."

"Please, call me Barick." He narrowed his eyes at Aodh. "I'm not here to get you into any trouble."

"We havnae done anything," Tina protested shrilly.

"Right, well..." Aodh sighed. "Why don't you have a seat? Hamish should be here soon." Aodh wondered if there was any way he could warn Hamish, and Mercy, before they ended up in this trap too. He glanced up to find Barick watching him closely, and realized that if this was a trap, Mercy and Hamish were already fucked.

"I just don't get it." Barick rubbed his forehead as he looked at the scribbles Aodh had drawn all over an image of the lower crypt that was informally known as the 'master bedroom'.

"Uuuunnngghhhh..." Aodh threw his head back. Barick rolled his eyes at Hamish, Mercy and Tina. Aodh was clearly a drama queen.

"These markings here... you think this is their alphabet? Why would it be here?" Mercy frowned.

"I don't know - I haven't been in there... out of context." Aodh balled his hands into fists. They all wanted him to figure everything out, and he was the only one who had never set foot inside Brecadh. Well, except Tina, but she didn't count.

"Look, we know this is a lot. Which other images would help?" Barick spread the pictures on the table out. Aodh looked over them and tried to remember how he had reached the conclusion that the markings were the alphabet.

"Something is missing." He cocked his head to one side.

'This is a crypt," Aodh said. The others looked less than impressed. "A crypt typically refers to a burial place, but that isn't what this is. This is a subterranean city."

"Right." Mercy opened up her palms.

"Mercy, have you found any bones, any burial sites?"

"We think they probably did a water burial or some kind of pyre - at least, that's our guess so far."

"We've been searching the surrounding waters for any related artifacts," Hamish volunteered.

"And?"

"Nothing."

"They wouldn't have nothing. There would be something for the dead." Aodh jabbed a drawing from another picture. "They respected life and death and the passage between them. They wouldn't throw their dead away. Something is missing."

Barick was shaking his head.

"What?" Mercy narrowed her eyes at him.

"Have you been... shut out lately?" Barick sucked in his cheeks, giving himself the appearance of a hawk.

"I don't think so," Mercy said, her suspicions of Barick deflated. "Have you?"

"Well, yes... I mean, we knew the WGM wasn't wanted there in the first place." He sipped his tea and took another ginger snap. "But the last two weeks... we've been pariahs."

"Uh huh - you said two weeks?" Hamish knitted his brows, "we got the request to do an artifact search from the cryptology department. They said they reckoned there was stuff in the surrounding waters."

"What? From what? There is literally *nothing* here that suggests that," Aodh said with exasperation.

"No one even ran that by me." Mercy looked flustered. "Although half my team has been replaced, so I've been slammed getting them up to speed."

"Och, sounds like someone disnae want somethin' to be found," Tina said, pushing back her chair and making her way into the kitchen. "I'm making a stew. There was nae much at the market, it's no gonna be great, but you're all welcome to stay."

Aodh pushed Barick and Mercy's cups back to the utmost edge of the table and rearranged the images, keeping his notes at the center.

"Oh my god!" Aodh gasped.

"What?" Mercy snapped her head towards him.

"Oh... no, never mind."

"Don't do that Aodh, you'll give me a heart attack!" Barick chided.

"I just can't tell a damn thing without bein' there."

"Well, you've got further than the lead cryptologist, and he *is* there," Mercy said with a black chuckle.

"We need to open Brecadh up to the public," Barick announced. "Get Aodh in there."

"We can't. The WG will put a stop to it."

"Not if we say we are giving permits to gifted researchers."

"A special permit," Mercy said, nodding along with Barick.

"Isn't it contaminated and cursed?" Tina said, throwing a glance at the TV, muted in the background. Another report about an unfortunate junior archeologist who had been crushed to death by debris in a tunnel was running on Sky News.

Mercy, Barick and Hamish exchanged a laugh. "No, it's all just fuss. The WG are letting it continue because it keeps lookie-loos away." Hamish said when Aodh pinched his arm. He hated being left out.

"Well, just tell the entire press and the world that, and bob's your uncle, I'm in." Aodh rolled his eyes.

"Oh Aodh, you're not wrong. We release information to the press saying that Brecadh is safe, we're short on information and we're thinking of allowing permits to gifted researchers. Once that ball gets rolling, even the WG will have a hard time stopping it."

"So, who releases it?" Tina was flushed with excitement.

"Has to be someone reliable, and close." Mercy frowned.

"I'll do it," Barick said. "No one will suspect me, and I do sound like a very, very reliable source." He smiled.

"Aye, and it's nae like the military have ever leaked information 'afore." Aodh hopped up from the table with a cheeky grin. "Now, I best be back to work so that when you lot get me in there I can figure this out."

Aodh rested his head back against his headboard and organized his notes. Whilst he was scruffy to the extreme when it came to clothes, hair and general demeanor, he was fastidiously scrupulous about his notes. Different notes on different topics were color coded and labeled, and corresponding research and images were tabbed with the right color. He had forced Tina to steal one of the large three-ring binders from her office for him to use.

He placed the binder on top of the unmade duvet and opened it at the first page. Barick, Hamish and Mercy hadn't been able to copy a blueprint, but they had worked together to draw him an accurate layout of Brecadh. This was followed by a series of images, numbered according to how Aodh had numbered each room. The walls were each covered with strange glyphs, or drawings that depicted scenes no one could understand.

"I'm missing something," Aodh mumbled to himself. Leaning forward and crossing his long legs in front of him, he looked like a praying mantis. He unsnapped the binder and began to lay everything out on his bed till he had a paper jigsaw.

The imagery in some of the pictures was shocking. Brutal killings, so the 'team' that Aodh wasn't part of had assumed they were a violent tribal culture. But nothing else added up to that. No death worship, or death-related gods, no bones found, no sacrificial chambers. And, many of the drawings were equally mundane; fishing, people with what seemed to be domesticated wolves, women dancing.

Aodh looked at the next row; crisp pictures of the glyphs that no one could decipher. He was sure the 'master bedroom' held the key to their alphabet. He just needed to work out how it paralleled their own alphabet in order to understand what everything meant.

Aodh ran his fingers over his notes. He had drawn each glyph out in biro, pressing hard on the paper so he could feel the indent like reverse braille. His fingers brushed over the top of each page and he closed his eyes. His eyelids flickered slightly as his brain ran through his database: Egyptian hieroglyphs, Pict runes, Greek alphabet, numerals, Norse runes, Man'ygana, Sanskrit… on and on the list went, but nothing matched.

Aodh snapped his eyes open. He shifted his puzzle slightly, tilting the images. They weren't aliens, as the news loved to hypothesize; they weren't magical or mythical or anything other than regular ancient humans. Yet somehow, they had gone unnoticed for thousands of years. And their city had survived under the North Sea. There were no bones, or any way of learning about the people themselves, the humans who had created an entire city. And there were no records of there ever being a landmass historically in that location.

Aodh sighed. Before he had started this little endeavor with Mercy, Hamish, Barick and Tina he had watched a show that claimed that the entire City of Brecadh was a hoax, an elaborate trick. They speculated it was for political subterfuge. Aodh hadn't believed it then, but the gaps in the information were starting to make him wonder.

"Aodh?" Tina hollered from the kitchen.

Aodh gritted his teeth. He felt almost constant frustration now that he was working on the Brecadh project. He wouldn't feel relief until he got to see it for himself.

"Aodh, QUICKLY!"

Something in Tina's voice sent him scrambling from his bed, forgetting his frustration and forgetting about keeping his notes in any kind of order.

MAY 2085

"I'm never getting in there," Aodh said glumly. They had met down at the beach behind the house so Bear could run around, but also so that they could meet discreetly. The past two months had brought a maelstrom of press and military to the isle. Both Barick and Mercy were acutely aware of how much trouble they would be in if they were caught handing 'sensitive, classified' information over to a civilian.

"I am working on it, Aodh. I promise." Mercy lobbed a tennis ball into the lapping waves and Bear charged in after it. "Morale is low. The anniversary of the discovery is in less than two months. The public want information and we don't have any. I'm thinking we release the idea then, or Barick does, and the public will clamor for it."

"The other deaths - were they really accidents?" Tina shielded her eyes from the low sun. It was chilly, and a brisk salty wind swept in over the beach.

"Of course!"

Aodh and Tina raised their eyebrows at one another.

"Hamish said the place seems cursed."

"Aye, especially after all those lovely remains they found," Aodh said with cutting sarcasm.

Barick glared at him. "We knew there had to be remains somewhere. Even you said that."

"Aye, a mass grave was nae exactly what I was talkin' aboot," Aodh said with a chuckle.

"The remains are still being processed," Mercy said neutrally. "We don't know it was a mass burial. It could've been a burial site into which remains were placed at different times."

"Mmm hmmm." Aodh inflected this with a particular type of sassiness that only he could muster.

"But I mean, four more people have died, and there's like three injured from the tunnel collapse." Tina frowned.

Aodh rolled his eyes. She was paranoid that something was going to happen to Hamish, even though he never really went inside Brecadh.

"Tina, honestly, tunnel collapses at subterranean dig sites are very common. Yes it's unfortunate, but it doesn't mean the place is cursed."

"What about..."

"The other deaths all have explanations too, contrary to what the media would have you believe. Two were killed in the tunnel collapse, one chap stayed after hours and drowned when a freak wave flooded the western cavern and the other death was someone who..." Barick paused and shifted to look out at sea, "someone who had a heart problem."

"So there isn't some deadly Brecadh virus that'll turn us all intae zombies then?" Aodh winked at Barick, who smiled back with relief.

"No, not any time soon."

Tina looked slightly appeased, but she still squinted out over the waves as if she might catch sight of Hamish's boat.

Mercy turned to them and crossed her arms. "Look, we're planning on releasing the idea about an anniversary permit to gifted archeologists, cryptologists, linguists, etcetera. We'll make sure as soon as it's official that your permit hits the desk as a definite yes. No more mucking around, Aodh. We need to know what those glyphs say, and fast. If one more bad thing happens at Brecadh, I dread to think what the WG will do."

JULY 12th 2085
First Anniversary of the Discovery of Brecadh

"So Ms. Davies, Mr Comey, you are the lead archeologists at Brecadh?" The presenter was in a shiny blue suit, nestling in the warmth of a studio, glad to be far away from the freezing island at five in the morning.

"Yes," Mercy smiled warmly at the TV presenter. "Doctor Comey specializes in sub-aquatic or underwater archeology." They were sitting in the makeshift command center that had been erected at the Lerwick Marine Institute.

"And Doctor Davies specializes in prehistoric archeology." Dr Comey grinned at Mercy.

Aodh was hopping from foot to foot in the kitchen. The smell of coffee mixed with the burnt odor that their heater gave off.

"Right, yes, of course, doctors." The presenter quickly recovered from his blunder.

"Come on, come on," Aodh mumbled to himself. Bear let out a strangled whine.

"So, this 'permit', it's unprecedented. We rarely see civilians, even extremely well-educated ones, being given access to a site as historically important as Brecadh."

"Well…" Mercy paused, "the anniversary permits aren't being given to random civilians, they are granted to those with exceptional ability within their field. We were clear to give the permit very specific parameters."

Dr Comey, with his thin, pale face and shaved head, looked strangely childlike, until he smiled, and you saw the impish charm that lay beneath. "And we always welcome fresh eyes and fresh minds."

Aodh could've sworn Mercy was stifling a smile and wondered if she had told Comey about him. The past month he had made significant headway into the glyphs and their meaning, although he hadn't told anyone. He knew he should have at least shared his theories with Mercy, but then another part of him wanted to emerge from Brecadh with his theory proven. Degree be damned, or lack thereof. It would be something he could shove in everyone's faces to prove he hadn't been broken by what had happened to him.

"And do you already have the candidates lined up?" The presenter's eyes were wide.

"We do. We have the first round of permit holders coming to check out the site today, to be briefed in security protocol, and to sign their lives away," Comey joked. The presenter looked momentarily shocked before realizing he was joking and giving an embarrassed chuckle.

Aodh knew this wasn't true. The signatures were liability waivers, covering everything from contracting syphilis to getting buried alive, and non-disclosure agreements.

"And how much will the permit holders be told about what you have already learned?"

"We will only be telling them things we know to be concrete facts." Mercy nodded her head stiffly.

"No conjecture, speculation or theorizing." Comey waggled an eyebrow.

"Such as?"

"Such as carbon date test results, layout, original structure, and where we found certain items."

"So not much."

"We do know more," Comey said softly, untroubled as to whether the presenter and the listening public believed him or not, "but much of it is still theory. We want to keep our minds open and not try to prove, disprove or even be colored by theories."

The presenter frowned. He had wanted something more salacious that could make headlines. "But isn't that why you've allowed these permits? Because you haven't discovered much?"

"We've discovered plenty," Comey said. "But most of it is just too boring to interest the public."

Aodh snorted. That was a lie. They had discovered some things, though 'plenty' was a stretch. And none of it was boring. They just didn't want the press going crazy with more insane theories: 'ZOMBIE VIRUS ENCASED IN BRECADH'S TOMBS!', 'CURSE OF THE CITY OF LIGHT SPREADS TO REST OF SHETLAND ISLE', (the locals had got a kick out of that one – two of farmer Taff's sheep had been killed by a wayward Labrador, hardly a curse.) 'DID ALIENS BUILD BRECADH?' 'IS BRECADH THE LOST CITY OF ATLANTIS?'

There was a knock.

"Yes!" Aodh yelped. "Come in!"

Hamish and Barick shuffled inside.

"Is it happening? Oh my god, please tell me it is?"

Barick raised an eyebrow. "Yes. It's happening."

"Is Bear ready?"

Aodh nodded. Bear's service vest was wrapped snugly around him.

"Do you nae need your notes?" Tina mumbled sleepily

from her bedroom doorway. Hamish went over and gave her a peck on the forehead.

Aodh raised his eyebrows. "They're seared into ma' brain, Tina."

"All right, I'm just checkin'."

"He wouldn't be able to bring them anyway. All bags are being searched for recording devices, cameras, and so on." Barick shook his head.

"You don't have anything like that?" Hamish looked sharply at Aodh.

"No, just a notepad, and Bear." Aodh rubbed Bear's monstrous head.

"Excellent. Let's go." Barick turned crisply on his heel and led them out of the cottage towards Brecadh.

"Here." A chubby woman with frizzy hair handed Aodh a sleek oblong of metal. "It's a recording device. State your name, position and area of expertise."

"What is this for exactly?"

"We'll collect them all at the end. You're not allowed to take any data off site." She spoke in a clipped voice with a strange accent that Aodh couldn't place.

"But..."

"Don't worry, you'll get credit if you discover anything," she sighed exasperatedly. She looked at Bear with distaste.

"He's a service dog. I was told he could come in with me." Aodh snapped.

"I can read!" The woman snapped back.

Bear looked up at her with his best gooey-eyed stare. It failed.

"Everything ready?" Mercy and Dr Comey smiled at

Aodh. They poked their heads into the cramped room.

"Commander Barick will be your chaperone."

"I need a chaperone?" Aodh looked disgusted.

"The Commander is a chaperone now?" The woman asked at the same time.

"Everyone wants to pitch in," Dr Comey said gently. His voice seemed to soothe frizzy hair for a moment.

"Aodh Campbell?" Barick stepped into the room. He was very convincing. "And this must be Bear?" He quickly leant down and showered the dog with affection to help disguise the fact that Bear had seemed excited to see him.

"You're not supposed to touch service dogs," Frizzy-Hair muttered half-heartedly.

"Sorry." Commander Barick stood up. "I'll be your chaperone, but just pretend I'm not there."

"And don't forget to use the recording device. For everything. No notepads. Talk us through it as you go through it."

Mercy's eyes were shining. "Dr Comey and I will be the ones going through them after."

"Ok then, take me into Brecadh." Aodh slid the recorder into his pocket, gripped Bear's leash and turned towards the door.

AUGUST 2086

"Here you are." Tina was standing in the doorway with her arms folded. Her eyes were red and puffy, but she still looked peeved. Hamish stood behind her, consciously looking anywhere but at the Campbells.

"Come on." Tina flapped a hand vaguely at the Campbells, who had snuck into the facility. The sleek comms box crackled in the corner of the room and everyone turned to look at it.

"We... dog... down here... what... fuck... low tide... it looks like that... service..."

"Oh fuck," Mrs Campbell made a fist. "Bear."

Tina covered her face with her hands and started to cry. Bear had been trying to run back to Brecadh ever since Aodh had vanished.

The comms crackled again, "something... in his mouth... holy shit... shit..."

A frizzy-haired receptionist grabbed the receiver. "Is everything OK down there?"

"Comey's... another... tunnels... new rooms."

"What?" Hamish strode over to the comms. "What was in Bear's mouth? And what the fuck do they mean they've found new rooms?"

"I don't know if we should allow civilians in here." The General tilted his head at the Campbells, Tina and Hamish.

"They're his family. They deserve to hear whatever is on the recorder."

The silver oblong, still stained with blood and sealed in a plastic bag, sat in the center of the table like an undiffused bomb.

"Mercy, look," The General started, but Mercy held up one, flat, immovable palm.

"General, there's something you need to know... you all need to know." Mercy took a deep breath. "Aodh knew a lot more about Brecadh than you thought. I and Commander

Barick had been giving him information about the glyphs and the discoveries."

"What?" The senior WG officials looked confused, outraged and aghast at the same time. "Why on earth would you need his help?"

"He's a genius," Mercy said simply.

"He had a brilliant mind," replied Hamish. "Has," he quickly corrected himself.

"The drop out?" one man said, his lips curling back in disgust. A few others from the WG opened their mouths to voice their own concerns, but Mr. Campbell cut them off. "Does it even matter anymore?" He said and the room fell silent.

Davina Porter, dressed in snug khakis and a thin long-sleeve top, surveyed the group. "I'm Dr Porter. You can call me Davina. We'll be sticking in groups of three as we head into the new tunnel system to explore the chambers. Comms are to be on at all times."

Her audience were not as excited as they should be about this groundbreaking discovery. The key to Brecadh was in these new rooms, she could feel it, and it would be she, Dr Davina Porter, who would uncover it.

"I know a young man and the Commander went missing, but they were most likely swept out to sea by a tidal flux," she went on. "There may be channels in these tunnels and chambers we don't know about. That is why you all are fitted with GPS devices in your kit vests."

"What if we find them?" A young man piped up. He was too weedy to be military.

"Them?"

"Aodh and Commander Barick," a young woman in camo said, glaring at Davina with steely eyes.

"Report it back to the base immediately and stay at that location till a recovery team arrives." Davina rolled her eyes ever so slightly. "Now, you all know the protocol, and you need to report back to me as each new chamber is entered. Understand?" She looked around the room; people nodded and mumbled assent. "Do you all understand?"

"Yes." The reply was more uniform, but edged with frustration. Davina didn't care.

"We'll play the tape once through - we can pause it for clarification. I will be transcribing as we go." The slim Eurasian man smiled warmly at all of them, and then perched on a small stool with a laptop. His long, graceful fingers tapped away at the keyboard for a moment. He smiled again, reaching forward and pressing the touch pad on the device to begin the recording.

"This is... I'm Aodh Campbell, I'm twenty-seven years old. I'm a... well, I know a lot about cryptology and linguistics. I applied for the permit because I'm a Shetland local, and obviously 'cause of all the stuff about crypto-linguistics... Do I really have to do this, Barick?"

(The Commander, whispering) "Come on Aodh. They'll be listening to this. Yes, all the permit holders have to do a full audio recording."

Aodh: "Right... well, we're just entering the main tunnel. Ohmyfuckinggod... ohmyholyfuckin'... This is amazin'! Nae wonder ye didnae want any random fuckers walkin' around in here."

"We should hook up the screen with imaging of the site," Mercy suggested to cover the chuckles in the room.

The General coughed. "I don't know." He looked over at the Campbells and Tina.

"Ye think we give a fuck aboot a fuckin' bunch of dirt? I wannae know what the fuck happened to my son," Mrs Campbell snarled.

The General nodded, and Mercy linked the large curved screen that filled one wall with her laptop. An image of the main entrance chamber appeared. It was cavernous with rounded ceilings, smoothed to an almost liquid chocolate texture. Thin grooves ran down the ceiling, and the walls, across the floor into a central well that collected water.

"These images look like there was either another civilization who took over, or a faction from within who uprooted the system. Matriarchal society, thriving fishing community. Advanced understanding of medicine. Even diving. They knew about water filtration systems... You can see the glyphs here, less so, but they do occur at the bottom and edges of some of these pictures. I would guess this was a meeting or ceremonial chamber... but Mercy knew that already."

"Aodh!" Barick chided.

"Their grasp of science was incredible. Solar and lunar movements, tidal flux, medicine... I want tae go this way. Right... this is the thermal spring. Jesus Christ on a cracker. See those alcoves Barick? They're essentially small gas valves, they could be ignited to create light."

The entire room was transfixed by Aodh's voice and the images. A huge pool of iridescent turquoise filled the room, with tiered ledges around the side. Off to the edges, two smaller pools that ebbed were kept separate by a carved wall.

"The pool is a natural hot spring, the two smaller ones are cold saltwater. They must have built up that wall to keep them separate - nae sure how. It's made of some kind of marble."

"What are those?" A WG man pointed a finger to the left of the screen. Mercy panned it sideways. Large flat squares were revealed that looked like small rice paddies.

"We think they're hydroponic farms," Dr Comey said.

Aodh's voice continued.

"This is definitely a hydroponic farm. See how some of the spring water was once diverted here, and that's what that drawing is out front... the third panel. Come on Barick, de ye nae pay attention? The third panel is a woman holding a bouquet of flowers, 'cept they're not, they're medicinal herbs, and she's lookin' up towards the sun, 'cept she's nae, she's looking at one of these gas balls... but there must've been another source of light in here... [long pause] Hmm... Anyway, at the woman's feet... in the picture Barick! At her feet, there are wooden tubes, with small holes. Same thing we use today. Pretty much. S'like a natural irrigation system. Incredible. Also, I am pretty sure those glyphs on the wall... they are what helped me crack everything."

"What?"

"Well, remember how in the master bedroom I said I thought there was the key to the alphabet, and none of ye gave a shite?"

"Aodh! People will listen to this… you could get myself, Mercy and Hamish into a lot of trouble!"

"That 'master bedroom' is nae a bedroom. It was for healing. I think healing was considered a sacred thing… I think that's why the room looked so… so regal."

"What does that have to do with all this?"

"The same glyphs are in the 'master bedroom' but in combinations. When I saw the lab reports about what was found in the scrapings from here it got me thinking that this was a farm… for medicinal plants, and that the glyphs musta denoted what was planted on each row." [Muffled sound – Aodh quietly recites the lab report word for word 'belladonna, marijuana, ferns, blood flower, hyssop and some plant matter that we can't trace back to an origin.]

"See how each glyph lines up with where a row woulda been. Right? Well in the room the combinations are medicines. Cures. Antidotes. Poisons."

"Oh my god… so… you just had to figure out what plant each glyph lined up with?" Even Barick sounded excited.

"Aye, it's like algebra… a wee bit trickier though, since in the master bedroom some of the glyphs mean other things… I think… like, quantities, times to 'marinate' or something… I'm still figuring it out, dosage, ailment.

"That's… that's fucking incredible Aodh."

"Aye… I bloody am." [long pause]. *"The thing that I cannae figure out is why would they need so much medicine. Huh, the layout is a part o' this too."*

"Clever boy," Comey chuckled.

"What? What is it?" Tina looked around frantically.

"The layout of Brecadh is very, very clever. It uses the

tide as a defense, as well as to channel fish into the settlement. Inside, light is filtered and projected through the use of polished glass, allowing the entire area to remain lit, most of the time." Comey steepled his fingers. "They even use the natural subaquatic tunnels to their advantage." He stopped there, and no one wanted to press him for an explanation.

"Why did they need defenses and secret tunnels and all this medicine?" A WG woman said. Her face was severe and her short hair was clipped close to her neck. "Who exactly were they afraid of?"

No one answered. Instead, Aodh's gentle Scottish lilt filled the room once more.

"The layout helps decipher the glyphs, there are instructions on the walls... like... you had to take certain herbs... I know it disnae make much sense, but it's like... they had to have medicine to go to certain parts of the settlement. Barick, has the whole settlement been uncovered?"

"What do you mean?"

"Like, has it all been mapped? Have they found more rooms, more... I dunno..."

"Why?"

"There is more to this place - we're missin' something. Anyway, right. Let's get tae the master bedroom, which is actually a hospital." [Recorder clicks on and off amidst the sounds of crunching footsteps.] "We're gonna be here for a while. I got most o' these semi-decoded. The triptych layout of the rooms holds part of the key... I couldnae set it up right with the images. Right... righty-o... OK, here are the ones I'd already done. This here, these are all for pain relief."

"How did they know about all this?"

"I dinnae ken... that's what I cannae figure out. Aye, maybe that's what everyone in that mass grave was for eh? Ha."

"Aodh, what did you just say?"

[Long silence] "Ohmifuckinggod... Barick, I think that's actually what it was. I cannae be sure since I don't know all the glyphs, but see this one here, it's beside all the other medicinal blends."

"What?"

[Rustling] "Look here, below this alcove. These glyphs above are usage, dose, how to make it, and the ones below are the ingredients that make the medicine - basically its name. But underneath, see this, this glyph I'm pretty sure is their symbol for subject/person/human, you know?"

"Right?"

"Well, it's underneath each one, beside this glyph, which I am pretty sure means 'test'."

"Test subject?"

"Oh god." The WG-appointed forensic pathologist paled. He was excellent, and specialized in fossilized remains. No one objected to him being on the team, even if he was World Government. "All the bodies were marked, scarred... they bore signs of either torture, warfare, sacrifice – I had no way of knowing."

"They were experimenting on their own people," Comey said. "Not uncommon, and that explains a lot."

"Were there two groups of them then?" An older man with tufts of gray hair dotted sporadically over his head peered at the screen.

"We can't figure that out." Mercy held up her hands in frustration. "Looking at the pictures, there was clearly some divide in their group. Mainlanders? Early Norse or Saxons? Even Picts?"

"Maybe a faction that broke away?" suggested Comey. "But, if so, where did they go? There aren't records of civilization on the Shetlands till much later."

"Let's say Aodh was right," the WG forensic pathologist cut in. "Could the newcomers have been people they captured?"

"No, look at the images." Mercy zoomed in on the first panel. "Here they are, living in quiet, basic domesticity. A small fishing community, on this tiny crop of land." Mercy looked around. Everyone was focused on her and Comey. Even the General looked interested.

Mercy flicked over a few more screens, "The newcomers were teaching them about tunneling, about hydroponics, about light refraction; one picture even looked like early metalworking."

"And apparently about lab testing and medicines and human subjects?" The typist arched one eyebrow and resumed the recording.

"There were other people who came to Brecadh."

"What? Who?"

"I don't know. This glyph, it's slightly different. Maybe a foreigner? It denotes a person, just not a person like them. Stranger, maybe?"

"What else does it say?" [Baricks' voice booming]

"It tells their story. The new people came and taught them about the sun, the moon and the stars. They taught

them how to grow, how to heal and how to live longer. They taught them architecture, physics and science."

"Where did they come from?"

"They didn't know. They thought they were gods because they knew so much, but the people explained that they weren't. This doesn't make sense. Maybe I... maybe I'm wrong."

"What?"

"It says the people wanted to teach them everything because the end of the world was coming, and this was the only way to survive."

"What – the – FUCK? Christ! Doomsday shit is the last thing Brecadh needs."

"This glyph... what is this?"

"I don't know."

"I wasn't asking you. The cure? So they thought a disease was coming. Well, that's nae that weird Barick. I mean, plague, Spanish flu, bird flu, aids, Ebola... lots o' diseases have been a global issue. Back then, even something small could'a been the end o' the world."

"So they left their people to escape this disease. They thought they could teach them how to survive it."

"Aye, or wanted to practice a cure to make sure they did. [Bear starts barking.] Shh bear. Bear, quiet!"

"What's he scratching at? Mercy'll have a fucking fit."

"Is that a door?"

"What?"

"At the end of the last panel... that part... it's not dirt, it's stone. It's in like, wee pieces..."

"Don't you dare, Aodh! Mercy will be furious and you'll end up arrested."

"It tells me too." [Scrabbling. Barick whispering unintelligibly and furiously, then the sound of falling rocks].

Davina pressed on down the tunnel. It was damp and chilly, but she was sweating under the kit vest. The other junior archaeologist was so close to her she wanted to stop short and smack the girl, and the soldier was snapping his rifle about like he had watched one too many horror movies.

"Tunnel's widening. Less air though," the soldier said.

Davina looked down at her oxygen meter. It had dropped about five points. Too many more and they wouldn't be able to continue.

"Like a pressure lock," the girl behind her remarked.

Davina made a waspish face but didn't turn around. "It's fine." She pressed forward. The tunnel was curving slightly, and she rushed onward in a funny half-jog. Her breath came short and ragged.

"Fuck!" She slapped a hand against the wall, "FUCK! A dead fucking end!" She screeched.

The soldier stepped forward. He tapped the wall with the butt of his rifle. Bits crumbled down. "Nah, it's just a blocked passage... or maybe a shitty door."

"Maybe they blocked it off?" The girl said softly.

Davina yanked her pickaxe from her vest.

"Shouldn't we..."

Davina cut them off with a look. She lifted her comms. "Team three, do you copy? Over." There was no reply. "Team three?"

"This is team one, left tunnel. We can't get hold of them."

"We can't wait for them. They're probably documenting what's down that branch." Davina lifted the comms to her face. "Your tunnel dead-ended, right? Over."

"Yes ma'am. Over."

"Are you a hundred per cent sure?" Davina was panting, from excitement or lack of oxygen she couldn't tell. "Over."

"Hundred per cent. Stone wall. You could hear water on the other side. Lapping... must go to some underwater cave. Could hear birds too. Over."

"Right, backtrack to the main chamber and go down the right tunnel to help team three. Got it? Over."

"Yes ma'am. Over."

"Let's get to work." She snapped at the soldier. He fiddled with his comms, uneasy. "Now!" She said, decisively swinging her pickaxe at the wall. Chips of rock and dirt scattered like confetti.

Back in the offices, Aodh's voice had resumed.

[Muffled banging, Barick hissing 'this is a bad idea', Bear snuffling, Aodh grunting.] "Oh my god! Look at this, Barick."

"Hold on."

"You should name this Aodh's room, since I found it."

"What is this place? Are those different glyphs?"

"Well aren't you the clever soldier. Some of these are ancient Pict runes. Huh. Yikes! Is that bone? Oh shite, this was a prison."

"Why are you sitting down? What does it all say?"

"I cannae breathe! Hold on a second... this is gonna take me a minute." [Long silence. Rustling. Bear crying, Barick petting him.]

"The guy was put in here for going against the newcomers. He calls them comet people, star people?"

"Like Gods?"

"Like... aliens."

"Oh god Aodh, you don't really believe that tripe?"

"Shh Barick. He writes that the star people came to 'help' them but it was a trick/an illusion. "They brought new things but also death and disease. They used them for disease." He must mean they used them as test subjects. He writes that they have a chamber where they throw the ones who are too weak or tested on and 'failed' and they leave them there to die."

"The mass grave? So they were testing some old disease?"

"Must be. He says, "the star people came to test out their main 'death weapon'. He says they wanted to see which land people would live."

"Must've been something like chicken pox. Or some type of flu. Long gone, but deadly back then no doubt." [Barick huffing] "You know... it sounds like some... like some kind of bioweapon testing facility."

"He writes "they keep it alive in the dirty plant." Dirty plant? Is that what he means? Rotten plant?"

"Mold?"

"Yes! Yes, he must mean mold. 'They keep it alive in the mold. There's a sealed room... separate.' Must mean another chamber... Barick, there must be another chamber. He writes "it lives for many moons and no one lives when they get sick... they aren't allowed to leave and the disease can fly". Must be airborne. Barick, that's exactly what this is... BEAR! No! Grab him, Barick!"

[Scuffling. Aodh screams] "BEAR! BEAR!"

[Clanging. Boot stomping. Faint crackle. Barick yelling in the distance.]

The recording died abruptly and the room was eerily silent.

The General stood up. "The disease, contained in mold, I mean… we need to notify the CDC and get everyone into quarantine."

"You don't think it's still alive?" the WG woman asked.

The forensic pathologist frowned. "If they kept it alive in mold, mold is a living thing - in a damp chamber with spring water, high humidity, relatively warm… I mean, 27,000 years would make it some old, old mold, but I suppose it isn't impossible."

The General paced back and forth. "I need to alert my men."

Mercy shook her head. "We need to alert Davina."

Davina could feel the barrier weakening, the rocks losing their stability as they began to tumble down of their own accord.

"We're close!" she grunted triumphantly. The soldier and the junior archaeologist said nothing. They were all sweating in the humidity, short on oxygen and cramped into the tunnel.

"Look at this." The girl leant in beside Davina. "It's a Pict rune. I think it says protection… safety… like… safe door?"

Davina pushed her aside, a manic grin on her face, "This must be where they kept their valuables." Images of Tutankhamen's tomb and Mayan gold danced in her mind. "Move." She swung her pickaxe and brought it down on the widening crack. With a shudder the packed dirt and stone tumbled away, leaving a wide chasm that opened into a new chamber.

The girl vomited. The soldier just managed to keep it together.

Davina recoiled. Sulfur and death. The rank fumes were pungent in the cramped space. She shielded her mouth and nose as she looked down. Small waves pushed up through a hole. Fish carcasses and spongy matter carpeted the floor. Davina forced a gag back down her throat.

There was a strange sound. A percolating, pulsing… the sound you get when you water a plant and listen to the soil as it's absorbed, like it's breathing.

"What is that *smell*?" The girl lifted herself upright, emptied of anything left to vomit.

Davina scoured the floor and recoiled. A shaft of light fell in from another tunnel entrance. A mound of fallen rocks freshly disturbed the mold that covered the walls. Someone had found another way into this chamber.

Not someone, Davina thought, as she stumbled backwards. Commander Barick and Aodh Campbell. Their corpses, or what was left of them, were hard to distinguish from the fish carcasses that littered the floor. Their skin had been eaten away and the exposed ligaments of their limbs were tangled together in a terrified embrace. Davina kept backing up until she banged into the junior archaeologist.

A fine mist clouded up and Davina felt it tickling her nostrils and throat.

"Oh my god, is that a body?" The girls' voice was high and full of panic.

"Back up!" Davina snapped. Her head swam and she felt her a strange popping in her eardrums as though she might faint. She turned to look at the pathologist but her vision clouded, and she could've sworn she saw billions of tiny white particles floating away down the corridor before her vision went black and she slumped down on the damp earth.

LIPS LIKE THAT

Procedures – 0
Twitter Followers – 212
Instagram Followers – 307

Rosie Dalkeith frowned at the papers scattered across her desk. Her fingers hovered over the new MacBook her parents had bought her as a congratulatory present for getting into the civil engineering program at Texas A&M.

"Fuck," she grumbled. She clicked the FaceTime application and hit her sister's name, 'Lily', adorned with a flower emoji.

"Hey Rosie. What's up?"

"Nothing, I'm just... whatever, how are you? How's home?"

"It's good. I miss you. Tank misses you, don't you Tank?" Lily spun the phone around to show a graying dog passed out on her bed.

"Yeah, he looks heartbroken. What've you been up to?" Rosie took her laptop over to her bed and leant back against the cheap plywood headboard.

"Nothing much. Mom is super happy I made varsity Cheer squad. I guess Dad has some big cattle ranchers' thing this weekend."

"Like something near here?" Rosie's voice ticked up hopefully.

"Nah... I dunno." Lily flopped on her bed and rubbed Tank's ears. "How's school? How's Alpha Pi?"

Rosie swallowed the lump in her throat. She was a legacy. Joining the sorority hadn't been much of a choice. "Good. Yeah... it's nice." Rosie faked a smile. In AP's defense, the girls were all lovely; it just wasn't really Rosie's thing. The girls were all about parties, make-up, marriage and shopping.

"Mom's so weird about it, she started wearing her aggies shirt and her AP sweater again." Lily wrinkled her pretty little nose. "Anyway, I gotta go, I said I'd meet Donovan tonight."

"Yeah... cool, send everyone my love."

Lily let out a wave and hung up. Her long blonde hair shimmered down, half covering her face for a frozen moment, before the screen went black. She wondered if she should have told Lily about the other night.

Rosie had been at a mixer, as opposed to a frat party. The entire Alpha Pi house had been invited and it was a low-key event. One of Rosie's old school friends, a guy named Jacob, had been there. She had been looking for him, just to say hi, when she had overheard the frat boys.

"So, the new Alpha Pi pledges are pretty fucking hot," one guy said.

"I'd bang them... well most of them."

"Maybe not that Rosie chick. You know her, right?"

Jacob coughed. "Yeah, we went to school together."

"How the fuck she'd get into Alpha Pi?"

"She's really smart - and a legacy. Her family are big ranchers up outside of Dinosaur Valley State Park."

"Huh, must've got in on her legacy status. Maybe her mom was hot," one guy mused.

Rosie, rooted in the hallway, wanted to die of shame. She heard Jacob laugh along with the other boys. "She's got super hot sisters. One older and one younger."

"How hot?" said a leering voice.

"Older sister is kinda tomboy, but really hot and a total badass. High-level army. Younger sister is insanely hot, cheer squad."

"Well let's just pray she gets in next year to make up for her dud of a sister."

"ROSIE!" She heard Jazmin shriek from down the hallway.

She closed her laptop and sighed, plastering a smile onto her face.

"OMG, ROSIEEEE." Jazmin, along with Gabriella and Fi, came barreling into her room. They had pledged together, and Rosie did like the girls, but she knew she wasn't in the same league as them.

"Look! Check it out!" Gabriella squealed and fanned her hands around Jazmin as she did a twirl.

"Oh my god! Wow, Jaz, you look…" Rosie's jaw hung open.

"Amazing, right?" Fi grinned.

"Yeah." Rosie was shaking her head. "Oh my god, how?"

"RET bayyybeee," Jaz squealed. "My Dad got it for me as a present for getting into Alpha Pi. It just took me forever to figure out what I wanted."

"Robotic Enhancement Technology?" Rosie swallowed hard.

"She got the Icy Fat Blast, Lip Fillers, EyesSoBright AND SuperGlow Face!" Gabriella crooned, surveying Jaz with envy.

Jaz shimmied around the room. "The Frat mixer tonight is gonna be so great."

Rosie took in the caramel skin, the honey blonde hair, and Jaz's lithe form, now accentuated by doe eyes, pearly skin and full, luscious lips.

"Aren't you… scared?" Rosie asked nervously.

They all giggled. "OMG RoRo, where have you been? RET machines don't cause brain damage, not unless you get like a million procedures. All that stuff about brain cells and whatever, it's like, not even proven." Fi plonked down on Rosie's bed. "Have you ever been to an RET clinic?"

"No."

"OMG, we have to take you to one." Jaz grinned. "Tomorrow, I have to go back for a checkup. We can all go, grab some lunch?"

"Perfect," Gabriella said without looking up from her cell phone. "OK, we have to get ready for the mixer. Dana wants us all ready by 9pm."

Rosie was about to say she wasn't really in the mood to tag along to yet another frat party where she got overlooked. Jaz, Fi and Gabby had already sauntered out of her room.

Procedures – 0
Twitter Followers – 214
Instagram Followers – 348

Rosie scrolled down her IG feed, and then clicked back to her own profile as another little heart pinged at the bottom of the screen. She had posted a series of pictures from the mixer. She had gained a slew of followers. People must have thought she was Jaz... or Gabby, or Fi, for that matter.

She opened the Wells Fargo app and logged in. Her savings account had $3800 in it. She had a partial scholarship to A&M. Her inheritance from her grandfather had just covered the remainder of her tuition. That savings account was all hers. She was saving it for a trip to Australia. Rosie and her other sister, Poppy, had wanted to go since they were tiny. She had enough for flights, and with some couch surfing, that $3800 would just cover a three-week trip.

"You ready?" Gabby poked her head around the door.

"Huh?"

"The RET clinic... Jaz's check up?"

"Right, yeah. Of course." Rosie hopped off her bed and followed Gabby out the door.

The RET clinic was ten minutes away. The sleek frosted glass was clean, with a laser-cut nautilus shell on the double doors. The words 'Nautilus Perfection Clinic' were in a modern typeface beneath.

Rosie swallowed as Jaz punched in a code. The sound of a metallic bolt clicked and the doors swung wide. Rosie felt her cheeks flushing as they entered the glass and metal lobby. She wasn't like her sorority friends, and she certainly wasn't like the people in this clinic. Everyone looked... polished, glossy, like something out of a magazine.

"Jazmin Jawar?" A slim man had appeared. He was older, but his face was still surprisingly smooth. He wore a close-cut charcoal suit rather than a white doctor's coat.

Jazmin stood. "Can my friends come in with me?"

Rosie thought the doctor would say no, but instead he beamed, "of course. Follow me ladies."

The room was spacious, and a long metal tube filled one wall. A row of blank monitors took up another wall. A large coffee table and two low profile sofas stretched out in the center.

"Ok Jazmin, let's get you in the machine and take a look at everything, shall we?"

Jaz hopped on the concave tube. A moment later she was encased inside. A series of different images popped up on the screens. The man scanned them all quickly and then pushed a button. He still hadn't introduced himself.

After about fifteen minutes, Jaz came sliding out. "All good, Doc?"

The doctor (Rosie felt a small wave of relief to hear that he actually was a doctor) smiled. "Everything looks great. Have you had any discomfort? Any itching? Any headaches, anything unusual at all?"

"Nope. I mean... I was kinda itchy from the chemical peel."

"Normal." The doctor smiled and slid his long fingers across the screen of his iPad. "Any questions for me?"

"How soon could I get another treatment?"

"Another?" Rosie blurted the word, then clapped her hand over her mouth. Thankfully, Jaz and the others all giggled.

"Which ones are you thinking of?" the doctor asked.

"Well... fat redistribution, maybe." Jaz frowned and tilted her head to one side.

Rosie scanned her figure. Jaz didn't have any fat to redistribute.

"We'd probably struggle with redistribution. We'd do what we could, but realistically it would be more like an implant procedure. I'd say you'd be safe to have that procedure done within a month."

"Great." Jaz beamed.

The doctor turned to Rosie, Gabby and Fi. "Now ladies, I don't think I introduced myself. I'm Doctor Nathaniel, or Doc. Do you have any questions, anything you'd like to know about RET?"

Gabby and Fi bombarded Doc with questions, while Rosie swallowed and tried to absorb all the information coming across. Neither of them needed anything done, not really. She was the only one who needed anything. She could feel Doc's eyes burning into her; into her fat stomach, into her dull, spotty skin, into her too-thin lips and her pendulous breasts, riddled with stretch marks.

"Does it like, affect your brain? RoRo here was all freaked out about that." Fi nudged her.

Doc cleared his throat. "That's a good question, actually. If you do RET treatments long term then there are some side effects."

Rosie peeked out at the others under her eyelashes, but they didn't seem remotely concerned.

"What kind of side effects?" Rosie asked.

"Difficulty concentrating, difficulty retaining short term memories. There have been some inconclusive studies about being able to retain new information." The Doctor cleared his throat again. "But this is all from synapse damage and cell damage that occurs after many, many treatments, and the majority of the studies haven't been conclusive."

Rosie nodded. Her uncle was a neurosurgeon up in Maine. She had heard from her parents that RET would turn your brain to jelly.

The doc was handing them all thick pamphlets. "Here is some information about RET and, a little bit of information about the Nautilus clinic. We do have some great pricing options." He winked. "Now, please excuse me but I have another appointment." He stood and ushered them out the door.

Rosie's legs felt hot and heavy as she clomped out of the room. The pamphlet was clutched tightly in her hand and she could hear Fi and Gabby chatting about what they were going to get.

"Rosie?"

"Huh?" She turned to Jaz.

"Look, they have a first timer's thing, if all three of you guys go you get a sweet deal, and I get a referral discount!"

Procedures – 0
Twitter Followers – 216
Instagram Followers – 343

Rosie's stomach churned as she walked through the door of the Nautilus clinic. She had agreed, without telling her parents or sisters, to go for an RET procedure with the girls, but they each had to have an individual consultation. For $500 each, they received a full consultation and two of the 'smaller' treatments offered. The options listed on the pamphlet were: Icy Fat Blast, EyeSoBright, Baby Skin, Perfect Pout or Forever Young. Rosie was scared as hell about the procedures, but she had known exactly which ones she wanted. In the privacy of her room at the sorority, she had been surprised by the glee she had felt once the money left her bank account and the consultation was scheduled.

"Hi, Rosie?"

A beautiful woman entered the room in a clean pale blue midi-dress. A nametag swung around her neck and platinum jewelry glinted in the warm lighting of the consultation room.

Rosie nodded.

"I'm Vivian, I'm going to be going through the consult with you today." She smiled warmly.

"OK."

"It's OK to be nervous. I promise, RET is painless and very safe."

Rosie gulped, "I've already paid and signed everything, so I guess there isn't much backing out now."

Vivian smiled gently again and reached out to place a warm dry hand on Rosie's arm. "I want Robotic Enhancement Technology to be a nice, enjoyable experience for you, OK? If you have any questions just let me know."

"Well... um... what is this consultation for?"

"We'll talk about the procedures you chose; Icy Fat Blast and BabySkin, we'll discuss if these are the best options, if these are the ones you really want or need, and what future procedures you might consider."

"Oh, I don't think..." Rosie murmured, but her voice trailed off.

"Now, tell me why you want the BabySkin."

"Um... I just... my skin is kinda rough, and I have some pretty bad stretch marks." Rosie felt her cheeks burning.

"Right, I see." Vivian bit her full lower lip. "The Icy Fat Blast does smooth skin a bit, so it will help with any roughness, but... can I be frank?"

Rosie nodded dumbly.

"BabySkin isn't designed to get rid of stretch marks or scarring, it is just to give you a nice, dewy glow. We do offer a larger treatment called Photoshop Perfection. Along with Cellulite Crusher, it eliminates over 80% of all blemishes, scarring and stretch marks. But that isn't covered by your package."

"Oh."

"Can I recommend Lip Fillers? They're subtle, painless, and would really add to the composition of your face. Much better value for you overall. Now, if you wanted to do Photoshop Perfection at a later date, I think that would be great for you and we could give you a great discount."

"Oh... right." Rosie felt herself nodding along dumbly,

trying to push Poppy's voice out of her head about fish lips and trout pouts.

"Excellent." Vivian beamed. "Now, let's go over the procedural stuff and then we'll get you in the RET machine."

"Now?" Rosie's voice sounded hollow and far away.

Vivian checked her expensive watch. "In about 30 minutes." She smiled warmly and Rosie smiled back.

Vivian began explaining how everything worked, but the words blurred. The next thing Rosie knew, she was nervously stripping off and drifting to sleep in the dark tube of the RET machine.

Procedures – 2
Twitter Followers – 298
Instagram Followers – 567

Rosie smiled at herself in the mirror and tossed her hair over her shoulder. She twisted and smiled coyly again. She brought her phone up to the mirror and snapped a few selfies.

She couldn't remember ever feeling this happy about how a selfie turned out. "Oh my god," She murmured. She was in a sundress, with Spanx, and she almost, almost looked hourglass shaped. Vivian hadn't been lying either, her skin was much softer after the Icy Blast. Her thighs were slimmer, her arms weren't as jiggly and even her fat belly was flatter. Her lips were the best part though. They had been thin and straight and just lips before. Now they were full, and when she applied a gloss they looked plump and juicy and she could see the guys in her engineering classes looking at them intently.

Her phone buzzed in her hand. Poppy's name flashed on the screen. FaceTime. Rosie quickly switched it over to voice call.

"Hey Poppy!" She said brightly.

"Did I not FaceTime you?"

"Yeah, my phone is being super weird."

"Oh, random. How are you? Dad said you're not coming home this weekend?"

"Yeah, I just… I have tons of work to do."

"How is schoolwork? Keeping up?"

Rosie looked at the stack of unfinished notes and unread library books on her desk. "Yeah, fine, just busy, y'know." She changed the subject quickly. "How's Fort Hood?"

"Good. I move over to Sniper school next week," Poppy sighed down the phone. "I'm bummed you won't be home. At this rate the next time I see you will be in Australia!"

Rosie said nothing for a long second, then "Yeah… um… I know."

"But I get it. Work is work, you gotta do it," Poppy said without a trace of judgment. She started chatting about life on the base.

Rosie gulped. Her mathematically-gifted, crack shot, badass sister was her best friend, but she also made her feel like a failure. Poppy was Dad's favorite. And Lily was just like Mom; big smile, cheer squad, permanently perky.

Rosie looked at herself in the mirror. Her phone buzzed and she pulled it away from her ear for a second. Since posting the new pictures of herself she had gained hundreds more followers on Instagram. Notifications filled her screen;

comments of clapping emojis, heart eyes, and little fireballs filled the comments.

"Hey, Poppy, can I call you back? I have to book a doctor's appointment real quick."

"Oh, uh... yeah, I mean, I have to... I'll just talk to you at the weekend."

"OK, great." Rosie quickly ended the call and found the Nautilus Clinic's number. She hurried over to her laptop and went to Wells Fargo. Before she had even connected the call, the money had been moved from her savings account to her checking.

"Nautilus Clinic, how can I help?"

"Hi, yes, this is Rosie Dalkeith, I was in last week? Yes. It's 07/07/2014... yes, that's me. I'd like to make an appointment for next week? OK... uh huh... perfect."

Rosie hung up and grinned.

A minute later she picked up her phone and opened Instagram again.

Procedures – 8
Twitter Followers – 547
Instagram Followers – 1815

"Oh. My. God." Fi looked completely gobsmacked.

"I am so fucking jealous!" Gabby's hands fluttered over Rosie. "How did you afford all this?"

"I had a bunch in savings just sitting there, not for anything, y'know... and I figured I might as well use it for something."

"Hell yeah!" Jaz grinned.

"So what did you get?" Fi's eyes were wide.

"Um, well…" Rosie tilted her head to one side. She had had the appointment yesterday but she frowned, as the names of the treatments eluded her. "Oh, yeah, I had Photoshop Perfection, Cellulite Blaster." Rosie frowned, that had been a waste. Her skin was smooth, but she wasn't any thinner. "Then I had a bit more lip filler, and EyesSoBright… oh, and they threw in this new hair thing… it like, smooths, thickens and lengthens hair."

"Girl, you look amazing." Jaz smiled. "We have to get a pic and tag Nautilus."

"Yes!" Gabby squealed. "With all of us. Maybe we can win that prize!"

"Prize?" Rosie's heart fluttered with excitement. There were two more treatments she wanted. Big treatments. Not hundreds of dollars, or even a few thousand, but $8000, $10,000 and even $20,000 treatments. She wanted the Luscious Sculpt. It was a massive procedure that involved liposuction and extensive sculpting, followed by breast and buttock implants with the extracted fat. It promised a natural, trim, hourglass shape. She also wanted rhinoplasty and facial sculpting.

"Yeah, Nautilus offers its own prizes for referrals, most liked pics, that kinda thing." Jaz was flicking through filters. "OK, smile!"

Jaz's phone made a flurry of clicks.

"Let me see." Fi peered over her shoulder.

"What do you mean 'its own prizes'? Rosie said, frowning.

"So, like, a bunch of places offer them as free prizes for

contests or challenges." Fi said distractedly as she checked the pictures.

"Yeah, it's super cool," Gabby continued. Y'know that chick Isla from Delta Delta? She won a competition from a Yoga clothing store. Their grand prize was a $10,000 gift certificate for RET. She got breast enhancement."

"Oh my god!" Rosie crowed.

"Yeah, my cousin works at Fashion Now and they offer gift certificates as bonuses and stuff."

Jaz grinned. "God yeah, I've heard loads of places do that now... even as part of the payment. Places like Fendlemen's Boutique and Java Lounge!"

Rosie pulled her quilt up to her armpits and propped the pillow behind her head as she opened another browser window. She had googled 'RET contests'. There was a wealth of results.

'WIN LUSCIOUSLIPS WITH KISS-ME-KUTE MAKE-UP!'

'FEELING FLABBY? ENTER THE 30-DAY FAT BURN CHALLENGE AND THE WINNER RECEIVES ICY FAT BLAST & CELLULITE CRUSHER!'

'BUY ACNE X-OUT FACE WASH AND BE ENTERED INTO THE RET PRIZE LOTTERY. 1ˢᵗ PLACE IS $5000 OF TREATMENT.'

Rosie kept scrolling down. Some of the contests had closed. She clicked onto their pages. The winners had posted a flurry of pictures on social media, all tagging the company. Rosie peered at them. They were all littered with hashtags; #blessed, #beautiful #confidence #hot.

Rosie went back to the search results. Everything was

for the $5K or less procedures. She had spent all her savings on those treatments already. Her tummy flipped.

'WANT TO HIT THE RET JACKPOT? MODEL FOR TRIPLEXXXHOT.COM AND WIN $10,000 R.E.T TREATMENT OF YOUR CHOICE*'

Rosie gasped and clicked the link. The terms and conditions were simple; the modeling pictures could be used and distributed by triplexxxhot.com at their choosing, and the treatment of choice would be subject to approval from the RET clinic and a specialist at triplexxxhot.com.

FaceTime startled the frown off Rosie's face and she hit answer without thinking.

"ROSIEEEEEEEE!" Lily and Poppy screeched in unison. The screen was pixelated for a moment and then their faces came into focus.

"Oh my god, Rosie, you look…" Poppy's voice was hollow.

Rosie felt a stab of panic, "Oh yeah, the girls wanted to do my hair and makeup for the house dinner… I look goofy," she blurted out quickly.

"You look amazing!" Lily shrieked. "Oh my god, what lip kit did they use? And what foundation?"

"That's all makeup?" Poppy's voice was doubtful.

Time to change the subject. "Uh-huh. What're you guys up to? I wish I could be home." Rosie guiltily glanced at the stack of unwritten papers, unfinished tests and unread books that had only grown since her last conversation with Poppy.

"We had a big barbecue last night, with everyone, y'know. And then we all went to the swimming hole in Dino Valley Park," Poppy said.

"We're having a shopping day tomorrow," Lily grinned. Poppy grimaced.

"Oh, that's so fun…" Rosie felt a pang of wistfulness. She couldn't go home. The other girls had all been invited to a frat party, but her invitation had never materialized. She quickly clicked on the entrance link for the triplexxxhot.com contest and began filling it out as her sisters chatted.

"How's the schoolwork coming along? You gonna be ready to build Dad a new cattle barn soon?" Poppy joked.

Rosie gave a fake smile. "Yeah, super good, super busy." She was too embarrassed to admit she was failing most of her classes.

"That's great. Mom and Dad are so happy about it. They brag to everyone about how you're at A&M. Mom loves that you're in her old sorority."

"I mean, Lily will be here soon. Cheer scholarship." A heavy lump settled in Rosie's stomach.

Lily smiled. "Maybe, I dunno. I spoke to Dad about maybe…"

"She's gonna be the family billionaire. Next Mark Zuckerberg right here." Poppy winked.

"What?"

"She and Donovan have been taking this advanced coding class. She's already developed all these amazing apps and plugins, it's insane." Poppy nudged their baby sister. Lily blushed.

Rosie felt like even more of a failure. She wasn't good at school anymore. She wasn't invited to the frat party. She wasn't swanning off on dates all the time. She wasn't a badass military tomboy. She wasn't anything.

"Hey, we gotta go. Dinner time."

Rosie said goodbye and hung up. She clicked back over to triplexxxhot.com. She could at least win this.

Procedures – 8
Twitter Followers – 3589
Instagram Followers – 5815

Since Rosie had entered the contest, her phone hadn't stopped buzzing. Every day more notifications. More hearts. She wouldn't tell a soul, but she had also found a way to get some of those clickbot things so all her pictures were flooded with likes.

She was a top contender in the triplexxxhot.com contest. They were posting her submitted pictures everyday and tagging her in all their promotions. She felt giddy, nervous, and somewhere beneath the excitement, terrified that her family would find out.

"Rosie!" The voice was sharp and unrecognizable and Rosie jumped out of her seat. She had been trying to study… kind of. Mostly looking at Instagram and the triplexxxhot.com polls.

A knock. The girls would never knock. "It's Dana, can I come in?" Her voice was sharp. She was president of the Alpha Pi sorority. Rosie gulped.

"Sure." She swallowed the lump in her throat.

Dana, in all her sleek, confident glory, strode in and towered over Rosie. She frowned. Rosie looked down at her textbooks.

"I wanted to talk to you."

"Look, I know my GPA has dropped, I've just been super busy." Rosie moved the mess of papers around in a semblance of organization.

"It's not that." Dana's voice was clipped.

"Right." Rosie swallowed again.

"I know it can be stressful when you start university and join a sorority, and I know you meet lots of new people and see and do lots of new things." Dana arched one manicured eyebrow. "But this... this is not Alpha Pi." She turned the screen of her phone around to face Rosie. Red lettering flashed and bright red kisses that faded to sparkles. 'WINNER' was in a bold typeface above Rosie's picture.

"I won?" Rosie couldn't stop the smile.

Dana looked horrified. "On triplexxxhot.com! It's a porn site that exploits women and girls by offering RET treatments. How many images did you send them? Nudes?"

Rosie's neck felt stiff as she tried to nod.

"They'll be all over the internet!" Dana shoved her phone into her back pocket and waved a hand in front of Rosie's face. "What were you thinking?" Her voice rose an octave. "Jesus Christ, Rosie. You're going to get kicked out of Alpha Pi."

"What?" Rosie was itching to look at her phone, but Dana's words shook her momentarily.

"It'll be put to a vote, but we can't have this type of thing associated with Alpha Pi. You'll have two days to find new accommodations. I'd start packing your things."

Rosie opened her mouth to argue, but Dana gave her a strange, sad look and walked out of her room.

Procedures – 10
Twitter Followers – 12,834
Instagram Followers – 17,951

Rosie looked around the sparse bedroom in the apartment. Two other girls and one guy occupied the other rooms. Thank god Jaz had known someone who lived off campus who was looking for a roommate.

She had ditched some of her classes, and had taken a job at a local bar to pay rent, which she thought would be fun. It turned out to be mostly being spoken at, not to, by beautiful girls, or being leered at and groped by gross drunk frat boys.

Her phone vibrated on the bed. She flipped it over and swiped away the thousands of likes. Since being featured on triplexxxhot.com and undergoing the rhinoplasty and facial sculpting, she was constantly getting DMs of dick pics, girls asking about her transformation, or sending her abuse.

She scrolled to the comments section.

'Uhhh... I'd be more interested if she hadn't been gross before' Followed by the laughing-crying emoji.

'I'd bang her now. Probs still rough without filters, photoshop and make-up though.' Followed by a row of beers.

'Fake.' That word was littered throughout the comments on all her pictures, usually with the puking emoji or the doctor's mask emoji. Jaz, Fi and Gabby told her those people were just jealous trolls or douche guys. Still, Rosie felt a wave of humiliation. It mingled with her anger and the urge to cry. She strode over to the mirror and adjusted her jeans

shorts and flowy top. She twisted left and right in front of the mirror. Her thighs were still chunky. Her stomach was still soft. Her butt was flat, yet it jiggled when she ran. She needed the Luscious Sculpt. That would make her perfect.

The liaison over at triplexxxhot.com had been so wonderful with Rosie when they were retouching her nude photos and making them tasteful, she wondered if they were going to run any more contests.

Her phone interrupted her thoughts. "Hey Mom." Rosie tried to sound cheerful, but her voice was flat.

"Hey sugar, how are you? You sound tired."

"Yeah, kinda."

"How's school? How's Alpha Pi?" Her voice was giddy.

"Um... fine, fine."

"Your father and I want you to come home this weekend." Her Mom's voice changed. It was lower.

Rosie's stomach lurched. Had they found out? "How come?"

"Granny died last night. The funeral is on Sunday."

Rosie sighed with relief.

"I know it's sad honey, but she was 104 and she'd been ill for a while now."

"Yeah, I... I'll come home."

"Great. Poppy managed to get leave, so the whole family will be home. Hey, you girls can plan your Australia trip, it was all Poppy talked about last time she was home. She's saved so much leave!"

Rosie felt her face flush and she gulped. "Cool... cool."

"Three beers, honey." The guy held up three waggling fingers at her and grinned suggestively. "Big tip if you bring 'em to Daddy fast.' Rosie fought the urge to grimace and instead smiled at him.

"Excuse me? Hello?" A skeletal girl in a slinky dress sneered at Rosie. "I've been trying to get attention for like 10 minutes. I want a drink."

"If you head on over to the bar they can help you out."

"Why can't you get me one?" The girl made a disgusted face.

"I only do table service." Rosie turned away from her and walked back to the bar.

She heard screeching behind her as the girl greeted her friends.

"Ugh, this place fucking sucks. The pig barmaid won't get me a drink," the girl said loudly.

Rosie shook her head and went to the serving end of the bar.

"Two… no sorry, three beers please Jake," she sighed.

"Hey, she's a bitch. Comes every Friday, tries to get table servers to get her drinks." Jake nodded his head towards the girl.

Rosie smiled. "Really?"

"Really."

Alan, the other bartender, popped up from hooking up another keg. "And she's a crap lay," he chimed in.

Rosie giggled. "Whatever."

"Trust him, he knows." Jake raised his eyebrows. "About pretty much every girl in here," Jake added as he handed a group their beers and change.

"'Cept you." Alan sidled over to Rosie.

"Uh huh." Rosie ignored him, but she felt her cheeks blushing. Guys like Alan never went for her. He was twenty-six, with long hair, dangerous green eyes, a chiseled body (she had snuck a look when he changed into his work T-shirt) and a semi-permanent tan.

"Think about it." Alan sauntered off.

Jake's face was clouded. "Watch out for him Rosie."

"Oh, he's like... totally joking." Rosie said, but she could feel her face set in a grin. "Better get these beers over to 'Daddy' at table 4." She fake-gagged and Jake's face relaxed into a laugh.

"He didn't actually?"

"Oh, he did." Rosie could still hear Jake's laugh as she left the bar. Was he laughing at her or the story, she wondered, as a frown creased her brow. Maybe he thought she was lying, and that no guy could possibly even try to hit on her.

Procedures – 10
Twitter Followers – 18,834
Instagram Followers – 27,951

Rosie's hands were clammy on the steering wheel. Her parents were going to freak out when they saw her. She hadn't worn make up or anything nice. She was dressed in baggy sweats and an old T-shirt. She had stayed up till 4am the night before deleting all her 'old' IG pictures, the ones she looked fat and disgusting in.

"I look better though. I look good now," she said out loud. "Now I can focus on my schoolwork... and I didn't even like Alpha Pi." She scrunched her eyes up. She was tired and stressed. She had lost her car keys that morning and spent forever looking for them, then she had forgotten a turn on the drive home and had to double back for ten miles.

Her phone buzzed, and she hit speaker. "Where are you?" Lily's voice wasn't her usual chipper pitch.

"Near."

There was a long silence. "I'm guessing Mom and Dad don't know about the RET or the stuff all over triplexxxhot.com," she snapped.

"Um… I…"

"Donovan said all the guys at school were showing the pictures round in the locker room. What the fuck, Rosie?"

Rosie was shaking as she pulled into the layby. "It isn't a big deal Lily, you don't understand…"

"I don't understand?" Her sister shrieked incredulously.

"No! I just… we can talk about this when I'm home. Don't tell Mom and Dad."

"I've looked at your IG feed, you look totally different. They're going to know."

"You said I looked good."

"I thought it was makeup, and that was before all the other stuff. It looks like you've had a million procedures. That stuff is so bad for you!"

"I have to drive, Lily." Rosie hung up before her sister could reply. She let out a shaky breath.

Her phone vibrated and she looked down, expecting an angry text, but it was a message from the triplexxxhot.com liaison.

Hi Rosie,
I wanted to let you know that the team at triplexxxhot.com
was going to run a contest with a winning prize of $20,000

worth of R.E.T treatment (that Luscious Sculpt you wanted would be yours!) The contest was 'Hottest TripleXXXHot Winners; Live in Action!'

However, after the incredibly positive reaction our fans and customers had to your pictures, we would love to offer you this opportunity as a contract instead. You would receive the $20,000 in exchange for making the film with us.

Let us know what you think soon, as I don't think this deal will be on the table for long!
AJ.
TripleXXXhot.com Contest Liaison'

Rosie scanned the text. The $20,000 seemed to jump off the page and vibrate in front of her eyeballs. Lily and Dana's voices mingled inside her skull – *what were you thinking? We can't be associated with this.* That was just about the nude pictures.

Rosie frowned. "The pictures were... tasteful," she said, as the word finally came to her. She opened up Twitter. It didn't sound like Lily had checked there. She typed fast and hit 'Tweet'. The blue bubble of text appeared beside her glamorous profile pic: 'Been offered a sweet contract w/the amazing peeps at triplexxxhot.com 2 b the star in a new film of theirs... Wat u guys think, shud I do it?'

She exhaled, unaware she had been holding her breath, and then she shoved her phone back in her bag and continued the drive towards home.

"What the actual fuck?" Poppy snarled. Her face was blotched and Rosie knew she was trying not to cry. "Mom can't even look at you, Dad's fucked off to the supermarket 'cause he doesn't know what to do, and... and... who even *are* you?"

Poppy's hair was styled in a neat pixie cut. Her square jaw was set angrily and her blue eyes blazed. Even out of her uniform, her jeans and T-shirt still looked crisp and formal somehow. Lily scuffed a toe of her Converse in the dirt of the barn.

"You... you don't look like you." Lily's voice was sad.

"No, I look better!"

Poppy scoffed. "Sending nudes in to triplexxxhot.com and having gross men leering over you, that's what you want?"

"It was one contest, it's not like I did that every time! I don't know why this is such a big deal. It's my body."

"Is this because of the girls at Alpha Pi? Jaz and... Fi?" Lily was frowning.

"No, they're super nice!" Rosie snapped.

"I'm not saying they're not, they're just... not like you!" Lily snapped back.

"What's that supposed to mean?" Rosie felt her breath coming faster and a prickling heat spreading under the makeup on her face and neck.

"You didn't used to give a shit about make-up and how you looked, you used to like hiking, and camping and engineering and books! Let me guess, you're failing school too!" Poppy said it sarcastically.

Rosie looked away.

"Oh my god, you are!" Lily sat down on a bale of hay.

"It's not a big deal, I'll get back on track soon. I just... I was super busy with my new job and... and..." Rosie trailed off.

Their mom appeared in the barn doorway. Her eyes were red and puffy. "How did you even pay for all this?"

"I used some savings. Mom this isn't a big deal." Rosie insisted.

"Wait, like... our Australia savings?" Poppy's voice was menacingly calm.

"I... I..." Rosie burst into tears and fled from the barn.

There was a soft knock on her door. "Rosie, it's Dad. Can I come in?"

Rosie was curled into the fetal position on her bed. It smelt of lavender, dog and the chili that Mom made every single Friday. More tears leaked from her eyes. "Fine," she snuffled.

"It's going to be OK, honey." Her dad, a big burly rancher, leant against her desk, still in his overalls. The pinboard above it was adorned with family pictures of camping trips, medals from winning science fairs, and mementos from school friends. Friends Rosie hadn't spoken to in months, not since she had overheard Jacob. Her dad held up his iPhone. "I spoke to Uncle Don." He sighed and shifted from one heavy boot to the other. "Your mother and I think you should head up to Maine for a little while and get checked over."

"What? No... no I can't leave school... and..." Rosie stammered. "There's nothing wrong with like... my brain." She waved her hands around her head, trying to phrase it better.

Her father frowned. "From what Lily and Poppy say, school is a bit... stressful for you right now. Maybe a break would do you some good."

"I... I don't want... " Rosie was crying again, but this time with frustration. She didn't know what she wanted and she didn't know how to make her family happy or how to get her sisters to forgive her, or how to do school anymore. "I... I..."

"I know honey." He enveloped her in a bear hug. He smelt of wood, diesel and cows, a safe, familiar smell that collided sickeningly with Rosie's perfume. She pushed him away. "Think about it, OK?" He stood up and left the room.

Rosie rolled back onto her side. She could hear Poppy ranting in the kitchen to Lily and her Mom.

She heard vibrating. She hadn't even checked her phone since she arrived. Her family had descended on her like vultures and torn her apart. She grabbed it from her bag and flopped back onto her bed. Her twitter had exploded.

OMG fuck yeah. Do it.

I'd def pay to see that!

Before or after more lipo?

Fake... and now a slut.

DO IT. YOU'RE A QUEEN!!

I wish I looked like you, I would so do it if I looked like you. Everyone saying other stuff is just jealous.

Yes!!

DO IT! DO IT! DO IT! Sincerely, guys everywhere.

You're so fuckin hot mama... please, please, please!

@triplexxxhot make this happen, she is amazing!

PLEASE GOD YES!

Kinda sad you're on here trying to validate more surgery and doing porn.

GOD DAMN girl, do it! Fuck the haters!

Her post had been liked thousands of times. There were hundreds, if not thousands, of comments. Heart-eye emojis, praying hand emojis, thumbs up and heart emojis. Her followers had boomed. Triplexxxhot.com had emailed her saying that they were willing to increase the RET contract to $25,000, since the fallout of her post was so positive.

Rosie relaxed back into her pillows and tried to concentrate on the smell of the house and the familiar smell of her dad, but her phone just kept buzzing. More IG followers. More DMs. More people telling her how much they loved her.

She opened Twitter and typed quickly. The blue bubble appeared. She felt a moment of peace. Everything would be OK now.

A moment later a gnawing anxiety took over. She picked up her iPhone. Comments were already flooding in on the latest tweet. It was pinned to the top of her feed. The retweets and likes were going up by the second.

She started tapping.

I love you guys! Stay tuned to triplexxxhot.com to see me star in a super-hot new vid! @triplexxxhot I love you guys too, let's do this!

www.ingramcontent.com/pod-product-compliance
Lightning Source LLC
Chambersburg PA
CBHW070157260626
47160CB00002B/369